THE INTERVAL

ALSO BY CHRIS BINNIX

DETECTIVE ROAN SERIES

Crimson Sand

Digital Grave

FORTUNE SERIES

Criminal Fortune - May 2026

Fortune & Forgery - Available Fall 2026

NOVELS

The Interval

NOVELLAS

The Farmhands

THE INTERVAL

CHRIS BINNIX

25 MEDIA

Identifiers:

LCCN: 2026903196

ISBNs:

979-8-9937336-6-1 (hardcover),

979-8-9937336-7-8 (trade paperback),

979-8-9937336-8-5 (ebook)

For Nolan, may every book you open plant a seed, and may you grow in ways I can only dream of watching.

THE INTERVAL

The only true wisdom is in knowing you know nothing.

Socrates

CHAPTER

I

THE DIGITAL NUMBERS on Bill Shaw's Garmin watch showed his heart rate held steady at 138 beats per minute. For a man of sixty-two with two reconstructed knees and thirty years of smoke inhalation from the Savannah Fire Department, staying under one-forty was the goal. He drew air in through his nose and pushed it out through his mouth.

The air in Savannah was heavy with river mud and the dew. The humidity filled his lungs with moisture that tasted of azaleas and the deep earth. Bill adjusted his pace, his feet landing strictly on the pavement of the Bull Street corridor.

Running this early was a ritual. The city belonged to the workers and the insomniacs, long before the tourists began to stir from their open-container cocktails in hotel beds. He had the route memorized down to the treacherous cracks in the sidewalk. His Hoka running shoes slapped the concrete in a steady rhythm. He focused on the breath, the physical exertion clearing the static from his mind.

Retirement had been a difficult adjustment. He missed the structure of the station, the jolt of the bell. He missed the absolute clarity of a fire scene where the objective was simple: get everyone out alive and put out the flames. Now, his enemies were cholesterol and the slow erosion of boredom.

The entrance to Forsyth Park rose ahead, its grand ironwork swallowed by the morning mist that hung low over the thirty acres of green. It obscured the far treeline, rendering the famous fountain at the north end a ghostly white shape in the grey light. The water jets were already running, their sound a low hiss that grew louder as he approached. A glance at his watch confirmed he was twelve seconds behind his usual pace.

Pushing a little harder, the familiar burn spread through his quads.

He passed the fountain, scattering a few pigeons into the air. The Spanish moss draping the massive live oaks remained perfectly still. In the absence of wind, it hung in long, grey beards that brushed the tops of the azalea bushes. The path curved around the white shell of the amphitheater.

His eyes stayed on the ground—scan, ever vigilant for the uneven pavers that could spell disaster. A turned ankle at his age meant six weeks of physical therapy and his wife, Maggie, finally winning the argument for a stationary bike.

He approached the Confederate Memorial, the bronze soldier standing high on his sandstone pedestal, staring north in perpetual vigilance. Up ahead, a large puddle of standing water blocked the walkway near the monument. The irrigation must have run long overnight.

Soaking his socks this early in the run would lead to blisters. He made a quick calculation. Veering left, he stepped off the pavement, aiming for the manicured grass between two massive oaks where the ground usually held firm, shielded from the heaviest dew by the canopy. He shortened his stride to navigate the uneven terrain, the thick grass cushioning his steps.

Something white flashed in his periphery.

Bill slowed, squinting into the deep shadows beneath the low-hanging branches of an oak about twenty yards away. The branches swept down toward the ground, creating a natural curtain of leaves and moss. Near a wrought-iron bench, a pale, long shape lay on the brick pavers.

He exhaled a sharp breath. Another one of the park's homeless population, sleeping late before the morning police sweeps. A flicker of irritation went through him. He didn't want to deal with it. He just wanted to finish his three miles and get his coffee.

Adjusting his trajectory to the right, he decided to give the sleeper a wide berth. No need to wake them, no need for a confrontation.

He turned back to check his footing.

His right Hoka planted on the grass verge, expecting the bite of earth. Instead, the world slipped out from under him. No friction. Just a violent slide that shot his leg sideways and dropped his center of gravity like a stone.

He hit hard, the breath leaving him in a wheeze, right hand slapping into the wet grass to arrest the slide. The impact knocked the wind from him, his right hip slamming into the earth and a jolt of pain shooting up his forearm from his wrist.

Bill lay there for a moment, staring up at the grey underbelly of the oak leaves, gasping for air.

"Damn it," he wheezed.

Rolling onto his side, he pushed himself up. His knee throbbed. This was what he had tried to avoid. A stupid, preventable fall because he was worried about wet socks.

He examined the grass to see what had taken him down.

The green blades were dark. He examined his right hand, the one he had planted firmly to catch himself. His palm was coated in something thick and warm. Dark red. Not mud. Mud was gritty—this was slick, coating his palm in a warm, tacky film. He rubbed his thumb against his fingertips, the texture all wrong for morning dew.

He brought his hand to his face, and the smell hit him—not the river, not the azaleas, but the sharp, copper tang of a penny placed on the tongue.

Blood.

Bill froze. The irritation vanished, replaced by a cold knot in his stomach. The firefighter training slammed back into place. *Scene safety. BSI. Patient assessment.*

He scrambled to his feet, his shoes sliding slightly in the gore. The patch of grass where he had slipped was a pool of red hidden among the green. He turned, searching for the source.

The white shape on the pavers was six feet away.

Bill took a step forward, Spanish moss brushing the top of his head. He ignored it, his focus locked on the figure.

It was a woman. Young, maybe late twenties, and completely naked. Her skin was the color of alabaster in the dim morning light.

She lay on her back on the hexagonal Savannah grey bricks. Her blonde hair was fanned out around her head, the strands combed flat against the stone in a perfect golden halo. It was deliberate.

He moved closer, his heart hammering against his ribs, far faster than one-forty now.

"Miss?" he said, his voice rough. "Miss, can you hear me?"

No movement. No rise and fall of her chest.

Bill stepped onto the bricks, avoiding the body as he moved toward her head to check for an airway, for a pulse, to start compressions.

Then her throat came into view.

He stopped. Put his hands on his knees, leaned down, and stared.

The anatomy of the neck was exposed. The tissue wasn't cut or sliced—it was gone. A crater had been carved from chin to clavicle. The severed trachea, the open esophagus, the white gristle of the larynx —all visible. The muscles were torn back in ragged strips. The carotid arteries were severed. The jugular veins were gone.

He studied her face. Her eyes were closed, her mouth relaxed. No grimace of pain, no rictus of terror. She appeared serene, as if sleeping. Below the chin, a ruin of meat and cartilage. Above it, a sleeping angel.

The contradiction made his stomach lurch.

He backed up until his spine hit the rough bark of an oak tree, the texture grounding him. A violent tremor started in his hands and traveled up his arms. He needed to call. Police. There was nothing for a paramedic to do here. She had been dead for hours. Rigor mortis had likely set in, her skin too pale, too grey.

He reached into the pocket of his running shorts, fumbling for his phone. His fingers were slick. He pulled the device out, but it slipped from his grip. He caught it against his chest, juggled it, then gripped it tight.

He tried to unlock it, but the biometric sensor failed. His thumb was coated in drying blood.

Bill gagged, a sour taste filling his mouth. He grabbed the hem of his grey shirt and scrubbed his thumb against the fabric, wiping the red smear away. He wiped the screen.

He entered his passcode, his fingers missing the numbers twice.

"Come on," he whispered. "Come on, Bill. Get it together."

He hit the green icon and dialed 9-1-1. Pressing the phone to his ear, he stared at the woman. He couldn't look away. The impossibility of the scene—the clean bricks, the peaceful face, the destroyed throat—held him captive.

The line clicked.

"911, what is your emergency?" The dispatcher's voice was calm, professional.

Bill slid down the trunk of the tree. His legs refused to hold him anymore. He sat on the damp grass, staring at the woman.

"I found a body," Bill said, his voice cracking. It sounded like a stranger's, thin and high. "Forsyth Park. Near the Memorial. A woman."

"Sir, are you safe?" the dispatcher asked.

Bill examined his right hand. The blood was drying in the creases of his palm, turning to rust.

"She's dead," Bill said. "She's... she's got no throat."

CHAPTER

2

DETECTIVE KARL RODECKER stepped out of his unmarked Ford Interceptor Utility and regretted the coffee he'd finished ten minutes ago. The acid churned in his stomach, joining the low-level irritation that had become his baseline state of being.

Blue lights from three patrol cruisers cut through the morning mist, bouncing off the low-hanging branches of the live oaks. Uniformed officers stood in loose clusters, shifting their weight and hands hovering near their belts. Something had them spooked. Beyond the yellow tape, the media crews assembled tripods and checked microphone levels. They sensed the story. They always did.

He ducked under the yellow crime scene tape near the Confederate Memorial. The bronze soldier atop the pedestal stared north. A rookie officer, sweat staining the underarms of his uniform, moved to intercept but stopped at the sight of the badge clipped to Rodecker's belt. The kid's shoulders dropped, and he stepped aside without a word.

"Detective Rodecker," a voice said.

Crime Scene Tech Miller walked toward him from the center of the lawn. Pale. His forensic coveralls were crisp, but his jaw worked like he was chewing something bitter. He gripped a camera in one gloved hand.

"Miller," Rodecker said. He kept walking, forcing the tech to fall in step. "Status."

"We're trying, Karl. But people were everywhere. Joggers. Dog walkers. It's Forsyth at dawn. We cleared them back to the sidewalk."

"The scene."

"It's... intact," Miller said. He hesitated. "I think."

Rodecker stopped. Miller didn't hesitate over "intact" unless the variables were wrong.

"You think?"

"You need to see it," Miller said. He pointed toward a massive live oak thirty yards away, near the fountain.

Rodecker started walking. The grass was slick with dew, dampening the cuffs of his trousers. As he cleared the trunk of the oak, the victim came into view.

She lay on her back on the brick pavers.

Rodecker stopped five feet away. Hands in pockets. He studied the face first. Her blonde hair fanned out around her head, strands catching the early light.

Caroline Marsh. He recognized her. Not personally, but he knew the face. She was local, involved in the arts scene and charity events. Her picture had been in the Savannah Morning News social pages enough times.

"Caroline Marsh," he said.

"Yeah, ID was in her purse," Miller said. "Found it on the bench. Untouched."

Rodecker crouched. His knees popped. He leaned closer.

Naked. Skin the color of milk, pale and waxy, stripped of vitality. Rigor had set in, locking her limbs. Arms crossed over her chest, left over right. Legs straight, ankles touching, bare feet pointing north toward the fountain.

The throat.

A ruin. The tissue torn away, leaving a gaping red opening where the windpipe and arteries should be. Not a clean slice. Something had excavated her neck. He had seen chainsaw accidents with less tissue damage.

"Massive arterial damage," Rodecker said. "Carotids, jugulars, trachea. Gone."

"The bricks," Miller said.

Rodecker lowered his gaze to the hexagonal pavers directly beneath her neck.

Dry.

He blinked. A wound like that pumped five liters of blood out in less than a minute. It sprayed. It pooled. It soaked into clothes, hair, and the ground.

The bricks were clean. A light sheen of dew coated them, catching the light, but there was no red. No sticky dark pools.

"Where is it?" Rodecker asked.

"Not here," Miller said. "Not underneath her. We checked the edges. Just... gone."

Rodecker extended a gloved finger, hovering an inch above the brick near her shoulder. He registered the dampness of the dew. Nothing else.

"Cleaned? With what?" Miller asked. "Bleach? Water? We'd smell it. The bricks would be wet. Check the gaps."

The sand between the pavers was undisturbed. If someone had washed the scene, the sand would be washed out or turned to mud.

Dry.

He stood up. The heat made his head swim.

Four white pillar candles sat on the bricks, forming a square around her. One at the head. One at the feet. One left, one right.

"Compass points," Rodecker said.

"North, south, east, west," Miller said. "I checked with my phone. Alignment is exact. Unlit. Wicks are white. Never burned."

"Someone was setting a stage." *But you couldn't stage the absence of five liters of blood.*

"Where's the witness?" Rodecker said.

"The firefighter. Shaw. He's over there." Miller pointed to a park bench outside the tape perimeter. "He found the blood."

"I thought you said there wasn't any blood."

"Not here," Miller said. He walked six feet away, toward the grass line. He pointed down.

Rodecker followed.

In the grass, six feet from the edge of the pavers, a patch of earth was stained dark. A smear, ten inches wide, where a shoe had skidded through something wet.

"He slipped," Miller said.

Rodecker examined the grass. Then he turned back to Caroline

Marsh. Six feet. No drag marks. No droplets bridging the gap. Just a solitary patch of blood on the grass, a void, and then a body.

"He says he didn't move her," Miller said.

"I'll ask him."

Rodecker walked toward the bench. Bill Shaw sat hunched over, a shock blanket draped over one shoulder. Running gear. His face had gone the color of ash. He wiped his hands with a wet towelette, scrubbing at skin that was already raw.

"Mr. Shaw," Rodecker said.

Shaw jumped. The towelette hit the ground. His eyes went wide.

"I didn't touch her," Shaw said.

"I didn't say you did."

"I slipped," Shaw said. He held up his right shoe. The tread was caked with dark, drying mud. Blood mud. "Running. Cut across the grass. Foot went out from under me. Went down on my hand."

He held up his hand. Scrubbed pink, but the cuticles were stained dark brown.

Rodecker sat on the other end of the bench.

"Bill," Rodecker said. "Exact sequence. You slipped."

"Slipped. Fell."

"Then what?"

"I saw her," Shaw said. He stared toward the oak tree, his gaze penetrating through it. "She was just... lying there. Sleeping. But the neck."

"Did you go to her? Check for a pulse?"

"Look at her. Why would I check for a pulse?"

"Did you move her? Tried to help and realized she was gone?"

"I stayed on the grass," Shaw said. His voice rose. "Stood up. Saw the candles. Saw the... the lack of mess. Backed away. Called 911. Waited by the tree. I didn't touch her."

Rodecker watched the man's face. Fear. Confusion. Hands scrubbed raw. If Shaw had dragged a bleeding body six feet, he would be covered in it. The grass would be torn up. The blood would be everywhere.

But it wasn't.

"Okay," Rodecker said.

Shaw let out a breath.

"Wait here, Bill."

Rodecker stood. He walked back to the tape. Miller waited by the body, holding a flashlight at an oblique angle over the victim's chest.

"Rodecker," Miller said. "Look."

Rodecker stepped onto the pavers. "What?"

"Spatter."

Rodecker leaned in. On the pale skin of Caroline Marsh's upper chest, below the ruined collarbone, tiny droplets of dried blood. High-velocity mist.

"Arterial spray," Rodecker said.

"Is it?" Miller asked. "Look at the tails."

Rodecker squinted. He leaned closer, face inches from the dead woman's chest. The air smelled like copper and something floral—perfume, maybe, something expensive that didn't belong on a corpse.

The droplets were elongated. In spatter analysis, the tapered end points in the direction of travel. If blood sprays out from a neck wound, the tails point away from the throat.

The tails on Caroline Marsh's chest pointed up toward the wound.

"Backwards," Rodecker said.

"Physics says blood flies out," Miller said. "Gravity says it falls down. These droplets... they were moving back toward the source."

"Suction?"

"Like a vacuum," Miller said.

Rodecker studied the wound. The flashlight beam cut across the torn edges. The jaggedness resolved into a pattern.

"The edges," Rodecker said. "Look, scalloped."

"I measured them," Miller said. "Regular intervals. Arc of four centimeters."

"Teeth?"

"Too big for a human," Miller said. "Too regular for an animal. A dog or coyote tears. This... this is punched."

"Garden tool," Rodecker said. "Hand rake. Cultivator. Something with tines."

"Maybe," Miller said. "But a tool leaves drag marks in the tissue. This is clean. Like a cookie cutter."

"It's a tool," Rodecker said. *It has to be. Tools come from hardware stores. Hardware stores have receipts. Receipts have names.* "Bag the soil samples from the grass. Everything."

"On it."

Movement at the perimeter. A woman ducked under the tape, holding a large cardboard cup of coffee. Detective Yolanda Pierce. Sharp. Irritated. Her blazer was crisp despite the heat. She marched toward them, heels clicking on the paved path like a countdown.

"Tell me the press isn't live yet," Pierce said.

"Channel 11 is setting up a shot with the fountain in the background," Rodecker said. "Artistic."

"Great," Pierce said. She took a drink of coffee. She studied the body. Her shoulders went tight. "Damn. Caroline."

"Yeah."

"Saw her three months ago. She was wearing blue then." Pierce stepped closer, careful not to step on the markers. "Candles?"

"Staging," Rodecker said. "Ritualistic."

"And the blood?" Pierce asked. "Where is it?"

"Don't know."

Pierce stared at him over the rim of her cup. "What do you mean, you don't know? Karl, her throat is gone."

"Bricks are dry," Rodecker said. "Miller checked. I checked. Clean."

Pierce lowered her cup. She studied the dry stones. She studied the patch of grass six feet away. She did the math, and the answer didn't make sense.

"Not possible," she said.

"I know."

"Drained somewhere else and dumped?"

"No drag marks," Rodecker said. "Shaw slipped on fresh blood. She bled here. Or... she died here."

Pierce turned her back to the body, facing the park perimeter, blocking the camera angles. Give them a wall of backs instead of a dead girl.

"Okay," Pierce said. Problem-solving mode. "Apartments. The row on Whitaker has a clear line of sight. Coffee shop on Bull opens at six. Someone saw something."

"Or someone saw nothing," Rodecker said. "Which is worse."

"I'll take the east side," Pierce said. "Start with the Collins Quarter. You take the residential block. Doorbell cameras. Teslas with sentry mode."

"We need to move her," Rodecker said. "Before the sun gets higher. Before the choppers launch."

"Do it," Pierce said. She flipped open her notebook. "I'll coordinate the uniforms. We lock this park down. No one leaves without ID."

She walked away, pointing at a pair of patrolmen.

Rodecker signaled the coroner's team. They brought the gurney across the grass, wheels rattling on the uneven ground.

"Miller," Rodecker said. "One last look before they lift."

Miller nodded. Camera ready. The two attendants, big men in blue jumpsuits, positioned themselves on either side of Caroline Marsh.

"On three," one said. "One. Two. Three."

They lifted.

Rodecker held his breath. *This is where we find it. The blood pooling underneath. The hidden stain. The answer.*

The body rose.

The bricks beneath her were bare.

Nothing. Just the grey stone, the pattern of the weave, and the dampness of the morning. No blood. No stain. No proof she had ever bled at all.

"Jesus," the attendant said.

"Bag her," Rodecker said. "Get her out."

They lowered Caroline onto the gurney and zipped the black vinyl bag. The zipper sound was final. The fountain kept running behind them, patient and indifferent.

Miller was on his knees by the grass patch, scraping soil into a plastic vial. The scraping sound grated on Rodecker's nerves like nails on a chalkboard.

The sun crested the tree line. The light hit the spray of the fountain in the distance—a Savannah morning. Tourists would be lining up for trolley tours in an hour, snapping pictures of the same fountain that had witnessed a woman with no blood.

Rodecker took his sunglasses from his pocket and slid them on. The world turned amber.

"Miller."

"Yeah, Detective?"

"Every grain of dirt. Every fiber. If a squirrel sneezed near this tree, I want to know about it."

"You got it."

Rodecker turned toward the street. The air felt heavy. Not just humidity. Pressure. He had felt it before, years ago, when a hurricane stalled off the coast—the waiting for the storm.

He walked toward his car, leaving the dry stones behind. He needed an answer that fit this scene. If he couldn't find one, he would have to accept that the rules had changed. And Rodecker didn't believe in magic.

He believed in evidence.

Even when the evidence was nothing but dry brick and unlit candles.

CHAPTER

3

Nadia Lopez straddled Nate's hips in the dim light of his Alexandria bedroom, her hands braced against his chest. Rich bronze skin caught the lamplight, muscle definition showing through even in shadow—the body of someone who competed, not someone who just trained. Her breasts swayed as she moved, nipples tight in the cool air. An athlete's frame, all compact power and control, thick thighs gripping his hips as she rhythmically moved against him.

She watched his face for a reaction that wasn't coming.

His hands rested on her waist—fingers pressing where ribs tapered to wide hips. He kissed her throat, trying to focus on the heat of her skin, the catch in her breath when his hands moved up her back to hold her nape. She was beautiful—objectively, undeniably beautiful. Sharp-minded, uncomplicated in the best way. This worked because neither of them wanted more.

But his eyes kept tracking past her shoulder to the open bedroom door, to the sparse living room beyond.

A single lamp by the window cast a yellow light on the cheap IKEA coffee table. The table held two things.

The first was a Saturday New York Times crossword puzzle, completed in black ink. No strike-throughs. No corrections. He had finished it in four minutes and thirty-seven seconds before Nadia arrived. The grid was complete—a block of ordered letters.

The second object sat beside it. A manila folder, corners soft and dog-eared from years of handling. The SCMPD logo stamped on the front had faded to a ghostly grey. A paperclip rusted to the top edge held a photograph of a nineteen-year-old girl in a SCAD hoodie. Sarah.

"Are you even here?" Nadia said, going still.

"I'm here." He pulled her down, kissed her throat, tried to anchor himself in the moment. She rocked against him. Her breasts pressed against his chest. He responded—his body knew what to do even when his mind was elsewhere. She made a soft sound and reached between them, her abdomen tightening as she moved, hand wrapping around him, guiding him inside her with a practiced ease that came from three months of this arrangement.

He gripped her hips, fingers digging into the curve of her ass as she began to move. He watched her face—dark eyes half-closed, full lips parted. This was good. This was normal. This was—

His phone buzzed on the nightstand.

Nadia's eyes opened. "Don't."

Another buzz. Then another.

"Don't answer that." Her movements slowed but didn't stop. She ground down, trying to reclaim his attention through sensation alone. "Nate. Whatever it is, it can wait ten minutes."

But he was already reaching. The shift in his attention was complete. She might as well have vanished. His fingers found the cold glass of the phone. He turned it over. The screen lit up the room with harsh blue light.

"Holloway," he answered, his free hand steadying Nadia's hip as she tried to continue moving, still wrapped around him.

"Holloway." Assistant Director Harran's voice was curt and commanding. "I need you on a plane. We have a situation in Georgia."

Nate sat up. Nadia had to brace herself against his shoulders. Her breasts pressed against him, her body slick with sweat. His focus was on Harran's voice.

"Go ahead," Nate said.

"Local PD has a body in a public park. Female, twenty-eight. Found at dawn by a civilian." Harran's voice carried the flat, rhythmic cadence of a man reading from a screen. "No signs of sexual assault. No defensive wounds. But the staging is specific. Victim was found nude, arms crossed over the chest, left over right. Four unlit candles placed at the cardinal points."

Nate stopped breathing. He stared past Nadia's shoulder at the manila folder on the table. The rusted paperclip caught the lamplight.

"Cause of death?" Nate asked.

"Massive trauma to the anterior neck. Tissue avulsion. The medical examiner's preliminary notes say the throat was destroyed. But here's the kicker, Nate. The scene is dry. The body is exsanguinated. We're talking ninety-plus percent blood volume loss with zero pooling at the site."

Nadia made a frustrated sound and climbed off him. The loss was immediate—warmth replaced by cool air hitting his skin where her body had been. She stood beside the bed, naked, all curves and toned muscle. Anger radiated from her in waves.

"Where?" Nate asked. The word came out like a rasp.

"Savannah," Harran said.

Nate stopped breathing. The hum of the refrigerator in the kitchen became a roar. The streetlights outside the window blurred. *Savannah.*

"Specifically, Forsyth Park," Harran continued, unaware of the silence on the other end. "Near the Confederate Memorial. The locals are spooked. They're asking for a profile, but they're already leaking details to the press about ritual killings. I need someone down there who can manage and give them a suspect that makes sense."

Nate stood up. He walked naked into the living room. The floorboards were cold under his feet.

He stopped at the coffee table, stared down at the crossword puzzle, and turned to the file.

"Nate?" Harran said. "You there?"

"I'm here."

"I know your history," Harran said, his tone shifting, softening just enough not to be insulting. "I know the file you keep in your desk. I know where you're from. If this is going to be a problem, I can send Greene. Or we wait for the GBI."

"No," Nate said.

"It's the same city, Nate. I checked the jacket. Sarah was found near Monterey Square. This is Forsyth. It's close."

"It's five blocks," Nate said. He didn't need a map. He could walk that route in his mind. He could see the live oaks, the Spanish moss dripping like grey rags, the shadows that swallowed light.

He'd walked it a thousand times in his nightmares.

"Are you compromised on this?" Harran asked. "Because I can't have you going down there and chasing ghosts. I need a federal agent, not a grieving brother."

Nate rubbed his face with his free hand. His fingers traced the scar bisecting his left eyebrow, a nervous habit he couldn't break.

"You said exsanguination," Nate said.

"Complete blood loss. That's what the ME says."

"And the candles. White pillar candles?"

"Yes. Unlit."

Nate examined the photo of Sarah. The hoodie she was wearing in the picture was blue. She'd been smiling. She'd called him two days before she died, complaining about her art history class.

"I'll take it," Nate said. "Send the file to my secure email. I'm leaving now."

"Nate—"

"I'm leaving now, Jeff."

He hung up. He dropped the phone on the table next to the folder and walked to the bedroom closet.

Nadia sat on his bed now, wrapped in the sheet. Her hair was a mess. Her face had gone rigid. She watched him pull a pair of dark slacks from a hanger, throw on and button a white shirt. She didn't look angry anymore.

"You're going," she said. It wasn't a question.

"Yes. Savannah."

He met her eyes then. She was smart. She was one of the best profilers in the unit. She'd witnessed the shift in him, the way the light behind his eyes had changed from desire to calculation.

"You heard," he said.

"I heard enough," Nadia said. She stood up. The sheet fell away—a last attempt. She stood naked in the center of his bedroom, exposed, her body framed by the low light. Nate couldn't bring himself to look her in the eye. "You're demonstrating classic cognitive distraction, Nate. Textbook definition. You perform the tasks of daily life—you eat, sleep, fuck—but your executive function is hijacked. You're not processing the present. You're running a background simulation of a past event. Constantly."

"It's a case," Nate said as he sat on the bed to tie his shoes. Double knot. Tight. "It's my job."

"It's not a case," she said. Her voice was calm, clinical. "Cases have file numbers. Cases have leads. That..." She gestured to the dog-eared folder. "...that is a shrine. You live in there. You don't live here."

Nate stood up. He grabbed his shoulder holster from the dresser. The leather creaked as he settled it over his shoulders. He performed a press check of the Glock's chamber. Brass glinted.

"A woman is dead," Nate said. "Same MO. Same city. If I don't go, who does? Greene? He'll write it up as a sex crime and move on. He won't examine the details."

"And you will?" Nadia asked. "You'll examine the details until you see Sarah in every shadow. You'll force the evidence to fit the ghost story you've been telling yourself for fifteen years."

"The details match, Nadia. Exsanguination. Staging. It's him."

"Or it's a copycat. Or it's a coincidence. Or it's something else." She adjusted the strap of her bag. "But you won't see that. You can't see that because you need it to be him. You need the puzzle to have a solution so you can finally stop counting the minutes since she died."

She walked to her clothes. Her steps were heavy on the hardwood and stopped with her hand on her jeans.

"I care about you, Nate," she said, gesturing between their bodies, at the bed they'd just shared, at her naked body he'd been inside minutes ago. "But my function in this arrangement is temporary stimulation. A way for you to feel a pulse before you go back to being dead with her."

Nate didn't answer.

Nadia stared at him. Then she nodded, a small, sharp movement. She turned away and began to dress. She pulled on her jeans and fastened them over her hips. She buttoned her blouse. She moved with the same efficiency he did.

She walked out of the bedroom without looking back. The front door opened and closed. The lock clicked.

He exhaled—a long breath that shuddered in his chest. He walked into the living room.

He sat down on the sofa, reached out, and picked up the manila folder. The paper felt dry and brittle under his fingers. He opened it.

The photo of Sarah looked up at him. She was laughing mid-sentence, her head thrown back. The picture had been taken two days before she died, before she was found in an alley off Tattnall Street. Before her throat was torn out. Before the blood was drained from her body. Savannah PD shrugged and called it a drug deal gone wrong or a transient attack.

Morning light crested over the Potomac and filtered through the blinds, washing out the yellow lamplight. It illuminated the ink grid of the crossword puzzle.

Four down. Eight letters. Cold, in a way.

"Unsolved," he said, staring at the word until the letters stopped meaning anything. Crosswords were kind in that way. They promised an answer existed.

He stood, shoved the manila folder into his bag, and walked out the door without a backward glance at the unmade bed. The crossword was finished.

The puzzle was all that mattered. And he never left a puzzle unsolved.

CHAPTER

4

THE AIR CONDITIONING in the SCMPD task force room was aggressive enough to preserve meat, humming with a mechanical rattle that vibrated through the cheap laminate of the conference table. Nate Holloway sat in a metal chair that offered no ergonomic support, hands flat on the table, spine straight. He did not lean back.

The room was a windowless box on the second floor of headquarters, institutional beige walls showing every scuff mark from chairs banging against the plaster. A large monitor dominated one end; a whiteboard covered the other. Blue painter's tape held maps of the Historic District to the wall, edges curling in the cold.

Chief Harold Dean stood at the head of the table, sweating despite the glacial temperature. A ring of perspiration had already darkened the collar of his uniform shirt as he wiped his upper lip with a hand-kerchief, eyes scanning the faces around the table with the look of a man drowning in shallow water.

"We treat this like any other homicide," Dean said, leaning his weight on his knuckles. His eyes darted to the woman pacing behind him. "We follow the evidence. We keep the circle tight. No leaks."

Councilwoman Patty Moffett stopped pacing near the door as if guarding it, her pale yellow suit expensive and crisp. Her hair was sprayed into a helmet of blonde armor that wouldn't move in a hurricane. She held a phone in one hand and a tablet in the other, her attention fixed on the screen with the intensity of someone monitoring a stock portfolio during a crash.

"The circle is already broken, Harold." Moffett didn't look up. "My inbox is full. The Chamber of Commerce is asking why there are crime scene tapes in Forsyth Park during peak season. I won't have headlines about bodies. I want headlines about swift justice. Or better yet. No headlines at all."

"We are handling it, Patty," Dean said.

"Handle it quietly." She finally looked up, her eyes hard. "We have the Music Festival coming up. We have weddings booked in that park for the next three weekends. Do you understand what that means for the tourism board?"

Nate remained silent, cataloging the players. *Dean, terrified. Moffett, an obstacle.*

Two detectives sat across from him.

Karl Rodecker looked like he had slept in his suit, a big man gone soft around the middle, his tie loose and his collar unbuttoned. He sat with his right leg extended under the table, rubbing his knee absent-mindedly with the distracted rhythm of chronic pain. He looked like a man counting the days until he could hand in his badge and disappear into a fishing boat somewhere quiet.

Yolanda Pierce sat next to him, younger and sharp, her blazer tailored and her notebook open with a pen poised above clean pages. She observed Nate with the assessing gaze of someone who knew how to read a room and didn't trust strangers with federal badges.

"Agent Holloway," Dean said. "Thank you for coming down so quickly."

Nate nodded. "Chief."

"You've been briefed on the basics?"

"I know where she was found," Nate said. "I know the condition of the body."

Dean flinched at the word *body* and glanced at Moffett.

"Right," Dean said, clearing his throat. "Detectives. Walk us through it."

Rodecker moved stiffly to the monitor and picked up a remote, his knee making him favor his left side. He clicked a button, and a grainy, timestamped image appeared on the screen.

A woman with blonde hair in a black dress stood on a sidewalk, laughing, looking back at someone out of frame.

"Caroline Marsh," Rodecker said, his voice gravelly from too many cigarettes or too little sleep. "Twenty-eight years old. Local. Worked in marketing for a logistics firm near the port and was part of the art scene—gallery openings, fundraisers, that crowd. This was taken outside The Rail Pub on Congress Street at eleven forty-three Thursday night."

He clicked again.

Caroline walked alone past a storefront on Whitaker, her posture relaxed, phone in her hand.

"She left the bar alone at midnight," Rodecker said. "Bartender confirms she had two drinks over two hours. Wasn't drunk. She paid her tab, left a good tip, and walked out like she owned the sidewalk. Her car was parked in the Whitaker Street garage three blocks north. She didn't go to her car."

"Where did she go?" Nate asked.

"She walked south." Pierce stood and moved to the map on the wall, tracing a line with a red marker. "She cut through the squares. Wright. Chippewa. Then she hit the dead zone."

Pierce tapped a large section of the map with the marker cap.

"We have cameras on the perimeter of the Historic District," she said. "We have them on the businesses—bars, hotels, the tourist traps. But once you get into the residential streets near the park, it gets dark. The moss blocks the streetlights. The cameras don't have the angles. It's like walking into a tunnel."

"She vanished," Rodecker said. "Last sighting was near the Mercer House at twelve twenty-one. She was walking toward Forsyth. Alone. No one following her. No one in the frame. Just her and the shadows."

"She walked into a park at two in the morning," Nate said. "Alone."

"That's the part that sticks out," Pierce said, her marker still hovering over the map. "Her friends say she was paranoid about safety. Pepper spray on her keychain. Shared her location on dates. She didn't take shortcuts through alleys. She didn't walk alone at night, especially not in the squares where the tourists don't go."

"But she did last night," Nate said.

"But she did," Pierce confirmed. Her pen stopped tapping.

Rodecker clicked the remote again. The screen changed to a crime scene photo.

Caroline Marsh lay on the brick path beneath the arching live oaks, Spanish moss hanging down like grey rags from branches that had seen two hundred years. She was naked, her skin pale against the red brick, every line of her body exposed to the morning jogger who had found her. Clothes missing. Her arms were crossed over her chest, left over right, hands positioned with care.

Four white candles stood in a square around her, unlit but placed with geometric precision.

Nate leaned forward, resting his elbows on the table, his focus narrowing to the screen. He studied the image, ignoring the face, focusing on the geometry and the angles—the precision.

"Show me the wound," Nate said.

Rodecker hesitated, glancing at Dean, who wiped his face again with the damp handkerchief.

"Show him," Pierce said.

Rodecker clicked. The camera zoomed in on the neck.

The tissue was destroyed. Not a clean slice, but a tear with ragged edges where something had ripped through skin and muscle. The trachea was visible, its cartilage white against the dark red of the muscle, windpipe exposed to air that no longer mattered.

A cold pressure settled in Nate's chest, a familiar weight he pushed down by focusing on the physics and the geometry, not the person who used to breathe through that throat.

"Where is the blood?" Nate asked.

Rodecker pointed at the screen. "That's the question, isn't it?"

"He killed her somewhere else," Dean said. "He dumped her there."

"Then where is the blood?" Moffett's voice rose, losing the controlled edge she'd been holding.

"It's gone," Rodecker said. "The ME estimates ninety-two percent volume loss. We found a few drops on the grass six feet away—that's where the firefighter slipped and contaminated the scene. But the body? Drained. Dry. Like something wrung her out."

"Ninety-two percent," Nate repeated, his mind running calculations. "That requires a pump. Or gravity and a lot of time. You can't do that on a park path in the middle of the night without leaving a swimming pool behind, without the ground soaking it up like a sponge."

"Unless you catch it," Pierce said.

Nate looked at her. She met his gaze, unflinching.

"Catch it."

"In a bucket," she said. "In a jar. In something. If it's not on the ground, it has to be somewhere. He took it with him."

Nate pushed his chair back, the metal legs scraping against the linoleum with a sound that made Dean wince. He crossed to the whiteboard and uncapped a black marker, the smell of solvent hitting him sharply and chemically. He erased the notes already there—timelines and officer assignments—wiping the space clean with broad strokes.

"We need a profile," Dean said. "Something to give the press."

Nate ignored him. He wrote a word in block letters, the marker squeaking against the smooth surface.

ORGANIZED.

"He didn't panic," Nate said, his back to the room. "He took her clothes. He took the weapon. He took the blood. He took the time to position the body and place the candles with a ruler's precision. This wasn't a crime of passion. This was a project. This was planned."

He wrote another word.

LOCAL.

"He knows the cameras," Nate said. "He knows the patrol schedules, knows exactly where the shadows are deepest in Forsyth Park after midnight when the streetlights can't reach through the moss. He didn't stumble into that spot by accident. He chose it. He owns it."

He drew a hard line under LOCAL, the marker tip squeaking.

"He was safe there," Nate said. "Safe enough to spend twenty or thirty minutes bleeding her out without rushing. He wasn't worried about being seen. That suggests arrogance. Or ownership."

"Ownership of what?" Moffett asked.

Nate turned around. "Of the city. Of the space. He thinks you are all guests in his house."

He turned back to the board and wrote two more words.

POWER. CONTROL.

"The sexual component is secondary," Nate said. "There was no rape kit evidence, correct?"

"Negative," Rodecker said. "No trauma. No DNA found yet, though the lab is still running tests."

"He doesn't need to rape her to possess her," Nate said. "Taking the blood is the possession. Taking a life is the act of intimacy he craves. The nakedness isn't about humiliation or sexual gratification. It's about stripping away her identity, making her a blank canvas for his ritual."

"Ritual," Dean said, the word tasting bad in his mouth. "You think this is a cult?"

"No. Cults are messy. Groups make mistakes, leave witnesses, talk to the wrong people. This was one man. The efficiency is too high for a group. The control too absolute."

He looked at the photo of the throat again. The ragged tear. The lack of blood.

"He wants you to see it," Nate said. "He staged her like art in a gallery. He wants the fear. He wants the awe. He wants you to know he can do this and walk away clean."

Nate wrote a final phrase on the board.

CLINICAL VAMPIRISM.

"What is that?" Dean asked.

"Renfield Syndrome," Nate said. "A psychological compulsion to consume blood. It's rare. Usually starts in childhood with animals—cutting them open, drinking from the wounds. It escalates. The subject derives sexual satisfaction or a sense of vitality from the act. They believe the blood gives them power, extends their life, connects them to something larger."

Moffett stepped forward, pointing a manicured finger at the board. "No."

"It fits the physical evidence," Nate said. "The blood is missing. It wasn't spilled. It was taken with purpose."

"You are not using that word." Moffett's voice climbed. "You are not putting 'vampire' in a press release. Do you have any idea what that would do? We have ghost tours on every corner selling stories about supernatural Savannah. If you tell them there is a vampire hunting women in the parks, you will destroy this city's reputation. You will turn us into a joke."

"I am not concerned with your ticket sales," Nate said. "I am concerned with catching a predator who drains women dry."

Moffet's eyes flare with anger at Nate's dismissal.

"It's a delusion," Nate added. "He believes he needs it, or believes he is something else. It doesn't matter what he believes. It matters what he does. And he will do it again."

"Why?" Pierce asked.

"Because he succeeded," Nate said. "He got away with it. The high was perfect. But the high fades. The hunger comes back. And he knows this city. He knows he can do it again."

An itch crawled between Nate's shoulder blades—a biological warning, the feeling of being observed. Not now, but by the city outside these walls, by something waiting in the squares and the moss. A *Local.*

"We keep the specific language internal," Nate said. "For the public, we say we are looking for a disorganized offender. Give them misinformation. Tell them he was sloppy, left evidence we're processing. We bruise his ego, make him angry. Maybe he makes a mistake and reaches out to correct the record."

"I can live with that," Moffett said. "Just keep the supernatural garbage out of it."

"It's not supernatural," Nate said. "It's psychopathology. A man with a knife and a bucket."

The conference room door opened, and a young man in a uniform stuck his head in, holding a pink slip of paper. His hand trembled.

"Chief?"

"Not now, Tyrell," Dean said, waving a dismissive hand.

"It's the phone lines, sir," Tyrell said. "The switchboard. I have a woman on line four. She's called six times in the last hour. She won't hang up until she speaks to the lead investigator. She's threatening to go to the press."

"Take a message."

"I did, sir. But she says it's critical. She says she knows the pattern."

Nate turned. "What pattern?"

Tyrell swallowed, his Adam's apple bobbing as he looked at Nate. "She says this happened before. She has records."

"Who is she?" Rodecker asked.

"Alicia Landry," Tyrell said. "She's with the Georgia Historical Society. She says the staging matches a killing from 1995. And one from 1980. And one from 1965."

Moffett threw her hands up. "Here we go. The ghouls and the ghost hunters, crawling out for their fifteen minutes of cable news fame."

"Take a number," Dean said. "Tell her we'll call her back."

"Wait," Nate said. He walked over and took the pink slip from Tyrell, the paper thin and cheap between his fingers.

Landry. Historical Society. Pattern.

"1995?" Nate asked.

"That's what she said," Tyrell confirmed. "And something about... she said to check the moon phase."

Dean groaned, rubbing his temples. "Great. Astrology. Just what we need. Next, she'll tell us to consult a psychic."

"Get her contact info," Nate said. "Tell her not to speak to the press, or I'll have her charged with obstruction."

The black conference phone in the center of the table lit up with a blinking red LED.

"That's Harran." Dean straightened his tie, staring at the phone. "He's been listening to the meeting."

He pressed the button.

"AD Harran," Dean said, his voice an octave higher. "We are wrapping up the briefing now."

"Put Holloway on," Harran's voice came through the speaker, tinny and sharp.

"I'm here," Nate said.

"I'm getting reports from the GBI liaison," Harran said. "They are hearing chatter about ritual elements. Are we containing this?"

"We are building a profile," Nate said. "It's organized. Predatory."

"I don't care about the psychology right now. I care about the narrative. I need you to squash the rumors before they metastasize. If this turns into a circus, if we have CNN down there talking about voodoo and vampires, I am pulling you out and sending someone who can control the message. Do you understand?"

"I understand."

"And this historian," Harran said. "Landry. The GBI says she's been pestering their cold case unit for years. Writes papers about violence cycles and patterns in Southern crime. Academic nonsense with no practical application."

"She called here," Nate said.

"Humor her. Go see her. Debunk her theories. Show her why she's wrong and shut her down before she goes to the papers with some ghost story that panics the tourists and costs the city millions. Keep the federal file clean, Nate. Facts. Only facts. No speculation."

"Understood," Nate said.

The line clicked dead. The silence that followed was heavy.

Moffett looked at Nate, a cold smile touching her lips. "You heard the man. No ghosts. No vampires. Fix it."

She picked up her tablet and marched out, the door slamming behind her with enough force to rattle the maps on the wall.

Dean slumped into a chair, the tension leaving him in a single, defeated exhale.

"Rodecker," Nate said. "Get the files ready. I want everything you have on the victim's movements for the last week—credit card transactions, social media posts, security footage from her building."

"You got it." Rodecker stood and cracked his knuckles.

"Pierce," Nate said. "Get me the address for the Historical Society."

"It's on Whitaker," she said. "Five minutes from here. Walking distance if you don't mind the heat."

Nate looked at the pink slip in his hand. *Pattern.* He looked at the whiteboard. *Clinical Vampirism.* He looked at the map, at the red line Pierce had drawn through the squares.

The cold air of the room bit through his shirt. He remembered the file in his bag, the photo of Sarah, the way the candles had been placed in the alley fifteen years ago.

He capped the marker.

"I'm going to see the historian," Nate said, and walked out of the room.

CHAPTER

5

THE HEAVY WOODEN doors swung shut behind Nate, sealing off the humid Savannah afternoon. The silence inside the Georgia Historical Society was instant and absolute, a sudden vacuum that pulled the street noise away. A wall of refrigerated air met him, drying the sweat on his neck and making his damp shirt cling cold against his spine. The building smelled of acidic old paper, and the sterile, recycled dust of a place that cataloged time rather than lived in it.

He bypassed the front desk, where a woman with reading glasses on a chain looked up, opened her mouth to ask for membership identification, then closed it when she saw the badge clipped to his belt and the set of his jaw. She pointed a manicured finger toward the double doors at the rear without a word.

Nate walked past glass display cases filled with Civil War muskets and ladies' fans, his heels clicking on the polished terrazzo. He checked his watch—quarter past three—and calculated he had allocated twenty minutes to shut this down. Twenty minutes to intimidate a local historian, dismantle her theory, and get back to the real work of building a profile on a very sick sexual predator.

The reading room was a cavern of shadows and amber light where rows of long oak tables stretched under a high ceiling. Green-shaded bankers' lamps illuminated the wood surfaces with pools of yellow light while leaving the rest of the room in gloom. The stacks rose in the back, metal shelves disappearing into the dark like the ribs of some fossilized creature.

He spotted her at a corner table in the far back, isolated from the two elderly men researching genealogy near the front. She had built a fortress around herself with archival grey boxes stacked three high on her left. Loose papers covered the surface in a chaotic spread that made sense only to her, a constellation only she could navigate.

Alicia Landry didn't look up as he approached, her attention fixed on the documents before her. She was younger than he expected, maybe early thirties, with dark hair pulled back in a messy bun that was already surrendering strands to gravity. A yellow pencil was pushed through the knot like a hasty afterthought. She wore an oversized cardigan wrapped tight around her frame, a shield against the building's aggressive climate control.

Nate stopped at the edge of the table and stood there for ten seconds, letting his shadow fall across her work. She turned a page in a leather-bound ledger, her movements precise and unhurried. Her fingers were stained with ink—blue smudges on the thumb, black on the index finger—markers of someone who still wrote things down by hand.

"You're blocking my light," she said without looking at him. Her voice was low, textured with a faint cadence that wasn't Savannah but something softer. Louisiana, maybe.

Nate pulled the pink phone message slip from his pocket and dropped it onto the open ledger, where it fluttered and settled over the handwriting. "Alicia Landry," he said, making it sound like an accusation. "You've been busy."

She looked up then, and behind tortoise-shell glasses, her eyes were dark and exhausted, circled by shadows that spoke of too much coffee and too little sleep. She looked at the pink slip, then up at him with no trace of apology or fear. She didn't blink.

"Agent Holloway," she said in a tone that suggested she'd been expecting him. "You took your time."

"I'm here now, and you wanted to talk about patterns." He let the pause stretch before continuing. "You have five minutes to tell me why you're calling my task force before I have you cited for interfering with a federal investigation."

She closed the ledger, moving the pink slip aside with a flick of her ink-stained finger. "I'm not interfering—I'm trying to stop you from chasing your tail while another woman dies."

"We have leads, and we have a profile," Nate said, his voice flat.

"You have nothing," she said without raising her voice, making it a statement of fact rather than an argument. "You have a body in Forsyth Park with no blood in it and a chief who cares more about the Music Festival than the victim. And you have a suspect profile that says 'organized sexual predator' because that's what the manual tells you to look for."

Nate pulled out the chair opposite her and sat down as the wood groaned under his weight. He leaned forward, resting his forearms on the table, invading her space with the deliberate pressure of someone used to getting answers. "We keep holdback evidence for a reason, Miss Landry, so if you know details about the blood volume, that makes you a person of interest, not a consultant."

"I know about the blood because I can read," she said, reaching into a stack of papers to slide a photocopy across the table. It was a page from a handwritten death register where the script was looped and ornate, the ink faded to brown.

"Chatham County Death Ledger, October 1890," she said, tapping the page.

Nate looked at the document and let his eyes adjust to the archaic handwriting that sprawled across the yellowed paper.

Entry 142. Unidentified Female. Found in the park extension. Age approx 20. Blonde. Throat rent as if by animal. Body strangely at peace. No blood found on soil.

The air conditioning unit gave a low thrum, a vibration in the floor that Nate felt through his shoes. He read the entry again, slower this time, letting the words sink in. *Throat rent. No blood.*

"1890," Nate said, grasping for the rational explanation his training demanded. "This is a yellow fever year when records were messy, and people died in the streets."

"Yellow fever makes you bleed from the eyes and nose," Alicia said, her tone patient as a teacher correcting a promising student. "It doesn't tear your throat out or drain the body dry without spilling a drop."

She placed another document on top of the first, this one a photocopy of a newspaper clipping from the *Savannah Morning News*. The headline was bold and grainy despite the decades. **VAMPIRE PANIC IN SQUARES**. The date was April 1935.

"Girl found in Chippewa Square," Alicia said, tapping the headline with one ink-stained finger. "Transient, blonde, throat destroyed—police blamed a wild dog pack, but dogs don't arrange the body."

Nate stared at the newsprint as the story described the body positioned with 'limbs composed' and 'candles stolen from the cathedral' placed nearby. The details were too specific, too familiar, too close to what he'd seen on the monitor an hour ago.

"Copycat," Nate said, keeping his voice flat and professional despite the unease creeping up his spine. "Someone read the old papers and recreated it."

"In 1935?" Alicia raised an eyebrow. "They were recreating an obscure death register entry from 1890 that wasn't public record?"

She dealt the next card like a gambler who already knew she'd won. A glossy black-and-white photograph that looked like a police evidence shot showed a woman's body on cobblestones, pale against the dark stone. Four white candles stood at the cardinal points with geometric precision.

"1995," Alicia said. "Coroner's inquest photo from a tourist out of Ohio—they ruled it a ritual killing by a local occult group, but never caught anyone. The group didn't exist."

Nate looked at the photo and felt his stomach tighten as he recognized the positioning. The crossed arms, left over right, the geometry precise and deliberate. It was the same scene he had looked at on the monitor in the task force room an hour ago.

"This is impossible," Nate said, but even as he spoke the words, his mind was already racing ahead. "The details, the candle placement—that wasn't in the papers."

"No," Alicia said. "It wasn't."

"Then how do you have it?"

"I'm a historian, Agent—I dig." She leaned forward, her eyes locked on his with an intensity that made him want to look away. "I found the inquest file in a mislabeled box in the county archives basement. 1890. 1935. 1995. Do the math, Agent Holloway."

Nate's mind resisted the calculation even as his training forced him to process the numbers. He wanted to arrest her and find out how she had accessed sealed files. But his brain, trained to find patterns, was already crunching the data despite his resistance.

"Fifteen years," he said.

"Fifteen years," she echoed, nodding. "1890, 1905, 1920, 1935, 1950, 1965, 1980, 1995, 2010, 2025."

"You skipped some," Nate said, seizing on the inconsistency. "You showed me three."

"I showed you the ones that fit on the table." She gestured to the wall of boxes beside her like a curator revealing her life's work. "I have the others—1920 was a prostitute on River Street, 1950 was a war widow, 1965 was a civil rights worker. The police didn't care about them because they were 'high-risk' victims, easy to ignore. But the wounds were the same, and the lack of blood was the same."

Nate sat back as the wooden chair dug into his spine, and he looked at the stacks of paper that represented years of obsessive research. It was a wall of noise, conspiracy theory logic like the people who connected JFK to Lincoln to 9/11 because they needed the world to make sense. He had seen it before.

"Correlation isn't causation," Nate said, falling back on his training. "You're cherry-picking data, and Savannah has a high violent crime rate. You look through enough records, you'll find throat wounds every fifteen years—it's statistical noise."

"With identical staging?" Alicia asked, her voice sharp now. "With the candles, with the blood volume anomaly, with the victimology?"

"Victimology," Nate said, latching onto the word. "You're using our words now."

"Blonde," she said, ticking them off on her ink-stained fingers with the precision of someone who'd memorized the list. "Petite, age eighteen to thirty, no defensive wounds, found near a square or a park. Naked and staged like a funeral."

She paused, watching him with those dark, exhausted eyes.

"That's not noise, Agent—that's a design."

Nate felt the itch between his shoulder blades again, the sense of being watched even though they were alone in the corner. The silence pressed against his ears like the weight of all those years, all those bodies, all those unsolved cases.

"A copycat," Nate said, needing it to be true more than he'd needed anything in years. "A multigenerational group, a family that passes the ritual down from grandfather to father to son. We see it in abuse cycles, and we see it in organized crime."

"A family that doesn't make a mistake for a hundred and thirty-five years?" Alicia asked, her tone reasonable despite the absurdity of what she was suggesting. "A family that kills every fifteen years exactly, then stops with no escalation, no cooling-off period variation? They just sleep?"

"People don't live for a hundred and thirty years, Miss Landry," Nate said, his voice harder now. "Cults do. Legends do."

"I didn't say it was a legend," she said, meeting his eyes. "I said it was a pattern."

She reached for a long roll of paper taped together from multiple sheets of graph paper, something that looked like an engineer's time-line. "I mapped it," she said as she began unrolling the document. "Geographically and temporally, the squares aren't random. He moves in a spiral, always inward."

She unrolled the spreadsheet across the table, covering the 1890 ledger with a grid of dates, locations, weather conditions, and names. The handwriting was tiny, precise, obsessive in a way that reminded Nate of his own case boards.

Nate scanned the columns as his eyes moved over the dates like a detective following breadcrumbs. 1965, 1980, 1995—the data was comprehensive with moon phases listed, tides recorded, temperatures noted. His eyes tracked to the next column, where a date caught his attention.

2010.

He stopped breathing.

The entry was typed in the middle of the page with the same clinical precision as all the others.

May 14, 2010. Monterey Square (Alley adjacency). Victim: Sarah Holloway. Age 19. Exsanguination.

The room seemed to shrink around him as the low thrum of the air conditioner faded into nothing. The smell of old paper turned into the smell of wet brick and iron, and suddenly he was back in the funeral home, standing over the closed casket while his father's hand pressed heavily on his shoulder. *Closed casket, son. It's better this way.*

Nate's hand shot out and slammed down on the paper, his palm covering the name as the slap cracked in the quiet room. The two elderly men at the front turned around while the librarian stood up, glaring at the disturbance.

Nate didn't see them because he only saw Alicia Landry.

"Where did you get this?" His voice was low and dangerous as he leaned over the table, his face inches from hers. The professional calm he wore like a uniform had evaporated, burned away by fifteen years of grief. "Where did you get her name?"

Alicia didn't flinch but sat perfectly still, looking up at him over the rim of her glasses. "It's a public record, Agent—unsolved homicide, Chatham County cold case file number 2010-449."

"She is not a data point," he said, the words tight in his throat like broken glass. "She is not part of your little science project."

"She is part of the pattern," Alicia said, her voice quiet and almost gentle. "I didn't put her there—he did."

"Stop." Nate grabbed the table, his knuckles straining white against the wood. "You don't know what you're talking about because it was a mugging, a gang initiation that went wrong."

"Is that what you tell yourself?" Alicia asked, and her voice wasn't mocking but sad. "A mugging with no stolen wallet? A gang initiation that leaves the body perfectly composed with lavender clutched in her palm?"

Nate recoiled as if she had struck him.

Lavender.

That detail wasn't in the papers or in the police report released to the public. It was in the private evidence inventory he had memorized and burned into his brain for fifteen years—a sachet made from her grandmother's recipe.

"How?" he said, the word a bare exhalation. "How do you know that?"

"Because he does it every time," Alicia said, her voice steady. "Jasmine, night-blooming cereus. However, lavender was only left once. He leaves flowers, and he leaves them peaceful."

She reached out as if to touch his hand, but he pulled back.

"Your sister wasn't random, Nate," she said, using his first name for the first time. "She wasn't in the wrong place at the wrong time—he hunted her, he watched her, he chose her."

Nate stood up and paced in a tight circle away from the table, his hands gripping his head. The stacks of books seemed to lean in, suffused with the weight of too much history pressing down on him.

He chose her.

The thought was a physical sickness that spread through his chest. For fifteen years, he had lived with the guilt of a random tragedy, torturing himself with what-ifs. If she hadn't walked that way, if he had called her five minutes earlier—randomness was cruel, but it was impersonal.

He turned back to Alicia and needed to destroy this theory, needed to break it into pieces so he could breathe again. "A copycat," he said again, desperation creeping into his tone. "A cult, or someone with access to the archives—someone like you. You have access to all of this, so maybe you're the one feeding the information to someone."

"I was fifteen years old in 2010," Alicia said, her voice patient. "I was in Louisiana—check my records."

"Then someone else, a generational obsession where a father teaches a son." He was grasping now, reaching for any explanation that didn't require him to accept the impossible. "They use the archives to pick the method."

"Why?" Alicia asked. "Why replicate a method that requires draining five liters of blood without spilling it? Why replicate the bite marks?"

"Bite marks?" Nate froze. "The autopsy said animal predation."

"The autopsy was wrong," Alicia said. "Or the coroner was lazy, or paid off, or scared—look at the wound photos again. The spacing, the arch—it's human dentition, Agent, just different."

She tapped the spreadsheet, right on top of Sarah's name.

"It's the same killer," she said. "1890, 1950, 2010, 2025—it is one individual."

"That's biologically impossible."

"I know," Alicia said, and for the first time, he heard the exhaustion in her voice. "And yet, here is the data."

She pushed the stack toward him like an offering he didn't want to accept.

"You want to catch him?" she asked. "Stop looking for a sex offender who hates his mother or a drifter passing through. Start looking for someone who has been here a long time, someone who knows the city better than the maps do."

Nate looked at the pile of papers—the ledger, the photos, the timeline—and saw Sarah's name peeking out from under the edge of the clipping. He felt a cracking sensation in his chest, the sound of a structural wall giving way after holding too much weight for too long. He had built his life around the FBI's logic of behavior, motivation, cause, and effect. The world was ugly, but it made sense.

This didn't make sense.

But the lavender did.

He reached out and grabbed the papers, folding the spreadsheet and crumpling the edges as he shoved the entire stack into the inside pocket of his jacket. "I'm taking these," Nate said, his voice hollow. "Evidence."

"I made copies," Alicia said without surprise. "I knew you would."

"If I see my sister's name in the paper," Nate said, pointing a finger at her with a tremor he couldn't control, "if I see one word about patterns or vampires or rituals on the news, I will bring the full weight of the federal government down on this institution. I will bury you."

"I don't want the news," Alicia said as she began to stack her remaining boxes, her movements methodical. "I want him stopped because I've been tracking him for ten years, and I'm tired of counting bodies."

She looked at him, her dark eyes magnified by the glasses.

"He's started the cycle, Nate—Caroline Marsh was just the first, and he needs more. He always takes more."

Nate didn't answer because he couldn't trust his voice.

He turned and walked away, marching past the genealogy researchers, past the display cases of muskets, past the woman at the front desk. He pushed the heavy doors open and stepped out into the world he no longer recognized.

The light was blinding, white, and harsh after the gloom of the archives, and he had to squint against the assault.

Nate moved to the side of the stairs, clutching the jacket pocket where the papers sat against his ribs. He felt the shape of them, the weight of them, the impossible truth of them.

Sarah.

He leaned against the warm brick of the building, gasping for air that tasted of exhaust and marsh. The city moved around him with trolleys ringing, tourists laughing, cars hissing on the pavement—all of it normal, all of it mundane, all of it oblivious.

It all looked the same as it had twenty minutes ago.

But the map had changed, and the grid had shifted.

He wasn't hunting a ghost anymore—he was hunting the man who killed his sister. And for the first time in fifteen years, he had a lead that made sense of the senseless.

Nate pushed off the wall and walked to his car, his hand trembling as he keyed the lock. He needed to see the map, needed to see the string, needed to see if the geometry held. He needed to know if Alicia Landry was a conspiracy theorist or the only person in Savannah who saw the truth.

CHAPTER

6

Nate Holloway stood near the Confederate Memorial, the bronze soldier atop the sandstone plinth staring north. Sweat gathered at his hairline and trickled down his temples despite the early hour. He held the map Alicia Landry had given him against the faint breeze, the paper heavy stock, creased and marked with her tight, angular handwriting. She had drawn vectors in red ink—lines of sight, egress routes, kill zones. She hadn't drawn a tourist map; she had drawn a firing solution.

Detective Karl Rodecker approached from the direction of the fountain, wiping his forehead with a handkerchief that had surrendered to the humidity an hour ago. Detective Yolanda Pierce walked beside him, tapping at a tablet screen that glared in the harsh afternoon sunlight.

"Ninety-two degrees," Rodecker said, stuffing the handkerchief into his pocket. "And eighty percent humidity, which means I'm breathing water out here."

Nate kept his eyes on the map, tracing the line Alicia had drawn in red ink, a vector cutting through the green space of the park.

"She entered here," Nate said, pointing toward the southern perimeter. "Caroline Marsh left the bar, and traffic cams put her on Drayton Street at one-forty-five before she vanishes from the grid."

Pierce scrolled on her tablet. "We have her on the camera at the corner of Gwinnett, but after that, nothing until the jogger found her."

"Because she stepped off the grid," Nate said, folding the map so the paper crinkled. "Walk with me."

He stepped onto the brick path that cut diagonally toward the fountain. The live oaks overhead stretched their massive limbs across the walkway, forming a canopy that blocked the sun. The shade offered no relief from the heat, only a dim, green-tinted gloom where Spanish moss hung like dead men's beards, motionless in the still air.

He stopped under the spreading branches of a massive oak where the path curved, obscuring the line of sight from the street. Nate looked up at a surveillance camera that stared down from a black pole twenty yards away.

"What does that camera see?" Nate asked.

Pierce tapped her screen, bringing up the feed history, and then frowned. "Nothing—the angle is bad."

"It's not the angle," Nate said, pointing at the heavy drapes of moss hanging directly in front of the lens. "It's the obstruction."

Pierce squinted at the camera. "Maintenance is supposed to trim that back every quarter."

"Convenient," Nate said.

Stepping off the brick path, Nate moved into the deep shadow of the tree trunk where the ground was soft, a mixture of sandy soil and decaying leaf litter that muffled his footsteps. He pressed his back against the rough bark and looked out at the path.

From this vantage point, the walkway was a kill zone where anyone walking past would be blinded by the transition from darkness to light, while the observer in the shadows remained unseen.

"He didn't just grab her," Nate said, his voice low. "He waited here, knew exactly where the camera couldn't see, knew the moss would block the lens, knew the lighting gaps."

Rodecker looked at the thick shrubbery at the base of the tree. "You think he scouted it?"

"I think he knows this park better than your maintenance crews do," Nate said.

A group of tourists wandered past on the path, wearing matching t-shirts and carrying plastic cups of beer, legal in the open container district. They laughed, pausing to take a selfie in front of the fountain where the killer had arranged Caroline Marsh less than forty-eight hours ago.

Nate watched them, his jaw tightening as they walked through the kill zone without breaking stride, unaware of the violence soaked into the soil beneath their sandals.

"Let's move," Nate said.

He walked out of the park, heading north on Bull Street, where the park's open space gave way to the city grid. Three-story brick and stucco townhouses rose, their walls crowding the narrow sidewalks.

"You mentioned a pattern back at the station," Pierce said, struggling to keep pace with Nate's long strides. "Something about the geometry."

Nate kept his eyes scanning the street, looking at the alley mouths, the service entrances, the gaps between carriage houses.

"Geographic determinism," Nate said, using the Bureau term. "Predators are creatures of habit who hunt where they are comfortable, where the terrain gives them an advantage."

"So he lives in the district," Rodecker said.

"He doesn't just live here," Nate said, gesturing down the long corridor of Bull Street. "He operates here—look at the layout, Oglethorpe's plan, a series of squares and open spaces connected by a grid that looks orderly but is full of blind spots, service lanes, and walled gardens." He paused. "It's a maze designed for privacy."

They crossed Gaston Street, and the traffic noise faded as they moved deeper into the residential quarter where the air felt older, trapped between the high garden walls.

"He moves inward," Nate said. "The historian, Miss Landry, mapped the previous cases she found, and the locations spiral toward the center of the district."

"You're putting a lot of stock in a historian's theory," Rodecker said. "She's been calling the precinct for years about this, and most of the guys think she's..." He trailed off.

"Crazy?" Nate said. "Maybe, but her data points match the body dump sites."

They reached the corner of Monterey Square.

The atmosphere shifted in a way Nate felt immediately—the trees here were denser, the shadows longer. The Mercer-Williams House dominated the western side of the square, its red brick façade imposing behind iron railings. A carriage tour rattled past, the horse's hooves clopping on the asphalt.

Nate stopped at the corner, looking at the Pulaski Monument in the center, the stone pillar rising out of the greenery.

"This is where the rough sleepers stay," Pierce said, pointing toward a secluded bench shielded by azalea bushes. "The ones who don't want to go to the shelters—we patrol it, but they know the schedule and fade back into the shadows when a cruiser rolls by."

"Invisibility," Nate said. "He picks victims who fall through the cracks—transients, tourists, people who aren't missed until it's too late."

"Except Caroline Marsh," Rodecker said. "She was a local, a socialite."

"Which means he's escalating," Nate said, "or he's getting arrogant."

He turned his back to the square, facing the detectives, aware that he had read the file a thousand times and memorized the crime scene photos until they were burned onto the back of his eyelids. But being here, standing on the physical pavement, required a different kind of strength.

He put his hands in his pockets to hide the way his fingers curled into fists.

"Where," Nate said, clearing his throat, "where exactly was the 2010 victim found?"

Rodecker blinked, as though the topic shift threw him. "2010? You mean the cold case?"

"The college student," Nate said. "Sarah Holloway."

Pierce looked up from her tablet and studied Nate's face, her eyes narrowing.

Rodecker scratched his chin. "Right, the SCAD girl—bad business, that was... yeah." He turned and pointed south, past the square. "Just over there, the service alley behind the carriage house."

Nate followed the line of Rodecker's finger.

The entrance to the alley was narrow, a dark cleft between two high brick walls where weeds sprouted from the cracks in the cobblestones. It looked unremarkable, like a place where people put their garbage bins.

Rodecker kept his arm extended, then looked back at Nate and saw the hard line of Nate's jaw, the pale blue eyes gone flat and distant. The name clicked into place. *Holloway.*

Rodecker's arm lowered. "Sarah Holloway—she was..."

Nate turned away from them and stepped off the curb.

"Nate," Pierce said, her voice soft, a warning or an offer of support.

He ignored it and walked across the cobblestones of the square while the heat seemed to intensify, pressing against his temples. His heart hammered a slow, heavy rhythm against his ribs.

He reached the mouth of the alley and stopped.

It was just an alley.

That was the horror of it—it wasn't a theatrical stage set or a movie scene but a utilitarian service corridor paved with hexagonal bricks that had shifted and buckled over time. A green plastic dumpster sat against one wall, and a rusted drainpipe ran down the side of a carriage house. The air smelled of wet rot, urine, and the sickly-sweet scent of jasmine blooming over a garden wall.

Nate stepped inside.

The sounds of the city—the traffic, the tourists, the distant tugboat on the river—faded to a low hum.

He walked to the center of the alley and looked down at the bricks.

The weeds vanished, and the damp brick dissolved as the smell hit him first—not the urine and rot of the alley, but the cloying sweetness of lilies and formaldehyde. *The mahogany box sat on the stand, closed.*

Better to remember her as she was. The funeral director's words.

Nate swayed, the ground beneath his feet insubstantial.

She called me at ten forty-two that night. He'd been studying for a torts exam when he saw her picture on the screen and thought, *I'll call her back in the morning.*

There was no morning.

He stared at the hexagonal bricks, the pattern looking like a honeycomb, while Alicia's words echoed in his mind—there was no blood on the soil. How do you tear a throat out and leave no blood?

A splash of color caught his eye, a purple flower crushed into the dirt between the pavers. Not lavender, just a weed.

But the smell of lavender hit him anyway, a phantom sensory memory triggered by the file in his pocket—the sachet, her grandmother's recipe.

He watched her and chose her.

Bile rose in his throat as his vision tunneled, the red brick walls pressing in. He wanted to break something, burn the city down.

A bell clanged—metal on metal, jarring and loud.

Nate's head snapped up.

A large orange and green trolley had turned the corner at the end of the alley, rumbling over the cobblestones with its engine grinding. It blocked the sunlight, casting a long shadow down the length of the corridor.

The vehicle was open-sided, packed with tourists fanning themselves with brochures while a loudspeaker mounted on the roof crackled.

The tour guide's voice boomed from the speaker, amplified into a tinny caricature of a Southern drawl.

"And on your right, folks, we have Monterey Square, considered by many to be the most haunted spot in Savannah."

The guide laughed, a practiced, rehearsed sound.

"Now, legend has it that Savannah has its very own vampire problem—over the years, bodies have been found drained of every drop of blood, right here in these squares." The voice dripped with theatrical menace. "Some folks say it's voodoo, some say it's ghosts, but we like to keep our windows locked at night, don't we?"

The tourists chuckled while a few snapped photos of the square. One woman pointed her phone directly into the alley where Nate stood.

"Of course, the police say it's just wild dogs," the guide continued, his voice dripping with cheap skepticism. "But I've never known a dog to lock the door behind him!"

The trolley rumbled past, its engine noise fading while the guide's last words hung in the humid air.

Legend.

Entertainment.

Sarah died alone in the dark on these bricks, terrified, and now she was a punchline in a script sold for twenty-five dollars a ticket.

Nate's vision swam at the edges as the red brick walls pulsed with the heat. His hands came out of his pockets and found the leather of his belt, his thumb pressing into the hard shape of his holster. The urge to run, to drag the guide from his platform, was a physical thing, a tightening in his chest.

A heavy hand landed on his shoulder.

Nate flinched, his body coiling, ready to strike.

"Holloway."

It was Rodecker, standing just inside the alley mouth and looking at Nate instead of the retreating trolley. His face was grim, sweating, and solid.

"Breathe," Rodecker said.

Nate stared at him, forcing air into his lungs before holding it and letting it out.

"Twenty-five bucks," Nate said, his voice gravelly. "Includes a bottle of water."

"I know," Rodecker said. "It's a business, and they don't know."

"They should know."

"If they knew, they wouldn't come," Rodecker said, "and the city needs them to come."

Pierce stepped up beside Rodecker and looked at the ground where Nate had been staring, then back at him. Her expression held no pity, only a sharp understanding.

"We find him," Pierce said. "We stop the story."

Nate closed his eyes for a second, forcing the alley's heat and smell to the front of his mind. The anger receded, boxed and shelved, and when he opened his eyes, the blue was flat and hard again.

He adjusted his jacket and wiped the sweat from his upper lip.

"The blind spots," Nate said, pointing to the roof of the carriage house. "No cameras on this alley in 2010?"

"None," Rodecker said. "Still aren't."

"He uses the service corridors and moves behind the façade," Nate said. "We need to canvass every business that backs onto these alleys, not just for yesterday but for the last week."

He walked past the detectives, heading back toward the light of the square without looking down at the bricks again.

"Get the traffic cam footage for a five-block radius," Nate said. "I want every vehicle that entered or exited this grid between midnight and four in the morning for the last three nights."

"That's thousands of cars, Nate," Pierce said.

"Then we'd better get started."

Nate stopped at the edge of the square and pulled the folded map from his pocket. He looked at the spiral Alicia had drawn while the geometry of the city spread out before him—the squares, the monuments, the rigid lines of the streets.

It wasn't a city plan but a game board, and the pieces had been moving for a long time.

He looked at the live oaks dripping with moss and at the shadows pooling under the branches.

"He's here," Nate said. "He's not a ghost or a legend—he's flesh and blood, and he makes mistakes."

He folded the map, the paper damp with his own sweat, and shoved it back into his pocket.

"Let's go to the next site."

Rodecker and Pierce exchanged a glance, then nodded and fell in behind him as he started walking north, back into the grid of the game board.

CHAPTER

7

Holloway drove the rental Ford Explorer with one hand on the wheel, his grip straining the dark plastic. The cold air blasted his face, a mechanical effort to hold back the Georgia summer.

Rodecker sat in the passenger seat, his bulk pressing against the door. He adjusted the vent so the stream of air hit his neck, his eyes closed behind aviator sunglasses. He smelled of stale sweat and damp cotton.

"Five miles," Rodecker said. He didn't open his eyes. "Georgetown. It's a straight shot down the parkway."

Nate nodded. He didn't speak. Speaking required loosening the tension in his jaw, and he wasn't ready to do that.

The landscape shifted outside the glass. The gothic canopy of the historic district—the strangling moss, the ancient oaks, the shadows that possessed mass and weight—gave way to the hard brightness of commercial zoning. Strip malls replaced carriage houses. Concrete replaced cobblestone. The sun hammered down on asphalt parking lots and chain restaurants.

They turned into the subdivision.

Beige vinyl. Manicured centipede grass. A maze designed to look identical from every angle. No moss here. No shadows. Just relentless exposure. Nate pulled the car into the driveway of a single-story ranch house that looked exactly like the one next to it. A sprinkler hissed somewhere nearby, a rhythmic, artificial sound that cut through the afternoon silence.

Nate killed the engine. The silence inside the car was sudden.

"You good?" Rodecker asked. He removed his sunglasses, squinting against the glare bouncing off the white garage door.

"I'm working," Nate said.

He opened the door. The air on the porch was solid water. It coated his skin instantly, smelling of hot asphalt and cut grass. Nate walked up the concrete path, his shoes making no sound. He adjusted his jacket, buttoning it over the shoulder holster. The brother who had stood in the alley was gone. The profiler had taken his place.

Megan Bacha opened the door before his hand reached the bell.

She stood in the threshold wearing grey sweatpants and a t-shirt that hung loose on her frame, the fabric stained near the hem. Her hair was pulled back in a knot that was coming undone, strands falling across a face scrubbed raw of makeup. Her eyes were red, the lids swollen, but her gaze was sharp, defensive.

She didn't ask for badges. She didn't ask who they were. She just stepped back, holding the door open, creating a space for them to enter.

"It's cold inside," she said. Her voice was brittle.

Nate stepped past her. The temperature drop was immediate and shocking. The air inside was frigid, refrigerated to a point that prickled his skin. It smelled of lavender, Fabuloso, and stale coffee, the scent of a house where someone was trying to scrub away grief.

"Thank you for seeing us, Ms. Bacha," Nate said.

She didn't answer. She turned and walked down the hallway, hugging her arms to her chest. Nate followed. The walls were lined with framed photographs. Megan and a blonde woman with a bright, open smile. Caroline Marsh. At the beach. At a bar. In graduation robes. The Caroline in the photos was vibrant, alive, incapable of ending up as a broken shape on the bricks of Forsyth Park.

They entered the kitchen. It was modern and sterile, with granite countertops that gleamed under harsh recessed lighting. A sliding glass door looked out onto a backyard surrounded by a high wooden fence. The sun beat against the glass, but inside, the air remained cold.

Megan sat at the round glass table, wrapping both hands around a ceramic mug that steamed in the chill air. She stared into the dark liquid.

Rodecker pulled out a chair, the legs scraping loudly against the tile. He winced at the noise. Nate sat opposite Megan. He kept his posture open, his hands visible on the table.

"I know this is difficult," Nate said. He pitched his voice to the quiet of the room. "But we need to understand Caroline's routine. We need to know how she moved through her life."

Megan nodded. She took a sip of the coffee. Her hands trembled, sending small ripples across the surface of the liquid.

"She was safe," Megan said. She looked at the refrigerator, where a magnetic calendar displayed a grid of shifts and appointments. "Annoying about it. That's what I told her. I told her she was paranoid."

"Paranoid how?" Rodecker asked. He had his notebook out, the pen poised.

"The locks," Megan said. "Three times. Every night. Front door, back door, windows. One, two, three. If she lost count, she started over." She let out a breath that shuddered through her chest. "She had a bat under her bed. Aluminum. She kept pepper spray on her keychain, the gel kind that sticks so it doesn't blow back in your face. She researched it."

Her fingers tightened around the mug. The knuckles turned white.

"She shared her location with me," Megan said. "Life360. If I turned mine off, she'd text me within five minutes. 'Where are you? Are you okay?' She wouldn't park in a garage if the lights were out. She wouldn't walk to her car alone after work."

Rodecker wrote, the scratch of the pen loud in the quiet kitchen.

"This level of caution," Nate said. "Was it recent? Or had she always been this way?"

"Always," Megan said. "Since college. She watched those true crime documentaries. She said the world was full of crazies."

Beyond the sliding glass, the backyard was empty. Just grass and a fence. A contained world. Safe.

"The night she died," Nate said. "She was in Forsyth Park. Two in the morning. On foot."

Megan slammed the mug down. Coffee sloshed over the rim, staining the glass table a brownish hue.

"No," she said. The word was a rejection of reality. "She wouldn't. She wouldn't go there. Not at night. Not alone."

"Her car was at the bar," Rodecker said, his voice low. "She walked."

"She didn't walk." Megan glared at Rodecker, tears spilling over her lashes. "She never walked if she could drive. She didn't like the dark. She didn't like the shadows under the trees. She called them blind spots."

"The evidence puts her there, Megan," Nate said. He didn't soften the blow. He needed her to confront the impossibility. "She left the safety of the lights. She walked into the dark. We need to know why."

Megan shook her head. She picked up a napkin and dabbed at the spilled coffee, her movements jerky.

"It doesn't make sense," she said. "It wasn't her. It's like talking about a different person."

Nate leaned forward. He rested his elbows on the table, commanding her attention. He needed to break the loop of denial.

"People break their own rules for two reasons," Nate said, his eyes locked onto hers. "Emergency. Or trust."

Megan froze. The napkin stopped moving.

"There was no emergency call," Nate said. "No 911 call. No panic text to you. She walked into that park calmly. She walked because she thought she was safe."

He let the silence stretch. The refrigerator hummed. The air conditioner cycled on, blowing a fresh draft of cold air across the table.

"Who did she trust, Megan?"

Megan looked away. She stared at the window, at the bright, hot world outside that Caroline was no longer part of. Her mouth worked, trying to form words she didn't want to say.

"She met someone," Megan said, her voice a thread of sound.

Nate didn't move. He didn't blink. "Who?"

"I don't know his name," Megan said. "She wouldn't say. She called him..." She hesitated. "She just said 'him.' Like he was the only man in the world."

Rodecker looked up from his notebook. His face was neutral.

"When did she meet him?" Rodecker asked.

"A week ago," Megan said. "Last Tuesday. There was a fundraiser at the Jepson Center. For the preservation society. Caroline volunteered to work the check-in table."

The Jepson Center. High society. Old money.

"She called me that night," Megan said. A small, sad smile ghosted across her face, vanishing as quickly as it appeared. "She sounded... giddy. Like she was sixteen, she said she met a man who actually looked at her. Not at her chest, not at his phone. At her."

"Describe him," Nate said.

"She said he was older," Megan said. "Not old, just... settled. Cultured. She said he knew everything about the city. He walked her through the gallery and told her stories about the paintings that weren't on the plaques. She said he was 'old money' but not arrogant. Refined."

The air conditioning cycled off, but the cold remained at the base of Nate's neck.

"And after that night?" Nate asked.

"She changed," Megan said. The sadness in her voice hardened into anger. "She blew me off. We were supposed to go to the movies on Thursday. She canceled. She missed work on Friday. Caroline never misses work. She forgot to pick up Leo—her nephew—from soccer practice on Saturday. Her sister had to go get him."

"Did you see him?" Nate asked.

"No," Megan said. "I asked. I said, bring him around. Let's get drinks. She said no. She said he was private. She said she wanted to keep him to herself for a little while."

"She was protecting him," Nate said.

"She was obsessed," Megan said. "I tried to call her on Sunday. She answered, but she sounded... floaty. Distant."

"What did she say?"

Megan gripped the mug again, as if seeking warmth from the cooling ceramic. She looked directly at Nate, her eyes wide and confused.

"She said time felt weird with him," Megan said. "She said hours felt like minutes. She said being with him was like being drunk without drinking. She said she felt safe. Safer than she'd ever felt."

Rodecker stopped writing. He stared at the page, his brow furrowed. He had heard descriptions like this before, buried in witness statements usually dismissed as drug-related or hysterical.

"Did she mention drugs?" Rodecker asked. "Alcohol?"

"No," Megan said. "Caroline barely drank. Two glasses of wine was her limit. She sounded sober. Just... gone. Like she was drifting."

Nate glanced at the photos on the wall again. The smiling girl. The girl who checked her deadbolts three times.

"Did she mention where they went?" Nate asked. "Where he lived?"

"She said he had a beautiful house," Megan said. "Downtown. With a wall garden and fresh jasmine, lavender, cereus. She said it was like stepping back in time."

Nate stood up. The chair slid back silently on the tile. He needed to get out of this cold, sterile house. He needed to think.

"Did she text you about him?" Nate asked. "Do you have the messages?"

Megan shook her head. "I looked. I checked my history this morning. The messages are gone. She must have used a disappearing app, or I deleted them by accident. I don't remember deleting them."

"It's okay," Nate said. "We can pull the records."

He took a card from his pocket and placed it on the glass table. It looked stark and white against the dark wood.

"If you remember anything else," Nate said. "Anything at all. Call me."

Megan nodded. She looked small in the large kitchen, diminished by the space her friend used to fill.

"Find him," she said, her voice low. "He did something to her. He changed her before he killed her."

"We will," Nate said.

They walked back down the hallway. The front door opened, and the heat of the afternoon met them. Nate welcomed it. It felt like the world where things rotted and burned, not the preserved chill of the house.

They walked to the Explorer in silence. Heat rose in visible distortion from the hood of the car. Nate unlocked the doors but didn't get in. He stood by the driver's side, resting his arms on the hot metal of the roof, looking across at Rodecker.

Rodecker leaned against the passenger door, putting his sunglasses back on. The lenses reflected the cookie-cutter houses of the subdivision.

"Psychological," Nate said. "Rapid bonding. He isolated her. Flooded her with attention. Shifted her sleep schedule. You can scramble someone fast if you know where to push."

Rodecker frowned, the corners of his mouth turning down.

"In a week?" Rodecker asked. "She went from checking backseats to walking into a dark park with someone she barely knew. Even for a master manipulator, that's fast."

Nate looked at the neat lawns, the sprinklers, the illusion of order. He thought about the phrase *drunk without drinking*.

"It's fast," Nate agreed. "It's efficient. He didn't just charm her, Karl. He dismantled her survival instincts. He turned off the alarm system in her head."

"Drugs?" Rodecker suggested. "Scopolamine? Something that makes you compliant?"

"Maybe," Nate said. "But the tox screen was clean for the usual suspects. And she was lucid enough to talk to her friend on the phone."

Nate opened the car door. The interior was baking, the air trapped inside stale and dry.

"He's not just a killer," Nate said, sliding into the seat. He gripped the steering wheel, ignoring the burn of the hot leather against his palms. "He's a collector. He collected her trust. He collected her safety. And then he collected her life."

Rodecker got in, groaning as he settled his weight.

"Old money," Rodecker said. "Jepson Center. Downtown house with a garden."

"We map the locations," Nate said. He started the engine. The A/C kicked on, blasting hot air that would slowly turn cold. "We check the donor lists for the preservation society. We find the man who lives in the past."

He put the car in gear and drove out of the maze of beige houses, leaving the grieving woman in her cold house, heading back toward the city where the moss hung heavy and the blind spots waited.

CHAPTER

8

THE MARSHALL HOUSE smelled of lemon Pledge and the faint chemical bite of iodine that never quite left buildings that had served as Civil War hospitals. It had been one when Sherman took Savannah, and a scent of that history still leaked through gaps in the hardwood.

Nate bypassed the elevator and took the stairs to the fourth floor, his footsteps muffled by worn carpet runners that had witnessed decades of guests who never stayed long to notice what the hotel remembered. Trapped between floors, the air in the stairwell felt stale and still, and he climbed with the muscles in his calves tight and burning from the day's stress. He reached the landing and paused, listening to the silence that filled the hallway.

Down the narrow corridor, the pale yellow walls absorbed the light from the sconces rather than reflecting it, and brass room numbers caught what little illumination survived the gloom. He stopped at Room 417 and slid the plastic key card into the slot. The lock clicked, disengaging, and he pushed the heavy door open and stepped inside, throwing the deadbolt without looking back.

Shadows pooled in the corners, and the air chilled him with the steady hum of the air conditioning unit rattling in the window. The machine sounded like a loose fan blade clipping its housing with every rotation. Nate leaned back against the wood of the door for a second and closed his eyes.

He pushed off the door and tossed his suit jacket onto the bed, where the mattress springs creaked under the weight. He walked to the desk by the window, where the lamp cast a yellow pool of light on the surface. Next to it lay the Saturday New York Times crossword puzzle he had finished days ago, the grid filled with black ink and no strikethroughs, no corrections—evidence of a simpler order, one where every clue had a definitive answer, and every box had a letter that fit.

He moved the puzzle aside and looked at the large corkboard he had mounted above the desk, purchased from an office supply store on Abercorn Street. It was a blank, brown surface waiting for data.

Nate unzipped his leather satchel, the sound loud in the quiet room, and reached inside to withdraw the files. He laid them out in neat stacks on the desk surface, organizing the chaos of the last forty-eight hours into piles. Caroline Marsh's file went on the left, the gloss of the crime scene photos catching the lamplight. Alicia Landry's historical documents went in the middle—photocopies of crumbling registers, grainy scans of microfiche, slick prints of digitized police records. Sarah's file went on the right, the manila folder soft at the edges from years of handling, the SCMPD logo stamped on the front faded to a ghostly grey.

He took a small plastic box of brass pushpins from his pocket and set it next to the lamp, then placed a spool of red thread beside it. Nate rolled up his shirt sleeves but did not remove his shoulder holster, the weight of the Glock 19M under his left arm a grounding pressure. He picked up the first photograph from Caroline's file—the wide shot of the body in Forsyth Park, where Caroline lay on the brick pavers, white skin against red clay and grey stone. The positioning of her pose was exact—arms crossed at the sternum, feet together, ankles touching.

He pressed a pin through the top center of the photograph, and the cork accepted the metal point with a dull crunch. He centered the image on the board, then picked up the close-up of the throat wound next. The jagged ruin of tissue, the clean bricks underneath—he pinned it directly below the wide shot, the visual evidence of the impossible blood loss staring back at him.

Nate picked up the stack of historical documents Alicia had given him at the archives, the paper heavy in his hand. He separated the top sheet and scanned the handwritten entry again—*Chatham County Death Register, 1890*—the script looping and archaic, the ink faded to brown in the photocopy. *Throat rent as if by an animal. Body strangely at peace. Found in the Park extension.*

He pinned the document to the far left of the board as the beginning, or at least the beginning of the records they had found so far. He picked up the 1935 newspaper clipping next, the headline bold and dramatic—*GIRL FOUND DRAINED IN CHIPPEWA SQUARE*—and the text described the lack of blood at the scene and speculated about a "maniac with a medical kit." He pinned it next to the 1890 register, leaving a gap of inches between them to show the passage of forty-five years.

Next was the 1995 police photograph, a Polaroid grainy and flash-lit, showing the victim inside a ring of four candles. The wax was white, and their placement was identical to Caroline's scene, marking the cardinal points—north, south, east, west. He held the photo up to the lamp, comparing the candle placement in the 1995 image to the 2025 image pinned in the center, and the angles were exact, the distance from the body consistent.

He pinned the 1995 photo to the board, and the timeline stretched across the cork in decades—1890, 1935, 1995, 2025.

Nate turned back to his bag and drew out the folded tourist map of the Savannah Historic District. It was large and detailed, marking every square, every street, every monument, and he unfolded it with the paper crinkling. He smoothed the creases against the lower half of the corkboard, covering the bottom section, and used four brass pins to secure the corners.

The city lay flat before him—Oglethorpe's colonial grid, an achievement of urban planning designed for order, for defense, for community. Squares spaced at regular intervals, streets running in straight lines. He traced the path through Forsyth Park with his index finger, found the spot near the Confederate Memorial where the firefighter had slipped on the blood, and drove a brass pin into the map at that exact location.

He went back to the documents and found *1890, Park Extension*, then located the area on the map at the southern end of the district and placed a pin. *1935, Chippewa Square*—he found the square in the center of the grid and placed a pin. *1995, Monterey Square*—he placed a pin.

Nate picked up the spool of red thread, found the end, and tied a small knot around the brass head of the 1890 pin. He drew the thread taut and wound it around the 1935 pin, then the 1995 pin, then Caroline's pin in Forsyth Park. The red line zigzagged across the map, creating a polygon with sharp angles.

Nate stepped back and retreated to the foot of the bed, crossing his arms over his chest and staring at the board. The string connected the deaths across time and space, turning separate tragedies into a single structure. But the shape was wrong—a piece was missing.

He walked back to the desk, and his hand hovered over the file on the right, the faded manila folder with the rust stain from the paper-clip on the top edge. He opened the file and found the photo of Sarah on top—nineteen years old, wearing her SCAD hoodie.

Nate picked up the photo, his fingers touching the glossy surface, and he held it for a long moment, looking at her eyes—the same shade of blue as his own. His hand felt stiff as he placed the photo on the timeline, between 1995 and 2025, the year marked *2010*.

He drove the pin through the white border of the photograph, pushing it deep into the cork, then looked down at the map. *Alley near Monterey Square.* He knew the spot because he had stood there today, had smelled the garbage and the damp brick. He located the alley behind the Mercer-Williams House on the paper grid, a narrow line between larger blocks, and placed a pin there.

He took the red thread again and unwound it from Caroline's pin, drawing it back to the 1995 location, then wound it around the pin marking Sarah's death in the alley. Then he drew it forward again to Caroline's location in Forsyth Park, tied the knot, and cut the string with a small pair of scissors from his travel kit.

Nate stepped back again, and the shape tightened, the intersecting lines now forming a center.

He picked up a clear plastic ruler from the desk supplies and walked to the map, placing the edge of the ruler along the line of the string connecting 1890 and 1935, tracing the trajectory. He moved the ruler and positioned it with the path between 1995 and 2010, then positioned it with the path between 2010 and 2025. The lines crossed, and the violence followed a pattern—not a scattershot distribution of opportunity, but a radial design.

He leaned in close, the lamp light reflecting off his pale skin, and followed the invisible lines radiating from the crime scenes. They all intersected at a single corridor, or they all bordered it—Jones Street.

The street ran east to west through the center of the southern historic district, called "the most beautiful street in America" by the guidebooks. Cobblestones, high stoops, Greek Revival mansions, and massive oaks arching over the road to form a canopy of branches. Nate pressed his index finger onto Jones Street on the map and tapped the spot twice, the paper giving under the pressure.

The pattern was clear—the lines all converged here.

He uncapped a black dry-erase marker, the sharp chemical smell of the solvent cutting through the lemon polish scent of the room, and turned to the white notepad section attached to the side of the corkboard. He wrote in block letters **CULT / FAMILY** and circled the words.

A multigenerational group, passing down the ritual from grandfather to father to son, maintaining the specific knowledge of the bite, the blood removal, the staging. Keeping the secrets of the locations would require discipline and fanaticism—a secret society operating within the high society of Savannah.

He wrote below it **GEOGRAPHIC DETERMINISM** and looked at the squares on the map. The city's layout forced movement into specific channels, and maybe the layout itself attracted a certain type of predator—the blind spots, the shadows, the isolation within the crowd. Maybe the city bred these killers independently, the environment selecting for the same traits over and over—convergent evolution.

He tapped the marker against his chin in a fast rhythm. *Tap-tap-tap.* He wrote a third option—**ARCHIVAL COPYCAT**—and considered the possibility. Someone with access to the old files, someone who knew about the 1890 case, the 1935 case. Alicia Landry had found them, so someone else could discover them too—a modern killer obsessed with the city's dark history, reenacting the past for his own gratification.

But the copycat theory failed on the forensics because a copycat could mimic the staging and buy the candles, but a copycat could not replicate the bite marks. A copycat could not drain ninety-four percent of the blood without a machine, unless the copycat were a surgeon or a mortician.

Nate wrote in the margins **BENEFIT?** and asked himself why anyone would do it, why maintain the pattern for 135 years. Power? Tradition? Some twisted religion?

He wrote **PURPOSE?** beneath it—to feed a need, to terrorize, to ritualize?

He looked at the red string again and traced the intersecting lines with his eyes. The center of the pattern was not a concept but a place —Jones Street. The man Megan Bacha described came back to him. *Old money. Cultured. House with a garden. Time felt weird.* A man who lived in the past, or a family that preserved it.

Nate leaned close to the map and drew a red circle around the Jones Street corridor, encompassing the blocks between Whitaker and Drayton. He wrote in clear, hard letters at the bottom of the board: **INVESTIGATE PROPERTIES - JONES ST.**

CHAPTER

9

"Tell me again about the paperwork," Rodecker said, mopping his face with a handkerchief that had long since surrendered to the weather. His voice was raspy, dry, and irritated. "Because I'm looking at these houses, and I'm thinking nobody lives here. They're just museums with better landscaping."

Nate checked the file in his hand. "Yolanda spent four hours in the courthouse basement for this. It's not a straight line. It's a maze."

"Rich people love mazes."

"This isn't just rich. It's paranoid." Nate tapped the top sheet. "The townhouse is held by Jones Street Preservation Trust, LLC, which is owned by Oglethorpe Holdings, registered in Delaware. Which is a subsidiary of a blind trust managed by a firm in Zurich."

"And the antique dealer?"

"Evan Carlisle is the sole beneficiary of the trust. He doesn't own the house. He doesn't own the car. On paper, the man owns nothing but the suit on his back."

Rodecker snorted. He stopped to stare up at the three-story brick facade of number 465. "Well, that's a nice suit to own. Place looks like it was built yesterday and scrubbed with a toothbrush."

Nate looked up. The Greek Revival structure rose three stories, imposing and severe, with white columns guarding a black lacquered door. The brickwork was clean, mortar lines precise as a surgeon's cut, not a chip or crack visible. Iron railings along the stoop gleamed with fresh paint. In a city that celebrated decay, where moss and peeling paint were badges of honor, the house stood out as an anomaly. It didn't look lived in. It looked preserved.

"Four shell companies to hide a house," Nate said. "Why go to the trouble?"

"Tax evasion," Rodecker suggested. "Hiding assets from an ex-wife."

"Maybe." Nate put the file away. "Let's see if he's home."

They walked up the stairs. The granite steps showed no wear. Nate lifted the brass knocker—a lion's head, heavy and cold—and let it fall. The sound was a solid thud, absorbed by the heavy wood, leaving only silence.

No sound of footsteps approaching. No barking dog. No muffled voices.

Nate waited and counted the seconds.

The lock did not click; it just opened.

It swung inward on silent hinges, revealing a slice of dim interior. A man stood in the opening.

"Gentlemen," the man said. "The heat is unforgiving today."

Evan Carlisle was taller than Nate had expected and wore a cream-colored linen suit that looked as though it had just come off a tailor's form, crisp and unwrinkled. His shirt was white, open at the collar. His hair was dark, silvered at the temples, swept back from a face where every feature aligned with geometric precision—too perfect, like a photograph instead of flesh. He looked to be in his early forties, fit and lean.

But it was his stillness that registered first. Most people fidgeted when opening a door to law enforcement. They shifted weight, glanced at badges, checked their watches. Carlisle stood without shifting his stance, without adjusting his posture, without the small fidgets most people made when standing under scrutiny.

Nate held up his credentials. "Mr. Carlisle? Agent Holloway, FBI. Detective Rodecker, SCMPD. We're canvassing the neighborhood regarding the incident in Forsyth Park."

Carlisle didn't look at the badges. He looked at Nate. His eyes were dark, the irises so deep brown they appeared black in the shadow of the doorway.

"The incident," Carlisle repeated. His voice was soft, carrying a cadence Nate couldn't place. It wasn't quite British, and it wasn't quite

Savannah. It sounded formal, like an actor reciting lines from an older play. "A polite euphemism for a tragedy. Please. Come in out of the sun."

He stepped back.

Nate crossed the threshold, and the heat vanished. The air inside was cool, dry, and still—the chill of a cellar, not of an air conditioner. The air smelled of beeswax, lemon oil, and something faint and floral —night-blooming jasmine, perhaps, or lilies.

Rodecker followed, exhaling a long breath. "A/C works good," he muttered.

"Thick walls," Carlisle said. He closed the door. The sound of the street—a distant siren, the hum of tires—cut off. "They keep the world at bay."

He led them into the parlor on the right. Nate's profiler instinct kicked in, scanning the environment. He expected wealth. He expected ostentation.

What he saw was a museum.

The floors were heart pine, wide planks burnished to a deep honey glow. The furniture was of the Federal period—sofas with slender curved legs, mahogany tables inlaid with satinwood, and wingback chairs upholstered in dark velvet. Nate knew enough about antiques to recognize reproductions. These were not reproductions. The varnish had a specific craquelure, the depth that came only with age. The silver candlesticks on the mantle were heavy, tarnished only in the crevices where a cloth couldn't reach.

"Please," Carlisle said, gesturing to the chairs. "Sit. Can I offer you iced tea? It is already prepared."

"We're fine," Nate said. He remained standing. He wanted to keep the dynamic uneven. "We won't take much of your time."

"Time is the one thing I have in abundance," Carlisle said. He smiled. The expression engaged his mouth but stopped at his cheek-bones, never reaching his eyes. He extended a hand. "I do not believe we have met, Agent Holloway."

Nate took the hand.

He held the grip a second longer than necessary, searching for a pulse in the wrist. He felt a rhythmic thud, slow and steady.

Bradycardia? Or an athlete's resting heart rate.

"You have a lovely home," Nate said, releasing the hand. "You've been here long?"

"The house has stood since 1852," Carlisle said. He did not answer the question. He moved to a sideboard and poured water from a crystal pitcher into three glasses, ignoring Nate's refusal. "I consider myself merely a custodian. Buildings like this require dedication. They demand a certain loyalty."

He handed a glass to Rodecker, then Nate. Nate took it. The condensation was cold against his palm.

"We're checking property records," Rodecker said, taking a sip. "Just routine. Trying to see who might have seen something. Your name came up on a few deeds."

"A few," Carlisle allowed. He leaned against the mantle, relaxed. "I dabble in preservation. The historic district is fragile. It requires protection."

"We're investigating the death of Caroline Marsh," Nate said. He watched Carlisle's face. "The body was found in Forsyth Park. Tuesday morning."

"Yes," Carlisle said. "I read the papers. A terrible business. Throat trauma, I understand."

"The papers didn't mention the specifics of the wound," Nate said.

Carlisle didn't blink. His gaze remained steady on Nate's face. "Savannah is a small town, Agent. Servants talk. Police officers talk. The air here carries whispers better than it carries sound."

"Did you know her?"

"Caroline? No."

"You used her first name."

"The papers used her first name. It fosters empathy." Carlisle took a sip of his water. "I did not know Ms. Marsh. However, I believe we attended the same function last Saturday. The Arts and Antiquities fundraiser at the Jepson Center. I attended with the new junior curator."

"You saw her there?"

"I see many people," Carlisle said. "It was a crowded room. Champagne, bad lighting, desperate social climbing. But yes, I recall her. She was wearing blue. Silk, I believe. She laughed at something the gallery director said and spilled her wine on the marble floor."

"Did you speak to her?"

"Briefly. If at all." Carlisle waved a hand, his fingers tracing a slow arc that dismissed the question. "I may have complimented her choice of wine. Or apologized for bumping into her. The memory is vague."

"Vague," Nate repeated. "You remember the fabric of her dress, but not the conversation?"

"I have an eye for aesthetics," Carlisle said. "Texture lingers longer than words."

Nate stepped closer. He invaded Carlisle's personal space, a tactic designed to provoke a reaction. A step back. A flinch. A blink.

Carlisle did not move. He stood perfectly still, his breathing imperceptible. His eyes tracked Nate, but the eyelids did not descend. Nate counted the seconds. *Ten. Twenty.* The man did not blink.

"She left the bar alone that night," Nate said. "She was careful. Paranoid, even. She wouldn't have walked into that park with a stranger."

"Then perhaps she walked with a friend," Carlisle suggested.

"Or someone she met at a fundraiser," Nate said. "Someone charming. Someone who made her feel comfortable."

"I am flattered by the implication," Carlisle said. "But I was here Tuesday night. Cataloging a collection of daguerreotypes. Alone, unfortunately. My staff leaves at six."

"Convenient," Rodecker said.

"Solitude often is."

Rodecker walked toward the window, looking out at the street. "You know a lot about the neighborhood. We got a witness saying they saw someone running near the old jail site. You know where that is?"

"Which jail?" Carlisle asked.

"The one on Habersham."

"Ah." Carlisle turned his head, the movement economical and controlled. "That structure was demolished in 1898. The police barracks replaced it. If your witness saw someone near the old jail, they are either confused or a student of history."

Nate narrowed his eyes. The tone wasn't that of someone reciting a fact from a book. It was the tone of someone correcting a tourist about a street name they walked every day.

"You know your dates," Nate said.

"It is my profession. The past is my inventory."

Nate turned his attention to the bookshelves lining the alcove. Floor-to-ceiling mahogany. Leather spines, gold leaf lettering. He scanned the titles. *History of the Colony of Georgia. Botanical Sketches of the Southern States. Mesopotamian cylinder seals.*

He pulled a book from the shelf. *A Journal of the Plague Year.* First edition. The leather was soft, worn by hands.

He opened it. The pages smelled of vanilla and dust.

In the margins, notes were scrawled in black ink. The handwriting was controlled, with a distinctive loop on the 'y's and 'g's.

1920 - The similarity to the London outbreak is overstated. The panic here is less... refined.

Nate flipped forward—another note, same ink, same hand.

1950 - The author misunderstands the nature of contagion. Fear travels faster than microbes.

He flipped to the end. A note on the flyleaf, the ink fresh, glistening in the light.

2025 - Repetitive. Humanity learns nothing.

Nate stared at the script. The slant of the letters. The pressure of the pen. It was identical—a hundred years of commentary, written by the same hand.

"Family heirlooms?" Nate asked, holding up the book.

Carlisle moved. He didn't rush, but he crossed the distance in three silent strides, close enough for Nate to feel the cool radiation of his body. He took the book from Nate's hand. He didn't snatch it, but the movement was firm.

"My grandfather was a voracious reader," Carlisle said. "As was my father. We share similar habits. Annotating is a vice."

"And handwriting?" Nate asked. "You share that too?"

"Genetics is a powerful force, Agent Holloway. We are often more like our ancestors than we care to admit." Carlisle slid the book back into its slot. He aligned the spine perfectly with its neighbors. "You are looking for a monster, Agent. I understand the impulse. A young girl, dead in a park. It requires a villain. Someone distinct. Someone to blame."

"I'm looking for a killer," Nate said. "I don't need monsters."

"Sometimes they are the same thing."

"Would you mind showing us the rest of the house?" Nate asked. "Just to be thorough."

"Of course."

Carlisle led them into the hallway. They passed a dining room with a table long enough to seat twenty. The surface was polished to a black mirror. No dust. No fingerprints.

"The kitchen and service areas are in the rear," Carlisle said, gesturing toward the back of the house. "The bedrooms are upstairs."

"What's in there?" Nate asked, pointing to a door in the rear of the kitchen,

"My cellar," Carlisle said. "It is in disarray. I am processing a new acquisition from Charleston. Dust everywhere."

"We don't mind dust," Nate said. He reached for the handle.

"I mind," Carlisle said.

His voice didn't rise. It didn't sharpen. It stopped. The air in the hallway thickened, the pressure dropping another few millibars. Nate looked at Carlisle.

The man was smiling, but the expression was fixed. It didn't touch his eyes. The muscles at the corners of his mouth were tight, a mask of politeness stretched over something hard and unyielding.

"Sensitive client files," Carlisle said, stepping between Nate and the door. "Attorney-client privilege applies to some of the provenance documents. I am sure you understand the legalities."

"You're not a lawyer," Rodecker said.

"My clients employ them. And they value discretion above all else." Carlisle checked his watch—a vintage Patek Philippe. "I hate to be rude, gentlemen, but I have a call to London in ten minutes. Unless you have a warrant?"

The question was soft, but it landed in the quiet hallway like a slammed door.

Nate stepped back. He cataloged the cellar door. The lack of blinking. The fundraiser.

"No warrant," Nate said. "Not today."

"Then I must bid you good afternoon."

Carlisle escorted them to the door. He opened it, and the Savannah heat punched Nate in the face, a humid, suffocating assault.

"Do let me know if you catch him," Carlisle said. He stood in the doorway, a creature of cool shadow framed by the bright violence of the sun. "I sleep better when the streets are safe."

"We'll be in touch," Nate said.

"I anticipate it."

The door closed. The heavy thud sealed the house tight.

Nate walked down the granite steps. His shirt was plastered to his back again. He resisted the urge to wipe his palms on his trousers. The air in the house had been clean, but he felt coated in something old and stale.

"Cocky son of a bitch," Rodecker muttered, putting his sunglasses on. "Rich, arrogant, and definitely hiding something in that cellar. Tax records, probably. Or porn."

"It wasn't porn," Nate said. He walked to the Explorer, unlocking it with the remote. He didn't get in immediately.

He stopped on the sidewalk. The sensation hit him between the shoulder blades. An itch. A prickle of electricity that lifted the fine hairs on his neck. He was being watched.

Nate turned. He looked up at the townhouse.

The windows on the second floor were tall, draped in heavy cream fabric. The glass was dark, reflecting the oak trees and the sky.

In the center window, the curtain stirred.

It wasn't a breeze. The air outside was dead still. It was a ripple, a disturbance in the fabric as if someone had been standing there, pressed against the glass, and had just stepped back into the dark.

Nate stared at the window. He imagined Carlisle up there. Watching. Unblinking.

"Nate?" Rodecker called from the car. "You coming? I'm melting here."

Nate turned back to the car. He opened the door and slid into the scorching interior. He started the engine and cranked the A/C.

"Put him at the top of the list," Nate said.

"Based on what?" Rodecker asked, pulling out into the traffic. "He was at a party?"

"He fits," Nate said. He stared out the window as the townhouse receded in the side mirror. "He fits the timeline. He fits the profile. And Karl?"

"Yeah?"

"He didn't blink," Nate said. "In twenty minutes, he didn't blink once."

Rodecker glanced at him, his brow furrowed. "Maybe he wears contacts. Nate, maybe you're just seeing things because you want to see them."

"Maybe," Nate said.

CHAPTER

10

THE RENTAL SUV's air conditioning died with the engine, leaving the silence to fill with the ticking of cooling metal. Through the windshield, Monterey Square sat heavy under the live oaks, the Spanish moss draping the branches like curing tobacco. Nothing moved outside except the heat waves rising off the asphalt, distorting the red brick of the Mercer-Williams House until the building looked ready to melt.

Nate stepped out, buttoning a jacket that was already too thick. Sweat pricked at his hairline as his gaze swept the perimeter of the square, a lingering hyper-awareness from Jones Street tightening the muscles at the base of his skull. He scanned the rooftops, the parked cars, the deep shadows between the trees.

The square possessed a stillness, the kind of quiet beauty found among old headstones. On the western side, the Mercer-Williams House loomed, its red brick facade a monument to the city's history of murder and secrets buried under money. It was a fitting stage for the current hunt.

Rodecker got out of the passenger side, slamming the door. He adjusted his sunglasses and wiped a hand across his damp forehead, his eyes tracking the street corners.

"My wife loves this square," Rodecker said, his attention fixed on the potential threats, not the architecture. "She likes the antique shops, says it feels romantic."

"It feels contained," Nate said. "An arena."

"That's the heat talking, or the company we just kept."

They walked toward the Casimir Pulaski Monument rising above the trees in the center of the square. Tourists clustered near its base, taking selfies and pointing at the Mercer House, oblivious to the population occupying the shaded benches on the periphery. Nate watched them, the rough sleepers and the displaced, the men and women who were as much a part of the scene as the statues, yet invisible to the visitors. They sat with a deep stillness, nursing water bottles and watching the world with flat, appraising eyes.

Detective Yolanda Pierce stepped out from the shadow of a massive oak to meet them on the brick path. Her blouse was crisp despite the weather, but a rigid set to her jaw betrayed the professional cool.

"You look like you're holding your breath," Rodecker observed.

Pierce ignored him, her focus landing on Nate. "See the guy on the west bench? Green jacket. Don't stare."

Nate kept walking, letting his eyes slide casually over the area. A man sat on a bench facing Bull Street, dressed for a deep freeze in the ninety-degree heat: a heavy green field jacket over a flannel shirt, a wool cap pulled low. He was rolling a cigarette with steady, sun-darkened hands.

"Booker Hayes," Pierce said, her voice dropping to barely above a murmur. "He sees what the cameras miss, and if it happens in the squares after dark, Booker knows about it."

"Reliable?" Nate asked.

"He's coherent and smart—did two tours in Iraq before the world came apart on him." Pierce stopped, turning her back to the tourists. "He trusts me, and he says one of his people is missing—a regular named Lucy Phelps."

"Missing how long?"

"Two days, three at the most. Lucy is a talker, non-stop, so her silence is an alarm bell."

Nate felt the familiar itch between his shoulder blades, the pattern locking into place. "Does she fit the profile?"

Pierce nodded once. "Small, blonde, thirty-five, but looks older—hard living. She's vulnerable, Agent Holloway, and she's just what you said we should look for."

Nate glanced back at the bench where Booker Hayes lit his cigarette, the flare of the match brief and sharp. The man didn't look around, smoking with a deliberate, contained focus.

"Let's talk to him," Nate said.

As they approached the bench, Nate hung back a few feet, letting Pierce take the lead. He didn't want to spook the man; he wanted to observe.

Booker Hayes had a face carved from teak, with deep lines bracketing his mouth and a closely cropped grey beard. His eyes were clear and sharp, tracking Pierce's approach without a flicker of surprise. He didn't stand.

"Detective," Booker said, his voice like grinding gravel.

"Booker," Pierce replied, crouching on the balls of her feet to put herself at his eye level. "These are the men I told you about—they need to hear what you told me."

Booker took a slow drag from his cigarette, exhaling a thin stream of blue smoke. His gaze passed over Rodecker before settling on Nate, lingering on the cut of his suit, the way he stood with his hands loose but ready near his waist.

"Feds," Booker stated.

"Agent Holloway," Nate said, stepping forward. "This is Detective Rodecker."

"You're dressed too warm for the weather," Booker observed. "Both of you."

"So are you," Nate replied.

A smile touched Booker's lips. "I wear everything I own because if I put it down, somebody takes it, but you wear that suit because you want people to know you're important. We're not the same."

"We're looking for Lucy," Nate said, moving a step closer and invading the man's personal space just enough to show intent. "Detective Pierce says you're worried."

Booker's faint amusement vanished. He leaned forward, resting his elbows on his knees as the cigarette burned down between his fingers, and he stared at an empty bench across the path.

"Lucy is a pain in the ass," Booker said. "She talks—Lord, she talks —about her grandmother in Macon, about the pigeons, about the weather. Likes the bread pudding from the cafe on warm Tuesdays when they give her the day-old stuff."

"When did you see her last?" Rodecker asked, his notebook already out, the pen clicking.

"Tuesday night, late, past midnight."

"Where?"

"Right there." Booker pointed with his chin to the empty bench. "She was holding court, or thought she was."

"Was she alone?" Nate asked.

Booker shook his head, dropping the cigarette butt and crushing it out with the heel of a heavy work boot. "No—she had a friend, a new friend."

"Describe him."

Booker looked up, squinting against the glare off the white pavement. "White fella, tall, dressed sharp in a linen suit—looked like he stepped out of a magazine, or a time machine. Nobody dresses like that just to sit on a bench at two in the afternoon."

Nate didn't move. The sweat on his back turned cold, a phantom draft from the Jones Street parlor cutting through the ninety-degree afternoon. "What was he doing?"

"Listening," Booker said. "Just listening while Lucy was rambling, you know how she gets—manic, highs and lows, talking about her grandma's silver set, stuff she hasn't had in ten years. And this guy sat right next to her, close, not leaning away like folks usually do."

"Did he say anything?"

"Not much—just nodded, watched her face like she was the most important person in the world, like she was a lady." Booker rubbed his jaw, the stubble rasping. "He brought her a box from a bakery, white box tied with string."

"Grooming," Nate said, the word sour in his mouth.

"He was feeding her," Booker corrected. "But not because she was hungry—it was precise, deliberate. He opened the box for her, handed her the pastry, wiped her chin when she got crumbs on it."

Nate visualized the act: the intimacy, the violation of boundaries disguised as kindness, a predator gaining trust through calculated touch. "Did you hear a name?"

Booker nodded. "Lucy called him Mr. Evan—she was all giggles, acting like a schoolgirl. 'Mr. Evan says I have nice eyes. Mr. Evan says he likes my stories."

Rodecker looked at Nate. The name hung in the humid air. *Evan.*

"Did you talk to him?" Nate asked.

"I tried." Booker reached into his pocket and pulled out a pouch of loose tobacco, his hands starting to work on another smoke—a nervous tic to keep them busy. "I went over there and told Lucy it was late, that she should come over to my side of the square. Safety in numbers."

"How did he react?"

"He didn't," Booker said. "That was the thing—most guys, you interrupt them with a street woman, they get aggressive, or they get scared and leave. This guy just looked at me."

Booker paused, licking the paper of his new cigarette to seal it. He held it unlit between his fingers.

"He smiled at me," Booker said. "Polite, real polite, but his eyes had nothing in them."

"Did you touch him?" Nate asked the question sharply.

Booker frowned, looking at his own hands as if they belonged to someone else. "Yeah, I reached out and grabbed his arm, told him he needed to move on, that Lucy wasn't looking for company."

"And?"

"Cold," Booker said, a full-body shudder spasming through him. "Through the suit jacket—like grabbing a bag of ice or dead meat. It wasn't right, man, not for a living man to feel that cold in Spring."

Nate looked at his own hand, a phantom chill radiating from his palm, the memory of stepping too close to Carlisle in the parlor on Jones Street. The air conditioning hadn't done that—the man was a void, a heat sink.

"What did Lucy do?" Pierce asked gently.

Booker looked at the ground, shame pulling at the corners of his mouth. "She got mad, told me to get lost, said I was jealous, that I didn't want her to have nice things."

"It's not your fault," Pierce said.

"I left her there," Booker's voice cracked. "I walked away. You see a wolf in the sheep pen, you know what comes next, but I walked away. I let him take her."

"Did you see them leave?" Nate asked.

"No—I went to my spot behind the church, and when I came back at dawn, she was gone. Her stuff was gone, even her cart. Lucy never leaves her cart."

"The bakery box," Nate said. "Was it still there?"

"Gone. Clean sweep."

Nate stood and walked to the edge of the path, staring down at the empty bench where a predator had played gentleman. He pictured Caroline Marsh and Lucy Phelps—blonde, petite, vulnerable. One educated and wealthy, one living on the street. The predator didn't care about tax brackets, only the type, only the vessel.

"Mr. Evan," Rodecker muttered, closing his notebook. "Evan Carlisle—it fits. The suit, the cold, the grooming."

"He fits the profile," Nate said. "He isolates them, makes them feel special, in thrall."

"In what?" Booker asked, looking up sharply.

"Charm," Nate corrected. "He's charismatic, manipulative."

"It was more than that," Booker said. "Lucy looked drunk, but she hadn't had a drop—she looked floaty, like she wasn't all the way inside her own head."

Nate turned back, crouching down again. He took a card from his pocket and pressed it into Booker's hand.

"If you see him again," Nate said, "or anyone who looks like him, or that white box—you call me, day or night. Don't engage him and do not touch him."

Booker looked at the card before tucking it into his flannel shirt pocket. "He took her, didn't he? He killed her."

"We're going to find her," Nate said, the lie he always told, hoping it sounded like the truth.

"Find her," Booker said, finally lighting the second cigarette. "Before he breaks her."

Pierce touched Nate's arm, pulling him back and guiding Rodecker with them. They moved ten yards away, near a fountain where the sound of water could cover their voices.

"You believe him," Pierce stated.

"I do," Nate said.

"It connects Carlisle to a victim," Rodecker said, "but it's hearsay. A homeless man's word against a wealthy antique dealer—the DA won't touch it."

"We need more," Nate said. "A location, physical evidence."

Pierce checked her phone, shielding the screen from the glare as she scanned the square. She lowered her voice further.

"I didn't want to say this in front of Booker, didn't want to spook him, but I pulled the 911 logs for the last week, looking for weird calls, disturbances in the squares."

"And?"

"Two nights ago," Pierce said. "Call came in at 11:45 PM—welfare check. Caller hung up before giving a name, but dispatch traced the cell."

"Location?"

"Apartment on York Street, just north of Wright Square."

CHAPTER

II

N ATE PARKED the Explorer hard against the curb on York Street, the tires scraping raw concrete, and killed the engine.

"Second floor," Pierce said, unbuckling her seatbelt. "Apartment 2B."

They stepped out into the wall of heat, and the air hit them like a cocktail of exhaust and the river's wet decay.

Rodecker moved to the sidewalk and put his back to the building, watching the street traffic through sunglasses that hid his eyes. The tension in his jaw was a knot of concrete.

They moved to the door, and Pierce pressed the buzzer—a buzz sounded, and the lock clicked. They pushed into the dim hallway where the air was cooler but stale with the smell of old carpet and frying onions.

The stairs groaned under their combined weight, twelve steps to a landing, twelve more to the second floor. Nate's eyes tracked the layout as they climbed: a single fire escape window at the far end of the hall, the stairs they'd just used. A perfect trap if things went wrong.

Pierce knocked on the door marked 2B, her knock gentle, not a cop knock. "Natalie?" she called. "It's Detective Pierce from the police department."

A chain rattled behind the door, and it opened two inches, revealing a slice of a face: one blue eye, messy blonde hair, pale skin stretched tight over sharp cheekbones.

"You brought people." The voice that came through the gap was a raw whisper, thin and frayed like old rope.

"Detective Rodecker," Pierce said, gesturing to the large man behind her, "and Agent Holloway from the FBI. We just want to talk, Natalie. We want to make sure you and Stevie are safe."

The eye darted to Nate, who held up his credentials, keeping his face a neutral mask. He let her see he was calm, that he wasn't going to force the door.

"Please," Nate said. "We believe you."

The chain slid back with a metallic scrape, and the door opened.

As they stepped inside, Nate's hand brushed the deadbolt, confirming it was thrown, his gaze tracing the doorjamb to check it was solid. The apartment was a small tunnel of a room with a window at the far end looking out onto the fire escape, its blinds drawn tight against the afternoon glare. A window unit air conditioner rattled in its frame, fighting a losing battle against the Georgia summer.

Toys littered the floor—Legos and action figures mingled with design portfolios stacked on a drafting table in the corner. It was the cramped space of two people living on top of each other, making do.

"Sit down, please." Pierce moved to the coffee table and perched on its edge, folding into herself to seem less imposing.

Natalie Ralston sank into the beige sofa, pulling her legs up under her like a child seeking protection. She wore Lululemon yoga pants and a grey t-shirt, and she looked like she hadn't slept in days—dark circles under her eyes, skin pale as paper. Her arms were crossed tight over her chest, her hands rubbing her biceps in a constant up-and-down motion that spoke of barely contained panic.

Rodecker moved to the window, parting the blinds with one finger to look down at the street, and he stayed there, standing guard.

In the corner of the room, a movement behind the sofa caught Nate's attention. A small shape huddled on the floor, knees pulled to chest, dark hair falling over his face. Big eyes watched them through the gap between the sofa and the wall, taking everything in.

Stevie. Eight years old. The witness.

Nate kept his attention on Natalie, his voice soft when he spoke. "Walk us through Tuesday night," he said. "Start at the gallery."

Natalie stared at the carpet, picking at a loose thread on the cushion, and for a moment, Nate thought she might not answer. "It was stupid," she finally said. "I don't know why I talked to him. I never talk to strangers, not with Stevie there."

"It wasn't stupid," Pierce said gently. "Tell us about him."

"He was wearing a suit—linen, cream colored, perfectly tailored." Natalie's fingers kept working the thread. "He looked… clean. Like he didn't sweat. Everyone sweats in Savannah in April, but he didn't. Not a drop."

Nate took a notebook from his pocket but didn't write anything yet, just held it in his lap. "He approached you?" he asked.

"We were outside the gallery on Broughton Street, looking at my piece in the window." Natalie's voice had gone flat, reciting facts. "He asked if I was the artist. Said he admired the composition of the piece, that the lighting was masterful. He knew about art—he talked about exposure, about negative space, things only someone who understands photography would mention."

"Did he ask where you lived?"

Natalie nodded, and her rubbing motions got faster, more frantic. "He asked if we walked here, and I said we lived near Wright Square. He nodded like he was checking a box, confirming something on a list he'd already made."

Nate glanced at Rodecker, and the detective turned his head slightly, catching his eye. Targeted selection. This wasn't random— Carlisle had hunted her specifically.

"Then what happened?" Pierce asked.

"He offered to walk us home, said it was getting dark, that the squares could be dangerous at night." A short, hysterical laugh escaped her throat. "He said he wanted to make sure we were safe. Can you believe that? Safe."

"Why did you say yes?" Nate needed to understand the mechanics, the exact point of compliance.

"I don't know," she whispered, and she started rocking slightly, a self-soothing motion. "The air felt thick, like I was breathing through cotton. My thoughts slowed down, like they were moving through water instead of air. It became easier to agree with him than to think for myself, easier to just nod and follow. It felt… peaceful, almost. Like floating."

Dissociation, Nate noted. Extreme suggestibility. Like Hayes described.

"Did he touch you?" Nate asked.

"He put his hand on my shoulder when we crossed Bull Street—said he wanted to guide me around a puddle." She shuddered, a violent spasm that shook her whole body. "He smelled like dirt," Natalie continued, and her eyes had gone unfocused now, seeing the square instead of the room. "Under the cologne—sandalwood, I think, something expensive that rich men wear—there was this other smell. Wet earth. Like a basement that floods every time it rains."

Nate wrote that down in his notebook: *Wet earth. Basement smell.*

"We got to Chippewa Square," she continued, her voice going even flatter, more distant. "The streetlights were out on the west side where the trees grow thick. It was dark under the branches—the moss hangs low there, blocks out what little light there is."

"He stopped?" Pierce prompted.

"He stopped walking, and he pointed to the shadows under the trees." Natalie's hands had stopped moving now, frozen on her arms. "He said he wanted to show me something beautiful, that it was just a few steps into the dark, that I'd never seen anything like it. His voice was so calm, so certain."

"And you went?"

"I turned toward the shadows. I took a step. I wanted to see it— God help me, I *needed* to see it like I needed air." Her voice cracked. "He was holding my hand by then, and his fingers were so cold they hurt, but I didn't care. I was going to follow him."

Nate looked at the space behind the sofa where the boy sat perfectly still. His gaze was fixed on Nate with an intensity that felt wrong for an eight-year-old, too focused, too aware.

"Stevie stopped you," Nate said. It wasn't a question.

Natalie looked at her wrist, and Nate could see four small, crescent-moon scabs marring her forearm where the skin was thinnest. "He dug his nails in hard enough to draw blood. He scratched me, and the pain—" She took a shaky breath. "It woke me up like a slap across the face. The fog cleared for just a second, maybe two. Just long enough."

"And then?"

"I grabbed Stevie, and I ran. I didn't look back, didn't think, just ran as fast as I could until we got inside and locked the door." She looked up at Nate, and her eyes were wet. "I didn't even say goodbye. I just ran."

"Did he follow?"

"I don't know. I didn't look."

Nate capped his pen and clipped it to the notebook, then looked at the floor behind the couch. "Stevie," he said, keeping his voice low and calm. "Can I talk to you for a minute?"

Natalie stiffened, reaching back as if to physically block him from the boy.

Pierce leaned forward, her voice gentle. "It's okay, Natalie. Agent Holloway is good at this. He wants to help."

Stevie stood up slowly, unfolding from his defensive crouch. He was small for eight, swimming in oversized basketball shorts and a superhero t-shirt that hung past his knees. His eyes were dark and wide, but he didn't look scared anymore—he looked serious in a way children shouldn't have to be.

Ignoring the protest of his suit trousers, Nate dropped to one knee, bringing himself down to the boy's level, and he kept his expression neutral. A fake smile would be an insult to a child this serious. "You were brave, Stevie. You saved your aunt."

Stevie didn't answer, just looked from Nate's badge to his face, studying him.

"Did you look at his face?" Nate said.

Stevie nodded and stepped out from behind the couch, moving closer with careful steps. "He looked at Aunt Nat while we walked. He kept looking at her."

"What about his eyes?"

Stevie shivered and hugged himself, his small arms wrapping tight around his chest. "They were wrong. They didn't blink... He stared like a fish does, all flat and dead. Like the big shark at the aquarium, the one that swims by the glass and looks at you, but doesn't really see you, just sees food. Shark eyes."

Nate nodded slowly, letting the boy know he understood. "Did he look at you?"

"Once," Stevie said quietly. "When I scratched Aunt Nat and broke her out of it. He looked at me then."

"What did he do?"

"He smiled, but it wasn't a happy smile." Stevie's voice got even quieter. "It was a hungry smile. Like when you're really hungry, and someone puts food in front of you."

Nate stood, his knees popping in the silence, and he looked at Rodecker, who held out a manila envelope he'd been carrying. Nate took it and moved to the coffee table, clearing away a stack of magazines to make room. He opened the envelope and slid out the sheet of paper inside.

A standard six-pack lineup—six white males with similar builds and dark hair arranged in two rows of three. Number four was Evan Carlisle, cropped from a society page photo where he wore a tuxedo and looked elegant and refined.

Nate placed the sheet on the table, smoothing it flat. "Stevie, I want you to look at these pictures. Take your time, look at each face carefully. Tell me if you see the man from the square."

Natalie turned her head away, unable to look.

Stevie walked forward with his eyes already locked on the page. He didn't scan the faces, didn't hesitate or second-guess. His small index finger came down hard on photo number four, pressing so hard the paper buckled slightly. "That's him."

Nate looked at the photo, and Evan Carlisle stared back with flat eyes—the camera flash caught in them, making them look reflective and dead.

"Are you sure?" Nate had to ask for procedure's sake, even though he already knew the answer.

"Yes."

Natalie looked then, unable to stop herself, and a gasp tore from her throat as she recoiled into the sofa cushions, her hand flying to her mouth. "Oh god. That's him. That's the man."

Nate looked at Stevie, and the boy hadn't moved his finger—he was pressing down on Carlisle's face as if trying to pin the man to the paper, to trap him there. The boy looked up at Nate, and his expression held no childish confusion or doubt. It was the look of someone who had seen a car wreck, who understood damage and death in a way no child should.

"He wanted to take us under the trees," Stevie said, his voice very quiet but absolutely certain. "If we'd went there in the dark, he would have eaten us."

The word hung in the humid air like a curse. *Eaten.*

Not killed. Not hurt. *Eaten.*

Pierce went completely still, and Rodecker stopped his pacing at the window.

Nate stared at the child, at the raw truth in his assessment. Children didn't have the filters adults spent years building—they didn't rationalize away the monsters or explain them into something safe.

"Why do you say that?" Nate asked, keeping his voice steady.

"Because," Stevie said, looking at Nate like it was the most obvious thing in the world, "he looked at us like food. Like we were chicken nuggets at McDonald's."

A wave of nausea washed over Nate, cold and sudden. He looked at Natalie—pale and blonde and small on the sofa, with the same delicate build as Caroline Marsh, the same terrified eyes as Lucy Phelps must have had, the same hair color as Sarah. Carlisle had a type, and he was hunting it.

Carlisle was escalating, Nate realized. Targeting a woman and a child together, hunting in the open in a public square, getting bolder.

Nate picked up the photo array and slid it back into the envelope with careful movements. "Thank you, Stevie. You did exactly the right thing—you saved your aunt's life."

He turned to Natalie, who was weeping silently, tears tracking through her makeup in clean lines. "He knows where we live," she whispered. "He walked us right to the door. He saw which apartment."

"We're going to have a patrol car stationed outside starting right now," Pierce said firmly. "They'll be on the street all night, every night, until we have him."

"You can't stay here tonight," Nate said, and it wasn't a suggestion. "Do you have family somewhere? Somewhere outside the city?"

"My sister lives in Pooler, about twenty minutes away."

"Go there," Nate said. "Pack a bag now, take what you need for a few days. Go while it's still light out."

Rodecker was already on his phone, stepping into the tiny kitchen to call in the patrol request, and his voice was a low, angry growl that promised violence to anyone who got in his way.

Nate looked at Stevie one last time. The boy had moved back behind the couch, but he wasn't hiding anymore—he was watching the door with fixed attention, standing guard, protecting the perimeter. "We're going to catch him," Nate told the boy. "I promise you that."

Stevie didn't answer, just kept watching the door like he expected it to open any second.

Nate signaled to Pierce with a slight nod, and they moved toward the door. They had done all they could here.

They walked out into the hallway, and the door closed behind them with a solid thump. The chain rattled into place with metallic finality, and the deadbolt slid home with a heavy thud that echoed in the narrow space.

The hallway was dim and close, and the smell of onions was stronger now, someone's lunch frying on a hot plate. Nate leaned against the wall, loosening his tie with one hand, feeling the air catch in his throat like he'd forgotten how to breathe properly.

"Shark eyes," Rodecker said, putting his phone away and joining them in the hall.

Nate stared at the door to apartment 2B, thinking about timelines. Two nights ago, before Caroline Marsh was drained in Forsyth Park, Carlisle had been hunting Natalie and Stevie. If the kid hadn't scratched her awake—

"He targets a specific type—young, blonde, delicate build. He uses some kind of hypnotic state to ensure compliance. He isolates them in darkness. And an eight-year-old kid says he wanted to eat them."

"It's not enough for a warrant," Rodecker grumbled. "Walking a girl home isn't a crime, no matter how creepy. Being cold isn't illegal."

"It's enough to focus on him," Nate said. "It's enough to burn his world down piece by piece until he makes a mistake."

He would have eaten us.

CHAPTER

12

CHATHAM COUNTY MEDICAL EXAMINER'S OFFICE

Autopsy Report - Preliminary Findings
Case Number: 2025-ME-0847
Decedent: MARSH, Caroline Elizabeth
Date of Birth: March 14, 1997
Date of Death: April 8, 2025 (estimated)
Date of Examination: April 9, 2025, 0645 hours

Examining Pathologist: Darnell Washington, M.D.,
Chief Medical Examiner
Assisting: Patricia Guillaume, Deputy Medical
Examiner

EXTERNAL EXAMINATION:
The body is that of a well-nourished, well-developed Caucasian female appearing consistent with stated age of 28 years. Body length measures 64 inches, weight 128 pounds. Rigor mortis is complete and generalized. Livor mortis is fixed, posterior distribution, minimal blanching—notable for marked pallor inconsistent with standard livor presentation. Body temperature at scene (0247 hours) recorded at 78.3°F, ambient temperature 64°F, suggesting time of death between 2100-2300 hours on April 8.
The decedent was found unclothed.

IDENTIFYING MARKS: Small surgical scar, right knee (approximately 3cm). Pierced ears, bilateral. Tattoo, left ankle—floral design, approximately 2x3cm.

TRAUMATIC INJURIES:

Anterior Neck Wound (PRIMARY): Catastrophic soft tissue destruction measuring approximately 11cm horizontally x 7cm vertically, centered 3cm below mandible. Wound margins demonstrate irregular tearing pattern with tissue avulsion rather than clean incision. Trachea and esophagus transected. Both common carotid arteries severed. Both internal jugular veins severed. Hyoid bone fractured bilaterally.

CRITICAL OBSERVATION: Within torn tissue margins, semicircular impressions measuring 0.8-1.2cm in spacing intervals, presenting with uniform repetition across primary wound site and secondary tissue disruption on posterior neck. Pattern suggests curved implement or biological dentition —curvature measures 4.0cm arc across widest point. Impressions show consistent depth and spacing beyond normal human bite parameters but below typical animal predation characteristics (submitted for forensic odontology consultation— Dr. Raymond Kessler, requested).

Minor Injuries: Perimortem bruising, inner aspects of both wrists, consistent with restraint or grip pressure. Minimal defensive wounds. Epithelial cells recovered from beneath fingernails (right hand, index and middle fingers— submitted for DNA analysis).

INTERNAL EXAMINATION:
CARDIOVASCULAR SYSTEM: Heart weighs 285 grams (within normal limits). All four chambers are EMPTY of blood. No gross anatomical abnormalities. Coronary arteries patent without significant atherosclerosis.

RESPIRATORY SYSTEM: Lungs show minimal hemorrhage despite major vessel trauma. Combined weight 820 grams (low-normal range). No evidence of aspiration.

HEPATOBILIARY SYSTEM: Liver presents with MARKED PALLOR, weight 1,420 grams (within normal range but appearance grossly abnormal). Consistency and architecture normal on sectioning, but coloration suggests profound anemia or exsanguination.

SPLEEN: Demonstrates SEVERE CONTRACTION, weight 95 grams (below expected range). Characteristic appearance of post-exsanguination organ collapse.

GENITOURINARY: Vaginal vault examination reveals presence of seminal fluid (swabs collected, submitted to forensic biology—single male contributor identified via preliminary screening, full DNA profile pending, CODIS submission initiated). No trauma to external or internal genitalia. Evidence of recent consensual intercourse.

VASCULAR EXAMINATION: Extensive dissection of peripheral vasculature demonstrates COLLAPSED CAPILLARIES throughout extremities. Major vessels (femoral, subclavian, brachial arteries) patent but empty. No evidence of:

- Venipuncture sites beyond standard
  medical examiner access
- Catheter insertion points
- Surgical incisions other than documented
  neck trauma
- Suspension marks or positioning trauma
  consistent with mechanical drainage

ESTIMATED BLOOD VOLUME LOSS: Based on body weight
(128 lbs/58kg), expected total blood volume
approximately 4,350ml. Based on organ presentation, cardiac chamber status, vascular collapse,
and tissue perfusion assessment, estimated
remaining blood volume: 260-350ml.
CALCULATED LOSS: 92-94% of total blood volume.
TOXICOLOGY: Samples submitted to FBI forensic labo-
ratory (requested expedited processing). Preliminary blood alcohol: 0.04% (below legal intoxication
threshold). Urine drug screen pending.

TRACE EVIDENCE:

- Epithelial cells (beneath fingernails):
  submitted for DNA analysis
- Seminal fluid: single male contributor,
  CODIS submitted
- Fibers: black synthetic (source unknown),
  three fibers recovered from dress fabric
- Environmental: Spanish moss articulate,
  soil consistent with Forsyth Park
  location

MICROSCOPIC EXAMINATION: (Preliminary) Tissue
samples demonstrate cellular architecture consistent with acute exsanguination. No evidence of

prolonged hypoxic state or agonal struggle beyond immediate trauma event.

CAUSE OF DEATH: Exsanguination secondary to traumatic anterior neck injury with major vessel transection.

MANNER OF DEATH: Homicide.

CONTRIBUTING FACTORS: Mechanism of blood volume extraction (92-94% loss) remains **undetermined** pending further investigation. Standard post-mortem exsanguination via cardiac pump mechanism accounts for approximately 40-50% blood volume loss before cardiac arrest. No mechanical, surgical, or positional methodology identified to account for degree of blood loss observed in this case.

PENDING:

- Forensic odontology consultation (Dr. Kessler)
- Complete toxicology panel
- DNA analysis (epithelial cells, seminal fluid)
- CODIS match confirmation

RECOMMENDATIONS:

1. Consult forensic odontology for bite pattern analysis
2. Full FBI forensic workup for trace evidence and biological samples
3. Review of comparative cases with similar

```
wound presentation (requesting archival
case file access)
```

Darnell Washington, M.D.
Chief Medical Examiner, Chatham County
Georgia License #ME-8847
Board Certified, Forensic Pathology
Date: April 9, 2025, 1347 hours

FROM: DWashington@chathamcountyga.gov
TO: N.Holloway@fbi.gov
SUBJECT: Marsh Preliminary - Off Record Concerns
DATE: April 9, 2025, 4:23 AM
PRIORITY: High

Agent Holloway,

Attached is the preliminary autopsy report for Caroline Marsh. The findings are documented according to standard forensic protocols, and I will testify to everything written above in any court proceeding.

WHAT FOLLOWS IS NOT for the official record.

I have been a forensic pathologist for thirty-one years. Eight years as an Army pathologist at Dover Air Force Base, processing casualties from two war zones. Fifteen years in Savannah. I have testified in over four hundred cases. I have seen bodies pulled from house fires, from the ocean after weeks of decomposition, from car accidents at highway speeds. I have documented homicides involving machetes, chainsaws, industrial equipment, and one memorable case involving a wood chipper that I still can't think about before meals.

I have never—not once in thirty-one years—written "mechanism undetermined" in the contributing factors section of a homicide autopsy.

I don't know how 92-94% of Caroline Marsh's blood volume left her body.

The math doesn't work. The human heart, even under ideal mechanical circumstances, cannot pump out more than roughly 50% of total blood volume before circulation failure. We've tested this in every configuration—hanging suspension, gravitational drainage, mechanical extraction, even extreme torture methodologies I reviewed during my military service. You cannot get a human body below 50% blood volume without leaving evidence of HOW you removed it.

There are no venipuncture sites. No catheter marks. No surgical incisions beyond the throat wound. No evidence she was suspended in a position that would facilitate gravitational drainage—and even if she had been, you still couldn't achieve this level of exsanguination without major surgical intervention.

Her liver looks like a teaching specimen for end-stage exsanguination. Her spleen is contracted to the point I initially thought it was pathologically diseased until I realized it was just *empty*. Her cardiac chambers contained nothing. Not residual pooling. Not coagulated traces. Nothing. I've performed field autopsies in 110-degree desert heat on bodies three days dead that had more recoverable blood volume than Caroline Marsh.

The wound pattern bothers me more than I documented. Those semicircular impressions—I called them "beyond normal human bite parameters" in the report, which is accurate, but insufficient. They're too uniform. Too precise. The spacing is mathematically consistent across multiple points of tissue disruption. I've seen human bite marks. I've seen animal predation. This is neither, but it's closer to human dentition than anything else—just *wider*. The curvature is wrong. The depth is wrong. But the pattern keeps repeating with the kind of precision that suggests deliberate methodology, not frenzied attack.

I've requested Dr. Kessler for forensic odontology because I need someone else to look at this and tell me I'm not losing my objectivity. I need someone who specializes in bite mark analysis to either identify this pattern or confirm that it doesn't match any known biological or mechanical source.

I've also requested full FBI forensic workup because your lab has resources I don't. I need someone to tell me if there's a mechanical extraction technology I'm not aware of—some medical device, some specialized equipment that could account for this. Because if there isn't...

I'm not a superstitious man, Agent Holloway. I'm a scientist. I believe in evidence. I believe in methodology. I believe that every effect has a cause, and that cause can be identified, measured, and documented.

But I'm looking at Caroline Marsh's body, and I cannot identify a cause that fits the effect I'm seeing.

The blood didn't drain. It didn't pool at the scene—your crime scene photos show minimal ground saturation, which is impossible given the degree of vascular trauma. It didn't soak her clothing in the volumes it should have. The spray pattern is wrong—those droplets you photographed arc *toward* the body, not away from the arterial source.

It's as if the blood *decided to leave*.

That's not scientific language. That's not forensic terminology. But it's the most accurate description I have for what I observed. The blood had agency in its departure. It wasn't forced out by mechanical means. It wasn't pulled by gravity. It *left*.

I don't know what that means.

I need you to understand—this is not in the official report because I cannot defend this language in court. A defense attorney would destroy me. But you need to know what I'm actually thinking, not just what I can formally document.

I've pulled two case files from the county archives—1985 and 1950. Both exsanguination homicides. Both with nearly identical wound presentations to Caroline Marsh. I'm having them couriered to your hotel this morning. Look at the photographs. Look at the wound descriptions. Then tell me I'm wrong about the pattern.

Call me when you've read this. I'll be in my office. I won't be sleeping.

—Darnell Washington, M.D.
Chief Medical Examiner
Chatham County, Georgia
Office: (912) 555-0147
Cell: (912) 555-0891
"The dead do not lie. But sometimes they don't make sense either."

CHAPTER

13

Ammonia and cold coffee coated the air in the windowless basement box SCMPD had generously labeled a task force room. Overhead, a fluorescent tube flickered, its high-pitched drone syncing perfectly with the throb behind Nate Holloway's eyes. He sat hunched over the metal table, pressing his thumbs against his temples, but the pressure didn't budge.

Darnell Washington's autopsy report lay open in the center of the table. Nate read the line again, letting the numbers burn into his retinas. *Calculated Loss: 92-94% of total blood volume.*

He ran the tip of his pen under the numbers, dragging the inkless point across the paper while his mind worked through the implications. The math was offensive, a violation of the basic laws of physics. The human body is a sealed container—puncture it, and the fluid sprays, pools, or soaks into fabric and earth. It doesn't evaporate, and it sure as hell doesn't vanish into thin air. *Where are the missing gallons, Darnell?*

Nate looked at the crime scene photos he had spread in a semicircle around the report, each one a piece of a puzzle that refused to fit together.

In the wide shot of Forsyth Park, the brick pavers beneath Caroline Marsh appeared damp with dew, nothing more. There was no red lake spreading between the stones, no saturation darkening the soil between the bricks.

He picked up the close-up of the spray pattern on her shoulder and the nearby grass, studying the elongated droplets with their distinctive tails.

Nate dropped the photo and rubbed his face with both hands,

feeling the grit of exhaustion in his eyes. Reaching into his messenger bag on the floor, his fingers brushed the worn edge of the manila folder he kept separate from the official files, the one that had traveled with him for fifteen years. He pulled it out.

He opened it slowly, placing his sister's autopsy summary directly next to Caroline Marsh's report. He forced himself to look at the words he had memorized fifteen years ago, words that still had the power to hollow him out. *Exsanguination. Mechanism undetermined. Minimal scene contamination.*

The medical examiner in 2010 had been lazy, writing it off. Darnell Washington was not lazy, and Darnell had done the math with the precision of a man who understood that numbers didn't lie.

Nate looked from one document to the other, his eyes tracking between the clinical language. The wording was different, but the math was the same, and the physics were the same.

Ninety-four percent.

He leaned back in the uncomfortable metal chair, feeling the metal press against his spine, and stared at the ceiling tiles. A brown water stain in the corner looked like a map of a country that didn't exist, all irregular borders and impossible geography.

Logic required a mechanism, and a mechanism required a method. If the blood was not on the ground, and it was not in the body, it had been removed through some process. Removal required a container, a container required time, and time required a lack of struggle.

Caroline Marsh had defensive wounds scraped under her fingernails, but no bruising on her arms, suggesting she had been held down for the hour it would take to drain a body this thoroughly.

The door swung open without warning.

Nate did not jump, just lowered his eyes from the ceiling. Detective Karl Rodecker stepped inside, holding two large Styrofoam cups, kicking the door shut with his heel before leaning against the wall. The detective looked grey, his suit rumpled, his tie loosened at the collar, and the bags under his hazel eyes were dark enough to be bruises.

"You look like hell," Rodecker said.

"I feel like I'm reading science fiction," Nate said, gesturing at the autopsy report.

Rodecker walked to the table and set one of the coffees down near Nate's elbow, steam rising from the plastic lid. "Black, two sugars—figured you needed the energy."

"Thanks." Nate wrapped his hands around the cup, letting the heat seep into his palms.

Rodecker gestured at the spread of photos with his chin. "You find the missing gallons yet?"

"No." Nate tapped the edge of the photograph against the metal table.

"Dean is asking for an update—wants to know if the lab found traces of a pump, a siphon, or a damn shop vac."

"No plastic residues, no mechanical lubricants, nothing consistent with medical tubing."

Rodecker took a sip of his coffee and grimaced at the taste. "So she just leaked."

"Blood doesn't leak up," Nate said, tapping the photo of the droplets with one finger. "It doesn't change direction mid-air."

Rodecker stared at the photo for a long moment, deliberately not looking at the picture of Sarah's file next to it. He knew better than to bring that up. He unbuttoned his jacket and hooked a thumb in his belt, near his badge. "People are talking, Nate—patrol guys, the ones who saw the body before the techs arrived. They're using the V-word."

"I know." Nate had heard the whispers in the hallway.

"It's on the blogs now—'Savannah's Vampire'—and that kind of thing catches fire."

"It's noise," Nate said flatly. "We ignore it."

"We ignore it," Rodecker agreed, nodding slowly. "But the people upstairs don't."

The door opened again, this time abruptly, and Officer Tyrell Jackson stuck his head in, looking nervous. His eyes darted from Rodecker to the photos on the table, then quickly away as if the images might burn him.

"Chief wants you," Jackson said quickly. "Conference room, now."

"Who else is there?" Rodecker asked.

"Councilwoman Moffett." Jackson's tone said everything about how that conversation was going to go.

Rodecker let out a long breath through his nose and looked at Nate. "Here we go."

Jackson retreated, closing the door behind him with a soft click.

Rodecker moved to block Nate from standing up immediately, leaning in over the table and lowering his voice. The room felt suddenly very small, the air thick with tension.

"Listen to me," Rodecker said, his voice barely above a whisper. "Patty Moffett doesn't care about forensics—she cares about the Music Festival next month and the fact that hotel bookings are down four percent since Tuesday."

Nate stood anyway, stacking the photos with slow, deliberate movements before sliding Sarah's file back into his bag. "She can care about whatever she wants, Karl—I have a federal mandate."

"You have a boss in D.C. who hates bad press," Rodecker countered, straightening to his full height. "Moffett talks to the Mayor, the Mayor talks to the Governor, the Governor calls the Director. Do not wave the freak flag in there, Nate—do not talk about blood flying backwards."

"You want me to lie."

"I want you to stay on the case," Rodecker said, his voice tight with urgency. He straightened his tie and ran a hand over his short, sandy hair. "If you spook them, they'll pull you and bring in someone who will write a report that makes everyone feel safe. And you'll be back in Virginia doing paperwork while this guy kills the next one."

Nate looked at the older detective, weighing the politics against the truth. Rodecker was right—the institution protected itself first, victims came second, and truth came third, if at all.

"Let's go," Nate said.

They left the room, pulling the door shut behind them.

The transition from the basement to the upper floor was jarring, a shift from one world to another. They rode the elevator in silence, neither man speaking. When the doors opened, the air changed completely— the basement smelled of old paper and cleaning fluid, while the administration floor smelled of expensive potpourri and carpet glue.

The drone of activity here was different, too, filled with the sound of phones ringing, keyboards clacking, and people speaking in hushed, urgent tones about budgets and schedules.

They walked down the wide hallway to the main conference room, their footsteps echoing off the polished floors. The walls here were glass, transparent, a design meant to project accountability.

Inside, the air conditioning was blasting, creating a significant drop in temperature from the rest of the building that raised goosebumps on Nate's arms.

Chief Harold Dean sat at the head of the long mahogany table, wearing his dress uniform with the collar looking too tight around his thick neck. Sweat beaded on his forehead despite the chill in the room.

Councilwoman Patricia Moffett stood by the window, looking out at the city skyline with her back to them. She wore a bright coral suit that seemed to vibrate against the neutral tones of the room, her hair sprayed into an immobile blonde helmet. Heavy gold jewelry clicked as she tapped her fingers against her tablet in an agitated rhythm.

She turned as they entered, her expression already set to combat mode.

"Sit," Dean said, gesturing to the chairs opposite him with a wave that brooked no argument. He did not look happy.

Nate sat, placing his notebook on the table in front of him. Rodecker took the chair next to him, settling in with the wary posture of a man expecting a fight.

Moffett did not sit, remaining standing as if height would give her power. She picked up her tablet and slammed it down onto the polished wood, the sound cracking through the room like a gunshot.

"Have you seen this?"

She pointed a manicured finger at the screen, the nail painted the same coral as her suit. Nate didn't need to look—he knew what it said.

"The crime blogs are calling it a ritual sacrifice," Moffett said, her voice sharp with the specific cadence of someone used to speaking into microphones. She paced behind the empty chairs on the other side of the table like a prosecutor working a jury. "They are using the word 'vampire,' and they are saying tourists aren't safe in the squares."

"It's an active investigation," Nate said, keeping his voice level. "We can't control online speculation."

"You can control the leaks," Moffett shot back. She stopped directly across from Nate, leaning forward to place both hands on the table. "Someone told the press about the blood loss, and someone told them about the neck wound."

"We are investigating the source of the leak," Dean said, wiping his face again with the handkerchief. "It won't happen again."

Moffett ignored him completely, her attention fixed on Nate. "This city relies on fourteen million visitors a year, Agent Holloway—three point one billion dollars in economic impact. If the narrative becomes that Savannah is a hunting ground for some supernatural freak, that money goes away."

Nate looked at her, seeing the calculation in her eyes with perfect clarity. She wasn't afraid of the killer—she was afraid of the deficit.

"A woman is dead," Nate said quietly. "We are focused on finding who killed her."

"Then find a man," Moffett said, her voice rising slightly. "Find a jealous boyfriend, find a drug deal gone bad, find something normal."

Sure, just find a man who can drink four liters of blood without vomiting and vanish into thin air. Easy.

"The evidence doesn't point to normal," Nate said.

"Make it point there," she said.

The room went quiet, the only sound the buzz of the A/C unit filling the silence with its mechanical hum.

Acid churned in his gut, the familiar feeling of the system protecting itself rising like bile. It was the same pressure he'd felt fifteen years ago when the Savannah PD closed Sarah's case without answers.

"I can't invent a suspect," Nate said. "And I won't ignore the profile."

"What is the profile?" Dean asked, leaning forward across the table, desperate for a lifeline.

Nate kept his voice flat, his eyes locked on Moffett to gauge her reactions. "We are looking for an organized offender—intelligent, local, someone who hunts in the historic district because he feels comfortable here. He feels a sense of ownership."

"That's fine," Moffett said, her posture relaxing slightly. "We can work with that."

"He likely suffers from a clinical delusion," Nate continued, watching her face. "Renfield's Syndrome—clinical vampirism. He believes he needs blood to survive, or he has a sexual fetish involving blood consumption."

Moffett flinched, her hand going instinctively to her throat to cover the gold necklace there. The physical reaction betrayed her composure like a tell in poker.

"You don't need to share that part with the press," Moffett said, her voice quieter now.

"The brutality of the crime is the reality," Nate said, deciding to push because he needed her to understand what they were dealing with. "He didn't just cut her throat, Councilwoman—he tore it out. He used his teeth, bit through the trachea and the carotid artery, and then he took the blood."

Moffett recoiled, taking a step back from the table as if physically struck. Her face lost its color beneath the heavy makeup, leaving her looking almost grey.

Dean looked sick, his hand pressed against his stomach. "Agent Holloway, that's enough."

"She wants to control the narrative," Nate said, not backing down. "She needs to know what the story actually is."

Moffett turned away, looking back out the window with her arms wrapped around herself. Her reflection in the glass looked ghostly against the bright sky outside, insubstantial.

"We cannot say 'vampire,'" she said, the word coming out as a bare whisper. "We cannot."

"We won't," Nate said, offering the compromise Rodecker had warned him about. "We call him a predator. We say he is a disturbed individual with a fixation. We emphasize that this is a human being with a mental illness—not a monster, just a sick man."

Dean exhaled, looking relieved at the diplomatic language. "That works—a sick man. We can catch a sick man."

Moffett turned back around, composing herself with visible effort as the mask slid back into place. "Fine—a disturbed individual. Is that understood?"

"Understood," Nate said.

"And Agent Holloway?" Moffett said, her voice hardening again. "Clear this up quickly, before the festival."

"We're doing everything we can," Rodecker said.

Moffett checked her watch, the gesture dismissive and final. She was done with them. "I have a luncheon—keep Chief Dean informed before you release anything to the media."

She walked to the door, her heels clicking sharply on the hard floor, leaving without a backward glance.

Dean stood up, smoothing his uniform shirt over his belly. "You heard her—keep it grounded. I don't want any more reports about impossible physics crossing my desk. Fix the timeline or fix the report, but make the math work."

Nate stood, picking up his notebook and tucking it under his arm. He didn't trust himself to speak to Dean right now.

"We'll handle it, Chief," Rodecker said.

They walked out of the conference room without another word.

The hallway felt miles long, the silence between them stretched thin and fragile. They passed a row of administrative assistants who didn't look up from their screens, absorbed in their own small dramas.

Rodecker waited until they were in the elevator and the doors slid shut, enclosing them in the metal box away from listening ears.

"You pushed her," Rodecker said.

"She needed to know." Nate leaned against the elevator wall.

"It's a strategy," Rodecker corrected. "It buys us time."

The elevator dinged, announcing their arrival at the ground floor. They stepped out, bypassing the basement, because they needed fresh air more than they needed their desks. They walked through the lobby and out the front doors of the precinct, escaping into the afternoon heat.

CHAPTER

14

News vans idled in double rows along Perry Street, their satellite dishes aimed at the grey dawn while cables snaked across the sidewalk like black vines. Nate settled his sunglasses on the bridge of his nose—no one needed to see the grit in his eyes.

Karl Rodecker walked beside him, the detective having abandoned his jacket in the car so that his shirt was already dark with sweat beneath the armpits. He moved with the heavy, forward-leaning momentum of a man preparing for a fight, using his shoulder to clear a path through a knot of cameramen setting up tripods on the sidewalk.

"Move," Rodecker said. It wasn't a request.

The perimeter of the square was a cacophony of camera shutters and the low murmur of a crowd hungry for a spectacle, with uniformed officers straining against a line of yellow tape. It wasn't press alone—tourists had spilled out of the nearby hotels, phones held high, their screens glowing in the dim light as they documented the horror before they knew what it looked like. The feed was live. The narrative was already out of his hands.

Nate flashed his badge at a young officer whose face was pale and slick with perspiration, and the officer lifted the tape. Nate ducked under, and the sound of the crowd receded, dampened by the canopy of live oaks and their thick hanging moss.

Tour guides called this the Forrest Gump square, a postcard of Southern charm that had transformed overnight into a kill box.

In the center of the square stood the bronze statue of General Oglethorpe, looking north toward the threats of yesterday. At the base of his pedestal, the medical examiner's team had set up a privacy screen, but it was too low, and the angles from the surrounding buildings offered a clear view.

Nate walked toward the monument, his movements precise while he felt the lenses of a dozen cameras tracking him. He focused on the ground where the brick pavers were uneven, pushed up by the roots of the massive oaks that had witnessed generations of Savannah's secrets.

Darnell Washington stood near the base of the statue, wearing blue coveralls and booties over his shoes. He was not writing in his notebook but staring at the ground, and when he saw Nate approach, he shook his head.

"Tell me," Nate said.

"See for yourself," Darnell replied.

Darnell stepped aside and reached down to pull back the corner of a sterile white tarp.

Nate crouched beside Lucy Phelps, who lay naked on her back against the red bricks, her skin the color of old parchment and drained of all vitality. The staging was geometrically perfect: arms crossed over her chest, left over right, fingers curled loosely against her collarbones, bare feet placed together with toes pointing toward the statue.

Four white pillar candles stood at the cardinal points around her body. Unlit.

The anatomy of her throat was wrong—the sternocleidomastoid muscles were severed mid-length, and the trachea showed more than a simple cut, with a section missing entirely. A cavernous, surgical void from chin to sternum exposed the anatomy of the neck to the open air.

A disturbed individual. A sick man.

Nate shifted his gaze to the bricks beneath the wound.

Savannah greys—porous and thirsty—should have drunk the five liters of blood Lucy Phelps held in her body. They should be black with it.

He took off his sunglasses because he needed to see the texture, then leaned closer until his face was inches from the ground. The brick was bone dry.

Nate touched a gloved finger to the brick next to Lucy's neck, and it came away clean, with a faint dampness from the morning dew alone.

"Where is it?" Nate asked, his voice low.

"It isn't here," Darnell said. "I've checked the storm drains, the soil in the planters, and the underside of the statue base—the scene is devoid of it."

Nate stood and walked a tight circle around the body, checking the alignment of the candles before pulling out his phone to open the compass app. The candle at her head was perfectly North, the one at her feet South, and the precision required time along with a lack of fear. The killer had stood here, in the middle of a public square, surrounded by hotels and windows, and performed a ritual that took minutes or longer.

"No drag marks," Nate noted.

"She walked here," Rodecker said from behind him, the detective scanning the windows of the surrounding buildings and looking for witnesses who hadn't come forward. "Or she was carried by someone she didn't fight."

"She was homeless, lived on the street, and would have been cautious around strangers," Nate said.

"Not if she knew him," Rodecker said.

"Or if she was charmed," Nate murmured, thinking of Megan Bacha's description of Caroline Marsh. *Time felt weird. Like being drunk.*

The noise at the perimeter spiked, going from a dull roar to a sharp, angry shout, and Nate turned away from the body.

A man was climbing onto a concrete planter box outside the police tape on the northeast corner of the square—large, broad-shouldered, wearing a black clerical shirt with a white tab collar. Sweat streamed down his face.

Reverend James Oden raised his hands, and the cameras swiveled while the chatter died. He had the presence of a man used to holding a room, though now he was holding a city block.

"Look!" His voice was a baritone thunderclap that cut through the humidity. "Look at what they cover with their tarps!"

Nate stepped away from the body, moving toward the sound with Rodecker right beside him.

"You have eyes!" Oden shouted, pointing a shaking finger past the police line, directly at the spot where Lucy lay. "But you do not see! You have ears, but you do not hear the crying of the blood from the ground!"

"Who is that?" Nate asked.

"James Oden," Rodecker said. "First African Baptist. He's been making noise about the missing women for years, though nobody listened."

Oden turned to face the crowd of tourists and reporters, and he did not look like a man seeking publicity but like a man breaking under the weight of a terrible truth.

"They tell you it is safe!" he cried. "They tell you to buy your tickets and ride your trolleys! But the wolf is in the fold! The bodies are drained dry while our leaders count their silver!"

The skin on the back of Nate's neck tightened. *Drained dry.*

"How does he know?" Nate asked.

"He doesn't," Rodecker said. "He's preaching."

"No," Nate said. "Listen to him."

Oden's voice dropped an octave, becoming more intense with each word. "This is not new! The ground remembers! The blood cries out from 1995! It cries out from 1980! And you stand there and take pictures while the demon feeds!"

It was Alicia Landry's ghost story, the pattern from the archives, but Oden wasn't reading from a spreadsheet—he was speaking it like scripture.

Detective Yolanda Pierce stood near the command post vehicle, thirty yards away, with a phone pressed to her ear. She looked furious, shouting something lost in the Reverend's sermon, and then she chopped her hand through the air, silencing whoever was on the other end, and shoved the phone into her pocket.

Pierce saw Nate and Rodecker and hurried toward them, her face tight with stress.

"Dean is losing his mind," Pierce said when she reached them. "He wants Oden arrested for inciting a disturbance."

"Bad move," Rodecker said. "Arresting a preacher at a crime scene looks like a cover-up."

"I told him that," Pierce said. "Moffett is screaming about message discipline and wants a statement out in ten minutes saying this is an isolated incident."

Nate looked back at the tarp. "It's not isolated, and it's far from disciplined."

"Wolves!" Oden shouted again. "Wolves in the clothing of men!"

Nate watched the Reverend, who wasn't looking at the crowd anymore but at the police, at Nate, with an accusation in his stare that hit harder than the heat.

Then Nate saw something else.

Standing at the edge of the police tape, in the shadow of a large oak, was a man who was not taking pictures or shouting but standing perfectly still, holding a dirty baseball cap against his chest with both hands. He wore layers of mismatched clothes despite the temperature.

He was watching the tarp.

"Pierce," Nate said, tapping her shoulder and pointing. "Look over there."

Pierce followed his gaze, and the tension left her shoulders, replaced by a sudden, sharp grief.

"Booker," she said.

Sunlight cut through the oaks and bleached the blue out of the tarp, making it a brilliant, clinical white against the grass.

Reverend Oden was still shouting, his voice hoarse now but no less powerful.

"They want silence!" he boomed. "They want you to look at the flowers! But the roots are fed on blood!"

Nate watched the tourists, who weren't leaving but were enthralled by the spectacle, filming Oden, filming the body, while the virality accelerated. Each second this scene remained active was a second the "delusion" narrative died.

You couldn't sell a delusion when the body was drained dry in the middle of a public square, and you couldn't tell people it was a confused mental patient when the staging was this precise.

Nate looked at the statue of Oglethorpe, where the founder of the colony stood high on his pedestal, sword at his side, gazing imperiously over the city he had designed—a city of grids, orderly and rational.

But down here on the bricks, rationality was gone.

"The killer is escalating," Nate said. "Forsyth Park was at night, in the shadows, but this is Chippewa Square—this is center stage."

"He's mocking us," Rodecker said, wiping his face with a handkerchief that was already soaked. "He knows we lied about the vampire angle and is rubbing our noses in it."

"He's showing us he can take anyone," Nate said. "A socialite, a homeless woman—it doesn't matter…"

Darnell walked over, peeling off his gloves with a snap.

"I'm done here," Darnell said. "We're moving her, but Nate…"

"Yeah?"

"The candles," Darnell said. "Beeswax, hand-dipped—you don't buy these at Walmart—and the wicks haven't been burned."

Nate looked at the three of them—Rodecker, sweating and angry; Pierce, grieving and guilty; Darnell, a man of science staring at something that defied physics. They were the ones who saw the truth of the scene while everyone else saw a tragedy, a headline, or a photo op.

"We need to get out of here," Nate said. "Before Dean comes down and tries to make us give a statement."

"Where to?" Rodecker asked.

"Back to the files," Nate said. "If Oden remembers 1995 and 1980, the records are there, and we stop looking for a suspect and start looking for a history."

He turned his back on the monument and the shouting preacher, ducked under the tape, and pushed past a reporter who shoved a microphone in his face. He didn't say a word but kept walking while the roar of the crowd faded.

CHAPTER

15

THE TELEVISION WASHED the hotel room in a pulsing blue light, and Nate sat on the edge of the unmade bed with his elbows resting on his knees, staring at the glowing pixels without blinking. He had muted the sound, but the chyron crawling across the bottom of the screen was a silent shout.

VAMPIRE STALKING SAVANNAH? ODEN DEMANDS ANSWERS.

CNN played the clip on a loop: Reverend Oden on the planter box in Chippewa Square, his face slick with sweat, his mouth wide in a declaration Nate could hear even in the quiet. *The wolf is in the fold.* The camera cut to the white tarp covering Lucy Phelps, then back to Oden, then to a panel of talking heads in an Atlanta studio. Their faces held gravity and excitement in equal measure.

Nate rubbed a hand over his face, the stubble on his jaw scratching against his palm as the clock crept toward four in the morning. He reached for the remote and pressed the button, and the screen went black.

Darkness swallowed the room.

The silence lasted three seconds before his phone vibrated against the nightstand wood. The harsh, mechanical buzz drilled into the quiet as the phone danced slightly on the veneer, and Nate stared at the lit screen where the name flashed white against black.

HARRAN.

Nate let it buzz twice before picking it up and standing, moving to the window where he could look down at the empty street. Wet pavement reflected the amber glow of the streetlights.

"Holloway."

"Tell me the news is wrong." Assistant Director Jeff Harran did not say hello, and his voice was tight, carrying the specific, clipped frequency of a bureaucrat watching his career slide off a cliff.

"Oden found the body before we did and controlled the narrative," Nate said. "The media ran with it."

"I don't care about the preacher," Harran said. "I care about the word *vampire* appearing on national television next to the FBI seal." Papers rustled on the other end of the line. "The Director just called me at home at four in the morning, Nate. And I am explaining to the Director why we have agents in Georgia hunting a creature from Gothic fiction instead of real criminals."

Nate turned from the window and paced the short length of the room until he stopped at the desk. The corkboard was a chaotic disarray of crime scene photos and maps, and under the desk lamp, the red string connecting Sarah to Caroline to Lucy was a bloody line.

"We aren't hunting gothic fiction," Nate said. "We are hunting a serial offender with a specific ritualistic pathology."

"Then find him and make sure he has a face people understand," Harran said. "I need a suspect with a name, a mugshot, and a history that doesn't belong in a horror movie."

"The evidence doesn't fit the usual profiles," Nate said. "The blood loss is absolute, and the staging is methodical. This isn't a disorganized drifter."

"Make it fit."

The order settled in the silence between them like a stone dropped in still water.

Nate's knuckles turned white as he gripped the phone. "Excuse me?"

"You heard me," Harran said. "Find a sex offender or a transient with a biting history. Find a meth head who likes knives and has priors. I don't care if the forensics are perfect or if it takes some creative interpretation. I need an arrest, and I need to show the public a mugshot of a dirty, broken human being so they stop looking at the shadows and blaming us for not catching the boogeyman."

"You want a scapegoat."

"I want closure, and I want this circus out of town," Harran said.

"The Mayor is calling the AG, the AG is calling the Director, and the pressure is building. If you can't give me a conventional suspect in forty-eight hours, I will find someone who can."

Nate stared down at the map on the desk and traced the line from Jones Street to the squares with his finger. The geometry was perfect, and the timeline defied logic.

"We have a person of interest named Evan Carlisle," Nate said. "He fits the geographic profile, has access to the victims' routines, and matches the witness descriptions."

"The antique dealer with the airtight alibis and the high-priced lawyer?" Harran's voice carried disbelief. "Don't be stupid, Nate. You go after a man like that with this nonsense, and he will sue the Bureau into the ground. Drop him."

"He's the guy, Jeff."

"Based on what evidence?" Harran's voice dropped, losing its heat to become cold and dangerous. "A ghost story? Your gut? Or is this about Sarah?"

Nate went rigid and stared at his own reflection in the dark window glass. A gaunt stranger with sunken eyes stared back.

"This is about the evidence," Nate said.

"Is it?" Harran asked. "Because when I look at your file, I see a pattern forming. You took this assignment when you should have recused yourself, and you are seeing ghosts where there are only criminals. You are letting a fifteen-year-old trauma dictate a federal investigation."

"The MO is identical."

"The MO is a copycat trying to get attention, or it's a coincidence," Harran said. "But you aren't seeing it clearly because you're looking for the monster that killed your sister. You are going to destroy your career trying to find him."

"I am doing my job."

"You have three days to bring me a drifter or a junkie or something real," Harran said. "Or you come back to Quantico and surrender your badge. I'm scheduling a psych eval for Monday morning."

The line went dead.

Nate lowered the phone as the quiet in the room pressed against his eardrums like water. He tossed the phone onto the bed, where it bounced once on the quilt and settled into the fabric.

He walked into the bathroom and turned the faucet handle, splashing cold water from the porcelain basin onto his face. He gasped at the chill and scrubbed hard, trying to wash away the exhaustion and frustration and the sound of Harran's voice still echoing in his ears. He grabbed a towel and dried his face, then stared at himself in the mirror where the red rims around his eyes were dark as bruises.

The phone on the bed rang.

Nate dropped the towel and moved quickly, assuming it was Harran calling back to twist the knife deeper. He reached for the device with his thumb hovering over the answer button, then stopped.

The name on the screen wasn't Harran.

MOM.

Nate froze with his hand hovering in the air as the phone vibrated against the mattress. The persistent, demanding buzz filled the room. It was a quarter past four in the morning, and Margaret Holloway did not call at this hour. She went to bed at nine and rose at five without exception.

He picked up the phone while his throat turned dry, and he cleared it.

"Mom?"

"Nathan." Her voice was quiet, not frantic or panicked, but empty. It sounded like it was coming from the bottom of a well. "Are you safe?"

"I'm safe," Nate said as he sat heavily in the armchair in the corner. The springs creaked under his weight. "Why are you calling so early? Is Dad okay?"

"Your father is sleeping through the night now," she said. "The pills help."

"Then what is it?"

"I turned on the news because I couldn't sleep," she said. "I wanted to watch the weather forecast. And I caught the report from Savannah."

Nate closed his eyes and tilted his head back against the chair while pinching the bridge of his nose. "Mom. Turn it off."

"They said the throat was torn," Margaret said, speaking the words with slow precision. "They said there was no blood on the ground, and they said the body was white as marble."

"It's just news reports exaggerating for ratings," Nate said.

"Don't lie to me," she said, her voice sharpening like a blade. "Do not lie to me, Nathan, not about this. It is exactly the same as Sarah. Isn't it?"

He opened his mouth to deny it and give her the lie Harran wanted for the public, but he couldn't. Not to her. She knew the details because she had read the autopsy report fifteen years ago, memorizing every injury on her daughter's body.

"Yes," he said, the word barely a breath. "It's the same."

The silence on the line stretched and filled only with the ragged, shallow sound of her breathing.

"You knew when you went down there," she said. "You didn't go for the Bureau or for justice. You went because you knew he was back."

"I suspected."

"You've been waiting for this," she said. "Fifteen years of waiting. You haven't come home for Christmas in three years, you don't have a wife, and you don't have a life. You just have those files and that obsession."

Nate stood because he couldn't sit with the jagged energy coursing through his body. He walked to the corkboard where Sarah's photo was pinned in the center, showing her smiling in her SCAD hoodie. The picture was taken two days before she died, and she appeared so young, so unaware of what was coming.

He touched the cool paper edge of the photo.

"I have to stop him," Nate said.

"Stop him?" Margaret let out a short, bitter sound that wasn't a laugh. "You aren't trying to stop him from killing again. You're trying to save her."

"I'm doing my job."

"You stopped being my son a long time ago," she said. "You became something else, this hunter with no life outside the hunt. You think if you catch him, it changes what happened in that alley? You think it brings her back to the dinner table on Sundays?"

"No," Nate said. "But it balances the scale."

"There is no scale to balance," she said. "There is just gone and not gone, and she is gone."

Nate turned from the photo to the empty hotel room where the shadows in the corners pressed deeper.

"I didn't answer," Nate said. The words came out before he could stop them, words he had never said aloud to anyone. Not to the grief counselors or his ex-fiancées or even to himself.

"What?" Margaret asked.

"The night she died, she called me around half past ten," Nate said, his voice cracking. He walked to the foot of the bed and sat on the floor with his back against the mattress, pulling his knees to his chest. He made himself small. "Two hours before they found her body."

"I know she called," Margaret said. "We reviewed the phone records with the police."

"I was studying in the law library with a torts exam the next morning," Nate said as the confession spilled out of him after being dammed up for a decade and a half. "My phone was sitting on the stack of books. It vibrated across the table, and I glanced at it and recognized her face on the screen."

He squeezed his eyes shut, seeing the library with its fluorescent lights and the smell of old paper, the phone buzzing across the table.

"I thought I'd call her back tomorrow," he said. "I pressed ignore and went back to reading about liability and negligence."

He put his head in his free hand, hiding his face from the empty room.

"If I had answered that call, she wouldn't have been in that alley," he said. "She would have been on the phone with me, talking about her classes or complaining about her roommate. She would be alive today. I killed her, Mom, because I wanted to be a lawyer more than I wanted to protect my little sister."

The line filled with a heavy silence, and then her voice returned without anger but with deep sadness.

"Oh, Nathan," Margaret said. "You think you're that godlike?"

Nate lifted his head and wiped his eyes with the back of his hand. "What?"

"You think you have the power of life and death?" she asked. "That is vanity and arrogance. If you had answered, maybe she would have talked to you for five minutes and then walked into the alley anyway. Maybe you would have stayed on the line and heard her die while being unable to help. Maybe the man was already watching her and waiting."

"I could have saved her."

"You couldn't have," she said firmly. "She is dead because a monster killed her. Not because of a phone call or a torts exam or any choice you made. A monster."

Nate stared at the dark window and at the reflection of a man sitting broken on the floor.

"Whatever this thing is, it broke us," Margaret said. "It broke your father, and it broke me, and it took my daughter. Don't let it take my son, too. Come home, Nathan. Just come home and let someone else chase this."

"I can't."

"Why?"

"Because he's still here in Savannah, and he's killing them the same way," Nate said. "And nobody else sees it for what it is. Harran wants me to pin it on a drifter and close the case. The police want it to go away quietly. I'm the only one who knows what he is."

"And what is he?"

"He's the thing that doesn't stop," Nate said.

He stood with his legs stiff and walked to the desk, where he stared at his badge and his gun. The Glock 19M lay heavy and black on the wood, a tool of the state and of justice, or just a tool.

"I'm not coming home until he's dead," Nate said.

"We can't bury you, too," Margaret said, her voice breaking. "I don't have enough left in me for another funeral, Nathan."

"You won't have to bury me," Nate said.

He picked up the Sharpie from the desk and uncapped it, then studied the map of Savannah pinned to the corkboard. He drew a thick, black line from Sarah's photo to Lucy Phelps's crime scene notation. Then he drew a circle around the townhouse on Jones Street, where the ink was dark and permanent against the paper.

"I will stop him," Nate said.

He didn't say *we* or *the Bureau* or *the law*.

"I will."

"Nathan—"

He pulled the phone from his ear and pressed the red button, severing the connection.

Nate placed the phone face down on the desk and stared at the circle on the map. The time for procedures was over, and the time for reports was over. Harran had given him three days to find a lie.

He would use them to find the truth.

CHAPTER

16

BOOKER HAYES MERGED with the deep gloom of the live oaks on the western edge of Chippewa Square. The air tasted of diesel exhaust and the dying azaleas, underlined by the sulfur-rotten scent of the river marshes. Sweat channeled down his spine, soaking the collar of the second-hand flannel shirt, but he did not wipe it away. Movement attracted attention. Tonight, Booker was wood. He was iron. He was part of the bench.

He was on watch.

Lucy Phelps was dead because he had failed to hold the line. The memory burned in his gut, hotter than the bad whiskey he used to drink to forget the desert. He had seen the wolf in the linen suit feeding her bread pudding and had done nothing because he was tired and invisible. Not tonight. Tonight, the square belonged to him. A few tourists dragged their feet through the humidity, searching for movie locations that didn't exist, eyes sliding over Booker as if he were just texture—urban camouflage.

Booker ran his sector scan, left to right, near to far, hunting for the anomaly.

The anomaly sat under the streetlight near the Oglethorpe monument.

Twenty-two, maybe. Blonde hair falling loose over her shoulders, catching the artificial yellow jaundice of the lamp. She sat on the brick wall surrounding the monument base, legs crossed at the ankles, a sketchpad resting on her knees. Her hand moved in quick, rhythmic strokes. Soft. That was the word. She looked clean and soft, and she had zero perimeter awareness.

A camera hung around her neck. Heavy glass lens. Expensive.

Booker shifted his weight on the slats. His hip ached, the dampness grinding into the bone. He checked the blind spots.

A trolley rattled past on Bull Street, bell clanging once. The sound faded into the heavy air.

Then the shadows separated.

No noise preceded him—just a shift in the darkness under the trees, and a man stepped into the pool of light—cream-colored linen suit, impossibly crisp. A figure cut from a magazine and pasted onto the dirty background of the night.

Mr. Evan.

Booker's hand gripped the bench edge until a splinter bit into his palm. Heart hammering a double-time rhythm against his ribs. The wolf had returned to the feed.

Carlisle didn't approach. He arrived. One second, ten feet away, the next standing at her shoulder. Stillness that human beings didn't possess. People fidgeted. They shifted weight. They breathed. Carlisle stood like a statue dressed in money.

The girl stopped drawing and looked up.

Run. The command screamed in Booker's head. *Get up and run.*

She didn't run. Her face lit up, a bright, open smile that twisted Booker's stomach. She closed the sketchbook, gathered her things, and stood.

They spoke. The words were lost to the distance, but the body language screamed dominance. Carlisle leaned in, commanding the space, a pale hand gesturing toward the north. Toward the river.

The girl hesitated.

She reached into her pocket. The phone screen bathed her face in harsh blue light. She checked the time or a text. Her thumb hovered over the glass.

Make the call. Call a cab. Call the cops.

Carlisle didn't grab her or snatch the device—he just reached out, fingers grazing her elbow. A touch barely there.

The girl went rigid.

She looked at Carlisle while the blue light died as the screen went black. She slid the phone back into her pocket without looking at it again. Her shoulders dropped. The tension drained from her frame, leaving her fluid. Dreamy. She nodded.

Carlisle smiled. Teeth, but no warmth.

They moved north, exiting the square. Carlisle led, the girl following close, her arm brushing against his linen jacket.

Booker counted. One-Mississippi. Two-Mississippi.

He stood, his knees popping with a sound loud in his own ears. He ignored the pain. Keeping the thick trunks between him and the couple, he moved. A ghost. A nobody. Following the wolf.

They crossed Liberty Street. The manicured lawns and historic markers dissolved into cracked sidewalks and buildings that hadn't seen paint since the Carter administration. Tourists didn't come this far. Streetlights spaced further apart, leaving long stretches of blackness that swallowed the road.

Booker stayed a block back, using parked cars and dark stoops for cover. Eyes locked on the white blur of the linen suit.

Humidity thickened near the river. The air tasted of salt and mud.

The blonde girl walked with a light step. She looked up at Carlisle, laughing once. The sound carried in the empty street, thin and dreamy.

They turned onto West Boundary.

The edge. The industrial fringe. The dead tooth of the city.

Brick husks loomed three stories high, blocking out the stars. Broken windows stared like empty sockets. Weeds reclaimed the asphalt. No trolleys here. Just the silence of abandoned commerce.

Carlisle stopped in front of a massive brick warehouse. Windows boarded over or blackened with soot.

Booker dove behind a rusted dumpster in the alley across the street. Low ground. Bad tactical position. He crouched in the muck, the smell of rotting garbage and old grease making his eyes water.

Through the gap between the dumpster and the wall, the scene played out.

Carlisle stepped to a heavy steel door and reached into his jacket pocket, producing a single, large key. Old iron. Heavy.

He slid the key into the lock.

Clack.

The tumblers turned with a heavy, mechanical sound.

The girl said something, gesturing loosely at the dark building. She laughed again, but the sound was brittle now. Nervous.

Carlisle placed his hand on the small of her back and guided her forward.

She stepped over the threshold.

Carlisle followed, not bothering to check the street, not caring who might see.

The heavy steel door swung shut.

Thud.

The sound of a cell door closing.

Booker let out a breath he didn't know he held. He checked his watch, a cheap digital thing from the shelter lost-and-found—quarter to nine.

He settled into the dirt.

Waiting. Always the waiting. In Fallujah, you waited for the mortar. You waited for the IED. You waited for the sun. The waiting gave you time to think about the things you tried to drown.

Lucy's shoes, soles worn through. The bread pudding.

A mosquito whined in his ear, and he swatted it away.

Legs cramping, he shifted and tried to keep blood flowing. The alley was dark, but the streetlamp down the block cast a sickly sodium-orange glow on the warehouse front.

Nothing moved. The city had turned its back on this place.

An hour passed.

You know what's happening, the voice in his head whispered. *You saw his eyes.*

Quarter past ten came and went.

A rat skittered across the alley mouth, pausing to sniff the air before darting into the shadows. Booker didn't flinch—just another piece of trash in the alley.

Two hours now. Nearly eleven.

Booker's back seized, and he rubbed the muscle, grimacing. Maybe they went out the back. Maybe he was guarding an empty box.

The latch clicked.

Sharp. Sudden.

Booker froze, pressing himself flat against the brick while his lungs halted.

The steel door groaned open.

Carlisle stepped out.

Alone.

Booker scanned the opening behind him, looking for the blonde hair, the camera.

Nothing but blackness.

Carlisle turned and locked the door with the iron key, then checked the handle. Precise movements. Unhurried. Suit unwrinkled. Hair perfect.

But he was carrying something.

A large canvas duffel bag hung from his left shoulder. Dark, heavy material. Military surplus or sailing gear.

Carlisle adjusted the strap, and the bag swung. Not clothes. Not art supplies.

It swung with a dense, shifting weight, hitting Carlisle's hip with a wet, heavy impact. *Thud.*

Booker stared at the canvas bulges while his mind tried to construct shapes. A head? A knee?

No. Just a bag. But the girl wasn't there.

Carlisle walked south, back toward the lights, back toward where monsters went when they were done. A bounce in his step. Energized.

He didn't look back.

Booker watched until the white suit vanished around the corner.

The street lay empty, the warehouse silent.

Booker stood on legs that wouldn't stop shaking. He grabbed the dumpster edge to steady himself.

The steel door.

Go in, the soldier said. *Breach. Clear. Assess.*

No weapon, the survivor whispered. *No backup. Locked tight.*

He took a step into the street, and gravel crunched under his boot. Too loud.

The warehouse felt awake. Watching him.

The girl was in there. Or she wasn't.

If she was in there...

Booker's throat closed while bile rose in his esophagus.

He couldn't go in. The certainty broke his heart. If he touched that door, if he tried to pick that lock, he died. The wolf would return. Or the building would swallow him whole.

Coward.

His hands were shaking so badly that he almost dropped the phone. The cheap prepaid brick Detective Pierce had given him. He pressed speed dial.

One ring.

Two rings.

Three rings.

Pick up.

The line clicked.

"You have reached the voicemail of Detective Yolanda Pierce. Please leave a message."

Beep.

Booker licked lips dry as dust and whispered into the plastic mesh.

"Detective. It's Booker."

He looked up and down the street. Exposed.

"A blonde girl," he said, voice cracking. He cleared his throat, keeping it low. "One with the camera. I saw her. Mr. Evan took her."

Breath hitched.

"West Boundary. The warehouse. Near the old cold storage. The brick one. West Boundary."

He needed to say more about the bag. The words stuck.

"West Boundary," he repeated. "He locked her in. Or... he took her out in a bag. I don't know. But she ain't came out walking."

He pulled the phone away. Call ended.

He shoved the phone into his pocket.

One last look at the steel door.

"I'm sorry," he whispered to the brick and the iron. "I'm so sorry."

He turned and ran, moving as fast as the bad hip allowed, shambling into the alley darkness. Away from the river, away from the thing he had seen and the thing he hadn't done. He ran until his lungs burned and the smell of rot faded into the smell of the city.

CHAPTER

17

PIERCE TASTED the recycled air in the SCMPD conference room, a stale mix of burnt coffee and the sharp chemical scent of dry-erase markers that sat heavy in her throat. Her lower back ached from the ergonomic chair that offered no actual support.

Chief Harold Dean stood at the head of the room, pointing a laser at a projected spreadsheet on the far wall, the red dot jittering over revenue projections for the Savannah Music Festival.

"Twelve million dollars," Dean said, his voice tight with the strain of a man defending an indefensible position. "That is the projected economic impact—we cancel, we lose that, we lose the tax revenue, we lose the goodwill of the hospitality association."

Mayor Thompson paced behind him, blocking the view of the whiteboard where someone had written *Talking Points* in blue ink. He stopped pacing to lean over Dean's shoulder, his cologne cutting through the stale conference room air.

"It is not just the money, Harold," Thompson said, his voice dropping into campaign mode. "It is the narrative—if we cancel, we admit we have lost control of the streets, we admit there is a predator we cannot catch."

Councilwoman Patty Moffett sat across from Pierce. She tapped a stylus against her tablet screen, the rhythmic *tick, tick, tick* against the glass like a metronome counting down to disaster.

"We need to control the vocabulary," Moffett said without looking up from her screen. "I am seeing the V-word on Twitter again, even on the local blogs—'Savannah Vampire'—it needs to stop. We cannot have a supernatural panic heading into the peak season."

Pierce stared at the wood grain of the table, a knot in the

mahogany that looked like a thumbprint. Her quadriceps tightened, the urge to kick the chair back vibrating in her legs—discussing vocabulary while bodies turned up with their throats torn out was insanity.

Her phone lay face down on the table in front of her.

It buzzed against the wood, a short, angry spasm of mechanics loud in the quiet room.

Pierce reached for it, her fingers brushing the cold metal case.

"Detective Pierce," Dean said, his voice sharp enough to cut the room's stale air. "We need your input on the patrol density for the squares—unless you have something more important on that screen."

Pierce froze, withdrawing her hand and placing it flat on the table. "No, Chief, just spam," she lied.

"Then pay attention," Moffett said. "We are discussing the safety of this city."

The phone shuddered again, longer this time—someone was calling.

Pierce watched the device shimmy slightly on the polished surface, every instinct in her twelve-year career screaming at her to pick it up. A call at this hour meant trouble, and trouble meant the job.

"The squares," Dean repeated, his marker squeaking against the whiteboard. "We need a visible presence in Chippewa and Monterey, but not aggressive—we want tourists to feel safe, not occupied. What is the sweet spot?"

"Uniforms on foot," Pierce said, her voice flat to her own ears. "Two officers per square, high visibility vests, keep the patrol cars on the perimeter so they don't block the sightlines for the tour buses."

"Good," the Mayor said. "Friendly, approachable."

The phone rattled a third time, then a fourth.

Pierce clenched her jaw, her molars grinding together as she stared at the black casing of the phone sitting there like a stone.

"What about the homeless population?" Moffett asked, her stylus still tapping that infernal rhythm. "If we have extra patrols, we need to make sure the aggressive panhandlers are moved along—nothing kills the vibe of a romantic weekend like being asked for change by someone shouting about demons."

"They are citizens, Councilwoman," Pierce said, the anger flaring hot in her chest. "They are also the ones getting killed."

"We are protecting them by moving them to shelters," Moffett countered. "For their own good."

The phone buzzed again, a double pulse—text message or voice-mail notification, Pierce couldn't tell.

Pierce looked at Dean, wiping his forehead with a handkerchief, exhausted like a man trying to patch a dam with duct tape.

"Can we wrap this up?" Pierce asked. "I need to get back to the street."

"We are not done with the press release," the Mayor said, his voice taking on that patronizing edge that made Pierce want to throw something. "We need a quote from you, Detective—something reassuring about the progress of the investigation, something that mentions 'leads' and 'person of interest' without getting specific."

"I don't have a specific person of interest I can name publicly," Pierce said. "And the leads are complicated."

"Make them simple," Dean said. "Draft something—we will review it before you leave."

Pierce picked up a pen and pulled a legal pad toward her, started writing words that meant nothing: *Diligent. Tireless. Focused.*

The phone buzzed one more time, then went still.

The lack of noise from the device felt heavier than the buzzing.

Time stretched, the air in the room thickening and pressing against Pierce's temples like atmospheric pressure before a storm. The Mayor argued about the font size on the public safety pamphlets, Moffett debated the color of the ribbons they would tie around the trees for awareness, and Dean stared at the revenue spreadsheet as if hoping the numbers would rearrange themselves into a solution.

One hour passed, then ninety minutes.

Pierce watched the second hand on the wall clock sweep around—*tick, tick, tick*—moving with agonizing slowness, every rotation a physical weight adding to the burden in the room.

Finally, Dean capped his marker and tossed it onto the tray. "Fine," he said. "We go with the draft—patrols start at 0800, we hold the press conference at noon on the steps. Dismissed."

Chairs scraped loudly against the linoleum floor, harsh and grating.

Pierce stood up immediately, her legs stiff, blood rushing back into her feet. She grabbed her phone but didn't check it in the room—she couldn't breathe in there anymore.

She hit the hallway, the heavy oak door cutting off the Mayor's drone, and the air out here was cooler, smelling of floor wax and old coffee, but it didn't stop the heat radiating from her collar. She didn't check the phone until she was ten feet down the corridor, back against the cinderblock, the screen flaring blue in the dim light.

The notification list scrolled down the screen.

Three missed calls, all from the same number.

Unknown Caller.

Then a voicemail icon.

Booker (Source).

Pierce stared at the name, a wave of nausea rolling through her gut. Booker never called—Booker survived by being invisible—and if Booker called, the world was burning.

She looked at the timestamp on the voicemail: *10:49 PM.*

She looked at the digital clock at the top of her screen: *1:15 AM.*

The math hit her harder than the heat—two hours, she had been sitting in that room listening to Patty Moffett talk about ribbon colors for over two hours while this message waited.

Pierce pressed the play button and held the phone to her ear, pressing her other hand over her free ear to block out the hum of the building.

The audio crackled—wind noise, street sounds, then a voice, low and trembling.

"Detective, it's Booker."

Pierce closed her eyes and pictured him, the weathered face, the eyes that had seen Fallujah and never really came back.

"A blonde girl," Booker said, his breath hitching on the recording. *"One with a camera—I saw her. Mr. Evan took her."*

Pierce pushed herself off the wall, her heart hammering a frantic rhythm against her ribs.

"West Boundary, the warehouse, near the old cold storage—the brick one. West Boundary."

A pause, a terrifying, heavy silence on the line.

"He locked her in, or he took her out in a bag—I don't know. But she ain't came out walking."

The message ended.

She ain't came out walking.

Pierce hit the redial button, her thumb shaking.

The phone rang—one ring, two.

"Pick up," she said into the phone. "Pick up, Booker, pick up."

You have reached a number that is no longer in service or is turned off.

She ended the call and tried again—same result.

"Shit."

He had turned it off, or the battery died, or he threw it away because he was terrified.

West Boundary, the warehouse.

She knew the area—a graveyard of industry on the edge of the city, empty buildings, dark streets, no witnesses.

Two hours.

If the girl was inside...

Pierce ran, hitting the stairwell door with her shoulder and bursting through, her footsteps clattering on the metal treads as she took them two at a time.

CHAPTER
18

Pierce bypassed the lock on her unmarked Explorer, tearing the door open and twisting the ignition before her hip even hit the seat, then slammed the car into gear and peeled out of the lot, tires chirping on the asphalt.

She drove toward the river, but not to the warehouse, not yet—she couldn't go alone, not against this.

She needed the Fed.

She blew through the intersection at Abercorn, the suspension bottoming out as the blurred lights of the cross-traffic smeared across her side window.

She screeched to a halt in the loading zone in front of the Marshall House, threw the placard on the dashboard, and was out of the car before the engine stopped ticking.

She ran through the lobby—the night clerk looked up, startled—but Pierce was already at the elevators, mashing the button, and when the doors didn't open fast enough, she turned and ran for the stairs.

Fourth floor, her lungs burning, her legs pumping.

She reached the hallway, quiet now, the patterned carpet absorbing the sound of her boots.

Room 417.

She hit the wood with the heel of her hand. "Nate! Open up!"

She didn't wait—she pounded again.

The lock clicked, the door swung inward.

Nate Holloway stood there in jeans and a black t-shirt, his feet bare, looking like he hadn't slept in a week, but his eyes were clear, sharp, alert.

A shoulder holster sat on the dresser behind him.

Pierce stepped inside without saying hello—she couldn't find the air for pleasantries.

"I missed it," she said, the words coming out in a rush, desperate and raw. "I was in the meeting with Dean, with the Mayor—I sat there for two hours, and I missed it."

Nate watched her without asking what she missed—he just waited.

Pierce held out her phone, her hand shaking. "Booker," she said.

She pressed play and put it on speaker.

Booker's voice filled the small hotel room, the fear in it raising goosebumps on Pierce's arms and tightening her throat, dropping the temperature in the room by ten degrees.

"*...saw her. Mr. Evan took her... West Boundary... she ain't came out walking.*"

Nate went still—not a passive stillness, but the stillness of a predator locating a threat, his gaze locked on the phone.

The door hadn't fully latched and swung open to reveal Karl Rodecker, his tie loose, shirt wrinkled—he must have seen Yolanda run out of the station.

"What is it?" Rodecker asked.

Pierce didn't answer—the message ended.

"Timestamp?" Nate asked, his voice quiet and deadly.

"10:49," Pierce said. "More than two hours ago."

Nate turned and moved to the desk, shoving a half-finished crossword puzzle to the floor, papers scattering as he woke his laptop, his fingers flying across the keyboard.

"West Boundary," Nate said. "Industrial district, warehouses."

"Booker said the brick one," Pierce said. "Near the cold storage."

"I know it," Rodecker said, moving into the room and closing the door behind him. "Old cotton warehouse—it's been derelict for years, fenced off."

Nate's screen cast a blue pallor over his face as he typed quickly, accessing databases that required federal clearance.

"Property records," Nate muttered. "Searching shell companies, linking addresses."

Pierce paced near the door, put her hands on her head, and pulled at her hair.

"I should have looked," she said. "The phone buzzed, I reached for it, Dean told me to focus, so I stopped—I let it sit there."

She looked at Rodecker, her eyes burning. "I let it sit there, Karl, for two hours."

"You didn't know," Rodecker said. "You were doing the job."

"The job is protecting people," Pierce snapped. "Not protecting the Mayor's poll numbers."

"Got it," Nate said.

He spun the laptop around.

A property deed displayed on the screen.

"West Boundary Warehouse and Storage," Nate read. "Owned by Aurora Holdings LLC."

He clicked another tab.

"Aurora Holdings is a subsidiary of a trust managed by a law firm in Delaware," Nate said, his voice flat and professional now. "But look at the local contact for tax purposes."

He pointed.

Evan Carlisle.

The name sat there on the screen—a confirmation, a challenge.

"He owns it," Nate said. "Booker saw him take a blonde woman inside."

Nate was already moving, snagging the holster from the dresser and buckling it over his t-shirt in one fluid motion, then picking up his badge and clipping it to his belt before turning to the corkboard on the wall.

A photo of Sarah Holloway hung in the center, her eyes watching him.

Nate looked at the photo, his expression unchanged, but the muscles in his jaw tightened, and a small pulse jumped in his neck.

"We go," Nate said. "Now."

"We need a warrant," Rodecker said—it was a reflex, thirty years of police work speaking.

"No time," Nate said, checking the magazine of his Glock and slamming it back into the grip. "If we wait for a judge, we're recovering a body—witness places a victim in the structure, imminent danger to life, that's enough to kick the door."

He looked at Rodecker, then at Pierce. "I'm going in—you coming?"

Rodecker looked at Pierce and saw the guilt carved into the lines around her mouth, pulling down her eyes, and saw the desperation.

He nodded.

"I'm driving," Rodecker said. "My truck has the ram bar."

Pierce pulled her weapon and checked the chamber—a brass round glinted under the slide.

"Let's go," she said.

They moved into the hallway with sharp, controlled urgency—no wasted motion, a current of electricity running through the group.

Pierce led the way to the stairs, not feeling the fatigue anymore, not feeling the heat or the hunger or the ache in her back.

She felt only the weight of the phone in her pocket, the weight of the message she hadn't answered.

Two hours.

Every minute they wasted in the car would be another minute added to that tally.

She hit the stairwell door and held it open for Nate and Rodecker.

They piled into Rodecker's unmarked truck, the heavy doors slamming shut.

Rodecker fired the engine but didn't use the siren, didn't use the lights—this wasn't a patrol, this was a hunt.

Nate sat in the passenger seat, staring out the windshield, his hand resting on the grip of his gun.

Pierce sat in the back and leaned forward between the seats.

"Booker said he locked her in," Pierce said. "He used a key."

"We'll open it," Nate said.

Rodecker turned onto Martin Luther King Jr. Boulevard, heading south toward the ramp that would drop them into the industrial fringe where the city lights began to thin out, and the historic charm faded into chain link fences and concrete.

Pierce looked out the window at the darkness that felt deeper here, thicker.

She touched the phone in her pocket again, a talisman of failure.

She ain't came out walking.

Booker's voice rang in her head.

Pierce made a silent vow to the glass and the passing streetlights: if the girl was dead, Pierce would burn the whole department down, would testify, would leak the emails, would destroy Dean and Moffett and the Mayor, would strip the varnish off this city and show the rot underneath.

But first, they had to open the door.

The warehouse district loomed ahead, brick skeletons rising against the night sky, silent and waiting.

Rodecker killed the headlights, the truck rolling forward in the dark.

"Which one?" Rodecker said, his voice low.

"The brick one," Pierce said. "Near the cold storage."

She pointed.

A massive structure sat on the corner of West Boundary, looking abandoned—windows boarded, weeds growing through the cracks in the pavement.

But there was a steel door on the side.

And across the street, a rusted dumpster.

Pierce could picture the shadows moving in the faint moonlight, could imagine Booker crouching there, watching, terrified, calling her.

"There," she said.

Rodecker pulled the truck to the curb a block away, the engine ticking as it cooled.

Nate opened his door and moved silently.

Pierce followed, drawing her weapon, the metal cold and heavy in her hand.

They moved toward the building—three shadows approaching a tomb.

The timestamp on Pierce's phone burned in her mind: *10:49 PM.*

It was now almost half past one in the morning.

Three hours.

They were late.

Pierce forced herself to breathe, forced herself to focus on the door, on the tactical approach.

She pushed the guilt down and packed it into a tight, hard ball in her gut—she would use it later, would use it as fuel.

Right now, she just needed to find the blonde girl.

Nate reached the door first, examined the lock, then looked back at them and held up three fingers.

One.

Two.

Three.

CHAPTER

19

Nate dropped his hand—the signal.

Rodecker moved with an efficiency that belied his size, covering the alley's mouth while Pierce took the near flank. Nate gripped the cold steel of the padlock, examining the hasp where bright, raw metal showed through—bolt cutters or a pry bar had recently forced it, the scratches glinting against the dull rust of the frame. Not decay. Access.

The hasp swung free, silent on greased hinges.

Nate pushed the heavy steel door inward, leading with his weapon into a void that swallowed the light.

His tactical light cut a cone into the blackness as Pierce and Rodecker filed in behind him. The door clicked shut, sealing them in with the humid Savannah night and the smell—bleach, industrial cleaner, and beneath it, the heavy, cloying sweetness of old blood. The air was a slaughterhouse scrubbed for inspection.

Nate swept his beam across the concrete floor. Clean.

"Clear," he said.

"Clear," Pierce replied from his left.

They moved down a narrow service corridor where the walls were bare brick, sweating with condensation. Pipes ran along the ceiling, wrapped in crumbling insulation, and the beam swept the floor, revealing no debris, no rat droppings, no trash. The hallway had been swept, and this space was maintained.

The double doors at the end of the corridor showed no light bleeding through the gap, and Nate nodded to Rodecker.

The detective took one handle, Nate the other, and they pulled the doors open onto a cavernous space—three stories of vertical darkness stretching to a ceiling of heavy timber beams.

Nate stepped into the loading bay and raised his light as the beam cut through the stagnant air, illuminating dust motes. On the far wall, rusted roll-up doors stood sealed against the night.

"My God," Pierce said, moving to the right and sweeping the perimeter while Rodecker took the left. Nate walked straight down the center.

An old freight elevator cage stood in the far corner, its wire mesh rusted black, and near the roll-up doors, a workbench sat empty and wiped clean. But the center of the room drew his attention—the concrete floor sloped toward a wide cast-iron drain set into the slab.

Nate knelt and ran his gloved hand along the concrete, finding grooves that had been cut into the slab, shallow but precise, forming a geometric grid that radiated outward from the drain. Channels.

"Nate," Rodecker said, his voice tight. "Up high."

Nate tilted his beam upward to where heavy iron hooks hung from the ceiling beams with chains dangling from them, ending in cuffs and spreaders. Eyebolts studded the brick walls at waist height in a layout that was specific, designed for suspension and restraint.

Pierce stood near the wall, her flashlight beam unsteady. "Hello, is anyone in here?" she called.

The name bounced off the hard surfaces and died in the upper rafters with no answer, no shuffle of movement, no breathing. The room was empty of life.

"She's not here," Nate said, the certainty settling like a lead weight in his gut.

"Booker said he brought her inside," Pierce said, spinning in a circle while her light jagged across the walls. "He said she didn't come out."

Nate looked at the drain, the truth crystallizing. "She didn't—not walking."

He pulled a small spray bottle of luminol from his tactical pouch, needing confirmation of the kill's geometry, not a forensic team.

"Lights off," Nate ordered.

Rodecker and Pierce killed their beams, and the warehouse plunged into blackness.

Nate sprayed the chemical across the concrete channels feeding the drain, then waited a beat before the blue chemiluminescence erupted in the dark.

It wasn't a smear or a few spots but the entire grid lighting up, the channels glowing with a fierce, electric intensity. The bleach had hidden the truth—victims had bled out here, their blood funneled down these channels and into the Savannah soil.

"Jesus," Rodecker breathed in the darkness.

Nate pulled his phone and snapped three photos: the glowing grid against the black, the drain, the hooks visible in the faint chemical light.

"We have enough," Nate said. "Back out. Seal it. Call it in."

He stood and reached for his flashlight when a mechanical clank echoed from the walls.

CHAPTER

20

THE WORLD DISSOLVED INTO A PURE, blinding white. Nate shielded his eyes, the spots dancing in his vision obscuring the room. The slam of the roll-up doors vibrated through the soles of his boots. Metal grinding on concrete.

Industrial floodlights mounted high on the beams washed out the room in harsh, shadowless brilliance, leaving Nate blinking against the spots dancing in his vision. Metal shrieked on metal as the roll-up doors ground downward, slamming into the concrete with a finality that vibrated through the floor.

"The door," Nate said.

Rodecker was already moving, sprinting back toward the double doors they had entered through before hitting the panic bar, but the doors didn't budge.

A heavy, motorized lock engaged on the other side as Rodecker slammed his shoulder into the wood. It held firm, solid.

"Sealed," Rodecker said, his voice tight.

A hissing sound started overhead.

Nate looked up at the sprinkler heads dotting the ceiling pipes, but water didn't rain down—a clear liquid sprayed in a fine mist, drifting down and coating the floor, the walls, their clothes.

The smell changed as the sweet rot vanished, replaced by the sharp, volatile scent of acetone and kerosene.

"Accelerant," Nate said, his voice flat. "Cover up."

The fire alarm erupted, the blaring klaxon beating against his skull, and a spark popped from a junction box near the ceiling fan.

The vapor caught with a concussive whoosh as a wave of heat slammed into Nate, knocking the breath from his lungs.

The fire raced along the floor, following the blood channels where the accelerant had pooled, and a grid of orange fire snapped into existence, separating them.

"Move," Nate said. "Away from the center."

Thick, oily smoke rolled down from the ceiling vents, dropping and cutting visibility to zero above waist height.

Nate dropped to a crouch where the heat was already blistering, and his skin pulled tight while his eyes watered.

"The drain," Pierce said, coughing with her sleeve pressed over her mouth. "Can we pull the grate?"

Nate scrambled toward the center, keeping low as the fire grid burned inches from his boots. He reached the cast-iron cover and grabbed the bars where the metal was already hot, then pulled, but it didn't shift. He pulled harder, straining his back, but rust and welds held it fast.

"Sealed," Nate choked out.

A timber beam overhead groaned as fire licked up the dry wood, fed by the accelerant, and a massive section of the roof support cracked and swung down, trailing sparks before crashing onto the concrete ten feet away. Embers sprayed.

"Can't go back the way we came," Rodecker said from his knees near the wall. "No exits on this side."

Nate scanned the room where the smoke was lowering and the heat rising—they had seconds before the oxygen burned out, or the fumes dropped them. His eyes found the corner where the freight elevator stood, a chimney, but a way out.

"Elevator," Nate said, pointing. "Go. Now."

He grabbed Pierce by the back of her tactical vest and shoved her toward the corner while Rodecker scrambled on hands and knees.

They reached the cage where the heat was intense but bearable, and Nate grabbed the accordion gate and hauled it back as it screeched in the tracks, but opened.

The shaft was a narrow brick throat rising three stories with a square of darkness at the top suggesting a roof hatch. A single, thick steel cable hung down the center, greasy and slack, with no car attached.

"Climb," Nate ordered. "Rodecker first. Break the hatch. Pierce second. Go."

"I can boost you," Rodecker said, his face streaked with soot.

"You're the only one heavy enough to breach that hatch," Nate said. "Move."

Rodecker didn't argue but jumped and grabbed the cable, wrapping his legs around the greasy steel and beginning to haul himself up while his boots scrabbled for tread on the brick walls before finding a rhythm on the cable itself.

Pierce waited until he was ten feet up, then looked at Nate with her eyes wide rims in a blackened face.

"He knew," she said. "He knew we were coming."

"Climb," Nate said.

She jumped, clamped onto the line, and pulled herself up into the shaft.

Nate turned back to the room where the warehouse was an inferno, with the floor a lake of fire and the beams falling one by one. The heat pressed against him, a physical weight trying to crush him into the floor, and he could feel the hair on his arms singing.

He holstered his weapon and wiped his hands on his jeans, trying to dry the sweat—useless.

He jumped.

His hands closed around the cable as pain flared through his palms where the steel strands were frayed, biting into his skin, and the grease was thick and slick, mixed with the soot. He slid down six inches before his grip held, the friction burning through the gloves.

He wrapped his legs around the line and pulled himself up.

The shaft acted as a furnace, sucking oxygen from below and blasting superheated smoke past them, and Nate couldn't breathe, taking only shallow, sipping gasps of the hot, toxic air.

"Keep moving," Nate said, his voice a rasp.

Above him, Pierce struggled as her boots slipped on the grease, but she kicked out, found the brick wall, and pushed herself up another foot.

Nate climbed hand over hand with the cable, digging into his flesh, while his shoulders screamed in protest. The heat from below cooked him, the soles of his boots softening against the rising temperature.

A sharp ping vibrated through the steel cable.

The line jerked.

Nate dropped six inches as Pierce cried out and slid while Rodecker grunted above them.

"It's giving way," Rodecker called from above.

"Don't stop," Nate said.

He clawed his way up where the grease made it a nightmare, and every foot of gain cost him everything he had, while his hands became numb layers of agony. Blood made the cable slicker.

He looked down to where the fire had reached the base of the shaft with flames licking up the brickwork, hunting him.

"Almost there," Rodecker said.

Impact—flesh and bone hitting metal—Rodecker was at the top, slamming his shoulder into the maintenance hatch.

Thud.

The cable vibrated with each impact.

Thud.

Another metallic ping as the cable dropped an inch, and the jerking motion nearly tore Nate's grip loose. He clamped his legs tighter while the rough steel wire shredded his jeans and cut into his thighs.

"Open it," Pierce said, her voice strained.

Crack.

A rusty screech came from above as a draft of cool, clean air rushed into the shaft, and Rodecker had breached the roof.

Nate looked up at a square of stars and Rodecker's silhouette, hauling himself up and over the lip.

"Pierce," Rodecker called down. "Give me your hand."

Pierce scrambled the last few feet and reached up as Rodecker grabbed her wrist and hauled her up with a grunt of exertion. Her legs kicked the air, then found the rim before she rolled out of sight.

Nate was alone in the shaft with the fire roaring below him, close now, and the heat searing his legs while the smoke blinded him.

He reached up, counting down the distance in his mind—five feet from the lip.

He pulled himself higher, his arms shaking. Four feet.

He pulled again, drawing on the last reserves of strength. Three feet.

The cable groaned, not the bolt this time but the strands unraveling, the heat weakening the steel.

Rodecker's face returned to the lip of the hatch.

"Reach," Rodecker said, extending his arm down into the shaft.

Nate let go with one hand and reached upward, his fingers brushing Rodecker's.

Snap.

The main anchor bolt sheared as the cable went slack, and gravity took him, his stomach dropping as the fire rushed up to meet him.

A hand clamped his wrist.

The jolt nearly dislocated his shoulder as Nate slammed into the brick wall of the shaft, but Rodecker held him—the detective was lying flat on the roof with his arm extended down the hole and veins popping in his neck, having caught Nate mid-drop.

"Got you," Rodecker said, his voice a raw grunt.

Another hand grabbed Nate's other wrist—Pierce, anchoring him.

They pulled, and Nate kicked his legs, trying to find a foothold on the smooth brick, scrabbling until he chinned the lip of the hatch.

He rolled onto the tarpaper and collapsed with the rough gravel of the roof digging into his cheek—cold, and it was wonderful.

Nate rolled onto his back and gasped for air while his lungs burned like they were filled with broken glass. He coughed, hacking up black phlegm.

Rodecker was on his knees next to him, his chest heaving, while Pierce lay spread-eagled, staring at the sky.

Nate held up his hands.

In the moonlight, they were ruined—the skin shredded with blisters already forming, bubbling up through the soot and grease, and blood welling in the deep cuts from the frayed wire. They shook uncontrollably.

A deep, structural groan came from below them as the roof under them vibrated.

A massive crump sounded from inside the warehouse as the floor of the room collapsed into the sub-basement, and smoke poured from the open hatch like a volcano while sparks danced into the night sky.

Nate sat up, forcing himself to look at where the warehouse was a blast furnace with the fire erasing everything—the channels, the hooks, the drain, the slate being scrubbed clean.

The blonde wasn't there. She never had been.

Nate stared at the flames licking the edges of the hatch.

Carlisle hadn't just set a trap but had sent a message.

You can't catch me. You can't hold me. I burn what I touch.

Sirens wailed in the distance, getting louder, and the flashing lights would reflect off the smoke soon.

Nate tried to make a fist, but his hands refused to close, the pain a white-hot line connecting him to the fire below.

He looked out across the rooftops of the industrial district where the shadows were deep, and the city was asleep.

Somewhere out there, in the cool safety of the distance, Carlisle was watching—the thought was a certainty.

CHAPTER

21

BLACK WATER DRIPPED from the toe of Nate's boot, marking the pristine linoleum with the filth of the warehouse. He watched the puddle widen, measuring time by the impact of each drop against the floor while a monitor in the next bay beeped a steady, mechanical rhythm.

Memorial University Medical Center hummed with a different frequency than the warehouse fire, which had been a roar of timber and accelerant. This was a low, electric buzz of fluorescent lights and ventilation systems scrubbing the air of everything except antiseptic and latex. Nate sat on the edge of the gurney, his feet dangling inches above the floor, watching the black puddle grow between his boots—a mixture of soot, grease, and the water from the fire hoses that had arrived too late.

A Nurse Practitioner stood between his knees, holding a pair of steel tweezers.

"Hold still," she said without looking at his face, her focus remaining on the ruin of his palms. She clamped the tweezers onto a curled shaving of steel wire embedded in the meat of his thumb and pulled.

Nate didn't flinch when the tweezers bit into his flesh; his nerves were a circuit board flooded with current, the specific points of contact lost in a general, throbbing numbness that made pain feel distant and abstract. The wire came free, coated in blood and heavy grease, and she dropped it onto a metal tray where it made a small *clink*, joining six other pieces already there.

"You're lucky," she said, grabbing a bottle of saline from the supply cart. "These cuts are deep, but they missed the tendons by a fraction of an inch. The friction burns are the real problem—second degree, bordering on third in the creases where the rope bit deepest."

She flushed the wounds with cool saline that hit the raw tissue like electricity. Nate's jaw tightened until his teeth ached, but he made no sound, just watched his hands as if they belonged to someone else now, two damaged tools at the ends of his wrists.

Through the gap in the privacy curtain, Rodecker sat shirtless on the adjacent gurney, his chest streaked with carbon and dried sweat. The skin over his ribs had been scraped raw where he'd slammed into the hatch during their escape, and a resident in blue scrubs was manipulating Rodecker's left arm, checking the shoulder that had popped out during the catch at the top of the shaft.

Rodecker grunted, his good hand gripping the edge of the mattress until his knuckles turned white. The resident rotated the arm in a slow, deliberate arc, and a dull pop sounded in the small space. Rodecker let out a long breath through his nose and slumped forward, sweat beading on his forehead.

"Socket is back in," the resident said, securing the arm against Rodecker's chest with practiced efficiency. "Ligaments are going to be angry for weeks, maybe months if you don't rest it. You need to keep this immobilized, no exceptions."

Pierce paced the narrow strip of floor between the gurneys and the nursing station, the only one still fully dressed. She had wiped the worst of the soot from her face with rough paper towels, leaving her skin red and scrubbed raw, and her hands flexed and unflexed at her sides as if searching for a weapon to draw or a throat to choke.

She stopped at the foot of Nate's gurney, her eyes moving from his bandaged hands to his face.

"The warehouse," she said, her voice low enough to carry under the ambient noise of the ER but not beyond the curtain. "Dispatch says the roof collapsed ten minutes after we got clear, and the floors pancaked into the sub-basement like a house of cards."

Nate watched the NP apply a thick, white layer of silver sulfadiazine cream to his palms, spreading it over the burned tissue with a tongue depressor. It looked like frosting spread over burned meat, and when it touched the raw nerve endings, it felt like ice pressed into an open wound.

"Everything," Pierce said.

"Everything," Nate repeated, his voice a wreck from the smoke that had scoured his throat raw during their crawl through the tunnels.

The NP began to wrap his hands in rolls of gauze, winding them tight around his palms and between his fingers. She separated each digit, wrapping them individually before binding them together into white clubs, and the dexterity he relied on disappeared layer by layer until he couldn't move his fingers at all.

"The blonde?" Nate said.

Pierce shook her head in a micro-movement that barely qualified as a gesture. "Fire crews can't even get inside yet—it's burning at twelve hundred degrees with accelerants feeding the flames. Old timber. Chemical storage. There won't be anything left to recover, not even bones."

Nate looked at the white clubs at the ends of his wrists, thinking about the blonde trapped in that room. The blood channels, the hooks, the biological trace of a century of murder—all of it was just carbon and heat now. Carlisle had destroyed the evidence with a match and walked away clean.

The NP tied off the bandage on his left hand and stepped back, crossing her arms over her chest.

"Listen to me," she said, her tone shifting from clinical to stern. "These need to stay dry and clean for at least a week, maybe longer, depending on how they heal. Infection is your biggest risk right now, and if bacteria get into those burns, you're looking at sepsis. And you cannot use them—no gripping, no lifting, no driving, nothing that requires finger movement. If you tear that new tissue before it sets, you're looking at skin grafts and permanent nerve damage. Seventy-two hours minimum of absolute rest, and I mean absolute."

Nate looked at her and nodded, which was a lie. He tested the flexibility of the bandages, feeling the gauze pull tight against the raw skin underneath, then lowered his hands to his lap, careful not to touch the denim of his jeans.

Rodecker's phone buzzed.

It sat on the metal tray table next to his gurney, vibrating against the stainless steel as the screen lit up with Chief Dean's name. The vibration sounded loud in the small bay, a rattling that cut through the hum of the hospital, and Rodecker stared at the screen without picking it up, then looked across the gap at Nate.

The resident was busy fitting a blue sling over Rodecker's head, oblivious to the decision being weighed in the silence between the two detectives.

They could tell the truth—report a kill room, evidence of a serial predator operating in Savannah for decades. They could say they were trapped in a burning building by a suspect who knew they were coming, who tried to kill them. And Dean would ask for the warrant, demand to see the probable cause, and request the physical evidence that was currently rising as smoke over the industrial district. He would fire them both and bury the investigation to save his pension and the Mayor's poll numbers.

Nate leaned forward, the movement pulling at the friction burns on his chest where the rope had caught him during the climb. His eyes hardened, and he looked at Rodecker and mouthed a single word.

Accident.

Rodecker let out a breath, reached out with his good hand, and picked up the phone. He cleared his throat, wincing at the pain in his chest, and answered.

"Chief," Rodecker said.

Nate watched him, and Pierce stopped pacing, standing near the curtain with her back to the hallway, blocking the view.

"Yes, sir," Rodecker said, his voice steady despite the pain. "We're at Memorial receiving treatment for smoke inhalation and some minor burns. We're clear—nothing life-threatening."

He listened, rubbing his forehead with his knuckles while his eyes stayed closed against whatever Dean was saying on the other end.

"We had a tip," Rodecker lied, his voice flat and professional, stripped of emotion. "Subject matching the description of a person of interest—we saw him enter the structure on Bay Street, and the door was open, so we pursued under exigent circumstances."

He paused, and Nate could hear the faint sound of Dean's voice rising in pitch through the phone's speaker. Rodecker's expression didn't change.

"We were conducting a sweep of the premises when the suspect fled deeper into the building," Rodecker said. "We didn't catch a face —it was too dark, and he knew the layout better than we did. Then the fire started in the northeast corner, and it went up fast, Chief. Old timber, exposed wiring, maybe some chemical solvents got knocked over in the chaos. The whole structure was a tinderbox waiting for a spark."

Pierce looked at the floor, her jaw muscles working as she ground her teeth together.

"No, sir," Rodecker said. "We barely got out before the roof came down. The structural integrity failed within minutes—floors collapsed into the basement. It's a total loss."

He looked at Nate, and there was something cold in his eyes.

"No shots fired," Rodecker said. "Just the fire."

It was the only play they had, and they both knew it. Claiming a suspect deliberately set the fire would trigger a federal investigation, bring in arson specialists and ATF agents who would pick through every piece of debris looking for accelerant patterns. It would draw attention they couldn't afford, raise questions they couldn't answer without evidence. An accident was tragic but explainable—an accident was tidy, and an accident meant the city could move on without digging deeper.

"Understood," Rodecker said. "We'll get patched up and file our reports first thing in the morning when we're clearer."

He hung up, dropping the phone back on the tray with a clatter that echoed in the small space.

"He bought it," Rodecker said, leaning back against the raised gurney. "Because he wanted to buy it, because it's easier than the alternative. He's already drafting the press release—dangerous structure, tragic loss of property, heroic officers injured in the line of duty while pursuing a lead."

Pierce turned to the wall-mounted television in the corner of the bay and grabbed the remote from the bedside table. She unmuted it, and the sound of a news anchor's voice filled the space.

"Channel 11," she said.

A red banner scrolled across the bottom of the screen: *INDUS-TRIAL ACCIDENT IN WEST SAVANNAH.*

Aerial footage from a news chopper showed the warehouse from a distance, the roof caved in to create a crater where flames still licked at the night sky. On the ground, a reporter stood near the perimeter tape with a Fire Marshal in full turnout gear, both of them lit by the orange glow of the fire behind them.

"Preliminary reports suggest accidental ignition," the Fire Marshal said, looking bored, like a man who wanted to finish his statement and go home. "This building has been cited for code violations multiple times in the past—exposed wiring, improper storage of industrial chemicals, structural deficiencies. It was a matter of time before something like this happened."

Nate watched the screen, seeing the warehouse burn in high definition. The fire erased everything—the blood, the chains, the DNA of a century of victims, all of it reduced to ash and smoke. Carlisle had known exactly which lever to pull, which match to strike. He didn't just destroy the evidence; he handed the city an excuse to look away and call it progress.

"He wins," Pierce said, staring at the fire on the screen. "He kills the girl, burns the evidence, and the city calls it an accident while we stand here with burns and bruises."

"He doesn't win," Nate said.

He slid off the gurney, and his boots hit the floor with a solid thump. His legs felt heavy, drained of strength, and he swayed for a second before catching his balance and standing next to Rodecker's gurney.

"We're alive," Nate said. "He missed his chance."

"He didn't miss," Rodecker said, adjusting the strap of his sling with his good hand. "He let us go because dead cops bring more federal heat. He wanted us to see it burn, to know that everything we found is gone."

Nate raised his bandaged hands and gestured at the television, where the Fire Marshal was still giving his statement.

"He thinks this is the end," Nate said. "He thinks because the paper trail is gone, we stop. He thinks because we can't get a warrant based on evidence that no longer exists, we stop. He thinks we're like Dean—that we care more about our careers than the truth."

The Nurse Practitioner returned with a clipboard and frowned when she saw Nate standing.

"I didn't discharge you," she said, stepping into his path. "You need to stay for observation—your oxygen levels were low when you came in, and smoke inhalation can cause delayed respiratory complications."

"We're leaving," Nate said, already turning toward the curtain.

"Sir, you have second-degree burns on your hands and significant smoke inhalation," she said, her voice rising with frustration. "Leaving now is Against Medical Advice, which means your insurance won't cover it if you have complications later."

Nate started for the exit without responding.

"Where do I sign?" he asked.

The NP sighed, realizing the argument was lost before it started. She held out the clipboard and a pen, but when Nate reached for it, his bandaged fingers were too thick and useless to form a grip. The pen slipped through his clumsy grasp and clattered to the floor.

He looked at his hands, wrapped in white gauze that might as well have been concrete.

Pierce picked up the pen.

"I'll sign for him," she said. "Witnessed."

She scrawled a signature on the AMA form and then signed another one for Rodecker, who was already standing and testing his balance. The resident handed Rodecker a prescription slip for painkillers, which he shoved into his pocket without looking at it.

"My jacket," Nate said.

Pierce grabbed his jacket from the pile of ruined clothes on the chair, the fabric stiff with dried sweat and soot. It smelled of smoke and chemical accelerant, and she draped it over his shoulders like a cape because he couldn't put his arms through the sleeves—the bulky bandages wouldn't fit, and the movement would tear the new skin forming underneath.

He caught his reflection in the dark glass of the sliding ER doors and saw a specter with a soot-streaked face, hollow eyes, and arms pinned to his sides by white bandages.

He turned away from the television, where the Fire Marshal was still talking about code violations and the inevitability of the collapse.

The city was already forgetting.

"Let's go," Nate said.

They walked toward the automatic doors—Rodecker on his left, favoring his shoulder, and Pierce on his right, her hand resting on her sidearm out of habit. They stepped out of the sterile white light of the hospital and back into the humid Savannah night, where the air smelled of rain on hot asphalt and the faint, underlying scent of burning timber drifting from miles away.

CHAPTER

22

The hallway of the Marshall House stretched out in dim silence, the carpet runners swallowing the sound of Nate's boots as he made his way down the corridor. His arms hung at his sides, the white gauze clubs that were his hands pulsing with a wet, rhythmic heat that matched his heartbeat. He stopped at Room 417.

The keycard was in his right pocket.

He stared at the wood grain of the door, the simple act of retrieval a logistical hell requiring coordination he no longer possessed. Turning his hip, he jammed the bandaged wedge of his right hand into his pocket. Friction burned the fresh skin beneath the gauze. He gritted his teeth, sweat pricking his hairline as he clamped the plastic card between the edges of the bandages, pinned it against his thigh, and managed to drag it out through sheer determination.

Leaning in, he slotted the card into the reader. The light blinked green.

Nate shouldered the door open and stumbled inside, kicking it shut behind him with enough force to rattle the frame. The heavy thud vibrated up through the floorboards.

Security protocol remained, even when the body failed.

He used his elbow to throw the deadbolt, and the metal slid home with a solid clack that echoed in the small room. He turned. The security chain hung silver against the frame. Manipulating the small slide was impossible, but he tried anyway, pincering the knob between the knuckles of his index and middle fingers. Pain shot up his forearm. He gasped, dropping his forehead against the door frame and forcing a breath through clenched teeth. He tried again, and the knob slid into the track.

Locked. Bolted. Chained.

Nate left the lights off, navigating the room by memory and the streetlights filtering through the heavy curtains like fog. He moved to the bed and sat, the mattress springs groaning under his weight. The smell of the warehouse clung to him: chemical, burned timber, melted plastic, and the copper tang of fear that had soaked into his clothes.

He couldn't undress. The buttons of his shirt were insurmountable obstacles. The shoulder holster dug into his ribs, the Glock 19M a comforting pressure against his side, even if he couldn't draw it.

He fell backward onto the mattress, and the ceiling became a dark nothing above him.

His hands throbbed as the ER's pain medication wore off, leaving a sharp, stinging clarity behind that made every pulse of his heart a small agony. He closed his eyes, listening to the hum of the window air conditioner and the settling creaks of a building that had stood since 1851.

Sleep pulled him under.

He was awake.

Not waking, but simply awake, as though someone had flipped a switch in his brain. The quality of the silence in the room had changed. There was a presence in it. The sensation of being watched crawled across his skin.

Nate opened his eyes without moving, keeping his breath slow and shallow as he scanned the darkness.

The desk lamp was on.

He hadn't turned it on.

In its harsh yellow pool of light, a figure sat in the desk chair, turned away from the desk and facing the bed with legs crossed comfortably at the knee. His cream linen suit was immaculate, without a single wrinkle to mar the fabric.

Evan Carlisle.

Carlisle held a manila folder in his lap, turning a page with a long, pale finger that moved with surgical precision. The slide of paper on paper was deafening.

Nate's heart hammered his ribs. He tried to scramble up, his right hand clawing instinctively for the grip of his gun, but the bandage fumbled against the leather holster. He couldn't find the release.

"Please don't," Carlisle said.

The voice was mild, conversational, like they were discussing the weather. He didn't look up from the file.

"We both know that would accomplish little," Carlisle said. "And I would prefer not to ruin the upholstery."

Nate froze, his hand hovering over the weapon like a threat he couldn't execute. The reality of the situation crashed into him. The door was bolted. The chain was engaged. He was armed. And the man he was chasing was sitting in his hotel room, reading a federal case file as though he owned the place.

"How," Nate said, his throat full of gravel. "The door."

"Locks are suggestions," Carlisle said, finally looking up.

In the lamplight, his eyes were wrong. They were dark, too dark, drinking the light instead of reflecting it. Deep in the pupils was a flat, mineral glitter. He didn't blink. He sat with a stillness that was heavy, like a statue carved into the corner of the room.

"I wanted to have a conversation," Carlisle said. "Without the theatre of warrants and lawyers and your colleagues listening through recording devices. This approach struck me as simpler."

He closed the file gently, placing it on the desk and squaring its corners with the edge of the wood in a gesture of fastidious precision.

"You are looking in the wrong places, Agent Holloway," Carlisle said. "All your evidence. Your patterns. Your timelines. Miss Landry has been helpful with those, I am sure, but you are still thinking this started recently. Perhaps a few generations back."

Carlisle stood.

The movement was seamless, without shift of weight or gathering of momentum. One moment he was seated, the next he was standing. He moved without a sound.

Nate pushed himself off the bed to stand, swaying slightly as the room tilted beneath him. He positioned himself between the intruder and the door, an instinct to block the exit that overrode the logic that this man didn't need one.

"What are you?" Nate asked.

Carlisle tilted his head, considering the question with the patience of someone who had all the time in the world. "A man who has walked this city longer than you might imagine. Someone who remembers when these streets were laid out. When that fountain was installed in Forsyth Park. I have watched Savannah grow from something raw and new into what it is today."

He took a step toward the wall, toward the corkboard Nate had constructed in obsessive detail.

"I was here when your sister arrived," Carlisle said.

The sweat on Nate's neck turned to ice, and his bandaged hands curled into useless fists.

"Don't," Nate said.

Carlisle ignored him. He stood before the obsession board, the web of red string crossing photos like a spider's work. Sarah's face was in the center. He reached out and touched the glossy photo of Sarah Holloway, his finger tracing the line of her jaw with terrible intimacy.

"She wore lavender," Carlisle said. "In a sachet around her neck. Her grandmother's recipe, she told me."

Nate stopped breathing. That detail wasn't in the reports. It wasn't in the papers. It was in an evidence box in a storage locker in Chatham County, a piece of information only the family knew.

"We talked for nearly an hour before... well," Carlisle said, his gaze fixed on the picture with something that might have been nostalgia. "She spoke of you. Her brother. The one who was going to be a lawyer, who always protected her. She was immensely proud."

A jagged, wounded noise tore from Nate's throat.

Carlisle turned, and the light caught the sharp angles of his face in a way that made him look like something carved from marble. His expression wasn't mocking. It was hollow, ancient.

"I remember them all," Carlisle said. "Every face. Every name. Every last conversation before the light left their eyes. The immigrant girl who dreamed of opening a bakery. The jazz singer who hummed while I... while she died. Your Sarah, who forgave me at the end."

He walked toward Nate, not hurried, but with a cold certainty that made retreat impossible.

"I have been doing this longer than your files can document, Agent Holloway."

He stopped three feet away, and the smell coming off him was distinct—not of the room or the city. It smelled of old earth, of turned soil, and beneath it, the faint, sweet scent of dried flowers.

"You cannot catch me," Carlisle said. "You cannot stop me. Your warehouse raid failed before it began. Your evidence will burn or disappear. Your witnesses will recant or die. I have outlasted empires, Agent Holloway. I have survived plagues and wars and witch hunts. I have watched civilizations rise and crumble to dust."

Carlisle moved closer, and his eyes were black holes in his face.

"What makes you think a federal agent with a dead sister will be any different?"

Rage broke the paralysis.

Nate lunged.

He didn't think about his hands or his gun or the impossibility of what he was doing. He threw his body forward, catching the lapels of the cream linen suit with his forearms and trapping the fabric between his wrists and chest. He drove his legs, slamming Carlisle backward into the wall near the door with enough force to shake the room. A picture frame rattled.

"You murdered my sister," Nate spat. "You son of a bitch!"

Carlisle didn't stumble or grunt or show any sign of being affected. He hit the wall with the solidity of granite. There was no give in his body; it was like shoving a block of iron.

Carlisle looked down at Nate, his expression one of boredom.

He raised his right hand with deliberate slowness. He didn't strike. He simply placed his palm on Nate's left wrist, right over the bandage.

The cold burned.

It wasn't the cold of ice but of absence, a place where heat had never existed and never would. It punched through the gauze, seared the burns beneath, and sank into the bone.

Nate gasped as his knees buckled, and the strength drained from his arms like water through a sieve.

"Yes," Carlisle said.

He was inches away, and his breath carried no warmth.

"I did," Carlisle said. "And I will kill again before this is finished. And then I will rest, and wake, and feed again when the cycle demands it. You cannot touch me, Agent Holloway. Go home. Mourn your sister. Let this go before I am forced to add Miss Landry to my collection. And those earnest detectives who follow you like loyal hounds. And you."

Nate tried to hold on, but his muscles refused to fire, and the cold paralyzed the nerves. His arms fell away, the linen slipping through his grasp.

Carlisle smoothed his lapels and adjusted his cuff with the care of a man preparing for a society event.

He reached for the doorknob. He turned it. The deadbolt slid back with a mechanical click. The chain rattled as it fell away. He opened the door to the hallway.

Pausing on the threshold, he looked back over his shoulder.

"Professional courtesy," Carlisle said. "I will not visit again. I have survived this particular dance for longer than you would believe, Agent Holloway. The odds are not in your favor."

He stepped out into the hallway. The door clicked shut.

Nate jerked awake.

He was on the edge of the bed, breath tearing from his lungs in ragged gasps that burned his throat. His heart hammered a frantic rhythm against his ribs.

Darkness.

The room was pitch black.

The desk lamp was off.

He scrambled backward across the mattress until his back hit the headboard, pulling his knees up to his chest in a defensive crouch. He scanned the dark, waiting for the cream suit to materialize from the shadows.

Silence. Only the hum of the A/C. The distant wail of a siren, miles away.

He looked at the desk but could see nothing in the blackness.

A dream. The pain in his hands was a throbbing, red noise that convinced him of reality. The smoke inhalation, the meds, the trauma. A nightmare born of guilt and exhaustion.

He sat for a long minute as his pulse began to slow and the adrenaline faded from his system.

He needed water. His mouth tasted of ash.

Nate slid his legs off the bed and stood on shaking, waiting for the dizziness to pass before taking a step. He walked to the desk, his movements stiff, and reached for the bottle of water he had left there.

His hand brushed paper.

Nate froze.

He hadn't left paper in the center of the desk—he was obsessive about organization. Files stacked left, water right, center clear.

He fumbled for the lamp switch, his bandaged fingers clumsy, and clicked it with his thumb.

Light flooded the workspace.

Sarah's file lay in the exact center of the desk, perfectly square with the edge.

Nate stared at it as the room tilted beneath him and nausea rolled through his gut.

He reached out with a bandaged hand, catching the cover with the edge of his thumb and flipping it open with a movement that made pain shoot up his arm.

The autopsy report was on top—the clinical diagram of a human body, the notes in the margins written in precise medical shorthand.

Resting on the paper, dead center, was a sprig of dried lavender.

The purple buds were faded and brittle, the stem brown with age. But the scent hit him, faint and impossible. It smelled like his grandmother's garden in Macon. It smelled like Sarah's dorm room.

Nate backed away, hitting the bed and stumbling.

"No," he whispered.

He walked to the door, the movement heavy, like wading through water that dragged at his legs. He looked at the deadbolt. It was engaged and turned right. Locked.

He looked up.

The security chain hung straight down. Unhooked.

He stared at the metal slide, and the memory came back—the pain of locking it, the struggle to pinch the knob, sliding it into the track. He never left a chain unhooked. Not in D.C. Not here. Not ever.

Nate put his eye to the peephole.

The hallway was empty. Fluorescent lights buzzed over a carpet patterned with beige and brown swirls.

He checked his watch.

Four in the morning.

Turning back to the room, he scanned the floor, and something caught the light near the wall—a glint of metal on the carpet. Right where he had slammed Carlisle into the plaster. Right where the struggle had happened.

Nate knelt, the movement pulling tight across his chest and sending fresh pain through his burned hands.

It was a pin. Small. Silver.

He pinched it between his bandaged palms and lifted it, and the metal was cold, sucking the heat from his skin.

He carried it to the desk lamp and held it under the bulb.

It was antique—old silver, tarnished in the crevices. The design was a strange crest or symbol. Around the rim, tiny characters were engraved into the metal. Too small to read, they didn't look like English letters. They looked like wedges.

Nate set the pin down next to the lavender.

The file. The flower. The silver.

He looked at the empty chair.

It hadn't been a dream. The monster had been here. He had walked through a locked door, sat in that chair, read the file, touched his wrist.

The cold. Nate looked at his left wrist, and the skin beneath the bandage was numb.

He looked at the unhooked chain again.

The message was clear. *I can get to you. I can get to anyone.*

Nate sat in the chair. He stared at the lavender, and he thought about Sarah, forgiving her killer at the end.

A lie. A manipulation designed to break him.

Nate looked at the silver pin and turned it under the light, studying the strange engravings. He didn't know what the symbols meant. But he knew someone who might.

CHAPTER

23

Booker sat on the wrought-iron bench near the Gordon Monument, elbows on knees, a heavy black plastic flashlight wedged between his boots. He'd scavenged the light from a dumpster behind the hardware store on Broughton Street—two pounds of solid metal that smelled of battery acid, but the beam cut through Savannah's night better than any city streetlamp ever could.

Grit scraped against his skin as he rubbed his face, twenty-four hours without sleep grinding behind his eyes. The steel door of the warehouse kept sliding shut in his mind, the blonde walking into the dark with that soft, confused smile while the man in the cream linen suit, *Mr. Evan*, guided her forward with one pale hand.

Booker squeezed his eyes shut, sparks dancing behind the lids. He'd stood across the street, counting the seconds, doing nothing.

His knees popped when he stood, a rifle-crack sound in the empty square that made him flinch. He shoved the flashlight into the pocket of his army surplus jacket—too warm for the weather, but the canvas wrapped around him like armor—and pulled his beanie lower over his ears.

He began the patrol.

The Mercer-Williams House took up the southwest corner, red brick dark behind the iron fence, where tourists came for the book murders, never knowing about the cold that radiated off a man in linen. Booker moved into the carriage lane shadows with his chin down, using the quiet shuffle he'd perfected over the years outside, a gait that didn't disturb the air or draw attention.

The alcove behind the old law office stood empty except for a pile of cardboard flattened against the wall.

He moved to the azaleas near Bull Street and clicked the light on, the beam yellow at the edges as it swept under the branches. Cigarette butts and a crushed soda can glinted in the dirt.

He clicked the light off to save the batteries.

South, then. The city's silence pressed against his ears in a way that didn't sit right—usually, Savannah breathed at night with highway hum and ship horns and palmetto fronds rustling in the wind, but tonight the Spanish moss hung grey and limp like dead rags on a line.

At the intersection, he looked toward the industrial district miles away, the direction pulling at his gut like a fishhook. The warehouse on West Boundary where he'd called Detective Pierce and left the message, two hours passing before she called back, and by then the door had closed, by then Mr. Evan had carried the canvas bag out to his car.

The bag had swung with a liquid weight.

"Coward," Booker said, and the word tasted like acid on his tongue.

He crossed the street, boots scuffing pavement as he made his way toward the Episcopal church where Old Man Henry sometimes slept in the back corner. Henry had a bad cough and couldn't run if trouble came looking.

Booker swept the area with his eyes, finding nothing but shadows and silence.

He looped back toward the Mercer-Williams House, the windows reflecting nothing but darkness. The narrow service alley behind the property beckoned him forward—hexagonal brick path, high walls, creeping fig vines, and a blind spot that made his instincts itch.

He stepped off the curb, and the ground texture changed under his boots where uneven bricks had been pushed up by tree roots.

The wrongness hit him all at once.

Not a sound, but the air pressure shifted, thicker here and colder, the humidity condensing into something with weight. The hair on his arms stood up the way it had in Fallujah, that split second before a mortar round dropped from the sky.

He gripped the flashlight hard enough that the plastic bit into his palm and pointed the lens into the alley, thumb resting on the switch.

The beam cut through the dark when he pressed it, hitting the brick wall first, then the tangled vines and moss in the mortar cracks. He moved the light lower across trash cans and a puddle of stagnant water that hadn't evaporated in the heat.

The light caught something pale on the ground.

Twenty feet ahead, not trash or paper but something with texture that absorbed the light instead of reflecting it back.

Booker took a step forward, heart kicking against his ribs like it wanted out.

Another step, and the pale shape resolved into legs—straight legs with heels on the bricks and toes pointing up.

He stopped, breath hitching in his chest as desperate hope flared for half a second. Maybe she'd escaped, maybe she'd run, maybe she'd collapsed here and was only sleeping.

"Miss?" he said.

No movement. The legs remained perfectly straight.

Booker forced his legs to carry him closer despite every instinct screaming at him to run. The beam trembled in his hand as yellow light traveled up the legs to the hips and torso.

The girl.

She lay on her back in the center of the alley, naked, her skin looking like marble in the harsh beam—white against the dirty bricks in a way that shouldn't be possible for human flesh.

Booker stopped six feet away, unable to make himself go any closer.

The light moved to her head, and stomach acid rose in his throat, hot and bitter.

Her blonde hair wasn't messy or matted with sweat the way it should be—someone had combed it, the strands fanned across the hexagonal bricks in a perfect golden half-circle around her head like a Renaissance painting or a museum display.

Booker lowered the light to her chest where her arms lay crossed, left over right, hands resting on her collarbones with fingers curled inward.

He moved the light around her body in a slow circle and found four white pillar candles standing on the bricks at cardinal points—

one at her head, one at her feet, one to her left, one to her right. The wicks stood white and unlit.

He forced the beam upward to her throat and immediately wished he hadn't.

The wound opened like a black trench where her throat should be, the entire structure of the neck destroyed and torn open side to side with ragged skin peeling back. In the harsh light, the interior looked charred, a cavern of ruined tissue where the windpipe and veins should have been but weren't anymore.

Booker stumbled back, his heel catching on a brick that sent him off balance. He threw a hand out and braced himself against the carriage house wall, rough brick scraping his palm as he tried to stay upright.

He retched, but nothing came up except bile that he spat onto the ground while sucking in air that wouldn't fill his lungs properly.

He wiped his mouth with the back of his hand and made himself look back at her.

He swept the beam across the bricks surrounding her shoulders, then down her sides and near her feet in a methodical search pattern.

Dry bricks everywhere.

A wound that deep empties the body of every drop—pints of blood that should pool in the cracks between bricks, soak into the dirt beneath, spread in a sticky lake that reaches for the walls. The bricks should be swimming in it, but instead, they looked clean, and she looked like something made of wax in a museum.

Unless someone took the blood on purpose.

The canvas bag, the way it swung heavy and liquid from Mr. Evan's hand.

Booker groaned, a sound pulled from somewhere deep in his chest, and squeezed the flashlight until the plastic creaked in his grip. He wanted to run, sprint out of the alley and out of Savannah, and keep running until his legs gave out.

But he couldn't leave her alone like this.

She lay naked on the cold bricks with no one to stand guard.

He reached into his jacket pocket with his left hand, fingers brushing the prepaid phone before he pulled it out and flipped it open. The screen glowed blue in the darkness, harsh and modern against the colonial brick.

Speed dial one.

He held the phone to his ear and looked at Nicole's feet to avoid her throat, waiting through the rings.

Booker stood rigid as a sentry, flashlight beam steady on the body.

"Pierce," the voice said, thick with sleep.

Booker wet his lips, tongue dry as sandpaper. "I found her."

Pause, then the rustle of sheets. "Booker? Found who?"

"The girl from the warehouse."

"Where are you?" Pierce's voice sharpened to cop clarity in half a second.

"Mercer-Williams," Booker said, looking up at the narrow strip of night sky visible between the buildings. No stars, only the orange glow of city lights reflecting off clouds. "The alley in the back, the service alley on the east side."

"Is she..."

Booker looked at the fan of hair spread across the bricks, the candles standing at attention, the ruin of her throat. "She's gone. She's all gone."

"Don't touch anything. I'm coming now—stay there, do you hear me? Stay exactly where you are."

"I ain't leaving."

"Five minutes, maybe less—Booker, stay with her."

"I'm here."

The line clicked dead in his ear.

Booker lowered the phone but didn't close it, letting his hand drop to his side. He kept the flashlight beam steady on the body while a cold detachment settled over him like a familiar coat—the soldier's switch that turned off the feeling and turned on the function, the part of him that could stand guard over the dead without flinching.

He turned his back to the body and walked to the mouth of the alley, positioning himself to face the square.

He scanned the shadows pooling under the oaks, checked the windows across the street for movement, surveyed the parked cars along the curb for anyone sitting inside.

Listened to the city breathing around him.

A street sweeper hummed on Bull Street with its rhythmic swish-hum, swish-hum, and a siren wailed miles away in the distance.

Booker waited with the flashlight gripped like a baton, hands steady, eyes on the dark.

The girl had sat on that bench sketching in her notebook, and she'd looked up when Mr. Evan approached, smiled at him with trust on her face before following him to the warehouse.

Booker looked at his own hands in the streetlight, dirt under the fingernails appearing black as old blood.

"I'm sorry," he said to the empty street, to no one and everyone.

An engine approached from the north, and a dark sedan turned the corner with headlights sweeping across the brick facades. Moving fast but controlled.

Booker raised his flashlight and signaled once with a quick flash.

The car slowed and pulled to the curb, tires crunching on loose gravel.

Detective Pierce got out dressed in jeans, a windbreaker, and a t-shirt with her badge on a chain around her neck. She looked small standing next to the sedan, almost fragile.

She walked toward him with purpose, looked at his face first, then past him into the alley's dark mouth.

"In the back," Booker said, stepping aside to give her room.

Pierce turned on her own flashlight and drew her weapon in one smooth motion, holding it low against her thigh as she walked past him into the alley. Booker followed in her footprints, his beam joining hers.

She stopped at the same spot where he'd stopped earlier, and her beam swept across the body in a professional assessment.

Pierce took a sharp breath that sounded like she'd been punched.

"Jesus," she said, the word barely above a whisper.

She holstered the weapon because there was no one to shoot, then stepped closer with her eyes scanning the ground around the body. Her flashlight lingered on the hair, the candles, the wound.

She crouched down, hovering over the bricks without touching anything.

"No blood," she said, and it sounded like an accusation against the universe.

"No blood," Booker confirmed. "Same as the other one. Same as Lucy."

Pierce looked up at him, face tight with stress and deep lines carved around her mouth. "You found her exactly like this?"

"Exactly like this."

"You didn't move anything at all?"

"No, ma'am."

"Not the candles, not her hands?"

"I didn't touch anything."

Pierce stood and looked at the body again, then at Booker. "You called me."

"I called you."

"I got your message late," she said, and her voice broke on the last word. "About the warehouse—I was in a meeting that ran long."

Booker met her eyes and recognized the guilt staring back at him because it matched his own. "We were both late."

Pierce nodded, then pulled her radio and brought it to her mouth, voice shifting back to hard professional clarity. "Dispatch, this is Detective Pierce. I have a 10-54 in the alley behind 429 Bull Street. Requesting crime scene unit and coroner immediately. Notify Chief Dean." She paused, thumb still on the button. "And get Agent Holloway on the line—tell him it's the pattern."

She released the button, and the radio crackled confirmation in electronic squawks.

Booker switched off his flashlight to save what remained of the dying batteries. He stood in the gloom, a dark silhouette against the darker alley, and kept watch over the detective guarding the dead girl. The night pressed down on them both with suffocating humidity.

He looked at the wall where creeping fig vine climbed the surface, each leaf clinging tight to the mortar as if afraid of falling.

"Mr. Evan," Booker said.

Pierce looked at him. "What?"

"He did this—took her time, took her blood, laid her out like a doll in a display case."

"We'll get him," Pierce said, but she sounded scared rather than confident.

Booker looked up at the Mercer-Williams House looming above them, the windows empty and black. How many other girls had lain on these same bricks over the years? How many times had someone scrubbed the stones clean?

"Handcuffs don't work on ghosts, Detective," Booker said.

He walked back toward the street because he needed air, needed to get away from the smell of damp earth and death.

"Don't leave," Pierce called after him.

"I ain't leaving," Booker said over his shoulder. "Just standing guard."

He reached the street and leaned against the carriage house wall, then slid down to the curb with his head in his hands.

The street sweeper turned the corner with yellow strobe lights flashing in the humid air—swish-hum, swish-hum—coming to clean the city the way it did every night.

Booker closed his eyes, and the warehouse door slid down again in his mind, the lock clicking into place while he stood across the street doing nothing.

He waited for the sirens that rose in the distance like a chorus converging on the square, loud and urgent and completely useless.

They were too late, all of them.

CHAPTER

24

Nate Holloway shut the door of his rental Ford with his elbow, his hands wrapped in thick gauze from the warehouse fire and throbbing with a dull, rhythmic pressure that spiked into sharp heat whenever he moved his fingers. He ignored it and locked his eyes on the scene ahead.

Red and blue lights washed over the red brick facade of the Mercer-Williams House, the colors pulsing against the creeping fig vines and the iron fences. The sirens had cut out long ago, leaving only the low idle of police cruisers and the static crackle of radios in the night air.

He walked toward the yellow tape stretched across the mouth of the alley.

The smell of wet earth mixed with exhaust from the idling Fords. Underneath that lay the faint, sweet rot of the city itself. A uniformed officer stepped forward to intercept him, saw the federal credentials clipped to his belt, and stepped back without a word.

Nate ducked under the plastic strip.

The alley behind the carriage house was narrow, with hexagonal pavers uneven from centuries of tree roots pushing from below. High brick walls rose on either side, slick with green moss that looked black in the shadows, and the space narrowed the sky into a dark strip above them.

Nate stopped, his breath hitching in his chest.

The texture of the brick walls, the width of the path, the way the shadows pooled in the corners—it was identical to the alley off Monterey Square where he had stood fifteen years ago, where his father had stood, where Sarah had lain.

He forced his feet to move.

Detective Pierce stepped out from the shadows near the privacy screens, looking smaller than usual with her shoulders hunched inside a dark windbreaker. In the flashing light, her face was grey and drawn tight around the eyes.

She blocked his path.

"Booker found her," Pierce said, rubbing her face with one hand. "He called me, but I was late getting the message."

"We were all late."

"You don't need to see this, Holloway. We can process it while you wait in the car."

"Move, Yolanda."

She held his gaze for a second, looking for a sign of instability, then stepped aside and fell in step beside him, keeping close to the wall to avoid the center of the path.

They approached the privacy screens where portable halogen work lights lit the area beyond, casting harsh, clinical shadows against the ancient masonry. The hum of the generator competed with the distant *swish-hum* of a street sweeper on Bull Street.

Darnell Washington knelt on a foam pad in the center of the light, wearing a white Tyvek suit that rustled as he moved. His medical bag sat open beside him, but he wasn't moving—he was just staring down at what lay between the hexagonal bricks.

Nate stepped into the light.

She lay on her back, naked, her skin pale under the halogens and looking like marble against the dark, dirty paving stones. Her blonde hair had been combed out and fanned around her head in a golden arc that caught the light.

Nate gripped his own wrist, digging his fingers into the bandage to use the pain as an anchor. It was Sarah all over again, the geometry of the body a taunt from 2010.

"Darnell."

The Medical Examiner didn't look up but pointed a gloved finger at the throat.

"Transected," Darnell said, his voice soft and shaking. "Just like the others—carotid, jugular, trachea completely destroyed. Look at the bricks, Agent Holloway."

Nate forced himself to lean in and shone his own flashlight on the wound. It was a gaping ruin, a black trench carved through the neck structure where the tissue wasn't cut but torn, with scalloped edges marking the skin where teeth had anchored. But inside the wound, the tissue was pale and drained.

"Ninety-plus percent volume loss," Darnell whispered. "Again, without a drop on the ground."

Nate straightened, the smell of the alley—damp, metallic, old— filling his nose as he watched Darnell reach for an evidence bag.

"We need to bag the hands. Protocol."

The ME reached out and took Nicole's right hand, which rested stiffly against her upper chest, and tried to pry the fingers away from the skin. Rigor mortis had begun to set in, offering resistance, but Darnell applied gentle pressure until the fingers uncurled.

Darnell froze, stopped breathing, his hand hovering in the air and trembling.

"What is it?" Pierce stepped closer.

Darnell didn't answer but stared at the dead girl's open palm before looking up at Nate, his eyes wide behind his glasses.

Nate stepped forward and shone his light into the girl's hand.

In the center of her palm, protected by the curled fingers, lay a tiny, dried sprig of purple flowers.

All he could see was the purple against the pale skin.

Lavender.

The scent hit him then, a ghost smell cutting through the rot of the alley.

He staggered back, his boot catching on an uneven paver, and slammed his shoulder into the brick wall. The pain flared hot and bright, but it felt distant.

"No." The word came out as a whisper.

Carlisle.

The image flashed in his mind—the hotel room at three in the morning, the unhooked chain, the file moved to the center of the desk, the lavender sprig he had found inside the autopsy report.

It was a message.

I know who you are. I know who she was. I am the same thing that killed her. And you cannot stop me.

The purple buds seemed to pulse before his eyes. Carlisle had reached into 2010 and dragged it into the present, and Nate couldn't breathe.

He slid down the wall a few inches, his knees buckling.

"Holloway!"

Pierce was there, her hands gripping his arms and holding him up as she shook him hard.

"Breathe. Agent Holloway, look at me."

Nate looked at her, watching her face swim into focus with terror written across it.

"He was in my room," Nate said, the words tearing his throat.

"Who?"

"Carlisle."

Pierce looked at the body, then back at Nate, her expression hardening as she understood. She grabbed his elbow and steered him away from the body, away from Darnell, toward the mouth of the alley where the air moved more freely.

"Okay. We handle this and nail him."

She leaned him against the hood of her unmarked sedan, the metal cool and damp, and pulled her phone from her pocket with her fingers flying across the screen.

"We get the link. We get the proof we need."

She hit dial and stabbed the speaker button, holding the phone up between them as the line rang once, then twice.

"Hello?"

The voice was tinny and wrecked—Savvy Johnson, the blonde girl's roommate.

"Savvy, this is Detective Pierce," Yolanda said, her voice shifting to become soft. "I have Agent Holloway with me, and we found her, Nicole."

A sob broke over the line, raw and ugly, echoing in the quiet street.

"Is she..."

"She's gone. I'm so sorry."

Nate pushed off the car and forced himself to stand straight, needing the anger to burn out the shock as he leaned toward the phone.

"Savvy, I need you to listen. I know this is hard, but we need to find the man who did this right now."

"He took her."

"Who? Tell me about the man."

"The gallery owner. She met him at the exhibition last week and couldn't stop talking about him."

Nate locked eyes with Pierce.

"Did she say his name?"

"No, she just called him the gallery guy. She said he was older, refined, like he was from a movie or something."

"What did they talk about?"

"Old pictures," Savvy said, blowing her nose, making the sound harsh over the speaker. "He knew everything about them—daguerreotypes, the chemicals. He talked about the people in the photos like he knew them, like they were friends."

The word hung in the air. *Daguerreotypes.*

Nate thought of the warehouse ownership records, the shell companies, the property on Jones Street held by the same family for a century.

"Where was she going, Savvy? Where did she go when she left you?"

"Coffee," Savvy whispered. "She said he invited her for coffee to see his studio, that he wanted to show her his collection."

"Did she say where the studio was?"

"No, just downtown near the squares."

Nate nodded to Pierce, who ended the call.

"Gallery. Studio. Daguerreotypes."

"Carlisle," Pierce said. "He's an antique dealer who specializes in 19th-century photography—it's in the file."

The gallery owner, the warehouse owner, the man who sat in Nate's hotel room and read Sarah's file.

"He's mocking us. He used the lavender to tell me he knows I'm watching, and he used the girl to show me he doesn't care."

Movement at the police tape caught his eye.

A woman was arguing with the uniformed officer, disheveled with her dark hair pulling loose from its bun as she clutched a leather satchel to her chest.

Alicia Landry.

Nate pushed away from the car and walked toward the perimeter, the pain in his hands feeling distant now and replaced by a cold, hard clarity.

Alicia spotted him, stopped arguing, and waved a hand with her face pale in the flashing lights.

"Holloway!"

Nate reached the tape and nodded to the officer, who lifted the plastic strip to let her through. Alicia ducked under, looking frantic, her eyes darting past him toward the alley and the privacy screens that blocked the view of the body.

"I heard the scanner—the location, Mercer-Williams, the alley."

"Go home, Alicia. You don't want to see this."

"I have to know." She stepped around him and moved toward the gap in the screens.

"Alicia, don't."

She didn't listen but walked to the edge of the privacy barrier and looked through the gap.

She stood there for a long moment, the blue light from the cruisers washing over her face and turning her skin the color of milk. She didn't scream or cry but stood frozen, staring.

Then she turned back to Nate with terror written across her expression.

She walked back to him, gripping the yellow tape in her hand and twisting the plastic until her knuckles turned white before leaning in close.

"The hair fanned out, the candles at North, South, East, West."

Nate nodded.

"Arms crossed, left over right."

"Yes."

"No blood."

"None."

Alicia looked him in the eye.

"He's recreating 2010. He's not just feeding, Nate—he's performing. He researched your sister, saw the photos in your file, and made this one look exactly like her."

"I know. He left the lavender."

Alicia's hand flew to her mouth. "Oh, god."

"He was in my room last night."

Alicia looked back at the alley where the darkness seemed to press against the brick walls, heavy and listening.

"It's a challenge. He's telling you that he remembers Sarah."

Nate looked at the alley one last time and memorized the scene—the clean bricks, the candles, the lavender in the dead girl's hand.

He wasn't an agent anymore or an investigator—he was the brother of Sarah Holloway, and he had an answer for the monster.

"He wants to play history," Nate said to the empty air. "I'm going to end his story."

CHAPTER

25

Nate Holloway leaned against the back wall, his shirt sticking to his skin, arms crossed low over his chest to hide the pressure of his shoulder holster against his ribs. The gauze on his hands felt tight, the burns beneath itching with the first promise of healing, and a dull ache throbbed in his lungs—a souvenir from the warehouse fire that wouldn't let him forget.

Beside him, Detective Karl Rodecker scanned the crowd with the methodical sweep of a man who had worked too many funerals. The detective looked worn down to the frame, the lines around his mouth carved deep, and his collar already soaked through.

At the pulpit, Reverend James Oden stood under the tube lights. The harsh glare bleached the color from the room, turning Sunday dresses and pressed suits a uniform, clinical grey that reminded Nate of autopsy lighting. Oden gripped the sides of the lectern with both hands, knuckles pale against the dark wood. He didn't use a microphone and didn't need it—his voice hit the back wall hard enough to vibrate the window frames.

"They tell us to be patient," Oden said. "They tell us the investigation is ongoing. They tell us to trust the process."

A low chorus of agreement moved through the folding chairs like a wave building strength.

"But while we trust the process, our daughters are disappearing." Oden leaned forward, the wood of the pulpit creaking under his weight, and Nate saw the tension in the man's shoulders—rage held in check by decades of practice. "While we wait for answers, bodies appear in our squares like discarded refuse."

Nate shifted his weight, feeling the anger in the room as a low hum he could sense in the floorboards.

"I have seen the police reports," Oden said, his voice rising with each word. "I have spoken to the families. And I tell you this: these are not random acts of violence. These are not accidents."

Oden paused, his gaze sweeping the room in a slow arc until it settled on the back wall where Nate and Rodecker stood.

"They tell us it was an animal attack," Oden said, his voice dropping to a gravelly whisper that somehow carried better than a shout. "But I ask you: what animal arranges a body with dignity? What animal lights candles? What animal crosses the arms of the dead?"

"Preach!" a woman in the front row shouted, rising halfway from her seat.

"We are being hunted," Oden declared, and the word *hunted* echoed off the walls. "And the shepherds paid to protect the flock are blind to the wolf. They look for a drifter with a knife, a stranger they can arrest and forget. But the dead talk to those who listen. And the dead are saying this is an old evil—an evil this city knows well."

He stepped back from the lectern, wiping his face with a white handkerchief that came away damp.

"We demand the truth," Oden said, his voice steadying into something harder. "Not the sanitized version for the tourists. Not the version that protects property values. We demand the blood truth."

Applause erupted, a scatter of claps that grew into a roar that shook the fellowship hall. People rose to their feet, the scrape of chair legs on linoleum deafening in the enclosed space, and flashbulbs popped near the front as local news crews scrambled for a shot of the Reverend.

"We need to grab him," Nate said, his voice barely carrying over the noise. "Before the cameras eat him alive."

Rodecker jerked his chin toward the side exit.

They moved through the crowd, Nate putting his shoulder forward and letting his size and the federal cut of his suit do the work. People glared but moved aside, creating a narrow channel through the press of bodies.

Oden was shaking hands near the front, heading for an exit into the churchyard with the patient grace of a man who had done this a thousand times. A reporter from WTOC thrust a microphone at his face, and Oden said something polite but firm and kept moving without breaking stride. Nate cut him off just as he reached the heavy wooden door, blocking the exit.

"Reverend," Nate said.

Oden stopped and looked at Nate with weary recognition that went deeper than tonight's speech. Up close, the man was exhausted in a way that went beyond sleeplessness—the whites of his eyes were yellowed, the skin beneath them sagging.

"Agent Holloway," Oden said. "I saw you standing in the back."

"We need to talk," Nate said. "Now. Not later."

"I have nothing to say to the FBI that I haven't just said to my congregation."

"You're referencing details you shouldn't have," Nate said, keeping his voice low under the noise of the dispersing crowd. "The candles. The positioning of the bodies. That information was held back to protect the investigation."

"Integrity," Oden repeated, and the word sounded like acid on his tongue.

"Who gave you those details, James?" Rodecker asked, moving to Oden's other side and using his bulk to shield the Reverend from the reporters who were circling closer. "You need to tell us."

Oden looked from the detective back to Nate, something shifting behind his eyes—calculation or resignation, Nate couldn't tell which. He pushed the crash bar on the door.

"Outside," Oden said.

They stepped out into the night, and the heat was worse than the hall—a suffocating blanket that smelled of wet asphalt and marsh rot. The noise from inside cut off as the door swung shut, replaced by a distant siren on Martin Luther King Jr. Boulevard.

Oden walked toward the massive live oak that dominated the churchyard corner, moving with the deliberate pace of a man who would not be rushed. Nate followed, his eyes scanning the perimeter for cameras or anyone who might have followed them out. Rodecker stayed by the door with his arms crossed, staring down a cameraman who had started to approach.

Oden stopped under the tree and turned to face Nate.

"You want my source," Oden said, not a question.

"I need to know if I have a leak in my task force," Nate said, "or in the ME's office."

"There is no leak, Agent Holloway, not unless you count the graves in Laurel Grove."

Nate's fists clenched, the gauze pulling tight against his burns and sending a sharp sting up his forearms. "Don't play games, Reverend. This isn't a sermon. Three women are dead."

"More than three," Oden said softly, and reached into his suit jacket. He pulled out a small, worn Bible with a leather cover so smooth it looked like water in the moonlight, the gold lettering faded almost to invisibility.

"You think this started with Caroline Marsh," Oden said, holding the Bible between them like evidence. "This month. This year."

"I know about the pattern," Nate said, his jaw tight. "I know about 2010 and the fifteen-year cycle. My sister died in 2010."

Oden's expression softened into something that looked like genuine grief. "Then you know what it means to lose someone to this. But you do not know the history."

He opened the Bible, bypassing the scripture to reach the flyleaves at the front and back—the blank pages meant for dedications and family trees. Nate stepped closer and pulled out his phone, turning on the flashlight to cut through the shadows.

The pages were filled with handwriting in different inks and different levels of fade. Some entries were in the shaky script of an old man, others in the firm hand of a younger one—names and dates stretching back across decades.

"Look," Oden said, pointing to a block of text. *May 12, 1995. Kelly Evans. Found near the rail yards. Throat torn, buried quietly.* He tapped the page with one finger. "The ME who handled her case confessed to me years later. He was told to write 'animal attack.' But he saw the body. The real report is here."

Oden's voice dropped to barely above a whisper. "He said she was drained—not a drop of blood left in her veins, not a drop of blood on the ground."

Nate stiffened, his breath catching in his chest. Darnell Washington had held back the details on exsanguination as a prosecutorial safeguard. The public knew the women's throats were cut, but they didn't know about the draining—that the bodies had been emptied completely.

"Who talked?" Nate whispered without looking at Rodecker.

"Not me," Rodecker murmured from his post by the door. "And not Pierce. Darnell keeps his files locked."

"Someone talked."

Nate moved the light up the page, his hand shaking enough to make the beam waver. *April 1980. Lucinda Williams. Throat destroyed. ME said wild dogs. Family said she was drained white.* The entries went back further, the handwriting changing with each generation, but the details remained constant—throat torn, drained, no blood.

"I have buried them," Oden said, his voice heavy with the weight of years. "For forty years. Before me, my father buried them. And before him, his mentor."

"Why didn't you come forward?" Nate asked, and the question came out sharper than he intended, edged with frustration.

"To whom?" Oden closed the Bible with a soft snap. "To the police in 1965? A black man coming forward when a white woman was found dead in this city, Agent Holloway. Even still, the investigation lasted as long as it took to type the report and file it away. They called it drug violence, animal attacks, the consequences of a high-risk lifestyle."

Oden stepped closer, and Nate could see the lines carved around the man's eyes—decades of grief compressed into flesh. "County medical examiners attend my church. Men who see things on their tables they cannot explain, things they are told to leave out of the official report. They talk to their pastor because they have nowhere else to take the burden. They unburden their souls. That is my source, Agent Holloway—the burden of confession."

Nate looked at the Bible in Oden's hands and understood what he was seeing. It was a parallel archive to the one Alicia Landry had built, constructed not from property deeds and city records but from funeral rites and whispered confessions.

"This matches," Nate said, his throat tight. "The dates. The interval between murders."

"1995, 1980, 1965," Oden recited like a litany. "And now 2025. The cycle turns again."

"We're looking for him," Nate said. "We have a suspect with connections to the properties."

"A suspect," Oden said, and there was pity in his voice. "You are looking for a man. For fingerprints and DNA and evidence that will hold up in court. You are trying to catch a storm with a net."

"We will catch him."

"Will you?" Oden gestured toward the lights of the historic district, where the trolley tours were probably starting their evening runs. "This city feeds on its ghosts, Agent Holloway. It sells them on trolley tours for twenty dollars a head. We invite the darkness in, dress it up in antebellum finery, and charge admission. When the darkness bites, we act surprised."

"I am not the city," Nate said. "And I am not the police department."

"You are the watchman."

Nate blinked.

"Ezekiel 33:6," Oden quoted, his voice taking on the cadence of the pulpit. *"But if the watchman see the sword come, and blow not the trumpet, and the people be not warned; if the sword come, and take any person from among them, he is taken away in his iniquity; but his blood will I require at the watchman's hand."*

"I tried to warn them," Nate said, his voice thin and stretched. "I told Harran. I told the task force what we were dealing with."

"You whispered," Oden said. "You need to shout. Tell the people what is hunting them—my congregation, the students walking home from work, the women who think they're safe. They need to know there is a wolf who looks like a gentleman."

"I can't," Nate said, and hated how defeated he sounded. "If I release the profile, if I validate this theory publicly, the investigation collapses. We lose credibility. We lose the resources to catch him."

"Credibility," Oden said, shaking his head with a profound, crushing pity that made Nate feel like a child. "You are worried about your badge. I am worried about the graves I have yet to dig."

"Give me the names," Nate said, reaching for something concrete he could use. "From the book. Let me cross-reference them with our databases."

"No." Oden slid the Bible back into his pocket, the motion final. "These names belong to God and their families. You have your files, Agent. You have your science. Use them."

"Reverend, if you go back out there and start talking about this to the media..."

"I will talk about evil," Oden said, cutting him off. "And I will pray for the watchman."

He turned and walked back toward the church, his robe swaying with his stride, moving with the unshakeable certainty of a man who preaches to the abyss and expects no answer.

Nate watched him go, the bile rising in his throat.

Rodecker walked over from the door, his footsteps heavy on the brick path. "What did he say?"

"He knows," Nate said, still staring at Oden's retreating back. "He's known for decades. His family has been tracking this since 1965."

"Is he going to stop talking to the press?"

"No."

Nate turned and walked toward the street, his strides fast enough that Rodecker had to hurry to keep up. The anger was back, burning through the exhaustion like alcohol on a wound.

"Where are you going?" Rodecker called after him.

"To make a call," Nate said over his shoulder. "To blow the damn trumpet."

He reached his rental Explorer and wrenched the door open with his bandaged hand, wincing as the gauze pulled at the burns. He slid into the driver's seat and slammed the door hard enough to make the whole car shake. The interior smelled of stale coffee and accumulated stress.

He pulled out his phone and checked the time. Harran would still be in his office, probably staring at the same reports Nate had sent him three times. Nate hit dial.

It rang three times.

"Harran."

"I need a warrant," Nate said without preamble. "Arrest warrant. Evan Carlisle. 465 Jones Street."

A pause on the other end, then the sound of a chair creaking under weight. "Nate. Slow down. What do you have?"

"Positive ID from a witness," Nate said, gripping the steering wheel so hard his knuckles went white. "Stevie Ralston. He identified Carlisle from a photo lineup with complete accuracy. Puts him at the scene of an abduction attempt three days before the first murder."

"The eight-year-old?" Harran's voice was flat. "The one who said the suspect wanted to eat them?"

"He identified the face, Jeff, without hesitation or coaching. The photo was in a lineup with five similar-looking men. He picked Carlisle immediately."

"A child witness isn't probable cause for a homicide arrest, and you know that better than I do. What else?"

"Property records," Nate said, forcing himself to slow down and present the evidence methodically. "The warehouse on West Boundary is owned by a shell company, 'Cypress Holdings.' The registered agent is a lawyer who has represented the Carlisle family for forty years. The townhouse on Jones Street is held by the same trust structure."

"Shell companies connect him to the building, not the bodies," Harran said, and Nate could hear him rubbing his temples.

"The fire," Nate said. "Someone rigged it. Someone knew we were inside."

"The fire marshal called it accidental—old wiring in a building that should have been condemned."

"It wasn't accidental!" Nate shouted into the phone, then lowered his voice when he realized he was screaming. "He trapped us. He burned the evidence. Jeff, listen to me. He matches the profile perfectly—organized, local, wealthy, with historical ties to the city. The timeline fits."

"The timeline," Harran sighed heavily. "You mean the 135-year timeline your historian friend keeps pushing in her reports?"

"I mean the murders happening right now in this city."

"Nate," Harran said, his voice taking on a patronizing tone that Nate hated more than anything. "I have the Deputy Director breathing down my neck about overtime and jurisdictional overreach. We have a Reverend on the six o'clock news talking about monsters and cover-ups. I cannot get a federal arrest warrant for a prominent businessman based on a traumatized child, a homeless person, and some property deeds."

"He's going to kill again," Nate said, staring at his reflection in the rearview mirror. "The cycle isn't done. We're only three victims in."

"Then find evidence," Harran said. "DNA. Fingerprints. A weapon. Something I can actually take to a judge."

"I can't get evidence if I can't get inside his house."

"We've been over this, Nate. We've been over this a dozen times."

"Jeff," Nate said, staring at his bandaged hands in the dashboard light. "Please. This is the guy. If we wait, another woman dies. Put it on me—I'll take the heat if it goes sideways."

"It's already sideways, Nate, and you know it. You're burnt out. Your objectivity is gone."

"Objectivity didn't burn my hands."

Silence stretched between them, broken only by the sound of Harran's breathing.

"I can't give you a warrant," Harran said finally, and Nate heard the note of finality in it. "The US Attorney won't sign it. But..."

"But what?"

"I can authorize a voluntary interview if he consents. Bring him in as a potential witness. Talk to him. See if he slips."

"He won't slip," Nate said, closing his eyes. "He's been doing this too long. He's had 135 years of practice."

"It's what I have, Nate. Take it or leave it."

"Voluntary," Nate repeated, and the word tasted like ash in his mouth.

"Do you want to bring him in or not?"

"Yeah," Nate said. "I'll bring him in."

"Good. And Nate? Keep the historian away from this. If I see her name on one more report, I'm pulling you off the case. Tonight."

The line went dead.

Nate lowered the phone and looked out at the church. The media vans were packing up their equipment, coiling cables, and breaking down lights. He had no warrant, no physical evidence that would satisfy a judge. He had witnesses the system would dismiss and a Bible full of dead names that would never be entered into evidence. The system was designed to catch men, built on the assumption of human frailty and rational motives. It had no mechanism for this.

Carlisle was protected by the laws Nate had sworn to uphold.

He started the car and put it in gear, the movement sending a sharp pain from his burned hand up his arm. He drove away from the church without looking back.

CHAPTER

26

Inside Interrogation Room 3, the stainless steel table gleamed under the light fixtures' buzz, bolted to the floor, waiting.

"He's early," Rodecker said.

The detective paced the narrow strip of floor behind Nate, and he smelled of nervous sweat and stale tobacco, opposed to the antiseptic chill of the room. Rodecker cracked his knuckles, the sound popping like dry twigs.

"Let him wait," Nate said.

"Blake called ahead, hard stop at four-fifteen, and if we stall, the lawyer walks him."

"It's a voluntary interview, Karl, which means he can walk whenever he wants." Nate turned from the glass, his shirt collar stiff with dried sweat, a souvenir from the humidity outside that the building's HVAC struggled to kill. He looked at his hands, thick white rolls of gauze encasing his palms and leaving only the fingertips exposed. The ER nurse had wrapped them tight, but the heat from the warehouse fire was still trapped inside, pulsing with his heartbeat.

"You ready?" Rodecker asked.

"No."

"Me neither."

They stepped into the hallway where the precinct hummed with a low-frequency tension. Officers walked past with their heads down, eyes fixed on paperwork or floor tiles, avoiding the observation deck because no one wanted to look at Nate.

The door to Interrogation Room 3 opened.

Evan Carlisle entered.

He wore a cream linen suit, pressed and crisp, defying the ninety-five-degree heat that was melting the asphalt outside. A pale blue shirt, open at the collar, showed skin as dry as parchment, and he didn't look around. He moved to the chair facing the mirror and sat, his motion efficient, wasting no energy.

Harrison Blake followed, a silver-haired pillar of the Savannah bar association, clutching a briefcase that cost more than Nate's car. He checked his watch—a gold Rolex—before taking the seat next to his client.

Nate waited and let the silence stretch. He let the sixty-two-degree air settle on Carlisle's skin, the temperature a tactic designed to make suspects hunch, cross their arms, seek warmth. It made them want to talk just to get out.

He pushed the door open.

The chill hit harder inside, and Rodecker followed, the door sealing them in with a solid thud. Nate took the chair opposite Carlisle, moved with deliberate care, keeping his hands elevated, and placing the bandaged bundles on the metal table.

Carlisle's eyes dropped to the gauze, dark irises, almost black, devoid of the usual flecks of light. They lingered on the injuries, then drifted up to Nate's face.

"Agent Holloway," Carlisle said, his voice smooth, a low baritone that sounded like it belonged to a different century. "I am relieved to see you recovered, as warehouse fires are treacherous things."

The phrasing landed like a scalpel. *I know you were there. I know I almost killed you.*

Nate fought the urge to pull his hands back. "Hazards of the job."

"One should be more careful," Carlisle said. "Savannah is an old city with old wiring, and accidents are inevitable."

Blake cleared his throat and clicked a gold pen. "Let's establish the ground rules here, gentlemen—my client is here voluntarily, as a civic duty, even after the harassment he has endured, and we have a hard stop at four-fifteen."

Nate glanced at the wall clock. Forty minutes.

"Understood," Nate said.

"You have questions," Carlisle said, leaning back, his chest open, arms resting easily on the armrests. He didn't shiver or hunch. "Ask them."

Nate leaned forward, ignoring the pull of the tape on his blisters. "Caroline Marsh."

"A tragedy," Carlisle said. "I read the papers, and she was a woman with promise."

"You met her at the Preservation Society gala a week before she died."

"I meet half the city at those events, Agent."

"You talked to her for twenty minutes, and witnesses said she was captivated when you discussed the restoration of the Mercer House portico."

A small smile touched Carlisle's lips, but didn't reach the dead zones of his eyes. "Ah, yes, I recall her now—she had a keen interest in Italianate architecture, which is rare to find in a young person who appreciates the distinction between cast and wrought iron. We discussed the effects of salt air on masonry."

Nate watched him, noting the recall was too sharp. A man like Carlisle met hundreds of donors, politicians, and socialites, so to remember a specific architectural debate with a nobody meant he had cataloged her.

"She changed after that night," Nate said. "Became distant, obsessed, stopped going to work."

"I cannot speak to her mental state," Carlisle said. "I never saw her again."

"You groomed her," Rodecker said from the corner where the detective stood with his back to the wall, arms crossed, radiating heat and anger. "You isolated her."

Carlisle didn't turn but kept his gaze on Nate. "Your detective seems agitated, and perhaps he should step out."

"He stays," Nate said, using his fingertips to slide a photo from the folder. Lucy Phelps in a driver's license picture, back when she was young and smiling, before the streets took her. "Do you know her?"

Carlisle glanced at the photo without leaning in. "The homeless woman from Monterey Square—Lucy, I believe?"

"You knew her name."

"One cannot walk the squares without noticing the less fortunate, and I gave her a sandwich once, from the bakery on Bull Street."

"Witnesses saw you sitting with her," Nate said. "Close, intimate, and she told people she had a gentleman suitor named Mr. Evan."

"I treat everyone with dignity, Agent, and if she mistook charity for courtship, that is a tragedy of her own mind."

"She was killed," Rodecker said. "Just like Caroline."

Blake tapped his pen on the legal pad. "My client is not here to discuss forensic details of crimes he did not commit, so next question."

Nate produced the next photo, Nicole Gladman, a SCAD student. "And her?"

Carlisle offered a mask of polite boredom. "So many artists come to Savannah, like silt in the river, and I couldn't possibly know them all."

"She was seen with you," Nate said. "Walking toward the industrial district."

"Mistaken identity," Blake snapped. "A blonde woman and a man in a suit describes half the population on a Friday night."

"The warehouse on West Boundary," Rodecker said, pushing off the wall. "The one that burned three nights ago—we know you own it."

Carlisle turned his head, a slow, hydraulic movement. "I own many properties, and I view myself as a custodian of Savannah's history. That warehouse was an architectural gem with 1847 original brick and heart pine beams, all irreplaceable."

"It was a kill room," Rodecker said. "We saw the drain and the hooks."

"It was storage," Carlisle said. "I lease it to various tenants, and I haven't visited in months, so the loss is substantial."

"Where were you the night of the fire?" Nate asked.

Blake slid a sheet of paper across the table, a photocopy of a guest ledger. "Coastal Heritage Society fundraiser at Old Fort Jackson with two hundred witnesses, and his signature is time-stamped eight forty-seven PM while the fire alarm triggered at eight fifty-two."

Nate read the signature, *Evan Carlisle*, in flowing, archaic script.

He looked at the man's hands resting on the table, fingers loosely interlaced, pale and still. No tremors, no tension, and he sat in a room designed to break people, facing two men who knew exactly what he was, looking like he was waiting for the opera to start.

"We need a DNA sample," Nate said, pushing a buccal swab kit forward. "Voluntary, to rule yourself out."

Blake's hand shot out, covering the kit. "No, you have no probable cause, and you are fishing."

"If he has nothing to hide—"

"We are done playing," Blake said. "We provided the alibi and explained the casual contacts, so unless you are charging him, that kit stays closed."

Nate watched Carlisle's pupils, looked for the dilation of stress, the widening of fear, but the black discs remained static.

"We have a witness," Nate said. "Stevie Ralston, eight years old."

Carlisle's head tilted, a micro-adjustment. "The child."

"He picked you out of a photo lineup with six photos, pointed to you, and said you approached him and his aunt, tried to get them under the trees."

"And what else?" Carlisle asked softly.

"He said your eyes looked like a shark's."

Carlisle chuckled, the sound dry, like dead leaves skittering on pavement. "A shark—children have potent imaginations, Agent, and they see a stranger in a suit, sense the anxiety of their guardian, then their minds fill the gaps with monsters from storybooks."

"He identified you," Nate said.

"He identified a fear," Carlisle said. "Suggestive procedures with a traumatized woman means any competent defense attorney would shred that identification before the jury was seated."

"He saw you," Rodecker said, his voice rising, cracking with strain. "He saw what you are."

"And what am I, Detective?"

Carlisle turned fully to face Rodecker, didn't blink, simply stared, a predator regarding prey that had forgotten its place.

"You're a monster," Rodecker said. "Three women are dead."

"And you have no evidence," Carlisle said. "You have shadows and stories, and you have two non-credible witnesses—a scared child and a homeless man with PTSD who fits the profile far better than I do."

"You trapped us in that warehouse," Rodecker said, stepping closer, looming over the seated man. "You tried to burn us alive."

"I was at a fundraiser," Carlisle said. "Drinking bad Chardonnay and discussing coastal erosion."

"Liar!"

Rodecker lunged.

He slammed both hands down on the metal table, and the sound cracked through the room like a gunshot. The floor vibrated, the plastic water pitcher jumped an inch, splashing water onto the steel, and Blake flinched, jerking back in his chair, hands coming up to protect his face. Nate's muscles locked, a hardwired survival reflex.

Carlisle did not move.

He didn't jump or blink, his shoulders didn't rise, and his hands remained loosely clasped on the table, right where the water pooled. He sat in the center of the violence, unaffected, a stone in a river.

The startle reflex is the oldest part of the human nervous system, bypassing the conscious brain. A loud noise, a sudden threat—the body reacts before the mind knows why, and it is biological law.

Carlisle broke the law.

Rodecker froze, breathed hard, face flushed, staring down at the man in the chair. The anger in the detective's eyes curdled into something else—fear, primal and cold.

He backed away. He had seen it.

The room went quiet, save for the hum of the air conditioner and the drip of water from the table to the floor.

Carlisle looked up at Rodecker, his expression holding a mild, polite disappointment. "Temper, Detective—stress kills."

Blake stood up, shoving his legal pad into his briefcase with shaking hands. "Interview over, this is intimidation, and I am filing a formal complaint with the Chief. We are leaving."

Carlisle stood, the movement liquid, a defying of gravity. He buttoned his jacket, checked his cuffs, and looked fresh, cool, untouched by the heat or the hate.

He turned to the door where Blake was already clawing for the handle.

Carlisle paused next to Nate's chair.

He looked down while Nate remained seated, his bandaged hands resting on the metal. He looked up into the dark eyes, and up close, the skin around Carlisle's eyes was too smooth, the texture wrong, like wax that had never known a wrinkle.

Carlisle leaned down and brought his face close to Nate's ear. He smelled of sandalwood and old, dry paper.

"Do take care of those burns, Agent," Carlisle said, his voice a whisper, intimate and deep, vibrating in Nate's chest. "Scar tissue can be so limiting, particularly for a man who works with his hands."

He straightened and offered a small, courtly nod.

"Good day, gentlemen."

He walked out.

The door clicked shut.

Nate stared at the empty chair where the metal was still cold, and the water pitcher sat in a puddle.

The door burst open.

Chief Harold Dean stormed in, followed by Russell Bennett from the DA's office, and Dean's face was a map of high blood pressure.

"Are you out of your mind?" Dean shouted, pointing a finger at Rodecker. "I watched the feed, and you assaulted the table, tried to physically intimidate a suspect with zero evidence and a lawyer present?"

"He didn't blink," Rodecker said, staring at the wall, his voice hollow. "Chief, he didn't blink."

"I don't care if he danced a jig!" Dean yelled. "Blake is on the phone with the Mayor, and you just handed them a harassment suit."

Bennett leaned against the mirror, rubbing his temples. "We have nothing, Nate—the alibi holds, the DNA is a non-starter without probable cause, and you can't hold him."

"He did it," Nate said. "He knows we know."

"Knowing isn't proving," Bennett said. "The timeline works for the warehouse fire, he has witnesses, and we have nothing."

"So we let him go?"

"He's already gone," Dean said. "And frankly, Agent, you're lucky you still have a badge, because this investigation into him is over, and we are pivoting."

CHAPTER

27

NATE STARED at the sixty-inch monitor on the far wall, at a bouncing geometric logo that promised a secure connection. Rodecker sat to his right, the detective having loosened his tie and unbuttoned his collar, but the heat of the room still pressed the air out of him. He spun a cheap ballpoint pen on the table. *Click. Spin. Click. Spin.* The sound was a metronome counting down to something terrible. Pierce stood near the door, her arms crossed against her chest, retreating into the shadows where the fluorescent glare didn't reach.

The screen flickered and cut to a quad-view grid. The Savannah feed was a cramped, dimly lit box, while the other three quadrants were windows into a different world—sterile, bright, well-funded.

Top right: Dr. Priya Thakker at Quantico. Her lab coat was pristine, the background a blur of stainless steel and glass.

Bottom right: Dr. Raymond Kessler at the GBI lab in Decatur. He looked older than his file photos, the skin under his eyes hanging in loose, dark pouches.

Bottom left: Dr. Darnell Washington. The Chatham County Medical Examiner sat in his office, framed by bookshelves and diplomas. He wasn't looking at the camera. He was looking down at a file folder.

"Audio check," Thakker said. Her voice was tinny, stripped of warmth by the compression algorithm. "Savannah, can you hear us?"

"We're here," Nate said.

"Dr. Kessler? Dr. Washington?"

"Present," Kessler said.

Darnell nodded, and when he finally looked up, the fatigue on his face was a mirror of Nate's own.

"Let's begin," Thakker said, skipping the pleasantries. "We have completed the expedited analysis on the biological and trace evidence submitted from the Marsh, Phelps, and Gladman cases. I want to start with the serology because it represents the most significant anomaly."

Thakker keyed a command, and the main view shifted, minimizing the faces and bringing up a spreadsheet filled with red data points.

"We ran the numbers three times," she said. "We recalibrated the equipment after the first run because we assumed a sensor error, but the results remained consistent."

Nate leaned forward, the pain in his hands spiking as the skin pulled.

"Caroline Marsh," Thakker read. "Estimated total blood volume prior to death, four point three liters. Volume recovered at scene and remaining in body, roughly three hundred milliliters. Lucy Phelps—estimated volume, four point eight liters, recovered four hundred milliliters. Nicole Gladman showed similar ratios."

"Percentages," Rodecker said, stopping the pen mid-spin.

"Between ninety-two and ninety-six percent volume loss," Thakker said. "Across all three victims."

The room in Savannah went quiet, the hum of the air conditioner filling the silence. Nate looked at the numbers on the screen, remembering the bodies—the skin translucent, sunken, like parchment pulled tight over bone. Seeing it quantified in a spreadsheet made it colder, more clinical, more impossible to deny.

"Talk to me about the mechanism," Nate said. "How did he do it?"

Thakker hesitated, looking off-camera for a second before returning her gaze to the lens. "That is the problem, Agent Holloway. We found no evidence of anticoagulants in the toxicology screens—no heparin, no warfarin, no citrate compounds. Nothing to thin the blood or prevent clotting."

"Mechanical extraction," Pierce said from the doorway. "A pump."

"We looked for that," Thakker said. "To remove that volume of fluid, you need access—venipuncture sites, catheter insertion points, large-bore needles accessing the femoral or subclavian arteries. We found none of that. The only trauma to the vascular system is the primary wound site at the throat."

She brought up a second graphic, a 3D rendering of the human circulatory system rotating slowly on the screen.

"The heart stops pumping after forty percent volume loss," Thakker continued, her voice gaining a rapid, nervous cadence. "Once cardiac arrest occurs, the pressure is zero, and gravity alone cannot drain a body to this extent. You would need to suspend the victim, manipulate the limbs, massage the tissues to get anywhere near sixty percent. To get to ninety-six percent without surgical intervention, without pumps—"

She stopped, taking a breath.

"It's beyond human capability," she said. "Not without leaving far more tissue trauma than we are observing."

Nate looked at Darnell's quadrant, watching the ME stare at the camera with a flat, unblinking intensity. He knew this. He had known it since the first autopsy.

"So where is the blood?" Rodecker asked. "If it's not in the body, and it's not on the ground..."

"It was removed, entirely," Thakker said. "The fluid was extracted and transported away from the scene, and the absence of containment vessels or spatter patterns is... unusual. It must be the explanation."

"Unusual," Rodecker said under his breath. "That's one word for it."

"Let's move to the odontology," Nate said, needing to push past the blood. The blood was a physics problem. The teeth were an identification problem.

Kessler cleared his throat, a wet and heavy sound over the speakers.

"I received the bite impression casts from Dr. Washington two days ago," Kessler said. "I compared them against the database of known animal predation marks, but nothing fit. Too wide for a wolf or large dog. Wrong curvature for a big cat. The spacing is uniform. Symmetrical."

"Human," Nate said.

"Humanoid," Kessler said. "The arch width is within the upper percentile of human male dentition, but the canines are elongated, sharp, not filed. Natural enamel structure, but wrong."

Kessler shared his screen, and the monitor displayed a topographical scan of the bite mark—high points in red, depressions in blue. Sharp, vertical incisors. Canines that extended four millimeters beyond the occlusal plane.

"This is the impression from Nicole Gladman's throat," Kessler said. "Note the inter-canine distance—four point one centimeters. Note the rotation of the lateral incisors."

He clicked a button, and a grainy black-and-white photograph overlaid the color map. The photo was old, the edges jagged. It showed a ruler lying next to a dark wound on pale skin.

"This photo is from the GBI cold case archives," Kessler said. "Savannah. October, 1950. Victim was an eight-year-old girl named Mary Alice Tremain."

The skin on Nate's arms tightened as Alicia Landry's timeline flashed through his mind—the 1950 cycle.

"Watch the overlay," Kessler said.

He slid the transparency of the 1950 photo over the 2025 digital scan, and they lined up with no margin of error. The red peaks of the 2025 rendering fit into the dark divots of the 1950 photograph. The arc was identical. The rotation of the incisors was identical. It was the same mouth.

"Dental friction ridges and alignment are as unique as fingerprints," Kessler said, his voice tired. "Teeth change over time—they wear down, gums recede, restoration work alters the profile. Over ten years, you expect drift."

"That's seventy-five years," Nate said.

"Yes," Kessler said. "Seventy-five years, and the dentition has not changed by a millimeter. The wear patterns on the molars are identical. The chip on the left premolar is identical."

"A relative," Rodecker suggested. "A son. A grandson. Genetics."

"Genetics dictates the shape of the jaw," Kessler said. "It does not dictate the specific wear pattern caused by grinding your teeth at night or replicate a traumatic chip on a specific tooth. This isn't a family resemblance, Detective. This is the same set of teeth."

Silence filled the room.

"So we have two impossible options," Kessler said, taking off his glasses to rub the bridge of his nose. "Option one is that your suspect is a man who has not aged or visited a dentist since the Truman administration."

He put the glasses back on.

"Option two is that you are dealing with a forensic forger of unprecedented skill, someone who has studied the 1950 case files, built a prosthetic appliance to match that specific bite pattern, and is using it to stage these murders."

"A prosthetic," Nate said. "Could a prosthetic apply the force required to tear out a throat?"

"It would be difficult," Kessler said. "The jaw pressure required to sever the trachea and the carotid arteries is substantial enough that a prosthetic would slip or break under that kind of torque. But physics says option two is the only one that exists."

"Physics is taking a beating today," Pierce murmured.

Thakker cleared her throat. "The DNA supports the historical connection."

Nate turned his attention back to the top right quadrant, where Thakker looked pale, shuffling papers as she searched for a chart she didn't want to show.

"We recovered biological material," she said. "Seminal fluid from Caroline Marsh and epithelial cells from under Nicole Gladman's fingernails. It's a single source profile. One male contributor."

"Carlisle," Nate said.

"We don't have Carlisle's DNA for a direct comparison," Thakker reminded him. "But we ran the profile against the database—no hits in CODIS. However, because of the bite mark connection, Dr. Kessler had the GBI pull the physical evidence from the 1950 Tremain case."

"Microscope slides," Kessler added. "Old swabs. Degraded. Kept in a basement that flooded twice."

"We used Next Generation Sequencing," Thakker said. "We managed to reconstruct a partial profile from the 1950 sample, and yes, it's degraded. But the loci we recovered—"

She put up a chart showing two columns of genetic markers that matched all the way down.

"It's the same donor," Thakker said. "The statistical probability of two unrelated individuals sharing this profile is effectively zero. With a direct descendant, you would see recombination, maternal DNA introducing variance. This is... it's a direct match."

"Ancestry?" Nate asked.

Thakker brought up a world map with a heat map glowing over the Middle East.

"We ran a biogeographical ancestry analysis," she said. "The markers are distinct, clustering in the Near East—the Levant. Specifically, the genetic haplogroups are consistent with populations from the Tigris and Euphrates river valley."

Mesopotamia.

Nate looked at Rodecker, watching the detective's face go grey as he stopped playing with the pen.

"Ancient Iraq," Nate said. "Syria. Southeastern Turkey."

"Yes," Thakker said. "Which is not uncommon. But combined with the 1950 match, the bite marks, and the blood volume—"

Thakker closed the file, folding her hands and aligning her thumbs with the edge of the desk as she straightened her spine. The FBI mask sliding back into place.

"The official consensus," Thakker said, her voice taking on a rehearsed cadence, "is that we are dealing with a highly sophisticated human offender who has access to the GBI archives. He has studied the 1950 Tremain case in obsessive detail, constructed prosthetics to mimic the bite pattern, and is planting DNA evidence—possibly synthesized or preserved historical samples—to confuse the investigation."

"Preserved samples?" Rodecker asked. "You think he's carrying around seventy-five-year-old jizz to sprinkle on crime scenes?"

"It is the only rational explanation, Detective," Thakker said. "We are writing the report to reflect a copycat profile—an offender driven by a compulsion to recreate a historical narrative. Vampiric delusion. Occult fetishism. He wants us to think he is a monster, staging the impossible to paralyze the investigation."

"He's doing a hell of a job," Pierce said.

"We will forward the full written reports within the hour," Thakker said. "Good luck, Agent Holloway."

"Thank you, Doctor."

Thakker cut the feed, her quadrant going black.

"I'll send the casts back by courier," Kessler said, looking at Nate with an expression where the scientific detachment slipped for a second. He looked like a man who wanted to apologize. "Get him, Agent. Whatever he is."

Kessler clicked off, leaving two quadrants black and only Darnell Washington remaining.

The ME hadn't moved, still sitting in his office in Chatham County a few miles away, though he felt distant. He looked at the papers on his desk one last time, then pushed them away and leaned toward the camera.

"Agent Holloway," Darnell said.

"I'm here, Doc."

"Thirty-one years," Darnell said, his voice quiet and heavy, lacking the tinny distortion of the other feeds. "Eight at Dover, processing war casualties, and fifteen here. I've testified in over four hundred homicide cases."

Darnell took off his glasses and set them on the desk, rubbing his eyes and pressing the heels of his hands into the sockets until he winced.

"I believe in evidence," Darnell said. "Methodology. The body tells the story, and the story is always true—physics doesn't lie, biology doesn't lie."

He looked directly into the lens, and it felt like he was staring straight at Nate's bandaged hands.

"But I am looking at these findings," Darnell said. "And I'm baffled."

Nate didn't speak, understanding the cost of that admission for a man like Darnell.

"The blood didn't drain by any mechanism I understand," Darnell said. "The DNA shouldn't match across decades, and the bite marks are identical across a human lifespan. Those things... they break the rules, the ones that are supposed to be absolute."

Darnell leaned back, looking small in his chair.

"If you find an explanation that makes sense, Agent Holloway, please share it, because the evidence is telling me something I don't have the vocabulary to accept."

Darnell reached forward, and the screen went black.

The light in the task force room died with the connection, the reflection of the fluorescent lights vanishing from the glossy screen and leaving only a dark mirror. Nate could see himself in the glass—a distorted shadow with white hands.

He looked at Rodecker.

The detective was staring at the blank monitor, his mouth a tight line.

"Seventy-five years," Rodecker said softly. "Seventy-five years and he hasn't lost a tooth."

"Mesopotamia?" Pierce said from the corner, stepping into the light. Her face was set, hard as flint.

"Yeah," Nate said.

"So the Feds are writing it up as a copycat," Rodecker said, picking up his pen again and gripping it like a weapon. "Sophisticated offender. Access to archives. That's the story."

"That's the lie," Nate said. "They have to tell it because the institution can't process the alternative."

"Can we?" Pierce asked.

Nate looked at his hands, flexing them and feeling the burn of the blisters—the reminder of the fire that had almost killed them. He thought about the coldness of Carlisle's touch in the interrogation room, the eyes that didn't reflect light, the alibi that was too perfect because the man could move faster than time allowed.

He stood up, the chair scraping loudly against the floor.

"We have the science," Nate said. "It gave us the answer we didn't want."

"It gave us a monster," Rodecker said.

"It gave us a target," Nate corrected. "Thakker and Kessler proved one thing, though they won't admit it—he's real, he's physical, and he leaves traces."

"He leaves bodies," Pierce said.

"And he's going to leave more," Nate said. "Unless we stop him."

"How?" Rodecker asked. "We can't arrest him, can't charge him. The DA won't look at this evidence without laughing us out of the room."

"We don't need the DA," Nate said, walking to the door. "We need the historian."

He pushed the door open, letting the noise of the precinct flood back in—phones ringing, voices talking about budgets and overtime, the sounds of a normal world that didn't know it was being hunted.

CHAPTER

28

THE HYDROCODONE TOOK twenty minutes to file the sharp edges off the nerve damage. It turned the throb in his hands into a dull, rhythmic pressure that matched the beat of his heart. The corners of the club sandwich on the tray had curled, the bread turning to stone.

Nate didn't look at the food. His eyes were pinned to the corkboard.

It dominated the far wall. A geography of violence mapped in red string and pushpins. Sarah's photo sat at the center, the dense mass that pulled everything else into its orbit. The string radiated outward to Caroline Marsh, to Lucy Phelps, to Nicole Gladman. It wasn't an investigation anymore. It was an altar.

Nate swallowed dry. The pill scraped down his throat.

He cradled his left hand against his chest. The ER nurse had wound the gauze tight, but the burn beneath felt active, feeding on the oxygen in the room. Every pulse sent a fresh wave of heat through the nerve endings. He stepped closer to the board and traced the line from Sarah to the warehouse address on West Boundary.

Three hard knocks rattled the door frame.

Nate turned, the movement pulling the skin on his palms. He hissed through his teeth. Housekeeping didn't knock like that at two in the morning. Carlisle wouldn't knock at all.

He walked to the door, the carpet dampening his footsteps. He checked the peephole. The fisheye lens bent the hallway into a tunnel, but the figure standing there required no identification.

Nate undid the latch and opened the door.

Nadia Lopez stood in the hallway. Her travel blazer was wrinkled, her dark hair frizzing from the Savannah humidity. A carry-on bag rested at her feet. She looked like she had been awake for thirty hours.

"Nadia," he said. His voice was a rasp.

She didn't wait for an invitation. She picked up her bag and walked past him, her shoulder brushing his chest. The contact was firm, a shock to a system that had been living in smoke for weeks. Nate closed the door and leaned back against it.

Nadia dropped her bag at the foot of the bed. She turned, her dark eyes scanning the room, cataloging the debris. She saw the curled sandwich. The empty mini-bottles of Jack Daniel's on the nightstand. The clothes piled on the chair.

Then she saw the board.

She walked toward the desk lamp, and the amber light caught the angles of her face as she stared at the web of red string. She looked at Sarah's photo. She looked at the timeline scrawled on index cards.

She turned to face him.

"You haven't slept," she said.

"I sleep."

"You pass out." She crossed the room, closing the distance between them. She reached out, her hand hovering near his chest, then dropping to his side. She looked at the thick white bandages enveloping his hands. "Let me see."

"They're fine."

"Don't lie to me, Nate." She took his wrist and turned his hand over, inspecting the seepage staining the gauze. "Third degree in spots, the report said. Chemical burns mixed with old timber. You shouldn't be out of the hospital."

"I signed myself out."

"Of course you did." She let go of his wrist and stepped back, putting two feet of dead air between them. "I called you. Three days, Nate. Radio silence. I had to pull the incident report from the Atlanta field office just to make sure you weren't in a drawer at the morgue."

"I've been working."

"Is that what this is?" She gestured to the room, her hand sweeping over the evidence of his fixation. "This isn't work. This is a collapse. Look at this place. Look at you."

Nate pushed off the door. He walked past her to the window, where the streetlights from Broughton Street filtered through the sheer curtains, painting stripes of grey across the floor. "I found the pattern, Nadia. It holds up. The forensics, the timeline, the property records. It's all him."

"I read the report you filed," she said to his back. "The multi-generational theory. The fixation of the antique dealer."

"It's not a theory."

"You're punishing yourself." She stepped into his space, her eyes wet in the amber light. "You think if you bleed enough, it makes up for not answering the phone fifteen years ago? You think if you burn, it balances the scales for Sarah?"

"Stop."

"No. I won't stop. Because you're going to get yourself killed, and for what? For a memory? For a cold case file?" She jabbed a finger toward the board. "You catch him. You kill him. Then what, Nate? Does she walk through that door? Does your mother stop grieving? Do you figure out how to be happy?"

"It stops him from taking another one," he said. He held up his bandaged hands. "It stops the next Sarah."

"And who stops you?"

She reached up. Her hands landed on his chest, palms flat against his shirt. She was shaking. He could feel the tremor running through her arms.

"I can't watch this," she said. "I can't watch you hollow yourself out until there's nothing left but the badge."

Nate looked down at her. The heat radiating from her was different from the cold emptiness he had been carrying since the warehouse fire. Exhaustion crashed into him, a physical weight that buckled his knees. He leaned forward and rested his forehead against hers.

"Nadia."

"Come back," she said. Her hands slid up his chest, wrapping around his neck. Her fingers wound through the short hair at the nape of his neck. "Just come back to me."

He didn't answer. The words stuck in his throat, blocked by the ash. Instead, he kissed her.

It wasn't gentle. There was no romance in it. It was a collision of needs. He pressed his mouth to hers, hunting for a connection that could tether him to the ground. She made a low sound in her throat and pulled him closer.

They stumbled backward. His legs hit the bed, and they fell together onto the twisted sheets.

The lamp cast long stretches of darkness against the wall. Nadia pushed his jacket off his shoulders, the fabric catching on his bandages. He hissed, but he didn't stop her. He needed the jacket gone.

She sat up, straddling his hips. Her hands moved to his shirt buttons.

Nate tried to help. He lifted his hands, but the thick gauze made his fingers useless clubs. He fumbled at the fabric, frustration spiking through the drug haze. He couldn't even undress a woman. He couldn't do the simplest human thing.

"Stop," she said. "Let me."

She brushed his hands away. Her fingers worked quickly, undoing the buttons, peeling the shirt from his body. She tossed it onto the floor. She reached for the hem of her own top and pulled it over her head.

She wasn't wearing a bra. Her skin was bronze in the lamplight, smooth and unbroken. No burns. No scars. She leaned down, her hair falling around them, shutting out the room.

She kissed his throat, her mouth hot against his skin. Nate reached for her. He wanted to feel the texture of her skin, the curve of her waist, but the gauze was in the way. He couldn't feel her. Not with his hands. The bandages were a layer of dead cotton between him and the living world.

He gripped her hips anyway, the pressure sending spikes of white-hot agony up his forearms. He welcomed it. The pain was focusing. It cut through the painkiller fog.

She moved against him, impatient. She shoved his jeans down, her hands urgent. He kicked them away.

When she sank onto him, the breath left his lungs in a rush.

It was a frantic rhythm. There was no tenderness, only a mutual need to drown out the silence of the room. Nadia moved with power, grounding herself against him, her eyes squeezed shut. Nate watched her face. He saw the grief there, and the anger.

He thrust upward, trying to bury himself in the sensation, trying to find a place where the logic of the case didn't exist. For a few minutes, there was no Carlise. No Jones Street. No Sarah. There was only the friction of skin, the smell of her shampoo, the sound of their breathing filling the empty spaces.

He gripped her harder, ignoring the wetness seeping through the bandages. He needed this. He needed to know he was still biological, still capable of something other than death.

Nadia cried out, a sharp, broken sound. She shuddered, her fingernails digging into his shoulders. Nate followed her seconds later, the release tearing through him, a temporary white noise that drowned out the world.

They collapsed.

Silence rushed back into the room. The air conditioner hummed, a mechanical drone.

Nadia rolled off him. She lay on her side, her back to the window, facing him. The sheet was twisted around their legs. Nate stared at the ceiling, watching the pattern of light thrown by the desk lamp. It looked like a cage.

Nadia reached out. She took his left hand.

She ran her fingertip along the edge of the bandage, tracing the line where the gauze met his skin. The flesh there was red, angry.

"It's bleeding again," she said.

"It'll stop."

"It won't heal if you keep using them. The tissue needs time. You need grafts, Nate. You need a sterile environment."

He didn't say anything. He closed his eyes, but the darkness was worse. In the dark, he saw the warehouse. He saw Rodecker and Pierce's faces.

"Come back to D.C. with me," she said. Her voice was small, hollowed out by exhaustion. "Tomorrow. There's a flight. We pack a bag. We leave the files. We go to Harran together, and we tell him you need medical leave."

Nate felt the pull of it. The seduction of a normal life. Coffee in the morning. A desk job. Sundays doing the crossword puzzle without a dead girl looking over his shoulder. It would be easy.

But then he thought about the lavender. The sprig tucked into Nicole's hand—the message.

I remember.

"I can't," he said.

Nadia went still. She didn't pull her hand away, but the heat seemed to drain out of her touch.

"You mean you won't."

"It's the same thing."

She let out a breath that shuddered in her chest. She moved closer, resting her head on his shoulder, avoiding the burns. She curled into him, defeated.

"I love you, Nate," she said into his skin. "I do. But I can't watch you die for someone who's already gone. I can't be the person who waits for the phone call."

"I know."

He stared at the wall. Across the room, the light illuminated the corkboard. The red string looked like arterial spray frozen in time. Sarah's face watched them from the center of the web, young and frozen and demanding.

Nadia's breathing evened out, falling into the rhythm of sleep. Nate lay awake. The pain in his hands returned, a steady, throbbing reminder of what he had touched and what he had lost. He watched the darkness lengthen as the night wore on, waiting for the dawn that would take her away.

CHAPTER

29

Morning light bled through the sheer curtains of Room 417, not brightening the space so much as exposing it. Yellow shafts cut through the stale air, illuminating dust motes that drifted like ash, settling on the unmade bed and the debris of an investigation.

Nate sat on the mattress with a ceramic mug cradled in his lap, the coffee inside tepid, a skin of oil filmed on its surface. He hadn't taken a sip in twenty minutes. His hands were clumsy paws of white gauze, wrapped tight by an ER nurse and re-wrapped by Nadia in the dark hours of the morning, yellow seepage staining the cotton where blisters had wept during the night. The heat from the mug seeped through the layers, creating a dull throb that registered less as pain and more as a continual reminder of the warehouse fire.

Near the wardrobe, Nadia moved with the cold efficiency of an agent clearing a scene. She folded a blouse, smoothing the fabric before placing it in her open carry-on, then added her toiletries kit next to it. The zipper hissed shut—a precise, final sound that marked the end of something. She was putting her armor back on: dark jeans, boots, the blazer that hid the shoulder holster she wasn't wearing because she was flying commercial.

She was leaving.

Nate watched her with a detached sense of observation settling over him. She was just movement on a screen now, a suspect packing up a life he wasn't part of.

"There is a flight at noon," Nadia said without turning. She picked up a pair of socks and examined them before speaking again. "We can make it if we leave in twenty minutes."

Nate looked down at the brown liquid in his mug.

"We go straight to the director," she said, placing the socks in the corner of the bag with deliberate precision. "Control the story. We tell Harran you were compromised by smoke inhalation and burns—medical leave, mandatory psych eval. We frame it as trauma response, not obsession."

She turned then, leaning against the wardrobe with her arms crossed, her face scrubbed clean of the night before. The openness was gone. In its place was the Behavioral Analysis Unit profile: competent, rational, problem-solver.

"It is the only way to save your badge, Nate. Pack a bag."

Nate didn't move. His eyes drifted to the nightstand, where his phone pulsed a slow, rhythmic blue next to the empty mini-bottles of Jack Daniels. Seventeen unread emails from Assistant Director Harran sat waiting in his inbox. Subject lines he didn't need to read: Status Update. Immediate Recall. The blinking light tracked the seconds of his career ticking away.

"Nate," Nadia said, her voice sharpening. "Did you hear me?"

"I heard you." His voice was a rasp of smoke and exhaustion.

"Then get up. Put on clean clothes. We are leaving."

His attention shifted to the corkboard on the wall, where Sarah's face stared back from the center of the web. Red string tethered her to the warehouse on West Boundary, to the alley behind Mercer-Williams, to the thing wearing Evan Carlisle's face.

"I can't just leave it," Nate said.

"You have tunnel vision on one suspect based on circumstantial evidence," Nadia said, stepping away from the wardrobe and entering his peripheral vision. "The moment Harran sees you've abandoned all other leads, you lose credibility—and then you lose the case entirely."

"Carlisle is the pattern."

"You're making connections that aren't there," she said, her voice tight with frustration. "When you present conspiracy theories instead of evidence, you hand Carlisle his defense." She reached for the mug, her fingers avoiding his bandaged palms, and set it on the nightstand next to the blinking phone. "Please."

The quiet that remained was broken only by the air conditioner rattling in the window. She was offering him a life—a career, a future where he didn't wake up screaming. All he had to do was stand up.

He shifted his weight. The mattress springs groaned.

A fist hammered the door.

Not a knock—a demand. Three heavy blows shook the frame.

Nadia's hand flew to her waist, grabbing for a weapon that wasn't there, her eyes narrowing as they locked on Nate.

He stood, the movement dragging the skin tight across his palms. He gritted his teeth against the flare of heat and walked to the door, his boots leaden on the cheap carpet. He didn't check the peephole— he knew that sound. It wasn't room service or the police. It was panic.

He reached for the latch, but his bandaged fingers were useless against the metal. He had to use the side of his hand, shoving the bolt back with clumsy effort before turning the handle.

Alicia Landry stood in the hallway.

Sweat plastered dark strands of hair to her forehead, escaped from their bun. Her cardigan was buttoned wrong, and she clutched a leather satchel to her chest with both arms, knuckles white, her breath hitching in her throat.

"I found it," Alicia said, pushing past him without waiting for permission. Her shoulder checked his arm as she brought the smell of old paper and courthouse basement dust into the air-conditioned room. "It's him—all of it is him. You need to see this."

Nate closed the door and turned. Nadia had stepped out from the narrow hallway, blocking Alicia's path, her posture rigid and her expression a mask of cold recognition.

"Hello," Nadia said. It wasn't a greeting.

Alicia stopped, blinking as if she was noticing Nadia for the first time. She adjusted her glasses with a shaking hand. "I'm sorry... I didn't know you were... it doesn't matter." She tried to step around Nadia. "I need the desk."

"This is an active federal investigation scene," Nadia said, not moving an inch. "You shouldn't be here."

"The investigation isn't going to wait for theories," Alicia said, her eyes wide and manic, fixed on Nate. "I found something incredible. Move."

Alicia dropped her shoulder and shoved past with brute determination rather than tactic. She reached the desk and swept her arm across it in one violent motion. The room service tray, empty water bottles, and a stack of unread case files clattered to the floor, the crash of plastic and glass loud in the small room.

"Hey!" Nadia took a step forward.

Alicia didn't hear. She unbuckled her satchel and upended it, sending a landslide of paper flooding across the desk—photocopies, original deeds, glossy photographs, index cards covered in scribbled notes.

"Look," Alicia said, her hands moving frantically, spreading the papers. "Look at the names."

Nate walked to the desk. Nadia hovered behind him, radiating disapproval, but she looked.

"Property records," Alicia said, jabbing a finger at a photocopy of a handwritten deed on yellowed parchment. "1853—purchase of the lot on Jones Street. Buyer is Edmund Carlisle."

She slid another paper over it. "1891. Transfer of deed to nephew, Edward Carlton."

Another paper. "1923. Transfer to son, Edwin Carver."

Another. "1953. Transfer to grandson, Evan Carpenter."

Another. "1983. Transfer to his nephew, Eric Chandler."

She slammed the final document down, a modern printout from the Chatham County tax assessor. "2019. Title transfer to Evan Carlisle."

"Shell companies," Nadia said, her voice flat. "Wealthy families use trusts to avoid inheritance tax—this proves nothing except they own good lawyers."

"Look at the signatures," Alicia said. She produced a magnifying glass from her pocket and thrust it at Nate. He took it, pinning the handle between his bandaged palms, and leaned over the documents.

The deed from 1891 displayed flowery Victorian script: Edward Carlton.

The 2019 tax document showed Evan Carlisle in modern pen.

The names were different. The handwriting was not.

The capital C began with a heavy downstroke, looped tight at the bottom, and finished with a sharp upward flick that crossed back over the letter—a specific, unnecessary flourish.

Identical.

"Muscle memory," Alicia said quietly. "You can change your name and your clothes, but you can't change the way your hand moves across paper after a hundred years."

"Forgery," Nadia said, standing beside Nate now. "If someone is trying to prove a claim to an estate, they practice the ancestor's signature."

"No," Alicia said, digging through the pile again. "Not just signatures—faces."

She slapped three photographs onto the wood.

The first was a grainy black-and-white from a crowded ballroom: Savannah Antiquarian Society Gala, 1923. Alicia pointed to a man on the edge of the frame holding a champagne flute—dark hair swept back from pale skin, high cheekbones catching the light.

The second was a news clipping: Courthouse Dedication, 1950. A man standing behind the mayor with the same dark hair, the same sharp jawline, the same unnatural stillness.

The third was a surveillance photo Nate had taken three days ago: Evan Carlisle leaving his townhouse.

The face did not change. Not the hairline, not the set of the eyes, not the way the ears sat against the skull.

"That is the same man," Alicia said.

"Grandfather, father, son," Nadia argued. "Strong genetics. It happens. You are reading pattern into coincidence."

"I am reading biology," Alicia said. "I am reading impossibility." She shuffled papers again, extracting a map of Savannah marked with red Xs. "The kill sites. We know he most likely used the warehouse on West Boundary, but look at the history."

She pointed near River Street. "1920. Textile warehouse—burned to the ground three weeks after the last body was found."

She pointed to the railroad yards. "1950. Meatpacking plant. Massive fire that destroyed all records and physical evidence."

She pointed to the old cannery district. "1980. Cannery fire. Arson suspected, never proved."

"He burns them," Nate said, looking at his bandaged hands. "He cleans the slate."

"He is doing it again," Alicia said. "The warehouse on West Boundary—he tried to burn you inside it. He is erasing the evidence."

"This is circumstantial," Nadia said, picking up the 1920s photo by the corner, her expression dismissive. "You show a family history of arson and tax evasion, a resemblance across generations, but you do not build a case a jury will believe."

"I can give you the key," Alicia said.

She reached into her pocket and dropped a heavy object on the desk.

Thud.

It was iron, old and pitted with rust, black with age. The bow was an elaborate trefoil, the shaft thick, the teeth complex.

"What is this?" Nadia asked.

"Master key," Alicia said. "Jones Street rowhouse—original 1850s hardware. I found it in a misfiled estate box at the Historical Society, labeled 'Carlisle Property - Do Not Catalogue'."

"You stole it," Nadia said.

"I borrowed it."

"You removed an artifact from a secure archive without authorization." Nadia dropped the photo, her voice rising. "Do you understand what you did? You broke chain of custody and larceny laws. Anything we find is fruit of the poisonous tree—it gets thrown out."

"It fits the lock," Alicia said, looking at Nate. "I checked the specs. The Jones Street house never updated the hardware on the service entrance—this key opens his back door."

"No." Nadia turned to Nate. "Tell her, Nate. Tell her this is insane. We cannot walk into a private residence with a stolen key based on a theory about immortal arsonists."

Nate looked at the key resting on the 1891 deed, iron against paper.

"The dental records," Alicia said to him. "You texted me Kessler's findings. The bite marks from the 1950s cold cases match Nicole Gladman—identical dentition."

"Mimicry," Nadia countered. "A copycat who studied the files and filed their teeth to match the legend."

"Across seventy-five years?" Alicia asked. "Who commits to the bit that hard?"

"Someone who wants us to react exactly like this," Nadia said, then turned to Nate and grabbed his arm, her fingers digging into his bicep. "Nate, listen to me. This is how you lose everything. You take that key and cross that threshold—there is no coming back. You become a criminal, and you go to prison."

Nate looked at the photographs. The face in 1923 stared back at him, eyes flat and holding no light—the same eyes that had looked at him across the interrogation table, the same eyes that had watched Sarah die.

"It matches," Nate said softly. "Everything matches."

Nadia recoiled, dropping his arm as if he'd burned her. She looked at him like he was a stranger. "You are considering this."

"The signatures," Nate said, pointing with a bandaged finger. "The fires, the teeth—it's too much for coincidence, Nadia. It's a pattern."

"It is a conspiracy theory!" Nadia's voice cracked as she gestured at Alicia. "She is feeding your obsession. She isn't an agent—she is an academic with a dissertation to prove. She wants this to be real."

Alicia went rigid. "I am trying to stop a killer."

"You are handing a loaded gun to a man who is suicidal," Nadia shot back.

"He kills every fifteen years," Alicia said, her voice shaking. "Caroline Marsh, Lucy Phelps, Nicole Gladman—he isn't done. The cycle isn't finished, and if we leave, another woman dies. He needs to finish before he goes dormant."

"So we get a search warrant!" Nadia yelled. "We build a case! We do not break and enter!"

"On what grounds?" Alicia asked. "The suspect has been doing this for a hundred and thirty years? Which judge signs that warrant?"

"We find something else!" Nadia said, her voice desperate. "Tax fraud, the arson, anything that builds a case a jury will believe."

"There is no time."

"There is always time to follow the law!" Nadia turned back to Nate, her eyes desperate and pleading. "Nate, please. You are hurt, and you are grieving. You are not thinking straight. Come to D.C., and we will put surveillance on Carlisle twenty-four seven. We do this the right way."

Nate looked at the iron key, thinking about the law and the oath he had taken. The framework that separated agents from vigilantes. Then he thought about the warehouse, the smell of gasoline, the heat that blistered his skin. The interview room and the night he came to 'chat'."

Carlisle feared nothing.

He looked at Sarah's photo on the corkboard. Fifteen years ago, the law had failed her, filed her away in a cold case box, and let Carlisle sleep.

"He'll walk," Nate said.

"What?"

"If we arrest him on tax fraud, he makes bail, and he'll produce abilis for every murder. He will disappear and then do this again in another fifteen years. Or a family member will. I don't think this is a copycat." Nate looked up, meeting her eyes. "I need to stay."

The fight drained out of Nadia, replaced by a cold and terrible understanding. She saw the decision in his face.

"Okay," she said, her voice barely above a murmur.

She stepped back, smoothed her blazer, and adjusted her collar—the armor returning to its place.

"I am filing a report with Harran as soon as I land," she said, her words formal and official. "I will note that you are mentally compromised, and I will recommend suspension of your credentials and surrender of your service weapon. I'm not doing it to hurt you—I am doing it to protect you."

She walked to the bed and picked up her bag without looking at Alicia or the desk covered in impossible evidence. She walked to the door and opened it so the hallway light spilled in, harsh and white. She paused on the threshold without turning around, her knuckles white on the handle of her bag.

"I hope Sarah would think this was worth it," she said. "Because you are trading everything she would want for you for a revenge that won't bring her back."

She stepped out.

The door clicked shut.

The sound was the end of a life, the end of a career.

Silence flooded the room. The air conditioner hummed.

Alicia stood by the desk, her hands shaking. "I didn't mean to..." she started. "I didn't want to ruin..."

"Show me the rest," Nate said. "Show me everything."

He sat in the chair Nadia had vacated without looking at the door or the phone.

He reached out with his bandaged hands and picked up the iron key. It was heavy and cold against his burned skin. It felt like the truth. "And there's something I need to show you."

CHAPTER

30

THE SUSPENSION COMPLAINED over the uneven bricks of Bull Street, and short, jagged gasps came not from driving but from the scene at the Marshall House that replayed behind her eyes.

You are trading everything she would want for you.

Nadia's voice looped in her head while she checked the rearview mirror for flashing lights or federal vehicles. Just a trolley tour lumbering through the humid afternoon haze. She wasn't an agent or a cop—she was an academic who had just instigated a rogue investigation and crossed lines that would possibly end her career.

But she had seen the pattern.

She swerved into a faculty spot behind the history department and ignored the sign. Killed the engine. Sat in the ticking quiet with hands shaking and fingers finding the evidence bag in her pocket, tracing the cold, hard edges of the silver pin.

She scrambled up the steps of the restored brick building, clutching her satchel as if it held state secrets. She moved past the closed doors through a network of corridors leading to the far corner where dim light and deeper quiet reigned.

Professor Frank Brandmeyer's door stood ajar.

She stepped inside without knocking and found the office lined floor to ceiling with books that hadn't moved in decades. A fire hazard of paper, dust that danced in a single beam of light from a gap in the velvet curtains, and in the center, surrounded by teetering stacks of monographs, Frank sat hunched over his desk.

He wore a thick wool cardigan buttoned to his chin against the building's cold, even in this season. A magnifying glass was clamped in one spotted, trembling hand while he studied a document with the intensity of a diamond cutter, his nose inches from the paper.

"Frank," she said.

He didn't look up but turned a page with agonizing slowness, the paper rasping in the quiet room.

"The translation of the cylinder seal is problematic," Frank said, his voice as dry as the dust surrounding them. "The scribe used a dialect that fell out of favor fifty years prior to the dating, which suggests either a forgery or a revivalist cult."

Alicia walked to the desk, her shoes clicking on the hardwood in a modern, urgent rhythm that seemed out of place in the unchanging space. She didn't want to discuss cylinder seals.

"I need you to look at something," she said.

Frank sighed, a long rattle in his chest, and finally raised his head. His eyes, magnified to owl-like proportions behind thick bifocals, blinked at her with mild irritation.

"Alicia, I assumed you were in the archives working on the Whitfield acquisition, which is still a shambles before Thursday's board meeting."

"Forget the Whitfield acquisition."

Alicia reached into her pocket and pulled out the plastic bag, opened it, and tipped the object onto the blotter directly in front of him.

The silver pin hit the desk with a heavy, dull sound.

It sat in the pool of lamplight, barely an inch across—a stylized crest or symbol, the metal dark with a dull, matte finish that absorbed the light.

Frank adjusted his glasses and reached out with a hand of parchment and blue veins. His fingers hovered over the object, then descended. He picked it up.

Alicia watched his face, needing him to tell her it was a reproduction or a trinket, needing him to tell her she was crazy so she could go back to the hotel and apologize to Nate.

Frank turned the pin over in his fingers and tilted it toward the window.

He stopped breathing, and the faint tremor in his hand ceased. The skin of his face went slack, taking on the color of wet ash.

"Where did you get this?" His voice was thin and reedy, stripped of everything but fear.

"Evidence from a scene," Alicia said, and the lie tasted sour. "I need to know what it is."

Frank didn't answer but fumbled in a desk drawer, wood screeching against the frame, and produced a jeweler's loupe. He screwed it into his eye and brought the pin up close, his breath fogging the metal. He scrutinized the reverse side, where minute engravings were carved into the silver.

His hand shook again, the tremor starting in his fingers and traveling up his wrist until the pin vibrated in his grip.

"Frank?"

He dropped it.

The pin clattered onto the desk, and Frank pulled his hand back and tucked it into the sleeve of his cardigan as if the metal had burned him. He stared at the object while his chest rose and fell.

"Where," he repeated, looking up at her with eyes wide and stripped of their academic detachment. "Tell me exactly where this came from, Alicia, and do not lie to me."

"I told you—it's connected to the murders, and the suspect dropped it."

Frank let out a sound that was half laugh, half sob, then pushed his chair back with legs scraping the floorboards. He stood with joints popping and shuffled to the bookshelf on the far wall.

"You shouldn't touch it or keep it here," he muttered while scanning the spines, his finger tracing the bindings. He pulled down a heavy volume bound in blue cloth—*The British Museum Catalogue of Ancient Near Eastern Antiquities, 1987.*

He carried it back to the desk and let it fall open, not needing the index, and flipped through the glossy plates while tearing a page in his haste.

"Here," he said, stabbing his finger on a color plate.

Alicia leaned over his shoulder and saw a photograph showing a display case containing fragments of pottery, gold leaf, and a row of silver pins. Corroded and eaten away by four thousand years of time, but the shape was unmistakable—the crest and lettering at the edges.

"Third Dynasty of Ur, approximately 2100 BCE, excavated from the Royal Cemetery," Frank said.

He pointed to the pin on his desk, which sat next to the photograph—the one in the book a relic, the one on his desk pristine.

"It's a priest's insignia from a specific sub-order called the *Kalu* priests, who were not high clergy but chanters and lamentation singers," Frank said, his voice barely audible.

"Lamentation singers," Alicia repeated. "What does the crest mean?"

"Passage," Frank said, sitting down heavily with the energy gone from him. He took off his glasses and rubbed his eyes. "Passage into the Netherworld, the land of no return."

He looked at the pin again without touching it.

"In the texts, these priests didn't just sing for the dead but managed the boundaries," he said, his voice so low Alicia had to lean in. "The Sumerians believed the dead could be dangerous if they died violently or had no one to pour water for them, because they came back."

"Came back how?"

"As *edimmu*—wind spirits, though that's a poor translation," Frank said. "They were the hungry dead who would drain the life from the living to sustain themselves in the void."

A coldness settled deep in her bones. "Vampires."

"No," Frank said, his academic precision a reflex. "Not vampires as Hollywood understands them—a vampire is a corpse that gets up and walks, but an *edimmu* is a spirit, a ghost that gains substance through forbidden rituals."

He trailed off, his eyes on the window.

"What rituals, Frank?"

"Binding rituals from forbidden texts," he said softly. "There were rumors in the scholarship about tablets that described a way to trap an *edimmu*, not to banish it but to bind it by tying the spirit to a living vessel."

"A living vessel," Alicia said. "A human."

"A volunteer or a victim—the text isn't clear on that point," Frank said, looking at her with eyes watery and terrified. "The binding would create a creature that wasn't dead but couldn't die because the spirit would animate the flesh, keep it from aging, repair it, though the cost was hunger—an unending, insatiable hunger for the life energy it was denied."

Alicia stared at the pin while images flooded her mind—the man in the 1923 photograph, the man in the 1950 newspaper clipping, Evan Carlisle, not a descendant or a copycat but the vessel himself.

"If someone bound it, how do you unbind it?" she said, her voice steady while her legs trembled. "How do you kill it?"

Frank laughed, a harsh, dry sound. "You don't, and that's the point, Alicia—it's a closed loop where you can't kill the body because the spirit repairs it, and you can't kill the spirit because it's already dead."

"Everything dies," Alicia said. "There must be a way, a flaw."

Frank looked at the pin. "Why are you asking me this?"

"Because people are dying right now, Frank, real people," she said, placing her hands on the desk and leaning into his space. "I need to know how to stop it."

Frank hesitated, looked at the door, then opened the bottom drawer of his desk and pulled out a manila folder thick with photocopies and handwritten notes.

"I taught a seminar on Near Eastern necromancy in 1978 that was unpopular, but I kept the notes," he said.

He opened the folder, and the smell of old toner and graphite rose up while he flipped through pages of cuneiform translations.

"Here—Tablet 44, which discusses the vulnerability of the *Gallu* demons, a related class," he said. "It implies the binding requires specific elements to maintain integrity, including blood and ritual observance tied to cycles."

"Fifteen years," Alicia said.

Frank stopped and looked up at her slowly. "What did you say?"

"The cycle is fifteen years—every fifteen years, he kills."

Frank closed his eyes. "The Venus cycle from the Tablet of Ammisaduqa," he said, his voice a low rasp. "The synodic period of

Venus is 584 days, so eight years is five cycles, and fifteen years aligns with the major conjunctions—astronomical, which means he's tied to the movement of the heavens."

"How do we break the tie?"

"I don't know because the text here is fragmentary," Frank said. "It mentions 'iron of the earth' and 'water of the deep,' but the specific operational details aren't in the standard canon since the British Museum doesn't possess the ritual tablets, which the museum staff considered too dangerous and too profane."

"Someone must possess them," Alicia said. "If he's here doing this, then the instructions exist."

Frank looked at the pin again. "If this is real, then the owner has been carrying it for four thousand years, which means he isn't a collector, Alicia—he's a relic, he is the history itself."

"Who possesses the tablets, Frank?"

Frank rubbed his face with both hands while the quiet in the room felt absolute. He looked at his books, his life's work, the safe world he had built for himself, then looked at Alicia and saw the desperation she couldn't hide.

"The Ashworths," he said.

"Reggie Ashworth?"

"His grandfather, Archibald Ashworth, a shipping magnate in the 1920s who financed excavations in Iraq before the antiquities laws were tightened," Frank said. "He brought back crates of material— statuary, cylinder seals, clay tablets."

Frank stood again and walked to the window, peering through the crack in the curtains at the live oaks dripping with moss.

"Archibald never catalogued the collection because he was eccentric and claimed the tablets spoke to him," Frank said. "After he died, the family locked it all away in the estate on East Broad, and Adelaide Ashworth runs the trust now, letting scholars in occasionally if they grovel."

"Do they possess the binding texts?"

"Archibald thought so," Frank said. "He wrote a letter to the society in 1928 claiming he had found the 'Key to Life,' though we assumed he meant a metaphor or possibly syphilis."

Frank turned back to the desk and picked up a pen, scribbling a name and a phone number on a scrap of paper. He didn't hand it to her.

"Dr. Landry," he said, and the title was a reminder of the world she was leaving behind. "If you go to the Ashworths and find these texts, you are looking for something that defies natural law—you are looking for a way to kill something that has survived empires."

"I know."

"Do you?" Frank's eyes were wet. "The myths say the *edimmu* doesn't just take blood but takes your fate and erases you." He picked up the pin one last time and weighed it in his palm. "This object feels heavy, heavier than silver should be."

He set it down and pushed the scrap of paper across the desk.

Alicia snatched the paper and grabbed the pin, shoving it back into the plastic bag and into her pocket. The absence of the object seemed to make the room lighter.

"Thank you, Frank."

"Don't thank me," he said, pulling the cardigan tighter and picking up his magnifying glass while his world shrank back to the document on his desk. "I didn't see you today, and this conversation never happened."

Alicia turned to the door.

"One more thing," Frank said.

She paused with her hand on the frame.

"The texts say the binding can only be broken by completing the cycle or by an intervention that meets specific ritual requirements," Frank said, his eyes fixed on the document. "Requirements I am not sure even the ancient priests fully understood."

He looked up then, and the fear in his face was absolute.

"You need a weapon, Alicia, but according to the lore, the weapon isn't sufficient on its own—you need the right hand to hold it."

"What does that mean?"

"I don't know," Frank said. "But be careful whose hand you choose."

Alicia nodded once and stepped into the hallway, the door clicking shut behind her. She walked fast with her heels clacking on the linoleum, clutching the scrap of paper like a map while the pin in her pocket felt like proof of something impossible.

She pushed through the exterior doors and fished her phone from her bag as she ran toward the car. The signal bars flickered while she dialed Nate's number.

It rang once.

"Holloway." His voice was flat.

"I found something—a name, the Ashworths," Alicia said, sliding into the driver's seat of the Corolla.

A pause stretched between them.

"Grab your gear," she said, turning the key in the ignition. "I'm coming back."

CHAPTER

31

THE ENGINE of the Toyota Corolla ticked in the silence of East Broad Street. Heat radiated off the asphalt, distorting the air above the hood in waves that made the world look liquid and unstable. Alicia Landry's palms were slick against the steering wheel, her fingers cramping. She took a breath that tasted of exhaust and humid decay. Beside her, Nate Holloway stared out the window at the house.

The Greek Revival house was dying. Paint peeled from the columns in long strips, revealing grey wood beneath. Resurrection ferns choked the live oaks in the front yard, heavy and brown in the dry heat, waiting for rain to turn them green again. Palmettos grew wild along the foundation, their fronds scraping against the brick like dry fingers.

"Ready?" Nate asked, though he didn't look ready. He held himself like he was waiting for a loud noise. He adjusted his suit jacket, checking the concealment of his weapon, then winced as the fabric brushed his bandaged hands.

"I have the citations." Alicia patted her satchel. "If they ask, it's a comparative study on nineteenth-century acquisition practices."

"If they ask, I'm federal law enforcement conducting an inquiry." Nate's voice had the flat authority of a man who'd used that line before. "Let me be the bad guy. You just find the clay."

They got out of the car. Alicia smoothed her skirt, wishing she had worn something more authoritative than a cardigan and a blouse that stuck to her back. They walked up the cracked pavement of the walkway where weeds grew through the fissures in the concrete.

Before they could reach the door, it swung open.

Reginald Ashworth III stood in the entryway wearing a seersucker suit that had been fashionable in 1980 and hadn't been cleaned since. Broken capillaries spiderwebbed across his nose and cheeks, his eyes watery and indistinct. He held a crystal tumbler filled with amber liquid that caught the morning light. It was eleven o'clock.

"Visitors!" His voice was wet and broad, filling the doorway. He swayed, catching himself on the doorframe. "Saw you pull up. Not often we get the law and the... well, whatever you are." He gestured with the glass, splashing bourbon onto the heart pine floorboards. "Come in. Come in out of the infernal damp."

They stepped into the foyer, where the air was cooler but heavy with a smell Alicia recognized from a hundred neglected archives—dust, old paper, wet dog, and, underneath it all, the acrid tang of gin and expensive whiskey.

"Reginald Ashworth," he said, extending a hand that felt damp and boneless when Alicia shook it. "But everyone calls me Reggie, except my sister, who calls me a disappointment." He laughed, a hacking sound that ended in a cough. "You're here for the collection? Grandfather's little treasures?"

"We are." Alicia straightened her shoulders. "I'm Dr. Landry, and this is Agent Holloway. We spoke on the phone."

"Of course, the scholars and the feds." Reggie turned, nearly tripping over a corner of a Persian rug that had been worn threadbare. He led them down a hallway that felt more like a tunnel. "Grandfather Archibald was a pirate, you know—a gentleman pirate. Went to Iraq in the twenties before the laws got all fussy. Brought back crates and crates!"

The hallway was a claustrophobic nightmare. Taxidermy heads—deer, boar, something that looked like an ibex—lined the walls, their glass eyes coated in a grey film. Cardboard boxes were stacked waist-high against the wainscoting. Alicia read the Sharpie scrawl on one: *Kitchen 1994*.

"He dug them up himself, or paid locals to do it—same thing really-ly." Reggie took a long pull from his glass. "Said the desert spoke to him. Said the clay tablets were hotter than the sand."

He stopped abruptly. A woman stood in the doorway of the parlor, blocking their path.

Adelaide Ashworth was sixty, all angles and tailored precision in a dress that cost more than Alicia's car. Her grey hair was pulled back so tightly that it pulled at the corners of her eyes. She looked at Reggie with exhausted contempt, then turned her attention to Nate with an expression both pointed and diagnostic.

"Reggie." Her voice was brittle. "Go to the kitchen. You've spilled on your lapel again."

Reggie looked down, brushed at his suit, and mumbled something about hydration. He drifted past her, disappearing into the shadows of the rear house.

Adelaide folded her arms and stayed planted in the doorway. "Federal Bureau of Investigation." It wasn't a question. "And a historian. An odd pairing for a social call."

Nate stepped forward and pulled his credentials from his jacket pocket, holding them up so the gold badge caught the dim light. "Not a social call, Ms. Ashworth. We need to examine specific items in your grandfather's collection, as we discussed on the phone."

"You discussed it with Reggie." Adelaide's tone could have etched glass. "Reggie would agree to a tour from the IRS if they brought a bottle. Why does the FBI care about clay tablets from Ur?"

Alicia stepped in. This was the pivot point. "It's about the homicide investigation, Ms. Ashworth. The ritualistic elements found at the crime scenes have historical antecedents. We believe the perpetrator is mimicking specific Mesopotamian motifs, and we need to verify the accuracy of the symbology to build a profile."

It was a good lie—close enough to the truth to hold water, academic enough to be boring.

Adelaide's eyes narrowed as she studied Alicia's satchel, then Nate's bandaged hands. "Mimicking motifs. You think a killer in Savannah is copying Sumerian artifacts that have been sitting in my library for eighty years?"

"We think he has access to specialized knowledge." Nate's voice dropped an octave, becoming the heavy, flat tone of authority. "We're trying to rule out connections. Unless you'd prefer we subpoena the collection logs? That takes time. It attracts press. I assumed you wanted to handle this quietly."

Adelaide's attention flickered from Nate's face to the chaotic hallway behind them, to the crates stamped *Basra*. A muscle in her jaw tightened. The Ashworth name was a fragile thing in this decaying house.

"Thirty minutes." She stepped aside, smoothing her skirt. "You have thirty minutes, and you do not remove anything. You do not break anything. If you damage a single seal, I will have you investigated, and you will be unemployable."

She pointed to a set of double doors at the end of the hall. "The library. Don't let Reggie in there. He knocks things over."

"Thank you." Alicia kept her voice neutral.

They walked past her, and Alicia felt the woman's attention on her back, pointed like a needle. They pushed open the heavy oak doors and stepped into the library.

The room was massive, with ceilings that soared twenty feet high, lined with built-in bookshelves that were sagging under the weight of books, papers, and random debris. The air here was thicker, heavy with the sweet, cloying scent of dry rot and mildew. There was no climate control. For a collection of organic materials and clay, it was a death sentence.

"Jesus." Nate kept his voice low.

The floor was a maze of wooden crates stamped with *Basra* and *Baghdad*, sitting open on the Persian carpet with packing straw spilling out like entrails. Fragments of stone statuary—hands, feet, the bearded face of a lamassu—lay wrapped in yellowed newspapers from the 1920s.

Alicia pulled a pair of white cotton gloves from her pocket and snapped them on. "Start looking. We need the tablets—flat, rectangular shapes, grey or reddish clay, dense writing."

She moved to a sideboard on the left wall, piled high with ceramics. She lifted a bowl carefully, and beneath it lay a stack of tablets piled like cheap coasters. Her heart hammered against her ribs. Any one of these could be four thousand years old, and they were treating them like junk mail.

She scanned the first stack—receipt tablets, grain tallies, administrative text. She knew the shape of the cuneiform for 'barley' and 'sheep' better than she knew her own phone number.

"Is this it?" Nate called from near the fireplace.

Alicia navigated the maze of crates. Nate was shining his flashlight into a wooden box where rows of cylinder seals were packed in sawdust.

"No, those are signatures." She shook her head. "Keep looking."

She moved to a large mahogany desk in the center of the room, its surface covered in maps and correspondence. Under a brass lamp that looked like it hadn't been turned on since the Depression, a smaller box sat waiting—a cigar box.

She opened it.

Inside lay a single broken tablet, roughly four inches by six inches, the clay dark and dense, the edges crumbling into reddish dust. The surface was covered in script so tight and precise it looked like machine work.

Alicia pulled out her phone and opened the photo gallery, scrolling to the auction record Frank had found—*Lot 404. Excavated Ur, 1922. Unclassified Ritual Text.* She held the phone up to the tablet. The break pattern on the top left corner matched, and the density of the text matched.

"I found it." Her voice trembled.

Nate was at her side in seconds, setting a portable LED evidence light on the desk, angling the beam across the surface of the clay. The shadows threw the cuneiform wedges into relief.

"Is that it?"

"It's the right era—Ur III period. The script is distinct." Alicia propped her phone against a bust of a Confederate general that sat on the corner of the desk and tapped the FaceTime icon.

The screen swirled, then resolved into the pixelated face of Frank Brandmeyer, who looked frail, hunched over his own notes in his university office.

"Frank, I'm looking at it."

"Show me." His voice came through tinny and distorted.

Alicia switched the camera view and held the phone steady over the tablet, moving it slowly so the light caught the depth of the impressions.

"The preservation is... nonexistent." Frank leaned closer to his screen. "The salt damage is extensive. Hold it steady, Alicia. Go to the top register."

"Translating now." Alicia leaned in, her eyes tracing the wedges. "It starts with an invocation—*Dingir*, a god sign, but it's reversed."

"A curse formula. Read the next line."

"To bind the shadow to the flesh of the..." Alicia stumbled over the complex grammar. "*Lu*? Man?"

"No, look at the determinative." Frank's tone sharpened. "It's not just man. It's *living* man—a willing vessel. Keep going."

Nate stood guard at the door, watching the hallway, but his eyes kept darting back to the clay.

Alicia moved her finger to the center of the tablet, hovering inches above the surface. "Here. There's a proper noun—two signs."

Frank squinted at the screen. "*Na-ram*—the cherished one. *E-kur* —House of the Mountain, or Netherworld. Naram-Ekur."

"Naram-Ekur." Alicia wrote it down in her notebook, underlining it twice. The ink bled slightly on the paper. The True Name, the name Carlisle had hidden for four thousand years.

"The text describes the binding." Frank's voice picked up speed. "It says the *edimmu* cannot cross the river—it has already crossed. It dwells in borrowed flesh. To sustain the binding, it requires tributaries."

"The cycle. Does it mention the time?"

"Lower left quadrant—the astronomical notation."

Alicia shifted the phone. "The Star of Inanna. Venus. Five cycles of three years, fifteen years total."

"It matches." The word came out of Nate heavy and certain. "It's the manual. It's exactly what he's been doing."

"The weapon." Alicia's pulse quickened. "Frank, look at the bottom edge—the destruction clause."

"Yes, it specifies the iron—*Bar-gal*, iron from the rock, not the sky. Bloomery iron. It must be birthed from fire, not alloyed. And quenched in water blessed by the name—water that hears the truth."

"And the wielder?" Nate asked. "Who has to use it?"

Frank hesitated. "The text is poetic here. It uses a metaphor—*Shu-nam-tar*, the Hand of Fate? No, that's not right. *Shu-mut*—the Hand of Death."

"Hand of Death." Nate let the words hang in the air. "What does that mean, an executioner?"

"It's ambiguous." Frank adjusted his glasses. "In the Ur III legal codes, it often referred to the King's justice or a soldier—someone authorized to kill, someone with lethal intent."

Nate nodded, staring at his bandaged hands. "Law enforcement. A justified kill. That fits."

Alicia moved the light to the right side of the tablet, where the clay was badly eroded, the surface flaking away in red scales. "Frank, there's more here—a secondary clause. It talks about the sustenance, the tributaries."

Frank leaned closer to his camera. "The binding endures through two streams, two types of blood."

Alicia's stomach turned over. "What types?"

"*Nig-sagg-ga*—treasures, vessels of beauty. That's the sustenance, the blonde women who feed the flesh."

"And the second?"

Frank was silent for a long moment. "*Nig-kug*—sanctified things, vessels of religious authority."

"Religious authority?" Alicia asked. "Like a king?"

"No, the context is clerical—*Sanga*, a priest, an administrator of the temple." Frank's voice dropped. "The text says, 'He who serves the death gods must consume he who serves the life gods. Priest must take priest, lest the binding weaken.'"

The room went cold, and the humidity seemed to vanish, replaced by a chill that started in Alicia's marrow.

Nate stepped away from the door, his face grey. "A religious figure—someone who serves a spiritual role."

"Not just any religious figure." Alicia's mind raced, connecting dots she hadn't known were there. "The pattern specifies consecrated authority—someone recognized by their community, a spiritual leader."

"In modern terms..." Nate's voice trailed off.

"A priest, a rabbi, an imam."

Nate pulled his phone from his pocket, his hands shaking so hard he almost dropped it. He tapped the screen, bringing up the victim profiles. "All the blonde women—Caroline, Lucy, Nicole, Sarah—they were food, just fuel."

"Frank, is there a timing requirement?" Alicia's voice was urgent. "When does he take the priest?"

"Look at the notation—the moon sign." Frank pointed to a damaged glyph near the edge. "It's cyclical. The consecrated vessel isn't taken randomly. It's the capstone, one of the last two. Before the binding can renew for another cycle, the priest must consume the priest."

"Are you finished?" The voice cut through the room like a whip.

Adelaide Ashworth stood in the doorway with a phone in her hand, her thumb hovering over the screen. Her face was tight with suspicion. "I said thirty minutes, and you have been in here for thirty-five." Her words were clipped. "And you are filming. I told you no recordings."

Nate lowered his phone without looking at her, his attention fixed on the tablet, his jaw set. The color had drained from his face, but when he spoke to Adelaide, his voice was steady. "Ms. Ashworth, we're not finished."

"You are." Adelaide took a step into the room. "I am calling my lawyer. You are trespassing. Get out."

Nate moved into her personal space without touching her, but the threat was physical. "If you call your lawyer, I will call the US Attorney. I will designate this entire house a federal crime scene. I will have a forensic team in here with evidence vacuums and chainsaws within the hour, and they will seize every crate, every paper, every piece of silver."

Adelaide flinched and stepped back, her hand dropping to her side.

"You have uncatalogued antiquities of dubious provenance." Nate's voice was low and dangerous. "Do you have the import licenses from

1922? Do you have the customs declarations? Because if we seize this collection, Ms. Ashworth, we will audit it, and I suspect we will find enough violations to keep you in court for the rest of your natural life."

Adelaide went pale, her eyes darting to the messy piles of crates, the legacy of a grandfather who didn't follow rules.

"Take your pictures and get out." She turned and marched down the hall, her heels hammering the floor like judgments.

"Quickly." Alicia grabbed a sheet of archival paper and a charcoal stick from her bag, laying the paper over the tablet. She rubbed the charcoal gently over the surface, the dark image of the cuneiform emerging like a ghost. "Got it."

She peeled the paper back and took three more high-resolution photos, catching the angles Frank had pointed out.

"Frank, we're leaving." She spoke to the phone. "I'll email the files."

"Be careful." Frank's voice was thin. "That clause about the wielder... be careful."

She killed the call and shoved the notebook and the rubbing into her satchel. She looked at the tablet one last time—the small, broken piece of clay that had sentenced so many women to death. It looked innocuous, just mud and time.

"Let's go."

They walked out of the library, down the tunnel of taxidermy, past the open door of the kitchen where Reggie was singing to himself. They didn't stop to say goodbye.

They burst out the front door into the blinding Savannah afternoon. The sun glared off the white hoods of passing cars.

They got into the Corolla. The interior was an oven, and Alicia threw her satchel into the back seat before gripping the wheel, her hands slippery with sweat and charcoal dust.

"We know." She started the engine, and the A/C blasted hot air into their faces. "We know what he is. We know his name. We know the rules."

Nate didn't answer. He stared through the windshield at the

peeling columns of the Ashworth house, then looked down at his bandaged hands and flexed them slowly.

Alicia pulled away from the curb, and the house receded in the rearview mirror, leaving them with the terrible weight of the truth.

CHAPTER

32

THE COROLLA's tires shrieked against the hot asphalt of Montgomery Street. Nate Holloway shoved the door open before the vehicle stopped moving, his dress shoes slapping the pavement. The midday heat wrapped around him, a thick weight that smelled of exhaust and ozone.

Alicia shouted something from the driver's seat, but he didn't hear it. His vision tunneled, the world dissolving at the edges until only the wide-open double doors of the First African Baptist Church remained. Rodekker had phoned him minutes after he and Alicia left the Ashworth Estate.

He took the stairs two at a time, his lungs burning with the ghost of old smoke. The bandages on his hands throbbed, a dull pulse in time with his heart, and he burst through the threshold and froze.

The transition from the brutal, bleaching glare of the Savannah sun to the cool, polished gloom of the sanctuary was a physical shock. His eyes fought to adjust while the air inside displaced the smell of the city —lemon oil, old hymnals, and the sharp, copper-penny scent of blood.

Silence pressed in, so heavy his ears rang. Somewhere in the back, a woman wept in a low, rhythmic sound that could only be Daisy Adams, the secretary who had arrived early for choir practice.

Nate stepped onto the runner carpet of the center aisle. High above, the stained glass windows depicting the Underground Railroad cast long, geometric shapes of color across the hardwood floor. He moved down the aisle, his footsteps striking the floor with a violence that violated the sanctuary's hush, eyes locked on the raised platform where the shadows gathered.

Ten feet from the steps, he stopped.

Reverend James Oden lay on his back on the stairs leading to the pulpit, positioned as if ascending, as if he had simply lain down to rest on his way to preach. His black clerical robes were straightened, the fabric falling in clean, heavy folds around his legs, and his arms were crossed over his chest, left over right.

Four white pillar candles stood on the steps around him, forming a perfect square at the cardinal points. The wicks were unlit.

Nate stared at the white clerical collar that was no longer white but a deep, wet crimson.

Nothing remained of the throat—not a cut but a ruin. Tissue torn away to expose the spinal column, the cartilage of the trachea shredded beyond recognition. The wound gaped like a dark mouth screaming silently at the church ceiling.

Nate looked at the floor beneath the body where the polished hardwood shone without a pool, without spray. A human body held five liters of blood, and Oden's throat had been opened wide, sufficient to drain it all in seconds.

The floor was clean.

The strength went out of his legs, and he locked his knees, forcing himself upright. The images of the blonde women flashed in his mind, their bodies arranged just like this, the positioning identical, the geometry precise.

The vibration of his phone in his pocket was a jolt. He pulled it out with hands that wouldn't stop shaking, the bandages making him clumsy as he swiped the screen, bringing up the notes Alicia had sent from the car.

The Ashworth tablet translation.

Priest must take priest.

He looked at the text, then at the body.

Lest the binding weaken.

It wasn't rage or retaliation. He had built his entire profile on the idea that the killer feared exposure, that Carlisle hunted in the shadows. Oden was a public figure in a crowded church that didn't fit the victimology.

But Oden fit the tablet.

This was the capstone—the blonde women were fuel, the batteries that kept the creature running. But the cycle couldn't close without the final piece, without the sacred authority.

A side door banged open.

Detective Karl Rodecker stumbled into the sanctuary, looking ten years older than he had yesterday. His shirt was soaked through with sweat, dark patches spreading under his arms and down his back as he ripped his sunglasses off and stopped at the edge of the pews.

He saw the body.

Rodecker made a wet, choking noise in his throat and braced a hand against the back of a pew, knuckles turning white. He stared at the candles, then at the crossed arms.

"Christ," Rodecker whispered, his voice thin in the quiet hall. "Don't tell me."

Nate didn't turn because he couldn't take his eyes off the clean floor. "It's the ritual."

Rodecker walked up the side aisle, moving like a man wading through deep water. He stopped next to Nate, wiping sweat from his eyes with the back of his hand before looking at Oden's face. The Reverend's eyes were closed, and he looked peaceful, except for the devastation below his chin.

"He went on TV," Rodecker said. "Called the guy out—this is a message."

"No," Nate said.

"Look at him, Nate—displayed in his own church."

"Not a message," Nate said, his voice flat, stripped of all inflection as he held up the phone. "A requirement."

Rodecker looked at the screen, then at Nate with widening eyes. "What?"

"This tablet," Nate said, pointing to the translation. "The text from 2100 BC specifies two victim types—*Vessels of beauty* and *Vessels of sacred authority*. The blondes sustain the binding, but to renew it, to go dormant again, he needs a priest."

Rodecker stared at him, the skin of his face turning grey and clammy. "You're saying he didn't kill him because he was loud, but because—"

"Because he was holy," Nate said. "Oden made himself a target, not by speaking out but by being what Carlisle needed to make the ritual complete."

Nate stepped into Rodecker's personal space, where the scent of fear and old sweat rolled off the detective. He shoved the phone toward him.

"Pull the records," Nate said.

"What?"

"Death records from Chatham County—1995, 1980, 1965. Look for clergy: priests, ministers, rabbis, anyone who died within weeks of the last blonde victim being found."

Rodecker blinked, then looked at the body on the steps. "You think he's been killing preachers for a hundred years?"

"Not alongside the women," Nate said, looking back at the altar. "After them—it's the final act, the period at the end of the sentence. Check the causes of death: heart attacks, strokes, falls, anything that looked natural, anything that could get signed off on without an autopsy."

Rodecker pulled a notebook from his pocket, but his hands shook so hard he dropped his pen. It clattered on the hardwood with a sound like a gunshot. He stooped to pick it up, his breath coming in short, shallow gasps.

"If that's true," Rodecker said, straightening up, "then we never had a chance—we were guarding the wrong people."

"I was guarding the wrong people," Nate corrected.

Footsteps approached from the main entrance, slow and measured.

Dr. Darnell Washington walked down the center aisle with his black medical bag in one hand. He wore his white lab coat over a dress shirt and a checkered bow tie, but didn't look at the stained glass or the architecture. He looked only at the man on the steps.

Darnell stopped beside them and set the bag down gently. He didn't speak to Nate or acknowledge Rodecker but walked up the first two steps and knelt beside the body.

He reached out, his long, gloved fingers hovering over Oden's shoulder before touching the fabric of the robe. Not an examination— a greeting.

"James," Darnell whispered.

Nate watched the medical examiner and saw the tremor in the man's jaw. Darnell Washington had performed four thousand autopsies, had seen bodies pulled from rivers and fires, and cataloged death in every conceivable form. But this wasn't a body—this was his pastor.

Darnell took a breath, composing his face into a mask of professional detachment, though his eyes remained wet behind his glasses. He tilted Oden's head back slightly.

"Exsanguination," Darnell said, his voice steady but thin. "Complete vascular collapse—the carotid and jugular are gone. The tissue avulsion is identical to Marsh and Phelps."

He pointed to the edge of the wound.

"Scalloped impressions," Darnell said. "Four-centimeter arc, uniform spacing—it's the same mouth."

He looked at the floor and ran a gloved finger over the polished wood, which came away clean.

"No pooling," Darnell said. "Five liters gone—he didn't bleed out here. He was drained."

Nate turned away because he couldn't look at the wound anymore. He walked in a small, tight circle near the front pew, running a hand over his short hair and gripping the back of his neck, where the skin was hot.

"You didn't know," Rodecker said. "You didn't possess the tablet."

"I'm the watchman," Nate said, looking at the stained glass window, at the image of escaping slaves following the North Star. "He quoted Ezekiel to me—*If the watchman see the sword come, and blow not the trumpet... his blood will I require at the watchman's hand.*"

He looked at his bandaged hands.

"I didn't blow the trumpet," Nate said.

"Nate," Rodecker started.

A sound cut him off—a low vibration in the floorboards that grew into a discordant, human cry. It wasn't traffic or wind but wailing, and it was getting louder.

Nate turned toward the vestibule where the glass doors separating the sanctuary from the entrance framed the bright world outside.

"Is that Luke?" Darnell asked as he stood, stripping off his gloves.

"Yeah," Roddecker said, walking to the glass doors. "That's Luke."

Through the glass, Nate saw the street where the crowd had gathered. Luke Oden, the Reverend's younger brother, stood on the sidewalk with his face contorted, shouting, tears streaming down his cheeks. Behind him, dozens of people pressed against the police tape, and the sound penetrated the thick brick walls—a chorus of grief from a city that had been pushed too far.

The sun reached its peak, burning away the shadows. One moment, Nate was in the cool silence of the church, and the next, he was on the hot pavement outside, everything exposed in harsh, unforgiving light.

The crowd had swelled from dozens to hundreds, possibly a thousand. A sea of people spilled off the sidewalks, blocking the intersection of Montgomery and Broughton.

Tactical units were staging two blocks down—Nate saw the black armored truck, the riot gear ready to deploy. This wasn't a homicide investigation anymore, but containment.

The chop of rotor blades beat the air as news helicopters circled overhead, their cameras trained on the church.

"Justice!" someone screamed. "We want justice!"

Luke Oden stood on the steps of the courthouse across the square, holding a megaphone. His voice cracked, distorted over the amplifier, but the rage was clear and undeniable.

"They watched him die!" Luke yelled. "They knew—he told them, and they let it happen!"

Nate stood just inside the yellow tape where the accusations hit like physical blows. They were right.

Three black SUVs pulled up to the curb, forcing the crowd back. The doors opened, and Mayor Thompson stepped out, adjusting his tie, his face a mask of grave seriousness. Beside him, Councilwoman Moffett emerged with her helmet-perfect hair. Chief Dean followed.

They walked to a podium that had been set up near the police line. Microphones waited, and the press pool surged forward.

Nate watched from ten yards away and saw Dean lean in to

whisper to the Mayor, saw the Mayor's quick, sharp nod—a decision made.

Dean stepped to the microphone, raising his hands for silence. The crowd quieted, but the tension hummed in the air like static.

"This is a dark day for Savannah," Dean said, his voice practiced and somber. "Reverend Oden was a pillar of this community, a voice for the voiceless."

He paused, looking directly into the news cameras.

"I want to assure the citizens of this city," Dean continued, "that the Savannah-Chatham Metropolitan Police Department, in conjunction with our federal partners, is working tirelessly. We identified a suspect."

Nate stiffened.

"We possess evidence," Dean said, "linking a specific individual to the murders of Caroline Marsh, Nicole Gladman, Lucy Phelps, and now Reverend Oden. This individual inserted himself into the investigation, sought attention, created a panic to feed his own need for notoriety."

Nate looked at Rodecker near the bumper of a patrol car. The detective had taken off his sunglasses, and his eyes met Nate's.

Rodecker gave a slight shake of his head, a grimace of disgust.

"We anticipate an arrest is imminent," the Mayor added, leaning into the mic. "We will possess this predator off our streets by tonight."

The crowd cheered because they wanted a monster, and the city was giving them one—a homeless veteran with PTSD, a man who couldn't defend himself—a scapegoat.

The heat seemed to vanish from Nate's skin as the noise of the crowd, the whir of the cameras, the politicians' voices—it all became sharp, unnaturally clear.

He looked at the politicians in their expensive suits, at the riot police gripping their batons, at the church where Oden's body still lay on the steps—the final offering to a creature that had been eating this city for a hundred and thirty years.

The system wasn't broken but was working as designed. It existed to protect the status quo, to keep the tourists coming and the hotels full. If that meant feeding an innocent man to the machine to cover up the impossible, the machine would do it without blinking.

Nate turned his back on the podium and the church.

He walked toward the edge of the crowd, pushing through the press of bodies, ignoring the shouts and the questions. He didn't look at Dean or the cameras.

There was no law here, not for this.

Nate Holloway walked away from the scene, away from the job, away from the man he was supposed to be.

CHAPTER

33

Fifteen people occupied a space designed for eight in the SCMPD conference room. Nate Holloway leaned against the back wall, his arms crossed to shield his bandaged hands. A dull, rhythmic ache throbbed from the burns, a pulse of pain that grounded him while the world dissolved into political theater. The conference room was a blur of grey suits and sweat stains, and his eyes burned from the fluorescent glare.

Chief Harold Dean sat at the head of the mahogany table, his suit jacket draped over his chair, his tie loosened around an unbuttoned collar. Sweat beaded on his forehead and upper lip, catching the harsh light, and he wiped it away with a handkerchief already damp and grey. His gaze stayed fixed on the table in front of him, refusing to meet the eyes of his detectives.

Two sixty-inch screens dominated the far wall, emitting a low hum that vibrated in the teeth.

On the left screen, Mayor Thompson's face filled the frame, red and distorted, his mouth open in a shout that the muted volume turned into a tinny, crackling stream of noise.

On the right, the air-conditioned silence of FBI Headquarters in Washington, D.C., offered a sharp counterpoint. Assistant Director Jeff Harran and Deputy Director Margaret Gardner sat in a room of glass and steel, their climate perfectly controlled, looking cool and distant like auditors reviewing a failed investment.

Gardner spoke, her voice crisp and clear through the speakers, cutting the humid air.

"We have reviewed the preliminary reports regarding the warehouse incident," she said, looking directly into the camera lens at Nate.

Nate held her gaze without blinking.

"The breach was unauthorized," Gardner continued, her tone flat and stripped of inflection. "The endangerment of local law enforcement personnel was extreme, and the intelligence leading to the breach was, based on our review, speculative at best."

Rodecker sat halfway down the table, staring at the wood grain while he dug his thumbs into his temples, the skin turning white as if trying to physically push a headache out of his skull.

"We also have concerning reports regarding your methodology, Agent Holloway," Gardner said, her words clipped and precise. "Communications from Agent Lopez indicate a loss of objectivity and a fixation on historical anomalies that do not align with Bureau profiling standards."

Nate's crossed arms tightened, the fabric of his shirt scraping against the gauze on his palms. *Nadia. She filed it.* The thought was cold and sharp in his chest, but he shoved it down because there was no room for it here.

Beside him, Pierce vibrated with barely contained fury, her heels coming off the floor, her weight shifting to her toes, ready to launch across the mahogany. She opened her mouth to speak.

Nate nudged her boot with his own in warning.

"The Bureau cannot support a rogue investigation," Gardner said, each word landing with bureaucratic finality. "One that produces casualties without results and draws connections to the 2010 case based on what we can only categorize as emotional projection."

Dean cleared his throat, a wet sound that filled the room, then stood and placed his palms flat on the sticky table. He addressed the screen with the Mayor, turning his shoulder to Nate and the other detectives as if he could hide from their judgment.

"We understand the Bureau's position," Dean said, his voice carrying the hollow ring of surrender. "And we agree that a new direction is necessary, given the complications of the current narrative. The public is scared and seeing patterns they don't understand."

"They see bodies," the Mayor's voice crackled through the speakers like breaking static. "They see a dead preacher on the news, and they're canceling hotel reservations. Fix it, Harold. Fix it today."

Dean nodded, wiping his face again with the soaked handkerchief. "We believe we are dealing with a copycat," he said, and the lie slid out greased with desperation. "Someone inspired by the local legends, a disturbed individual mimicking the folklore to gain notoriety, which explains the similarities to historical cases without suggesting institutional failure."

Councilwoman Patty Moffett sat to Dean's right with her fingers flying across a tablet. The blue light illuminated her face, but she didn't look up from the screen.

"We can work with that," Moffett said without stopping her typing, the words mechanical and efficient. "A copycat implies a singular, containable threat and removes the suggestion of a serial predator operating unchecked for decades. 'The Savannah Mimic.' We can spin that narrative because it suggests the danger is novel, not chronic."

Russell Bennett, from the District Attorney's office, leaned back in his chair and tapped a gold pen against the table. He checked the time on a watch that cost more than Booker Hayes would earn in ten lifetimes.

"The narrative matters less than the resolution," Bennett said, his tone carrying the cold calculation of a man who measured human suffering in economic projections. "We have the Savannah Music Festival opening in four days with projected revenue of twelve million dollars, and cancellations are already ticking up. If we don't have a suspect in custody within twenty-four hours, the economic impact will be catastrophic."

Bennett stopped tapping and pointed the pen at the whiteboard where photos of Caroline Marsh, Nicole Gladman, Lucy Phelps, and Reverend Oden stared back with dead eyes.

"We need a name," Bennett said. "We need a face. And we need it now."

The room fell quiet, the hum of the projector seeming to grow louder as the heat pressed in and the air grew thick.

Dean looked at his notes, shifting his weight from foot to foot, his eyes searching the room for anything except the faces of Pierce or Rodecker.

"There is a name," Dean said, his voice low and rough. "Someone who has been present at multiple scenes, someone with a documented history of mental instability, someone who inserted himself into the investigation."

Nate went still because he knew what was coming, had seen the machinery gearing up for this since the arrest at the church.

"Booker Hayes," Dean said.

Pierce pushed off the wall and stepped into the light. "No."

Dean flinched but kept his eyes on the table like a coward.

"Booker Hayes is a witness," Pierce said, her voice shaking with the effort to keep it level and professional. "He called me to warn us about the warehouse, found Nicole because he was looking for her when we weren't, and he didn't kill anyone."

Bennett turned his chair to face her, a small and dismissive smile on his lips that made Nate's hands curl into fists. "He placed himself at the scenes, Detective, and 'found' the bodies, which is textbook injection behavior according to every profile of killers who help the search party."

"He's a homeless veteran with PTSD who barely has shoes," Pierce shot back, slamming her hand on the back of an empty chair. "You think he orchestrated a complex ritual murder inside a locked church and staged these scenes without leaving a trace?"

"He has the motivation," Bennett countered, leaning forward with the confidence of a man who had never been wrong because he'd never faced consequences. "Relevance. He wants to be important, so he creates a villain—this 'Mr. Evan'—and then tries to be the hero who stops him. When no one listens, he escalates."

"That's bullshit," Pierce said, the profanity sharp in the formal space. "We have physical evidence from the warehouse and a link to Carlisle."

"You have a burned-out building and a dead end," Gardner's voice cut in from D.C., cold and clinical. "The Bureau has reviewed the file on Hayes, and his psychological profile is consistent with delusion and deflection. He creates a fantasy suspect to mask his own culpability, and a wealthy white man who leaves no evidence is a classic projection of powerlessness."

Gardner's voice filled the room with the weight of institutional authority, the voice of an organization deciding what was true regardless of the facts.

"He fits the profile, Detective," Gardner said, ticking off the points like a prosecutor. "He is transient. He is unstable. He is violent. And most importantly, he is there."

Nate watched Gardner on the screen, her calm face a mask of bureaucratic certainty, then looked at Harran sitting silently beside her. They didn't care about the truth or justice or Booker Hayes as a human being. They cared about the file, about closing the loop, and Booker Hayes fit the box while Evan Carlisle did not. Therefore, Booker Hayes was the killer.

Moffett looked up from her tablet, her expression calculating. "The public will understand this," she said, already drafting the press release in her mind. "A tragedy involving a mentally ill veteran is sad but understandable, and it doesn't scare the tourists the way a phantom does. It resolves the fear."

"It's a lie," Pierce said, turning to Dean with desperation bleeding into her voice. "Chief. You know this is a lie. You saw the wounds. You saw the precision."

Dean picked up his water glass with a hand that shook, the ice clinking against the side in an irregular rhythm. He took a sip, set it down with deliberate care, then looked at Pierce with empty eyes.

"The Mayor wants this closed," Dean said quietly, each word an admission of defeat. "The city needs this closed."

"At the cost of an innocent man?" Pierce asked.

Bennett leaned forward, his gold pen spinning between his fingers. "He's not innocent. He's convenient. And right now, convenience is what saves this city."

The Mayor's face on the screen turned a deeper shade of purple, his jowls shaking with rage. The audio crackled. "Enough debate!" he shouted, spittle probably flying on his end of the connection. "I want an arrest! I want a press conference at five o'clock! Do your jobs!"

Dean closed his eyes for a second, took a breath that sounded like surrender, then opened them with the last of the detective gone and only the politician remaining.

"Draw up the papers," Dean said to Rodecker, his voice flat and administrative. "Bring me everything—the proximity timeline, the witness statements, the psychological evaluation recommending a competency assessment. We charge him tonight."

"Chief," Rodecker said, his first words of the meeting, his voice like gravel grinding. "Don't do this."

"It's done, Karl," Dean said, standing to gather his jacket. "It's done."

Pierce stepped forward, her body coiled and ready, looking like she might grab Dean by the lapels and shake sense into him.

Rodecker moved fast, his chair scraping loudly against the floor as he reached out to grab Pierce's forearm with a grip hard enough to bruise. She looked at him, her eyes wide and vibrating with fury, and he shook his head in a tiny, almost imperceptible movement. *Not here. Not like this.*

Pierce stopped, the fight draining from her shoulders as she looked from Dean to the screens to the whiteboard with the dead women. She didn't relax so much as realize the walls were too thick to punch through.

"Meeting adjourned," Dean said.

The video screens went black, the hum stopped, and the resulting quiet in the room was thick and wet like the air before a storm.

Moffett stood immediately and walked to Bennett, and they huddled together whispering about press releases and talking points, rewriting history before they even left the room. They walked out the door without looking back at the wreckage they'd created.

Dean lingered, organizing his papers and straightening his tie with trembling hands before walking past his detectives with his eyes fixed on the exit sign like a man fleeing a crime scene.

The room cleared, but the smell of sweat remained, along with the ghost of cowardice.

Nate pushed himself off the back wall, his legs stiff from standing motionless for so long, and looked at the empty chairs and the blank grey faces of the monitors where the authority had been. The system wasn't failing because it was working exactly as designed. A machine doesn't care about guilt; it cares about friction. Booker Hayes was friction. Evan Carlisle was a ghost. The machine couldn't handcuff a ghost, so it would eat the homeless man instead.

Nate walked out of the conference room into air that felt like breathing through a wet towel.

The hallway was cooler because the air conditioning worked out here, the corridor stretching long and beige, lined with closed doors and framed commendations for officers who had once believed in the job.

Rodecker waited by the water fountain, leaning against the wall while staring at the ceiling tiles, his face the color of old ash. The lines around his eyes were carved deep like canyons.

Nate stopped beside him.

Rodecker lowered his gaze, and for the first time all day, there was no evasion in his eyes, just a man looking at the wreckage of his profession.

"Thirty years," Rodecker said softly. "I gave this department thirty years."

Nate said nothing, letting the silence hold the weight of three decades of service ending in betrayal.

"I stood in that room," Rodecker said, his voice barely above a whisper, "and I watched them decide to kill him. They aren't going to execute him, but they're going to kill him by burying him in the system until he rots."

"Yes," Nate said. "They will."

Rodecker pushed himself from the wall, adjusting his holster in an automatic reflex that no longer meant anything because the badge had become worthless.

"If they're going to railroad Booker to save the Mayor's poll numbers," Rodecker said, his voice dropping to a murmur that didn't carry past the two of them, "then I'm done following orders and done with the badge that used to mean something."

He glanced down the hall toward the Chief's office, then back at Nate with eyes that had made a decision.

"Whatever you're planning," Rodecker said. "With the historian."

Nate looked at him and saw the resolve, not the hot anger Pierce carried, but the cold, heavy certainty of a man who had nothing left to lose because the thing he valued had just been sold for twelve million dollars in festival revenue.

"You know what it means," Nate said.

"I know," Rodecker said. "Count me in."

Rodecker turned and walked toward his desk to type up the arrest warrant that would destroy an innocent man and end his own career, and he didn't look back.

Nate stood alone in the hallway, touching the bandage on his left hand where the pain was sharp and real and the only honest thing left in the building. He turned and walked toward the exit, leaving the conference room and the cowards behind.

CHAPTER

34

Nate Holloway stood in the deep shade of a live oak on the southern periphery, his back against the rough bark, the texture biting into his jacket. He kept his hands deep in his pockets, where the gauze bandages wrapping his burns throbbed a dull, rhythmic counterpoint to his pulse.

Forty yards away, Booker Hayes sat on a bench near the Mercer-Williams House, the mansion's red brick rising behind him like a monument to old money and older sins. Tourists clustered on the sidewalk, pointing lenses at the famous windows, hungry for the ghost stories they paid twenty dollars to hear. They didn't look at the man on the bench. Real tragedy doesn't sell tickets.

Booker ignored them, smoking a cigarette down to the filter, elbows on his knees, movements slow and deliberate, conserving energy he knew he wouldn't need later. He wore mismatched layers despite the heat—a heavy coat over a flannel shirt—looking like debris the city hadn't swept up yet.

Nate remained in the shadows, refusing to step forward. The machine had already started its gears; intervention now would only hasten the crush.

Yolanda Pierce entered the square from the south, her stride choppy, trying for a casual stroll even though the cords in her neck were tight enough to snap. Her eyes passed over the gloom where Nate stood, zeroing in on the bench. She dropped onto it next to Booker, invading his personal space, leaning in until their shoulders touched. Nate watched their profiles, unable to hear the words but knowing the script. *Run. Hide. Get off the street.*

Booker didn't turn his head, taking a long drag from the cigarette and exhaling a thin stream of blue smoke into the stagnant air before shaking his head slowly.

He reached into his pocket, pulled out a fresh cigarette, and lit it off the dying ember of the old one before crushing the butt under the heel of a worn sneaker. He wasn't running. He settled back against the bench in a posture of resignation, a man who had stopped fighting gravity.

Pierce grabbed his arm, speaking faster, her hand chopping the air in sharp, desperate gestures.

Booker placed his hand over hers and patted it gently, said something short, then turned his face toward the sun and closed his eyes.

The convoy turned the corner.

Three SCMPD patrol cars rolled into the square in formation, no sirens, just the hum of engines and the crunch of tires on pavement. The light bars strobed a violent, artificial blue and red against the greenery, boxing in the western edge of the square, blocking the street, and stopping traffic.

Two news vans pulled up immediately behind the blockade—someone had tipped them off. Cameramen jumped out, hoisting gear onto their shoulders with practiced efficiency, running to get the angles while a walking tour group stopped to watch. The guide pointed toward the police activity and incorporated it into the show. *Look, folks. Excitement in the Hostess City.*

Chief Harold Dean stepped out of the lead car, buttoning his suit jacket and smoothing his silver hair in the reflection of the window glass. He didn't look at his officers. His eyes were locked on the red tally lights of the news cameras. He adjusted his tie and walked into the square with the stride of a man accepting an award.

Two uniformed officers flanked him, hands near their holsters as they marched toward the bench where Pierce had risen to her feet.

She put her body between Booker and the approaching line.

Dean didn't break stride, projecting his voice not to the man on the bench but to the lens positioned behind him.

"Booker Hayes," Dean announced, his voice carrying over the traffic noise. "You are under arrest."

Booker stayed seated, taking another drag from his cigarette.

"For the murders of Caroline Marsh," Dean recited, "Nicole Glad-man. And Reverend James Oden."

The cameras swiveled. Shutters clicked in a wall of noise.

Dean stopped five feet away, gesturing broadly to ensure the lens caught his profile and the righteousness etched into his expression. "This individual inserted himself into the investigation," Dean said, pitching his voice for the microphones. "He sought to control the narrative. He discovered bodies he himself killed. He created a panic to feed his own need for notoriety."

"That's a lie!" Pierce shouted, stepping toward Dean, her face dark with blood. "He called me! He called me before she was even missing!"

Dean didn't look at her, signaling the uniforms instead. "Secure the suspect."

"He's a witness!" Pierce screamed, shoving one of the uniforms back hard enough to make him stumble. "He tried to warn us! You can't do this!"

"Detective Pierce," Dean said, his voice cold and hard. "Stand down."

"He told us about the warehouse! He told us about the girl!"

"He knew because he put her there," Dean said, turning back to the cameras with the smooth pivot of a politician at a press conference. "He created an elaborate alternative suspect. A phantom. 'Mr. Evan.' A classic deflection tactic used by serial offenders."

"He's innocent!"

Pierce lunged, but two uniforms intercepted her before she reached the Chief, grabbing her arms and hauling her back. She struggled, kicking at their shins, her blazer tearing at the shoulder.

"Get off me!" she yelled.

Dean stepped into her space, turning his back to the media pool so the cameras couldn't catch his expression. He leaned close to her face, his voice dropping to a hiss. "Detective Pierce," he said, "if you cannot maintain professional objectivity, remove yourself from this scene. You are done here."

Pierce stopped struggling, her chest heaving as she looked at the officers holding her—men she worked with, men she drank with. They wouldn't meet her eyes.

Booker Hayes stood up.

The movement was slow, magnetic, drawing the camera focus away from the Chief and the struggling detective. He dropped his second cigarette and ground it out on the pavement next to the first, dusted ash from his heavy coat, looked at the officers, then at Dean. Not afraid. Just exhausted.

He held out his wrists.

The cuffs came out. The steel ratcheted shut. *Click. Click.*

Booker looked past the uniforms, past Dean, and locked eyes with Pierce across the distance between them. For a second, the square went quiet.

"I tried to help," Booker said, his voice gravel and smoke. It didn't carry to the cameras, but it carried to Pierce. "I called. You were two hours late."

Pierce flinched as if struck.

The officers grabbed Booker's arms and marched him toward the waiting cruiser, his limp visible with every third step, his head up, not hiding his face. The cameramen swarmed, jockeying for position, wanting the perp walk, wanting the monster, and they got a disheveled Black man in dirty clothes. It fit the narrative.

Dean positioned himself near the car door, arranging his face into a mask of solemn competence before nodding to a reporter who had pushed to the front of the media scrum. Effective. The man knew his angles.

They shoved Booker into the back seat, an officer's hand on his head to guide him in, and the door slammed with the finality of a coffin lid. The convoy moved, lights flashing against the storefronts, and disappeared onto Bull Street.

The show ended.

Reporters lowered their cameras and started typing captions, already crafting the narrative for the evening news. *Arrest made. Vampire killer caught.*

Pierce stood alone on the sidewalk, released by the officers, her hands clenched into fists as she stared at the empty street. She looked small, destroyed.

Nate pushed himself off the tree bark.

He looked north, toward Jones Street, and could almost picture the townhouse with its immaculate brick facade. He could see Evan Carlisle sitting in his parlor, a cup of tea in hand, watching the news on television with a smile curling at the corners of his mouth.

Carlisle hadn't just evaded capture or killed four people—he had turned the city's protectors into his personal cleanup crew, corrupting the institution so thoroughly that it was now feeding him victims to keep its own hands clean.

A cold, hard knot formed in Nate's stomach. Not anger. Cold certainty. The law didn't work here. The law was a set of rules for people who played by them, and Carlisle owned the board.

CHAPTER

35

NATE WALKED the Chatham County Detention Center corridors with a stride that felt mechanical, his left hand throbbing inside its gauze wrapping. The burn from the warehouse fire was a steady, rhythmic pulse of pain that synchronized with his heartbeat. He didn't take the pain medication the ER doctor had prescribed—he needed the throb. The pain kept him sharp, kept Evan Carlisle from becoming a theory in a file and kept him what he was: a man who burned things.

The detention center reeked of industrial pine cleaner and microwaved burritos, the scent of a place where time stopped.

Nate swiped his credentials at the heavy steel door of Block C. The lock disengaged with a loud clack that echoed down the concrete hallway. He pushed it open.

Interview Room 3 was a windowless box painted a glossy, institutional beige that seemed to sweat under the fluorescent lights. The buzz of the ballast was audible, a low-frequency drone that vibrated in his teeth.

Booker Hayes sat at the bolted metal table.

They had stripped him of his mismatched layers, his heavy coat, and his street clothes, replacing them with a bright orange jumpsuit that hung loosely on his frame. The fabric was stiff and cheap. Without his layers, Booker looked smaller, diminished. The shower they had forced on him had washed away the grime of the squares, revealing the grey in his stubble and the deep, carved lines of exhaustion around his eyes. Without the grime and the layers of wool, he looked younger—exposed.

Steel cuffs locked Booker's wrists together. A short chain ran from the shackles to a loop welded into the table, dragging his shoulders forward, but he sat upright. He didn't slump or lean. He maintained a quiet, rigid dignity that seemed completely out of place in the orange scrubs.

He wasn't alone.

A woman sat next to him, her side of the table cluttered with manila folders and legal pads. She looked barely thirty, her suit jacket rumpled and her hair drawn back in a messy knot that suggested she had been awake for twenty hours. Eva Crenshaw. Public Defender. She looked up as Nate entered, her eyes narrowing behind wire-rimmed glasses.

"Agent Holloway," she said, her voice sharp and defensive. "My client has not been arraigned yet. You've got no business here."

Nate let the door close behind him. The sound sucked the air out of the room. He didn't look at Crenshaw but at Booker instead, at the chains dragging Booker's hands down to the metal.

"This isn't a state interrogation, counselor," Nate said, his voice rough in the small room. "This isn't about your murder charges."

Crenshaw stood up and moved her body between Nate and Booker, a physical shield. "Don't give me that. Everything he says to you ends up in the DA's file. I watched the press conference. I know what Chief Dean is spinning. You want him to confess to being a serial killer so everyone can go home to dinner."

"Mr. Hayes is a material witness in an ongoing federal case," Nate said, his voice flat. "Human trafficking. Interstate crime. I need to verify his account of the warehouse."

"He's charged with three counts of capital murder," Crenshaw snapped. "He's not a witness—he's a scapegoat. And I am not letting you badger him into a confession that puts a needle in his arm."

It made Nate's chest ache.

"I'm not looking for a confession," Nate said, looking over Crenshaw's shoulder to meet Booker's eyes. "I'm looking for the truth about the warehouse, about the girl. I need to know what you saw, Booker, not what they said you saw."

Booker watched him. The man's eyes were dark and steady, not like a man facing the death penalty but like a soldier waiting for a shelling to stop.

Booker nodded once—a small, careful movement.

"It's okay, Miss Eva," Booker said, his voice gravel scraped raw by smoke and silence. "Let him sit."

Crenshaw hesitated, looking from Booker to Nate and weighing the risks. She gathered her files, stacking them with sharp, aggressive movements.

"I'm timing this," she said to Nate. "Ten minutes. If I hear you raise your voice, if I hear you trying to coerce him, I'm coming back in with the guard, and I'm filing a formal complaint with the DOJ."

"Understood," Nate said.

She touched Booker's shoulder, a brief, human gesture in the cold room, and walked out. The heavy door clicked shut, sealing them in.

Nate drew out the metal chair opposite Booker and sat down, placing his hands on the table. The white gauze on his left hand stood out starkly against the grey metal. He didn't try to hide the injury.

Silence stretched between them. The buzz of the lights seemed to grow louder.

Nate didn't open a notebook or turn on a recorder. He just watched the man the system had chosen to eat.

"They've got a story," Nate said, his voice low. "I just left the task office room. I heard what they're writing up."

Booker looked down at his chained hands but didn't speak.

"They're going to say you've got paranoid delusions," Nate continued. "They're going to say 'Mr. Evan' is a phantom you invented to feel important, a projection of your own guilt. They'll say you inserted yourself into the investigation because you craved attention, that you found the bodies because you put them there, that you called Detective Pierce because you wanted to play the hero."

Nate paused, watching a muscle jump in Booker's jaw.

"They're painting you as a homeless man with a history of mental instability who snapped," Nate said. "The DA's got a plea deal on the table—manslaughter, diminished capacity, twenty years. You take it, the case closes, the tourists keep coming, and the Mayor gets re-elected."

Booker turned his hands over, and the chains rattled like loose change in a dryer. He traced a groove in the metal table with a calloused thumb.

"That's the court version," Nate said. "Tell me the truth."

Booker looked up, his eyes clear and holding no madness, only a terrible, crushing fatigue.

"The truth don't change nothing," Booker said.

"It changes what I do next," Nate said.

Booker studied Nate's face, looking at the burns, looking at the shadows under Nate's eyes. He seemed to reach a decision.

"I was sitting on my bench," Booker began, his voice low and rhythmic. "The sun was going down, and the light gets gold right before it goes grey. She was there—the blonde girl, Nicole."

Nate nodded. "With the camera."

"She was sketching the monument," Booker said. "Just a kid who looked like she was waiting for something good to happen. Then he came."

"Carlisle."

"Mr. Evan," Booker corrected. "He moved quiet—professional quiet. He sat next to her, didn't touch her, but he crowded her space. You understand? He looked at her the way a man looks at a steak on a plate, checking the cut."

Booker paused, licking dry lips.

"She knew him," Booker said. "Or she thought she did. Her face lit up, and she put her sketchbook away. She stood up like he'd yanked her with a string. They started walking."

"Where did they go?" Nate asked, though he knew.

"North," Booker said. "Toward the river, past the lights, past the tourists. I followed them and kept back. He never looked around because he didn't need to—he walked like he owned the pavement."

Booker's finger traced a line on the table, mapping the route through the city's veins.

"They went to the West Boundary," Booker said. "That old brick building with the windows blacked out. He had a key—a big iron key. He opened the side door, and she went through ahead of him. She was laughing. She thought it was an adventure."

Booker stopped and stared at the spot on the table where his finger rested.

"The door closed," he said softly. "It made a sound like a vault. Then nothing—no screaming, no fighting. Just quiet."

Nate leaned in. The air in the room felt heavy, pressurized.

"How long?" Nate asked.

"Ninety minutes," Booker said. "I counted the streetlights coming on, counted the cars passing on the overpass. Ninety minutes."

"Then what?"

"The door opened," Booker said. "He came out alone."

Nate's pulse hammered in his throat. "Did you see anything else?"

Booker gave a slow nod and raised his hands as far as the chains would allow, miming the grip of a handle.

"He was carrying a bag," Booker said. "Canvas, military-issue, green."

"Was it full?"

"It was heavy," Booker said, looking directly at Nate. "But not like clothes or books. It swung different."

"Different how?"

"Liquid weight," Booker said. "It moved when he moved, sloshed around. Heavy, like carrying two gallons of water in a sack, but he carried it like it was precious."

Nate felt a chill that had nothing to do with the air conditioning. *Liquid weight.* The autopsy report flashed in his mind. *92% blood volume loss.* Carlisle hadn't just killed Nicole in that warehouse—he had drained her, filled containers with her life, and walked out into the Savannah night carrying it like groceries.

"What did you do?" Nate asked.

"I waited," Booker said. "I stayed there and watched the door."

Booker's face crumbled a fraction. The dignity fractured, revealing the raw wound underneath.

"I called the detective," Booker said. "Detective Pierce. I called her number, and it went to voicemail. I left a message saying I'd spotted the girl, saying where they were."

"She didn't answer," Nate said.

"Two hours," Booker said. "I sat behind a dumpster for two hours waiting for the police, waiting for the blue lights. Nothing came."

"Why didn't you go in?" Nate asked. The question was brutal but necessary.

Booker looked down, his shoulders slumping, the orange fabric bunching around his neck.

"I wanted to," Booker said quietly. "I told myself to stand up, told myself to kick that door. I kicked doors in Fallujah—I know how to kick a door."

He swallowed hard.

"But I felt it," Booker said. "The cold, even from across the street. That building wasn't empty. It felt like a mouth. I knew if I went through that door, I wasn't coming back out, that I would die in the dark."

He looked up at Nate, tears standing in his eyes.

"I was scared," Booker said quietly. "I'm a grown man. I've been to war. But I was scared of that door, so I sat there and let her die."

The confession hung in the cold air.

Nate looked at the man across from him and recognized the shame that was eating him alive. But he also recognized the reality—if Booker had gone through that door, he would be dead. His blood would be in a jar in Evan Carlisle's cellar, and his body would be ash.

"You're alive," Nate said. "That's why you're here—you're the only witness who survived him."

Booker laughed, a short, bitter bark of a sound, and gestured with his chin toward the door where the public defender had exited.

"Look where alive got me," Booker said. "They've got papers out there saying I did it, got a deal saying if I admit I'm crazy, they won't kill me—they'll just lock me up until I die of old age."

Nate looked at the file Crenshaw had left on the table. The plea deal was a neat, sterile document that reduced the horror of what Carlisle had done into a manageable bureaucratic process. It was the machine digesting the problem.

Booker leaned back, and the chains went taut.

"Optics," Booker said. "That's what the detective said later—she was in a meeting about optics. That's why she didn't come. The girl died for optics."

Nate felt the anger rise in his chest, not the hot flare of temper but a cold, solid thing like an iron bar in his spine.

"The system is protecting itself," Nate said. "It can't catch Carlisle because he doesn't play by its rules, so it's catching you."

"I know," Booker said. "I'm the debris."

Nate stood up. The chair scraped loudly against the concrete floor, and he placed his hands flat on the table, leaning in until his face was level with Booker's.

"I will fix this," Nate said, his voice low and intense. "I will prove you didn't do this. I'll tear their story apart."

Booker looked at him and smiled, but it was a smile full of pity, the smile of a man who had watched good intentions crushed by reality a thousand times.

"You're a good man, Agent Holloway," Booker said quietly. "You want it to be right, but good men don't fix broken systems."

Booker shook his head.

"They just break themselves trying," he said.

Nate stared at him and thought of Pierce, sidelined and screaming, thought of Rodecker watching his career dissolve, thought of Sarah fifteen years gone.

"I'm not asking for permission," Nate said. "I'm telling you what happens next."

Nate turned and walked to the door without looking back at the table, without looking back at the orange jumpsuit or the man chained to the steel loop.

He gripped the handle. The metal was cold.

He stopped.

He turned his head, looking back over his shoulder.

"The man who killed those women," Nate said, "I'm going to stop him. And when I do, you walk free."

Booker just watched him, silent in the humming room.

"That's not a promise," Nate said. "That's a fact."

Nate tugged the handle and stepped out into the corridor. The heavy steel door swung shut behind him, sealing with a final, definitive thud.

As the latch engaged, Nate heard a sound from inside the room—faint, muffled by the heavy door, but unmistakable.

It was the metallic rattle of chains scraping in the empty silence.

CHAPTER

36

The rental Explorer's air conditioning rattled, a mechanical death rattle that did nothing against the Georgia heat. Nate kept his eyes on the road instead, guiding the car through the grid of the historic district where live oaks reached over the street, their branches heavy with moss that hung dead still in the windless afternoon. Sun cut through the leaves, catching the dust on the dashboard in shafts of gold.

He parked on the street near the Mercer-Williams House. The engine ticked as it cooled, the only sound in the sudden quiet. He sat there, breathing in the scent of stale coffee and rental car plastic, staring at his hands on the wheel. The gauze wrapping was grey with soot he hadn't washed off.

He got out and walked toward the narrow opening of the lane behind the house, stepping from the golden light of the square into the grey shadow of the service corridor. Brick walls rose high on either side, blocking the sun, and the temperature dropped by ten degrees. The trolley bells and tourist chatter faded, deadened by the masonry.

He stopped where she had died.

No crime scene tape. No plastic markers. The property owner had been thorough; the hexagonal pavers were wet and dark, scrubbed clean of the violence from three days ago.

Nate crouched, his knees popping with a dry crack in the silence. He leaned closer to the ground. The smell hit him then—not blood, but bleach. Sharp, chemical, antiseptic. It masked the damp earth and the mold living in the mortar, but deep in the cracks where the pressure washer failed to reach, he saw it—faint, dark stains in the grout.

He reached out with his hand, felt the brick cold and slick beneath his palm. He traced the line of the grout, feeling the grit. The creeping fig vine clinging to the wall brushed against his shoulder, the leaves stiff and waxy.

Nicole Gladman had lain here.

He didn't need to close his eyes to see it. The geometry of the scene arranged itself over the wet bricks—arms crossed left over right, bare feet pointing north, candles burning at the cardinal points with wax dripping onto the stone. Her throat torn open.

Then the face changed.

It wasn't Nicole anymore.

The brick texture under his boots was the same, the silence pressing against his ears identical. Sarah, lying on the cold stones, her life drained away into the Savannah soil.

Nate kept his hand on the damp earth as the sensory memory washed over him, drowning out the present. He felt the weight of the casket handle digging into his shoulder, the sharp edge of the wood biting through his suit. He smelled the lilies in the funeral home, cloying and sweet, failing to cover the formaldehyde. He heard the undertaker's voice, a soft, apologetic rasp.

We had to use a scarf, Mr. Holloway. The damage to the neck...

He stood up stiffly and paced in a small circle in the narrow confines, boots scraping against the stone. The high walls trapped the air and trapped the history.

Carlisle had been here.

Nate stopped pacing and looked at his bandaged hand. The warehouse hadn't been an investigation but a trap—Carlisle had lured them there, toyed with them, and then tried to burn them alive. The burns weren't injuries but a signature.

He looked back at the spot on the ground where the lavender sprig had been found in Nicole's hand.

It wasn't just a ritual element; it was something specific. The dried variety matched the sprig in Sarah's evidence file, the file he kept in his hotel room.

Carlisle had been in his room.

He had stood over Nate while he slept, had read the files, and had taken lavender and placed it in Nicole's hand.

I know you. I know your pain. I remember her.

Nate leaned his back against the rough brick and felt the grit dig into his jacket. He looked up at the narrow strip of sky between the rooflines, turning the color of a fresh bruise as evening approached.

The man wasn't just killing to feed but performing. He was mocking the investigation, mocking Nate's grief, mocking the idea that he could be stopped.

And the law could do nothing.

Nate ran the facts through his mind one last time—the autopsy reports, the blood volume loss that defied physics, the lack of defensive wounds, the timeline stretching back to 1890, the bite marks matching across a century.

Booker Hayes sat in a cage somewhere, wearing an orange jumpsuit, waiting to be sacrificed because the system needed a body. The Mayor needed a win. The tourists needed to feel safe.

If Nate followed the rules, Booker would go to prison, and Carlisle would wait out the heat, then slip into dormancy or move on. He would kill again in fifteen years or thirty.

The badge in Nate's pocket felt heavy. It felt like a lie.

He pushed himself off the wall as the exhaustion weighing on him for weeks seemed to burn off, replaced by something cold and hard. The conflict between the agent and the brother ended.

Nate reached into his pocket and pulled out his phone. The screen lit up, casting a pale blue glow on the wet bricks.

He scrolled through his contacts, went past Assistant Director Harran, went past the BAU Duty Desk, and went past Nadia.

He stopped at the name *Landry, Alicia.*

He pressed the call button.

He lifted the phone to his ear and listened to the ring, a digital trill too loud in the quiet lane. He stared at the dark stain in the grout, the blood that wouldn't wash away.

She answered on the second ring.

"Holloway?" Her voice was tight, expectant. She knew. She had known before he did.

Nate looked at the creeping fig, at the walls that had hidden a monster's work for a century. He didn't introduce himself. He didn't explain.

"How can I end this?"

CHAPTER

37

THE ELEVATOR DOORS slid open on the fourth floor of the Marshall House with a grinding shudder that vibrated through the soles of Nate's boots and echoed down the empty hallway. He stepped out into air that smelled of old carpet and mildew, a faint trace of lemon polish failing to cover a century of absorbed humidity. The dim corridor stretched before him, his footsteps muffled by the worn runner, and the gauze wrapping his left hand felt tight against skin that throbbed hot where the wire cable had chewed into his palm.

He rounded the corner toward Room 417 and found two silhouettes waiting outside his door.

Karl Rodecker leaned against the wall, his weight slumping into the cheap drywall, out of his department store suit, and wearing worn denim jeans with an Atlanta Braves T-shirt that looked tight across the shoulders. Without the badge and jacket, the sag in his posture was more pronounced. Yolanda Pierce paced the narrow strip of carpet in front of him, her movements sharp and contained, dressed in black running clothes that absorbed the low light. Her hair was pulled back severely and tight, and she stopped moving the moment she saw Nate, her eyes locking onto his with an intensity that made his chest tighten.

Neither of them smiled.

Nate didn't ask why they were there, just reached into his pocket with his good hand and fished out the key card. The plastic click of the lock was loud in the quiet hall, and he pushed the door open and stepped aside to let them pass into what had become his temporary war room.

The small hotel room had been transformed into something that looked more like a detective's obsession than a place to sleep. Alicia

Landry sat at the small desk, the hotel stationery and room service menu discarded on the floor around her, replaced by property records, translations from the Ashworth estate, and high-resolution photos of the tablet arranged into a precise grid. The corkboard on the wall was no longer just a collection of crime scene photos but a timeline, a web of red string connecting dates that spanned three centuries of violence.

Alicia stood as they entered, smoothing her skirt with fingers stained with ink. Her stance was defensive, shoulders squared like she expected an argument, but her eyes were steady and unflinching.

Rodecker didn't sit, just stood in the center of the room with his hands shoved deep into his pockets, staring at the floor where the carpet met the baseboard. When he finally spoke, his voice was flat, stripped of the professional cadence he used at crime scenes. "Dean is fast-tracking the arraignment. DA wants Booker charged formally by Friday morning, and they're skipping the prelims so they can get a statement ready for the six o'clock news cycle."

Nate locked the door behind them and leaned back against the wood, letting its coolness seep through his jacket. "Friday. That gives us forty-eight hours."

"Less than that," Rodecker said, his jaw working like he was chewing on something bitter. "Once he's arraigned, he goes into general population at the county jail, and if he survives the weekend in there with the charges they hung on him, he pleads out on Monday. Case closed, and we all go back to working the Music Festival security detail like none of this happened."

Pierce moved to the window and stared out at the streetlights of Broughton Street, her reflection a ghost in the dark glass. "I ran six miles before I came here," she said without turning around, her voice tight with something close to desperation. "My lungs burned, and I thought it would clear my head, but it didn't."

She turned to face them, and her face was bare of makeup, her eyes raw and red-rimmed. "Twelve years a cop—Beat, Vice, Homicide— and I believed the system worked. Slow, ugly, but it worked." She took a sharp breath that sounded painful. "Today I watched them put chains on a man I know is innocent, watched Chief Dean smile for the cameras, watched them sacrifice Booker to protect the Mayor's approval ratings." Her hand fell to her side, fingers curling into a fist. "I'm done believing."

Alicia cleared her throat and gestured to the corkboard with a sweep of her hand. "The system relies on precedent," she said, slipping into the lecture hall tone she used to command a room full of under-graduates. "It relies on things making sense—motive, opportunity, means—but what we have doesn't fit in a case file, doesn't fit in any file that anyone would believe."

Her eyes scanned the wall, and Nate's followed to the three photographs pinned in a vertical line. A photograph from 1920 showed Edward Carlton standing beside a Model T, his expression cold and aristocratic. A photo from 1950 showed Edwin Carver at a society function, champagne glass in hand. The current surveillance shot showed Evan Carlisle leaving his townhouse in designer clothes.

"The face is the same," Alicia said, and her voice carried the weight of someone who'd spent months verifying impossible facts. "Not similar—the same. The biometric analysis on the ear shape and facial landmarks confirms it beyond any statistical doubt. It is the same man."

She picked up a stack of property deeds, the papers yellowed with age, and spread them across the desk like a card dealer revealing a winning hand. "The townhouse on Jones Street has had continuous ownership under variations of the same name since 1853. The signatures don't age, the handwriting doesn't degrade, and the pattern repeats every fifteen years without fail—1890, 1905, 1920, 1935, 1950, 1965, 1980, 1995, 2010."

She turned to face them with the kind of expression a scientist might wear when presenting data that violated every law of physics. "We have the Ashworth tablet translation, which describes the binding of an *edimmu*—a Mesopotamian demon. We have forensic impossibil-ities that no lab can explain—bite marks identical across seventy-five years, DNA that matches degraded samples from 1950, blood spatter that violates the laws of gravity."

Rodecker shook his head and stepped away from the board, moving toward the dresser and putting distance between himself and the wall of evidence. He looked trapped, cornered by facts that didn't make sense in the world he'd spent thirty years navigating.

"I'm a cop," Rodecker said, his voice rough with frustration. "I deal in fingerprints, ballistics, witness statements—things I can put in front of a jury. You're talking about mythology and ghosts." He rubbed the back of his neck hard enough to leave red marks. "There has to be a rational explanation somewhere in this mess—a family resemblance, a sophisticated copycat with access to old records."

"Karl," Pierce said, and she stepped away from the window into his line of sight, forcing him to look at her. "We were in that warehouse together."

"I know where we were," Rodecker said, his voice tight and defensive.

"The fire started while we were inside, and the doors were rigged shut," Pierce said, her words coming faster now. "The building was a trap, and something knew we were coming, knew exactly when we'd be there. A copycat doesn't move like that, doesn't plan with that kind of precision. A human suspect doesn't vanish from a locked building with every exit covered."

Nate pushed himself off the door and walked to the desk, his boots heavy on the thin carpet. He picked up the plastic evidence bag containing the dried sprig of lavender that had been found clutched in Nicole Gladman's dead hand and held it up to the light.

"He was in this room," Nate said.

Rodecker's head snapped toward him. "Who was?"

"Carlisle," Nate said, and the name felt like poison on his tongue. "A couple of nights ago, I woke up and thought it was a dream at first —he was sitting in that chair by the window, watching me. He told me I couldn't stop him, told me he remembered Sarah like she was someone he'd met at a party last week."

Nate placed the bag on the desk and reached into his pocket to pull out the small lapel pin, the ancient priest's insignia he'd found among Sarah's belongings. He pinned it to the corkboard next to Sarah's student ID, the metal catching the lamplight. "He put this lavender on Gladman, the same way he did on my sister fifteen years ago. He placed it on Nicole's body as a message. He knows everything we know, sees everything we do."

Nate turned to face them and held up his bandaged hands so they could see the white gauze wrapped around his palms. "When you slammed your hand on the table during the interview, Carlisle didn't blink, didn't flinch, didn't show any autonomic response. His heart rate didn't spike, and his skin temperature was ten degrees below what it should have been—I checked the thermal scan twice." He looked directly at Rodecker. "I felt his breath when he leaned close to me during questioning. It was cold, not cool, but cold like air from a freezer, like something that had never been alive."

Rodecker stared at Nate for a long moment, then looked at the pin on the wall, at the burn dressing on Nate's hand, at the evidence bag with its withered sprig of purple flowers.

Alicia placed her hands flat on the desk, fingers spread wide like she was steadying herself. "I am a historian," she said, her voice calm and measured. "I verify sources, cross-reference documents, check authenticity. Every document I've found for one hundred and thirty-five years says the same thing—this man does not age, does not die, and he kills every fifteen years with the same methodology." She paused, and when she spoke again, her voice was softer. "At what point do we accept what the evidence shows instead of what we want to believe?"

The room went silent except for the hum of the air conditioner and the distant sound of a trolley bell clanging faintly on Bull Street.

Rodecker sat heavily on the edge of the unmade bed, springs creaking under his weight. He stared at his sneakers for a long moment, then cracked his knuckles one by one—sharp pops that sounded skeletal in the quiet room.

He took a breath, let it out slowly through his nose, and looked up at Nate with shoulders that were rounded but eyes that had gone hard. "Thirty years I've spent following rules, believing the institution would do right by people, that the system worked even when it was slow." He looked at Pierce, and his expression was bitter. "Today I watched them manufacture a case against a guy who tried to warn us, watched them railroad him to save the Mayor's poll numbers. At least

Carlisle doesn't pretend to be a public servant while he bleeds people dry."

He stood and cracked his neck, the sound loud in the small room, and looked at the photo of Carlisle on the wall. "I don't care what you call him—vampire, *edimmu*, demon. He's a monster, and he needs to go down."

Nate nodded once, a sharp movement, and began to pace the small strip of floor between the bed and the desk. "We can't arrest him through normal channels, can't get a warrant because no probable cause exists that a judge would sign. He's legally untouchable—money, lawyers, layers of corporate shielding. He'll outlive every prosecutor, every witness, every piece of evidence we could gather. He'll kill again in fifteen years, and then fifteen years after that, forever."

Alicia picked up a stack of papers, her hands shaking slightly, but her voice remained clinical and precise. "There is a way to stop him. The tablet specifies the binding ritual—the creature is bound to a stolen body by an ancient curse, and it's sustained by blood taken in cycles tied to the lunar eclipse."

She looked at Nate, and her eyes were fierce behind her glasses. "To end it, we have to break the binding, and the ritual requires four specific things." She held up one finger. "Iron, but not modern steel— iron smelted without impurities using the bloomery technique, the old way before industrial processes." She held up a second finger. "Water, specifically the blade, must be quenched in running water." She held up a third finger. "The name—we have to speak his true name when we strike: *Naram-Ekur*."

"And the fourth?" Pierce asked, her voice steady despite the tension in her shoulders.

Alicia consulted her notes, adjusting her glasses with one hand. "The translation is specific about this part—it requires the 'Hand of Death,' *Qāt mīt* in the Akkadian, and it refers to the wielder of the weapon." She looked up from the papers. "An executioner, a lawman who judges, someone who wields the weapon with lethal intent and is authorized by society to take life."

Rodecker snorted, but there was no humor in it. "So we need a weapon, a name, and an executioner."

Nate stopped pacing and rubbed his face with his unwrapped hand, feeling the grit of the day on his skin and the exhaustion settling into his bones. He looked at Sarah's photo on the wall, at the red string connecting her to Nicole, to Lucy, to Caroline—a line of bodies stretching back through decades.

"I tried to make it fit the profile like any other serial case," Nate said softly, his voice barely above a whisper. "But the profile is broken, because he's not a man and never was."

He looked at Alicia. "You're absolutely sure about the iron?"

"The text is explicit," Alicia said without hesitation. "Modern alloys contain carbon and other elements that disrupt the ritual purity. It has to be pure iron or the binding won't break."

"Then we need a blacksmith," Nate said.

"I know a blacksmith," Alicia said. "I'll contact him. His name is Zeke."

Pierce stepped away from the window and into the circle of light cast by the desk lamp, her face half in shadow. "We need to be clear about what we're discussing here," she said, her cop voice coming back. "You're talking about entering a private residence without a warrant, attacking a civilian who has not been charged with a crime, and killing him with premeditation and planning. You're talking about murder."

"Yes," Nate said, and he didn't look away from her eyes.

"That's murder in the first degree," Pierce said. "Premeditated, planned, executed."

Nate met her eyes and held them. "I'm talking about executing a combatant who has declared war on this city and has been killing its people for over a century."

The word hung in the air between them like smoke. *Murder.*

Rodecker drew himself up to his full height, and when he spoke, his voice had the weight of finality. "What do you need from us?" The question wasn't procedural or hypothetical—it was acceptance.

Nate looked around the room at each of them in turn, needing them to understand the full price they would pay. "I need to know you're in—all the way, no hesitation, no turning back. There's no coming back from this line we're about to cross. If we do this, we become criminals in the eyes of the law we've spent our lives serving."

Rodecker stepped forward, his jaw set. "My pension, thirty years of service, a comfortable ending to my career—I'm throwing it all away. But I won't watch another innocent person get destroyed by this system while a monster walks free. I'm in."

Pierce's face was set hard as stone, and when she spoke, her voice didn't waver. "My badge, this job, my identity—everything I've built since I was twenty-three years old. I'm ending my career for this, burning it down. If being a good cop means letting Booker take the fall while a monster walks free, then I don't want to be a cop anymore. I'm in."

Alicia came around the desk, and she looked small standing next to the two detectives, but her eyes were fierce and unafraid. "My academic position, my safety, my reputation—if we fail, I'm complicit in murder, and I'll lose everything. I've spent fifteen years building my career, and I'm risking it all." She touched the papers on the desk, her fingers gentle on the ancient translations. "Because someone has to witness this, someone has to remember what really happened."

Nate looked at them, then down at his bandaged hands, at the evidence of how close he'd already come to dying. "I already lost everything that mattered fifteen years ago when Sarah died. I've got nothing left to lose except the chance to make her death mean something more than just another victim in his collection. My career's already over—Harran is recalling me to DC. I'm all in."

"If we do this and it works," Rodecker said, his voice grim, "we don't get medals or commendations. We get investigated, prosecuted, destroyed. Best-case scenario, we lose our jobs and our pensions. Worst case, we spend the rest of our lives in prison."

"I know," Nate said.

"And if it doesn't work?" Pierce asked. "If the ritual fails or we can't get to him?"

"Then we die," Nate said simply. "And Carlisle keeps killing for another century."

A long silence settled over the room like a physical weight. No one moved, and the only sounds were the air conditioner, the distant traffic on the street below, and the shared breath of four people who'd just chosen to cross a line they could never uncross. It was a contract sealed not with signatures or handshakes but with a shared, unbroken gaze that said more than words ever could.

The moment passed like a held breath releasing.

"I'll go to the blacksmith tomorrow morning," Alicia said, breaking the spell that had held them. She gathered the translation notes and diagrams into a folder, her movements quick and efficient. "I need to prepare the exact specifications for the blade—length, weight, composition."

"I'll secure perimeter intel," Rodecker said, his cop mind already working through logistics. "Shift schedules, patrol routes, security cameras. We need to know exactly when that street is quiet and for how long."

"I'll get the hardware we need," Pierce said. "Breaching tools, backup weapons. If we're going in, we're going in fast, and we're going in hard."

They moved with purpose now, the hesitation and doubt burned away by the fire of commitment.

Rodecker and Pierce exited into the hallway, their footsteps fading down the corridor toward the elevator. Alicia paused at the door and gave Nate a final, steady nod that said everything that needed saying, then slipped out into the dimly lit hallway.

The door clicked shut with a sound that seemed too loud.

Nate stood alone in the center of the room, and the silence rushed back in like water filling a hole, heavy and suffocating.

He turned slowly to the desk where his FBI credentials sat on the polished wood. The leather wallet was open, and the gold badge caught the lamplight, gleaming with authority and legitimacy. *Federal Bureau of Investigation. Special Agent.* Years of rules, procedures, protocols. An oath to uphold the Constitution, to serve justice, to be the man he'd always believed he could be.

He picked it up and felt the weight of it in his palm, heavier than it should be. He closed the wallet with a soft snap and set it deliberately on the nightstand next to the hotel Bible, two books of laws he was about to violate.

He picked up his Glock 19M from where it lay on the desk. The metal was cool against his skin, familiar and comforting in the way only a weapon you've carried for years can be. He pressed the magazine release and felt it slide out, heavy with rounds, and checked the brass —full load, no misfires. He slammed it back home with a sharp click that echoed in the empty room, then pulled the slide back just far enough to check the chamber. Brass gleamed in the lamplight, ready and waiting. He let the slide ride forward with a metallic snap.

He gripped the weapon in both hands, feeling the balance and heft of it. Not a tool of federal law enforcement anymore, not a symbol of justice and order. Just a gun, just a piece of metal and polymer designed to kill.

He looked at his reflection in the darkened window glass, and the man staring back at him had hollow eyes and grey skin stretched tight over bone. He wore a suit, but he wasn't an agent anymore—he was something older, something more primal. A hunter tracking prey. An avenger seeking blood. An executioner preparing to kill.

Nate reached out with one hand and switched off the desk lamp.

The room plunged into darkness.

CHAPTER

38

T HE SERVICE LANE off Broughton Street smelled of stagnant water and wet brick, a narrow channel where shadows lay long across the uneven pavement. Nate Holloway trailed Karl Rodecker with Alicia Landry a step behind, the three of them moving in single file through the urban canyon. An overflowing dumpster from a nearby restaurant choked the path, forcing Nate to step over a puddle of oil that held a greasy reflection of the grey sky. His eyes scanned the rooflines and the darkened windows of the buildings pressing in, threat assessment becoming his new baseline—a low-grade hum he couldn't turn off.

Rodecker stopped at a nondescript brick facade, the wall scarred by decades of delivery trucks scraping past. Above a reinforced steel door, a hand-painted sign with peeling paint and a bracket streaked with rust read *Tatum Forge: Restorations & Custom Ironwork*. Rodecker checked the street behind them, his attention sweeping the fire escapes before he gave a slight nod and said, "Clear."

Alicia reached for the handle and swung the heavy door open. They stepped inside, and the world changed in an instant. The humid, heavy air of Savannah vanished, replaced by a wall of dry, intense heat that slammed into them like a physical blow. It sucked the moisture from Nate's eyes and dried the sweat on his neck. Nate flinched as the skin beneath the bandages on his palms throbbed in protest of the dryness.

They stood in a small front office where dust motes danced in the shafts of light cutting through a grime-caked window. A glass partition separated them from the dark cavern of the forge, and it shook with a low, rhythmic thrumming from the workshop beyond—metal on metal, fire on iron, the percussion of industry.

A woman sat at a cluttered metal desk with ledgers and invoices stacked in organized piles around her like fortifications. She looked up over the rim of her reading glasses, her sharp, assessing eyes taking them in with the practiced efficiency of someone who'd spent decades reading people.

Ruby Tatum did not smile, and she didn't stand right away. When she did move, she went to the door connecting the office to the workshop and crossed her arms over her chest to block the path.

"Help you?" she asked, her voice flat. Her eyes flicked to Rodecker, noting the way he stood and the way his hand hovered near his belt—a cop's stance, unmistakable. She looked at Nate next, taking in the rumpled suit and the rigid posture of federal authority. Then she studied Alicia with her satchel and nervous hands.

"You got a work order?" Ruby asked. "Or did you bring a search authorization?"

"Neither," Alicia said, stepping forward with her hands visible and non-threatening. "I called earlier about the restoration project."

Ruby studied Alicia's face for signs of deception, her attention returning to Nate for a final assessment before she made her decision.

"You're the historian," Ruby said, a statement rather than a question.

"Yes," Alicia said. "Alicia Landry."

Ruby held her ground for another moment, weighing the threat level and deciding they were either harmless or simply unavoidable. She turned and hit a buzzer on the wall, and the lock on the partition door clicked open with a metallic snap.

"He's in the middle of a heat," Ruby said. "Don't touch anything, and don't distract him until the hammer stops."

She opened the door, and they walked into the main workshop. The noise was a physical presence that pressed against their eardrums. The rhythmic *clang, clang, clang* of metal on metal rang off the brick walls, while the roar of a forced-air blower filled the spaces between hammer strikes, like a beast breathing. The air tasted of sulfur and coal dust—the smell of industry from a century ago, before automation and safety regulations.

The workshop was a long, high-ceilinged space that looked like it belonged in another era. Chains and tongs hung from the rafters beside racks of iron bars lining the walls, and there were no computer-controlled cutters or clean assembly lines. Just fire and iron and the strength to bend one to the other.

In the center of the room, a coal forge burned with an orange heart. A man stood at the anvil with his back to them, holding long-handled tongs in his left hand while a hammer rose and fell in his right as he struck a piece of red-hot iron. Sparks sprayed across the concrete floor in bright arcs, dying before they reached the walls.

Ezekiel "Zeke" Tatum was in his late sixties, his white hair cropped close to his skull, and a leather apron covered his chest and legs over a faded, soot-stained work shirt. He brought the hammer down again, the muscle in his forearm cording with the effort despite the thinness of his frame. He struck the iron one last time, turned, and thrust the metal back into the coals before looking up.

Wiping soot from his forehead with a grey rag, Zeke propped himself against the anvil. His face was deeply lined, his dark eyes sharp in the gloom despite his age. He didn't speak, just watched them with the patience of someone who'd seen everything at least twice.

Alicia approached a workbench covered in sketches, calipers, and soapstone markers. She opened her satchel and drew out the diagram she had created from the tablet translation, laying it on the scarred wood with reverence.

"Mr. Tatum," Alicia said, raising her voice over the drone of the ventilation fans. "Thank you for agreeing to see us."

Zeke looked at the paper but didn't move toward it, his expression unreadable.

"Ruby said you needed something custom," he said, his voice a rasp of gravel grinding together. "Said it was time-sensitive."

"It is," Alicia said.

Zeke walked to the bench and picked up the diagram, squinting at the specifications and the notes Alicia had written in the margins with painstaking detail.

Bloomery iron. No flux. Folded forty times. Quenched in running water.

A dry, rattling sound escaped his throat and ended in a short cough. He tossed the paper back onto the bench and walked to a coal bin, shoveling new fuel onto the fire.

"This is nonsense," Zeke said, turning his back to the flames. "You want bloomery iron? You know what that involves? Building a furnace from scratch. Smelting ore. Reducing it to a sponge, then hammering the slag out by hand over the course of three days before you can even start shaping a blade."

"We know," Alicia said.

"Why?" Zeke asked.

"It has to be made the old way," Alicia said.

"For a reproduction?" Zeke shook his head with disgust. "University folks always want it exactly like the original until they see the bill." He looked at Nate with suspicion. "Or until they realize the old ways produce dirty metal full of slag inclusions."

Nate stepped closer, keeping his bandaged hands deep in his pockets as the heat from the forge warmed the front of his suit. "We're conducting a forensic reconstruction," Nate said. "We need to test the tensile strength of historical weapons against modern body armor, which means it has to be chemically accurate to the period."

Zeke stopped cleaning his hammer and held the tool loosely in his hand, studying Nate with new interest. He looked at Nate's suit and at the way Nate stood with his weight balanced on the balls of his feet like a fighter. He looked at the bandages peeking out from Nate's pockets, then picked up a pair of calipers and pointed them at Nate like an accusation.

"Don't feed me a line about forensics, son," Zeke said. "I've been making historical reproductions for forty years—wall hangers for tourists, re-enactment gear for hobbyists, and museum pieces for glass cases." He tapped the diagram on the bench with one knuckle. "This balance," Zeke said, "the tang construction, the edge geometry—this isn't for a wall, and it isn't for a test."

Zeke looked Nate in the eye and didn't blink. "This is designed to cut through flesh and bone," Zeke said. "Now get out of my shop."

The blower droned. The coals crackled. Nate didn't move.

"We can't," Nate said.

"Then I'll call the real police," Zeke said, gesturing at Rodecker. "Not whatever costume department sent you."

"Mr. Tatum—" Alicia began.

"I don't care what credentials you've got or what university sent you," Zeke said, his voice hardening. "I know what this is. Someone wants to hurt someone, and they want me to be part of it." He turned his back to them and picked up his hammer. "I've got two months left on this earth. I'm not spending them in a courtroom or explaining to federal prosecutors why I forged a murder weapon."

Ruby appeared in the doorway from the office, her arms crossed. "You heard him," Ruby said. "Time to go."

Alicia looked at Nate with desperation in her eyes. Nate drew his hands from his pockets and held up the bandaged palms.

"A man named Evan Carlisle did this to me," Nate said. "Three nights ago. He lured us into a warehouse, chained the doors, and set it on fire while we were inside."

Zeke stopped with the hammer halfway to the anvil.

"We barely made it out," Nate continued. "The building burned to the ground, and when the fire marshal went through the rubble, there was no evidence he was ever there. No fingerprints. No DNA. Nothing."

"So arrest him for arson," Zeke said without turning around.

"I can't," Nate said. "Because he's protected—money, lawyers, a paper trail that goes back a hundred and thirty-five years. He owns half of Jones Street, and he's been killing women in this city since 1890."

Zeke turned slowly. "1890," Zeke repeated, his voice flat with skepticism.

"The same man," Nate said. "The same face in photographs from 1920, 1950, 1980, 2010. We have biometric analysis proving it's not descendants or lookalikes—it's *him*."

"That's impossible," Ruby said from the doorway.

"We thought so too," Alicia said. She opened her satchel and pulled out a folder, spreading crime scene photos across the workbench. Nicole Gladman. Lucy Phelps. Caroline Marsh. "Until we started looking at the pattern."

Zeke stepped closer to the bench, his eyes moving over the photographs. His jaw tightened.

"Throats torn out," Alicia said. "Exsanguination. Positioned in the squares like offerings. Every fifteen years, the same methodology, the same signature."

"Every fifteen years," Ruby said softly.

Something in her voice made Nate turn to look at her. Ruby was staring at the photos, her face gone pale.

"1995," Ruby said. "Fifteen years before 2010."

"Yes," Alicia said.

Ruby walked slowly into the workshop, her sensible shoes clicking on the concrete. She stopped at the workbench and picked up one of the photos with shaking hands.

"There was a girl," Ruby said, her voice distant. "Jenna Colfax. She worked at the art gallery on Broughton—came in here once to ask about custom hinges for an exhibit frame."

Nate felt his pulse quicken.

"She was twenty-three," Ruby continued. "Pretty blonde thing, always smiling. She talked about moving to Atlanta, about getting out of Savannah." Ruby set the photo down. "They found her in Monterey Square in October of 1995. The police said it was a drifter, some transient passing through."

"They always say that," Rodecker said quietly.

Ruby looked at him, then at the crime scene photos spread across the bench. "She looked like them," Ruby said, pointing at Caroline, Lucy, and Nicole. "Same hair, same build." Her voice cracked. "I went to her funeral. Her mother couldn't stop crying—kept saying Jenna had been so excited about a man she'd met, some gentleman from the historic district who appreciated art."

The workshop was silent except for the hiss of the forge.

"Jones Street," Ruby said. "She mentioned Jones Street."

Nate nodded slowly.

Ruby turned to her husband. "Zeke," she said. "There were others. Before Jenna."

Zeke stared at the photos, his expression unreadable.

"My father told me something once," Zeke said, his voice rough.

"Back in the '60s, when I was learning the trade. He said a man came to the shop asking for a special commission—a blade made the old way, bloomery iron, specific dimensions."

Zeke looked at the diagram on the bench. "My father refused. Said there was something wrong about the man, something off. He told me to never make weapons for anyone from Jones Street."

"Did he say why?" Alicia asked.

"He said the old families knew things," Zeke said. "Whispers about a gentleman who didn't age, who'd been in Savannah since before the War Between the States. My father called it superstition, but he was scared enough to turn down the money."

"It's not superstition," Nate said. "We have a Mesopotamian tablet that describes the binding ritual—an *edimmu*, a demon that steals bodies and feeds on blood. The tablet gives the method to break the binding."

Zeke picked up the translation Alicia had laid out, his eyes scanning the ancient script and the annotations.

"This is insane," Zeke said, but his voice lacked conviction.

"The police arrested a homeless veteran named Booker Hayes yesterday," Nate said. "They're charging him with three murders because the Mayor needs a win before the music festival. Booker tried to warn people about Carlisle, and now he's going to prison for trying to help."

Zeke set down the translation.

"Even if I believe you," Zeke said, "even if this is real, you're asking me to forge a murder weapon. You're asking me to be complicit in killing a man."

"Not a man," Alicia said. "The thing wearing Evan Carlisle's face hasn't been human for centuries."

"And you expect me to just accept that?" Zeke asked. "On faith?"

"On evidence," Nate said. He gestured to the photos, the property records, the biometric analysis. "We have forensic impossibilities—bite marks identical across seventy-five years, DNA that matches degraded samples from 1950, blood spatter that defies physics. We have witness testimony going back generations. We have your father's warning."

Ruby walked to the shelf near the grinding wheel, where a row of amber pill bottles sat coated in a fine layer of iron dust. *Oxycodone. Ondansetron. Gemcitabine.* Oncology medications and pain management. She picked up one of the containers and turned it over in her hands before setting it down.

She looked at her husband. "Jenna Colfax was twenty-three years old," Ruby said. "Her mother buried her only child. I held that woman while she sobbed in the pew, and I had no answers for her."

Ruby's voice hardened. "If this is real—if there's even a chance this is real—we can't walk away."

"Ruby—" Zeke began.

"You're dying anyway," Ruby said, her voice sharp enough to cut. "The doctor said six months. That was four months ago. You've been sitting here waiting for the cancer to finish the job, and you're miserable."

Zeke flinched.

"I've watched you waste away," Ruby continued, tears standing in her eyes. "I've watched you count down the days like a prisoner waiting for execution. If you're going to die, Ezekiel Tatum, at least die doing something that matters."

The silence that followed was suffocating. Zeke looked at his wife, at the photos on the bench, at the diagram with its precise specifications. He picked up the translation and read it again, his lips moving silently.

"Iron smelted the old way," Zeke said. "Quenched in running water. The name spoken at the moment of the strike." He looked at Nate. "And the wielder must be the Hand of Death, an executioner."

"I'm FBI," Nate said. "I'm authorized to use lethal force."

"Not like this, you're not," Zeke said. "This isn't a justified shooting. This is premeditated murder, and if you're wrong, you go to prison for the rest of your life."

"If we're wrong," Nate said, "then a serial killer who's evaded justice for a century goes free, and another person dies. I'll take that risk."

Zeke looked down at the anvil and ran a hand over its smooth, hardened steel face as though drawing strength from the tool. A cough built in his chest, starting low and growing in intensity. He bent over the anvil, the cough racking his frame with violence—a deep, wet sound, like air trapped in damaged lungs. His shoulders shook as he pressed the rag to his mouth, and the sound filled the space under the high rafters with the promise of mortality.

Nate watched him without looking away.

Zeke straightened in increments, wiped his mouth, and crumpled the rag in his hand without hiding the red spots on the grey cloth. His breaths came in shallow, careful gasps, and he rested against the brick wall for support.

"Even if I believe you," Zeke said, "you want me to spend what's left sweating over a bloomery fire. Forging a weapon based on an ancient tablet and a ghost story."

"It's not a story," Nate said.

"Prove it," Zeke said.

Nate held his gaze. "He was in my hotel room two nights ago," Nate said, his voice low and steady. "I woke up, and he was sitting in the chair by the window, watching me sleep. He told me I couldn't stop him. He told me he remembered my sister, Sarah, who died fifteen years ago in Chapel Hill."

Nate's jaw tightened. "He described the way she died. The way her throat looked. Details that were never in the press, never in the reports. He knew because he killed her."

Nate reached into his pocket and pulled out a plastic evidence bag containing a dried lavender sprig. He placed it on the workbench next to the photos.

"He put this in Nicole Gladman's hand after he killed her," Nate said. "The same way he put lavender in my sister's hand fifteen years ago." Nate's voice cracked. "He wanted me to know. He wanted me to understand that he's been watching, that he's been here the whole time, and that I'm powerless to stop him through legal means."

Zeke picked up the evidence bag and held it to the light, studying the withered purple flowers.

"The thermal scan during his interview showed his skin temperature was ten degrees below normal," Nate continued. "His heart rate didn't spike when we accused him of murder. When he leaned close to me, his breath was cold—not cool, but cold like air from a freezer."

Zeke set down the bag.

"And you think this will work?" Zeke asked, tapping the diagram. "You think a piece of iron I hammer out in my yard will kill something that's survived for over a century?"

"The tablet says it will," Alicia said. "The ritual is specific—the iron must be pure, folded to align the grain, quenched in running water, and wielded by someone with the authority to execute. Every element matters."

"And if it doesn't work?" Ruby asked.

"Then we die," Nate said simply. "And Carlisle keeps killing."

A long silence settled over the workshop. Ruby walked to her husband and took his hand, the one still holding the soiled rag. She looked at the blood spotting the grey cloth, then up at his face.

"I think about that sometimes," Ruby said softly. "Jenna's mother. Her face at the funeral." She squeezed Zeke's hand. "If we can stop another mother from burying her daughter—even if it sounds insane, even if it's dangerous—don't we have to try?"

Zeke stared at his wife for a long moment. Then he looked at Nate.

"If I do this," Zeke said, "I'm not making a wall hanger or a museum piece. I'm making an executioner's blade, and you need to understand what that means."

"I understand," Nate said.

"Do you?" Zeke asked. "Because once I start this process, once I commit the iron to the fire, there's no going back. You'll have a weapon, and you'll have a choice—use it or walk away. But that choice will define the rest of your life."

"My life was defined fifteen years ago," Nate said, "when Sarah died, and no one could tell me why. If using that blade means her death finally means something, then I'll carry that weight."

Zeke searched Nate's face for doubt and found none. He turned to Ruby.

"You're sure?" Zeke asked her.

"No," Ruby said. "But I'm sure about you, and I'm sure about what happened to Jenna." She touched his face with her free hand.

"And I'm sure that if we do nothing, we'll regret it for whatever time we have left."

Zeke closed his eyes and took a shallow, careful breath. When he opened them, they were clear and focused. He released Ruby's hand and walked to the coal bin, picking up a shovel.

"Three days," Zeke said. "I'll need bog iron ore, charcoal, clay for the furnace, and running water for the quench."

"We'll get everything," Alicia said, her voice shaking with relief.

Zeke turned to face them, and despite the grey pallor of his skin, he stood straight.

"But I want something in return," Zeke said.

"Name it," Nate said.

Zeke looked at Ruby, then back at Nate. "When this is over," Zeke said, "whether it works or it doesn't, whether you kill him or he kills you—I want the truth recorded. I want someone to know that Ezekiel Tatum spent his last days forging a weapon to stop a monster, not wasting away in a hospice bed." His voice grew fierce. "I don't want to be a footnote or a casualty. I want my work to be remembered."

"I'll make sure of it," Alicia said. "I promise."

Zeke nodded slowly. He looked at the diagram on the bench, at the specifications written in Alicia's careful hand, at the translation of the ancient ritual.

"Bloomery iron," Zeke said, almost to himself. "Forty folds. Quenched in running water." He picked up his hammer and tested its weight. "I haven't done this in thirty years. It might kill me before the cancer does."

"Then you'll die at the anvil," Ruby said, her voice steady despite the tears on her face. "Not in a hospital bed."

Zeke looked at his wife and managed a ghost of a smile. "I can live with that," he said.

He turned to Nate and extended his hand. Nate took it, feeling the callouses and the tremor beneath the grip. They shook once, firm and final.

"Three days," Zeke repeated.

"We'll be here," Nate said.

Zeke released his hand and walked to the forge. He cranked the handle of the blower, sending air rushing into the fire pot and making the coals burn brighter. The orange light intensified until it hurt to look at directly. He picked up the shovel and fed the beast.

Ruby stood beside her husband, watching him work.

Nate signaled to the others. They turned and walked back through the office, leaving Ruby and Zeke to their preparations. They exited through the heavy steel door and stepped back into the humid, grey light of the service lane.

Nate looked back through the grime of the window and saw the dark shape of Ezekiel Tatum framed by the rising flames. He raised the hammer with deliberate care. He brought it down with purpose.

The ring of iron on iron followed them down the alley.

CHAPTER

39

THE HEAT of the forge clung to Nate's clothes as they moved away from the shop, the smell of coal smoke embedded in his nostrils and masking the scent of damp garbage.

Rodecker checked the corners as they emerged onto Broughton Street, where the late afternoon pedestrian traffic was picking up. Tourists with shopping bags moved between boutiques while a trolley tour rumbled past, the guide's amplified voice carrying over the traffic.

"...and some say the spirits still walk these streets," the guide said.

Nate watched a group of college students laugh at the story without any idea of how close to the truth it was.

"He's dying," Alicia said, her voice low as she walked beside Nate and clutched her satchel to her chest. "The tablet says the wielder must be the 'Hand of Death'—*Qāt mīt.*"

"We talked about this," Nate said, his eyes moving across the faces in the crowd in never-ending assessment. "It means an executioner, someone authorized."

"I know," Alicia said. "But I get the feeling we were meant to come here. And watching him cough up blood and looking at those pills—"

"He's a craftsman," Nate said dismissively. "He wants to finish strong, so don't overthink it."

Rodecker fell in step on Nate's other side.

"You think he can do it?" Rodecker asked. "Three days is fast for that type of work, and that's for a healthy man."

"He'll do it," Nate said. "He has to."

"And what happens when he dies in the middle of it?" Rodecker asked.

"Then we finish it," Nate said. "Somehow."

They reached the corner where the Marshall House was visible two blocks down, the flag above the entrance hanging limp in the still air.

"I need to get the iron ore," Alicia said. "Zeke has a supplier for the raw bog iron, but we need to pick it up from a warehouse near the port."

"I'll drive," Rodecker said. "My truck is inconspicuous."

"Do it," Nate said. "Get him whatever he needs—charcoal, clay, moon rocks, whatever."

Nate stopped and looked at his reflection in a shop window, where the suit appeared expensive but hung wrong on him now. He looked like a man wearing a costume, and the bandages on his hands were dirty with forge dust.

He thought of Booker Hayes sitting in a cell and of the plea deal on the table.

"I'm going to see Booker," Nate said.

"Is that smart?" Rodecker asked. "Dean will check the visitor logs."

"I don't care," Nate said. "He needs to know we haven't given up and that the cavalry is coming."

"The cavalry being a dying blacksmith and three disgraced public servants?" Rodecker asked.

Nate looked toward the forge in the distance, where the smoke from Zeke's chimney was just visible against the grey sky, a thin dark line rising straight up.

"Those are the only kind worth having," Nate said.

He turned and walked toward the parking garage with heavy steps. The burn in his hands was a continual throb, a reminder that he was still alive and could still fight.

He got into his rental car, where the interior was hot from sitting in the sun. He tossed his jacket onto the passenger seat and started the engine, the A/C blasting warm air that would take minutes to cool. He gripped the steering wheel despite the way the gauze slid against the leather.

Three days.

Zeke Tatum was working, and Nate just hoped the old man could finish the job before his body gave out.

Nate merged into traffic and became invisible again—just another suit in a sedan. But under the seat, wrapped in a towel, lay his service weapon. And in his mind, the plan was solidifying into something hard and sharp.

Iron. Water. Name. Hand.

The formula for murder or salvation, depending on who wielded it.

He drove toward the jail as the sun began to set and the long shadows of the live oaks lay across the road. The city was getting ready for the night.

So was he.

CHAPTER

40

THE FORGE WAS dark when Alicia returned with the ore, the streetlights buzzing overhead like dying insects. The industrial block was empty at this hour, the machine shops and welding yards locked behind chain-link and razor wire. Only the Metalworks showed light —a dim glow seeping from beneath the steel roll-up door.

Alicia knocked on the steel door. The sound echoed in the empty street.

Ruby opened it while holding a mug of tea, steam rising in the cool night air. She wore an old flannel shirt over jeans, her grey hair pulled back in a braid. She looked past Alicia to the boxes of raw bog iron in the bed of Rodecker's truck, then nodded once.

"Bring it around back," Ruby said. "He's prepping the furnace."

Rodecker pulled the truck through the side gate and into the gravel yard behind the shop. The space was cluttered with scrap metal, rusted drums, and the skeletal frames of half-finished projects. But in the center, illuminated by a single work light, stood something that didn't belong in the twenty-first century.

Zeke had built a structure out of clay bricks that looked primitive, ancient—like a beehive or a small chimney rising from the earth. The bloomery furnace stood roughly four feet tall, its walls thick and hand-shaped, the clay still damp in places where he had sealed cracks. A bed of charcoal glowed red at its base, and the air shimmered with heat.

They carried the heavy boxes across the yard, boots crunching on gravel. Zeke was packing more charcoal into the base of the furnace and didn't look up when they entered. He wore a leather apron over his thin frame, his arms bare despite the chill. Sweat darkened his shirt at the spine.

"Is that it?" Zeke asked, his voice rough.

"Bog iron," Alicia said, setting down her box. "From the riverbeds near Ebenezer Creek. Three different sites, like you said."

Zeke straightened slowly, joints popping, and moved to the boxes. He pulled out a chunk of the ore—dark, rust-colored, porous like volcanic rock. He turned it over in his calloused hands, examining it in the work light, testing its weight.

"Good," he said. "Pure. No industrial contamination."

He set the ore down carefully, almost reverently, then turned back to the furnace. He coughed—a deep, rattling sound that came from the bottom of his lungs—and spit into the dust. The phlegm was dark.

"Go home," Zeke said. "This part takes time—I need to bake the moisture out of the clay, get the heat up in stages. Can't rush iron. You rush it, it's brittle. Brittle won't kill what you're hunting."

"We can help," Alicia said. "I've read about the process—"

"No," Zeke said, cutting her off. He turned to face her, and in the firelight, his face looked skeletal, the skin stretched tight over bone. "You can't—this is between me and the fire. Always has been."

He looked at the clay tower, at the glowing building in its belly.

"Come back tomorrow," Zeke said. "Late afternoon. Bring the water."

"Water?" Alicia asked.

"For the quench," Zeke said. "You said running water or sacred water, whatever the text said. You bring that, and I'll have your blade."

Alicia felt the weight of what he was offering. Not just a weapon, but a piece of himself—his knowledge, his craft, his remaining time on earth poured into steel.

"We can use the water from the stream nearby," Alicia said.

Zeke looked at her with an intensity that made her want to look away, but she held his gaze.

"Make sure it's right," he said. "The metal will remember the water that births it. I've got one shot at this because my lungs won't last for a second try."

Alicia nodded. "I understand."

"Do you?" Zeke asked. He gestured to the bloomery. "This is old magic, Dr. Landry. Older than your books. Iron from the earth, fire from the forge, water from the living world. You're not making a knife —you're making an answer."

"An answer to what?" Rodecker asked from behind them.

"To something that shouldn't exist," Zeke said. He turned back to the fire. "Now go. Let me work."

Alicia walked back to the truck where Rodecker was waiting, wiping his hands on his pants.

"He good?" Rodecker asked.

"He's working," Alicia said. She looked at the smoke rising from the yard, grey against the sodium lights. "He's dying to do this."

"Aren't we all," Rodecker said quietly.

He put the truck in gear, and they drove away. In the rearview mirror, Alicia watched the fire in the yard grow brighter, casting long shadows against the brick walls. Zeke Tatum stood in the light, feeding charcoal into the furnace's mouth and talking to the flames in a voice too low to hear.

CHAPTER

41

THE CHATHAM COUNTY DETENTION CENTER was a fortress of concrete and razor wire west of the city, sitting in an expanse of scrub pine and marshland where it was designed to be forgotten. Nate parked in the visitor lot and walked to the intake center, where the fluorescent lights buzzed in a room that smelled of floor wax and hopelessness.

He flashed his credentials at the plexiglass window. The desk sergeant, a thick-necked man with grey stubble, examined the badge with narrowed eyes, then looked at Nate like he was measuring him for a cell.

"You're the fed from the warehouse," the sergeant said, not a question.

"I need to see Booker Hayes," Nate said.

The sergeant picked up a phone, spoke in low tones that Nate couldn't hear, then set it down with deliberate slowness. "Captain says five minutes. No recording devices."

"Understood."

The buzz of the door lock was harsh and final. The power of the badge still held weight here in this forgotten corner of the justice system, but it was fraying at the edges.

He waited in a small interview room where the table was bolted to the floor, and the chair was cold steel. The walls were cinderblock painted institutional beige, scuffed at shoulder height where men had leaned into despair. The air was stale and recycled, thick with the accumulated exhalations of a thousand confessions.

The door opened.

Booker Hayes shuffled in wearing an orange jumpsuit that hung loose on his frame, the fabric stiff and cheap. His wrists were shackled to his waist, the chain clinking with each step. Without his layered coats, without the bulk that had made him seem solid and immovable on his bench in the squares, he looked diminished. Smaller. They had forced him through intake showers that stripped away more than grime—they had stripped away his armor.

His limp was more pronounced without his worn sneakers, the jail-issue slides offering no support. A purple bruise spread across his left cheekbone, fresh enough to still be swollen. His head had been shaved down to grey stubble that revealed the shape of his skull, the sharp angles of a man who had lost weight he couldn't afford to lose.

But it was his eyes that hit Nate hardest. On the street, even in his exhaustion, Booker's eyes had held awareness, vigilance, the sharp focus of a man who survived by seeing threats before they materialized. Now they were flat, dulled by fluorescent light and concrete walls and the soul-crushing mathematics of capital murder charges.

The street had weathered him, but the cage was breaking him.

A guard stood by the door with his arms crossed.

"Give us the room," Nate said.

The guard hesitated and said, "He's high risk—capital murder charges."

"I'm a federal agent," Nate said, putting every ounce of command he had left into his voice. "Step outside."

The guard shrugged and stepped out, the heavy door clanging shut behind him.

Booker sat with the chains rattling, looking at Nate with eyes that had gone dull.

"You come to tell me to take the deal?" Booker asked.

"No," Nate said.

"Public defender says I should," Booker said. "Says living is better than the needle, and nobody beats three bodies."

"You didn't kill them," Nate said.

"Doesn't matter," Booker said, his voice carrying the flat resigna-tion of a man who understood the machinery that was grinding him down. "Dean needs a win, Mayor needs a win, and I'm the convenient win."

Nate felt the words like a fist to his sternum. He was looking at a sacrifice, at a man being fed to a system that valued optics over truth. He thought of Sarah, of standing in a different room fifteen years ago, being told there were no leads, no suspects, no justice coming. He thought of how that helplessness had calcified into obsession, how it had consumed every relationship he'd tried to build.

He wouldn't let it happen again. Not to Booker. Not to anyone.

Nate shifted forward and put his bandaged hands on the table where Booker could see them. The gauze was still white, changed this morning, but his palms throbbed with the memory of fire.

"We found a way," Nate said.

Booker looked at the bandages and then at Nate's face with dawning comprehension.

"Mr. Evan?" Booker asked.

"We know what he is," Nate said. "We know how to stop him, and we're building the tool now."

Booker studied him and saw the fatigue and the desperation written in every line of Nate's face.

"You going to kill him?" Booker asked.

"Yes," Nate said.

Booker nodded and settled back against the chair, something like relief passing across his features.

"Good," Booker said. "He needs killing."

"It's going to take a few days," Nate said. "You need to hold on—don't sign anything, don't confess, just wait."

"I'm good at waiting," Booker said. "Spent a year doing it in Fallujah. Spent ten years doing it in shelters. What's a few more days?"

Booker looked at the two-way mirror on the wall and at his own reflection staring back at him—a ghost in orange, a man already erased.

"You sure?" Booker asked.

Nate hesitated. The weight of the word hung between them, heavy as the chains on Booker's wrists. He thought about all the variables, all the ways it could go wrong. But he also thought about walking away from this room, leaving Booker to rot for crimes he didn't commit while the real monster walked free.

"I promise," Nate said.

Booker's expression shifted, something sad and knowing entering his eyes.

"Don't promise," Booker said, his voice dropping to barely above a whisper. "Promises are for people who still believe the world works right. I've heard promises from the VA, from social workers, from cops who said they'd look into things. Promises don't unlock doors, Agent Holloway. Promises don't stop judges. Promises just make it hurt worse when they break."

The words settled into the space between them like stones dropped in still water.

"Then I won't promise," Nate said, holding Booker's gaze. "I'll just do it."

Booker studied him for a long moment, then nodded once, a small movement that carried the weight of trust given against better judgment, "And then it's over?"

"Yes," Nate confirmed.

Nate stood and signaled the guard through the small window. The door opened, and the guard stepped in, keys already in hand.

"Stay safe," Nate said.

Booker laughed, a hollow sound that echoed in the small room and died against the cinderblock walls.

"I'm in a box, Agent Holloway," Booker said as they pulled him to his feet. "I'm the safest man in Savannah—you're the one walking around with the monsters."

The guard led him toward the door, and Booker looked back over his shoulder one last time.

"Don't get bit," Booker said.

Nate watched them lead Booker away, the orange jumpsuit disappearing down the grey hallway, the shuffle of his feet and the clink of chains fading into the institutional silence. The door closed with a hollow boom that seemed to echo in Nate's chest.

He stood alone in the interview room, staring at the empty chair where Booker had sat, at the scuff marks on the table where countless shackled hands had rested. The fluorescent lights buzzed overhead, indifferent and eternal.

He had made a promise he wasn't supposed to make, to a man who didn't believe in promises anymore.

Now he had to keep it.

CHAPTER

42

ZEKE TATUM STOOD at the center of the inferno. The blacksmith had transformed his workspace into something archaic, something that belonged in another century. The electric lights were off, and the only illumination came from the angry orange throat of the clay furnace Zeke had built by hand over the last forty-eight hours. Shadows jumped against the brick walls, stretching and snapping back with the rhythm of the bellows like living things responding to an unseen conductor.

Zeke gripped the wooden handle of the primary pump and pulled down. Air rushed through the clay tuyere pipe at the base of the furnace, and the fire roared—a deafening rush of combustion that vibrated through the floor and up through Nate's boots. Zeke released the handle, and the leather lung of the bellows expanded with a wheeze. He pulled again.

Down. Roar. Up. Silence. Down. Roar.

Zeke's apprentice, a young man named Isaiah, worked the secondary pump on the other side of the furnace. They moved in sync, bodies bowing and straightening like penitents before an altar of mud and fire, locked in a rhythm older than the country they stood in.

Alicia Landry stood three feet from the furnace with a sheaf of papers in one hand and her phone in the other, using the screen's flashlight to read her own handwriting. The blue-white LED beam cut through the haze of coal dust like a knife through smoke.

"Temperature is holding," she said over the noise. "Keep the airflow steady. Do not spike it."

Nate watched her from across the shop. Her cardigan and glasses seemed too clean for a room that smelled of burning rock and ancient chemistry, yet she didn't flinch when sparks popped from the vent and scattered across the concrete. She stared at the clay walls of the furnace as if she could see the atomic structures shifting inside, as if she could read the transformation happening at the molecular level.

Rodecker and Pierce stood behind Nate, pressed against the jamb of the open door to catch the draft from the alley. Rodecker had his hand near his waist, eyes scanning the dark service lane outside—old habits from twenty years on the street. He was looking for a shooter or a suspect, but the threat wasn't coming from the alley.

The threat was the process itself.

Zeke stumbled.

His boot caught on a piece of charcoal scattered on the floor, and the rhythm of the bellows faltered for a second. The roar dropped in pitch, and Ruby Tatum started forward from the office doorway. She stopped herself after one step, her hands gripping her apron so hard the knuckles showed white. She knew the rules better than anyone. If the air stopped, the heat dropped, and if the heat dropped, the iron wouldn't separate from the slag. The bloom would die in the womb.

Zeke recovered, hauling down on the handle with a grunt that Nate heard over the fire. The roar returned, building back to full volume, and the old man's face was a mask of soot and strain. His mouth hung open, gasping for oxygen that the fire was consuming first.

Nate checked his watch. Four hours since they started pumping. Four hours of this brutal, monotonous work.

"How much longer?" Nate had to yell to be heard over the roar.

Alicia checked the translation notes again, then looked at the color of the flame venting from the top of the stack. It had shifted from yellow to a blinding white that hurt to look at directly.

"The slag has to liquefy," Alicia said, her voice high to cut through the noise. "It has to drop to the bottom. If we pull it too early, it's just a rock. If we wait too long, the iron re-oxidizes."

She looked at Zeke, and he was staring at the furnace with glassy eyes that reflected the firelight.

"Now," Zeke said. His voice was a rasp that cut under the noise like a blade under skin.

He let go of the bellows, and Isaiah dropped his handle. The silence that rushed into the room was sudden and ringing, broken only by the settling crackle of the coals.

"Break it," Zeke said.

Isaiah grabbed a heavy iron pry bar leaning against the wall and jammed the chisel tip into the dried clay at the base of the furnace. He heaved, and the baked mud cracked with a sharp report like a gunshot.

Heat flooded out in a wave that slammed into Nate's chest.

He shielded his face with his forearm as the air in the shop rippled with the assault. Zeke moved toward the furnace and picked up a pair of tongs that looked big enough to pull a railroad tie. He jammed them into the hole Isaiah had made, twisted his torso, and braced his legs against the concrete floor. The muscles in his neck stood out like cords under the skin.

He pulled.

Something came out of the fire.

It didn't look like a sword or a weapon or anything that belonged in the modern world. It was a jagged, dripping mass of orange sponge that wept liquid fire onto the floor, where it hissed and sputtered. Slag pooled beneath it—molten glass and rock.

The bloom.

"Anvil," Zeke said, his voice a ragged whisper.

He dragged the mass across the floor, lacking the strength to lift it fully, and swung it up onto the steel face of the anvil with a grunt that sounded like it tore something inside him.

"Clear out," Zeke told Isaiah, and the apprentice scrambled back toward the wall.

Zeke dropped the tongs, reached for the hammer—not a power hammer but a four-pound cross-peen hand hammer with a handle polished smooth by decades of work—and raised it over his head.

He brought it down.

CRACK.

The sound rang in Nate's ears like a church bell. Liquid slag exploded from the bloom in a shower of yellow sparks that sprayed across the shop, bouncing off the brick walls and stinging Nate's exposed neck. He didn't move, didn't flinch, just watched as Zeke raised the hammer again.

CRACK.

Zeke swung again, consolidating the iron and beating the impurities out of the sponge while it was still at welding heat. It was brutal work that required strength and precision in equal measure, and Nate could see the toll it was taking.

CRACK.

Nate watched Zeke's arms as the hammer rose and fell. They were thin, the skin hanging loose over the muscle like fabric draped over wire, but the geometry of his swing was perfect. He used the rebound of the anvil to lift the hammer for the next strike, trading his remaining life for velocity.

The bloom began to flatten, changing from a sponge to a brick as the glow began to fade from white-hot to cherry red.

"Heat," Zeke said, his voice barely audible over the ringing in Nate's ears.

He shoved the iron into the coal forge—not the bloomery furnace, but the open forge he used for daily work—and cranked the blower. Sparks shot up the chimney like fireflies escaping captivity.

Alicia moved closer, counting under her breath in a rhythm that matched the bellows.

"No flux," she reminded him, her voice shrill with tension. "The tablet is specific. No borax. No modern chemical binders. The weld has to be pure."

Zeke didn't look at her, just watched the color of the metal in the coals with the focus of a man reading his own death sentence. He knew what he was doing. He was welding with heat and strength alone, the hard way, the old way.

He pulled the billet out and went to work.

Hammer. Strike. Turn. Strike. Turn.

He drew the brick out into a long bar, then stopped and set a chisel at the center of the bar. He struck it hard, cutting the bar halfway through, then folded the metal back onto itself.

"First fold," Alicia said, almost to herself, her voice barely a whisper.

Zeke brushed the scale off with a wire brush and put it back in the fire.

This was the ritual. Heat. Hammer. Fold. Heat. Hammer. Fold.

The repetition was monotonous, broken only by the danger of flying sparks and Zeke's visible exhaustion. With every cycle, he moved a little slower, his chest heaving with the effort of drawing breath in the oxygen-depleted room. The coughing started during the third heat.

It was a wet, rattling sound that shook his whole frame. Zeke bent over the anvil, gripping the edge with one hand and the tongs in the other, and coughed until his face turned grey under the soot.

Ruby was at his side before Nate could move.

She stepped into the workspace with a plastic cup and put a hand on Zeke's back. She held the cup to his lips without saying a word.

"Drink," she said, and her voice was steady despite what Nate could see in her eyes.

Zeke drank, water spilling down his chin and cutting paths through the grime on his face. He nodded to her and pushed her hand away with more gentleness than Nate expected.

"Iron's getting cold," he said, his voice a wheeze that came from somewhere deep in his chest.

He went back to the hammer without another word.

Ruby stepped back to the wall and crossed her arms. Her face was granite, every line carved from stone, and she was watching her husband kill himself, strike by strike. She wasn't stopping him because she understood what Nate understood—this was the only thing left that mattered.

She was letting him finish.

Nate looked at the metal taking shape on the anvil.

It was changing with every fold and every strike. The folding process was homogenizing the carbon, driving out the last of the slag, and transforming the iron into something harder and sharper. It was becoming steel.

Zeke worked for another hour, and the rhythm of the hammer slowed, but the strikes never lost their accuracy. *Ring. Ring. Ring.* The sound became the heartbeat of the room, a pulse that Nate felt in his chest.

The concrete floor hummed against the soles of Nate's shoes, and he felt the vibration in the burns on his palms through the bandages.

The blade began to take shape under Zeke's hammer.

He drew out the point with careful, deliberate strikes, then beveled the edges and used a flatter tool to smooth the surface. It was a short sword, perhaps fourteen inches of blade, double-edged and leaf-shaped with a thick, tapered tang.

It looked rough, looked ancient, looked like something dug out of a peat bog. The surface wasn't mirror-polished like modern steel—it had a texture, a grain that ran through it like petrified wood that had caught fire and been frozen mid-burn.

Zeke leaned his weight on the tongs, his entire body sagging against the anvil. "Final heat."

His shirt was soaked through with sweat, clinging to his ribs and showing every bone in his chest.

He put the blade back into the coals one last time and watched the color change. He wasn't looking for bright orange now—he was looking for the temperature where the steel lost its magnetism, where the crystal structure changed at the atomic level and became something new.

Alicia stepped forward and held up her phone with the translation notes visible on the screen.

"The quench," she said, her voice tight with something between fear and excitement. "Running water. Not a bucket. It has to be the living current."

Zeke nodded once, then pulled the blade from the fire. It burned a dull, menacing red that painted his face in shades of hell.

He didn't put it on the anvil this time.

Instead, he grabbed a strip of wet leather from the water trough and wrapped it quickly around the hot tang, his hands moving with muscle memory that overrode pain. He gripped the leather-wrapped tang and dropped the tongs with a clatter.

"Door," Zeke said.

Rodecker kicked the back door open, and cold air rushed in.

Zeke moved faster than a dying man should be able to move, carrying the red-hot steel in front of him like a priest carrying a relic.

They poured out of the shop into the alley in a ragged procession.

The transition was jarring, brutal in its contrast. The air outside was cool and thick with humidity, and the smell of the tidal creek hit Nate like a slap—salt mud and decaying marsh grass and the mineral tang of the Savannah River. The sky to the east was turning the color of a bruised plum as dawn crept toward them.

Zeke led them down the narrow path behind the shop, his boots crunching on gravel. The ground was uneven, covered in weeds and broken glass, but he didn't stumble or hesitate.

They reached the bank of the creek.

The water was a dark vein cutting through the marsh, feeding into the Savannah River a mile downstream. The tide was moving out, pulling the water with it, and the current was black and fast and looked deep.

Zeke stopped at the edge of the mud, and his boots sank slightly into the soft earth.

He held the blade up, and the red light illuminated his face from below. His eyes were wide, staring at something Nate couldn't see, and he looked like a priest on a ziggurat about to make an offering to gods that no longer had names.

Nate stood ten feet back with Alicia beside him. She was trembling, her breath coming in quick, shallow gasps.

"Do it," she said, her voice barely audible over the sound of the water.

Zeke didn't hesitate, didn't pray or speak or acknowledge the moment.

He thrust the red-hot steel into the black water.

A high-pitched shriek tore through the quiet morning—a sound of pure thermal shock that set Nate's teeth on edge. A plume of white steam exploded from the water and rose up in a violent column, obscuring Zeke completely.

The water around the blade boiled and churned like something alive was thrashing beneath the surface.

A vibration traveled through the ground, up Nate's legs, and settled in his teeth like the aftermath of an explosion.

The shriek faded to a hiss, then to silence broken only by the sound of the creek.

The steam began to disperse, carried away by the river breeze.

Zeke stood motionless, bent over the water with the blade submerged. He held it there for a long count of ten, then pulled it out.

The red light was gone.

The blade was black as old iron, dripping water that looked like ink in the low light.

Zeke turned slowly, his steps heavy and uncertain, and walked up the bank. He stopped in front of Nate and Alicia and held the blade out between them.

"Check it," Zeke said, his voice a shadow of what it had been.

Alicia reached out with trembling fingers and touched the flat of the blade. She pulled her hand back as if she'd been shocked, her eyes wide.

"It's humming," she said, her voice shaking with something between awe and terror. "It's vibrating."

"It's cool," Zeke said, and there was satisfaction in his voice despite the pain. "Hard."

He wiped the blade with the wet leather rag, and the black scale revealed a pattern underneath—swirls of grey and silver like oil on water, like the watering pattern of wootz steel or something older that had no name in modern metallurgy.

Zeke's knees buckled.

It happened in slow motion, like watching a building collapse. The adrenaline that had sustained him for twelve hours evaporated all at once, and the cancer reclaimed him with interest.

He folded forward.

Nate lunged, but Ruby was faster despite the distance. She caught him under the arm and took his weight, bracing her hip against his and keeping him upright through sheer determination.

Zeke hacked, and it was a terrible, tearing sound. He doubled over, his body convulsing with spasms he couldn't control, and pulled the rag from his pocket to press it to his mouth. He coughed until he couldn't breathe, until his eyes bulged and his face turned purple.

When he pulled the rag away, Nate shone his flashlight on it without thinking.

Bright, frothy red stained the fabric.

Arterial blood, oxygenated and fresh.

Zeke stared at the blood on the rag for a long moment, then wiped his mouth with the back of his hand. The motion smeared red into the soot on his face like war paint.

He looked at Nate, and his eyes were clearer than they had any right to be. There was no fear in them, no regret or second-guessing—only a cold, hard satisfaction.

He reversed the blade and held it by the steel itself, offering the leather-wrapped tang to Nate.

"Take it," Zeke said, his voice a rattle in his throat.

Nate reached out, and his bandaged hand closed around the leather grip.

The weapon was heavy, heavier than a knife, heavier than a gun. It felt dense, as if the metal contained more mass than its volume should allow, as if the weight came from somewhere other than the physical world.

Nate looked at the black iron, then at the dying man leaning against his wife.

"Use it right," Zeke said, and his voice was barely a whisper. He gripped Nate's forearm with a hand that felt like a claw made of bone and skin. "Make it matter."

Nate looked into Zeke's eyes and saw the transaction laid bare. Zeke had poured his remaining days into the fire, had shortened his life to forge this death, and now he needed to know it would count for something.

"I will," Nate said, and he meant it with everything he had left.

He didn't say thank you because thank you wasn't adequate for what had just happened.

Zeke nodded once, then slumped against Ruby with the last of his strength gone.

"Get him inside," Nate told Rodecker, his voice rough. "Help her."

Rodecker moved to Zeke's other side, and together he and Ruby half-carried, half-walked the blacksmith back toward the shop. Zeke's boots dragged in the dirt, leaving tracks in the mud.

Nate stood by the creek with the iron blade in his hand.

The sky was lightening minute by minute, turning from purple to grey to the pale gold of early morning. The city was waking up around them—delivery trucks on Bay Street, the first tourists heading toward River Street, the normal world going about its business. Somewhere in a townhouse on Jones Street, a monster was sleeping in the dark, unaware that the weapon of its destruction had just been born.

43

Nate watched from the doorway of the office as Ruby settled Zeke onto the worn leather sofa in the corner. Rodecker stood awkwardly by the filing cabinet with his hands hanging uselessly at his sides, and the big detective looked helpless in the face of this particular kind of violence—the kind that medicine couldn't stop and badges couldn't prevent.

Zeke's breathing was a shallow rattle that filled the small room. His skin was the color of old parchment, yellowed and thin.

"Go," Ruby said without looking up. She was wiping Zeke's face with a clean towel, removing the soot and sweat with gentle strokes.

"We can call a bus," Rodecker said, his voice uncertain. "Get him to Candler."

"No hospitals," Zeke said with his eyes closed. "Home."

Ruby looked at Nate, and her eyes were dry despite everything. "You have what you came for. Go do what you said you would do."

Nate nodded and backed out of the room without another word.

He walked through the silent shop, past the cooling furnace where the clay was already cracking as it contracted. The air still smelled of sulfur and sweat and the acrid bite of quenched steel.

He stepped out into the alley where Alicia was waiting by Rodecker's truck. She was staring at the blade in Nate's hand like it was a live wire.

"It's real," she said, her voice filled with something close to wonder. "The translation, the ritual—it actually worked."

"We'll see," Nate said, because he'd learned not to trust anything until it was tested.

He opened the back door of the truck and grabbed a roll of

oilcloth from Rodecker's tool kit. He wrapped the blade with care, not wanting to touch it directly because it felt like holding something that shouldn't exist.

Rodecker came out a moment later, and he looked shaken in a way Nate had never seen.

"He's tough," Rodecker said, his voice quiet. "But he's not lasting three days, not like that."

"He lasted long enough," Nate said, and it was the truth.

"Friday," Alicia said, checking her phone. "That's tomorrow night. The cycle peaks."

"We need to get ready," Nate said, already thinking through the logistics. "We need to scout the Jones Street house again."

He looked at the wrapped bundle in his hand, feeling the weight of it.

"Let's go," Nate said, moving toward the truck. "We have work to do."

They got into the truck, and Rodecker started the engine with a cough of exhaust. As they pulled away, Nate looked back at the forge one last time through the rear window. The windows were dark, the fire was out, and the building looked like any other industrial shop on the block.

The cost had been paid in blood and breath and years of life.

Rodecker drove them back to the Marshall House without speaking, his eyes fixed on the road ahead. The morning traffic was building on Bay Street—delivery trucks making their rounds, commuters heading to work, the normal world going about its business like nothing had changed.

Nate felt the disconnect like a physical thing in his chest. He was sitting in a Ford F-150 with a piece of Iron Age technology on his lap that was supposed to kill a Sumerian demon, and the rest of the world was worried about coffee and traffic.

He looked at his hands, at the bandages filthy with soot and sweat. He needed to change them, needed to sleep, but the vibration of the blade seemed to travel through the oilcloth and into his legs.

It kept him awake.

Rodecker dropped them at the hotel entrance and left the engine running.

"I'll coordinate with Pierce," Rodecker said, his voice back to business. "We'll set up the staging area on Whitaker Street."

"Keep it off the radio," Nate said, because the last thing they needed was official attention.

"I know the drill," Rodecker said, then looked at Nate with concern in his eyes. "You okay?"

"I'm fine," Nate said, and it was a lie they both recognized.

"You look like hell," Rodecker said.

"Fits the job," Nate said, and got out of the truck.

Alicia followed him through the lobby, both of them ignoring the look from the night clerk who was wondering what they'd been doing. They took the stairs to the fourth floor because the elevator felt too slow.

Nate unlocked the door to Room 417 and pushed it open.

Nate cleared the desk with one sweep of his arm, sending papers and notes to the floor. He unwrapped the blade with deliberate care and laid it down on the wooden surface.

Under the electric lights, it looked even more crude and ancient. Lumps of slag were still embedded in the crossguard where Zeke hadn't had time to clean them, and the edge was rough and unpolished.

But the pattern in the steel caught the light and twisted it. The metal seemed to shift and eddy like water flowing over stones.

Alicia stood beside him, staring at the blade.

"You have to be the one," she said, her voice quiet but certain.

"I know," Nate said, because they'd been over this before.

"The tablet was specific," she said, reciting the translation from memory. "The hand of death must wield it."

Nate looked at Sarah's picture on the corkboard, then back at the blade. He picked it up and tested its balance. It was tip-heavy, designed for chopping rather than thrusting—a tool for severing, for separation, for cutting things away.

He swung it slowly through the air, feeling it hiss.

Alicia went to the door and paused with her hand on the knob. "I'm going to get some sleep. You should too."

"I will," Nate said, another lie they both recognized.

She left, and the door clicked shut behind her.

Nate sat in the chair by the window and held the newly forged weapon across his lap. He watched the sun come up over Savannah, painting the sky in shades of purple and gold, turning the city from shadow to light. The tourists would be out soon, wandering the squares and taking photos, living their normal lives.

CHAPTER

44

THE GAUZE STRIPS PULLED at the raw skin of Nate's palms, a hot circuit of pain flaring up his wrists as he peeled them away. He gritted his teeth and dropped the soiled bandages into the hotel trash can, watching pink fluid from the warehouse cable burns stain the white cotton. He poured antiseptic over the wounds, his hands shaking from the damage to the muscle and the systemic shock that hadn't quite faded since the fire. He wrapped fresh gauze around his palms.

Alicia Landry stood by the desk, a tremor in the hand she used to tap a photograph on the wood surface. Her hair was pulling loose from its bun, dark strands framing a face pale from lack of sleep.

"This was yesterday," Alicia said, her voice scratchy from exhaustion. "Four p.m., and she was inside for three hours."

Nate moved to the desk and flexed his stiff fingers, testing the range of motion before he looked at the photo. It was a grainy telephoto shot taken from a vehicle, showing a woman on the sidewalk outside 465 Jones Street—a blonde, petite woman in a gallery-chic black dress that looked expensive.

"Zoe Kaplan," Alicia said. "Junior curator at the gallery on Broughton, been in Savannah three months after transferring from Atlanta."

Alicia slid a second photo across the desk, this one clearer, taken through the window of a coffee shop where Zoe sat at a small table with a leather-bound notebook open in front of her, writing furiously.

"I got close enough to see the header on the page," Alicia said. "She titled it *The Carlisle Collection*."

Nate stared at the image, watching Zoe's face angled down while the profile remained distinct enough to recognize. He looked from the photo in his hand to the corkboard wall, his eyes tracing the line of Sarah's jaw, then Caroline Marsh's, then Lucy Phelps's—the slope of the nose, the set of the chin all matching in ways that couldn't be a coincidence. Carlisle wasn't just hunting for an opportunity; he was ordering from a menu.

"In the frame, her weight was on her heels, head lolling back slightly like the posture of a drunk, but her hands were empty," Alicia said. "She stumbled when she hit the pavement, like she had to remember how to use her legs."

"Disorientation," Nate said, picking up the photo with the tips of his bandaged fingers. "Time distortion and sensory overload."

"The thrall," Alicia said.

"Call it what you want," Nate said, dropping the photo back on the desk. "It's the pre-capture phase where he isolates her, makes her feel special, makes her feel seen, and she's the next link in his chain."

Alicia looked at him with eyes that wanted him to say something different. "We have the blade and the plan for the house, so we don't need her."

"We need probable cause," Nate said. "Rodecker can't kick down that door on a hunch, not with his badge on the line, and we need a live victim in distress to justify exigent circumstances."

"She's a civilian, Nate."

"She's already a victim who just doesn't know it yet." Nate turned to see Detective Pierce leaning against the wall, cleaning her service weapon as the slide clicked back, the smell of gun oil sharpening the air. She hadn't looked up during the exchange.

"Bring her in," Nate said. "Quietly, no sirens, no uniforms—make it a voluntary community safety interview and tell her we're screening women in the arts district."

Pierce snapped the slide forward, the metal click loud in the quiet room before she holstered the weapon.

"You know what this is," Pierce said, still not looking at him, her eyes fixed on the door.

"I know," Nate said.

"We put her in play—we might not get her back."

"If we don't put her in play, she's dead anyway, and at least this way she has a tracker."

Pierce stared at him for a long second with eyes gone hard before she opened the door. "I'll get the car."

Zoe Kaplan looked out of place against the institutional cinderblock in her silk blouse and tailored trousers, though the polish was slipping. Her hair was mussed on one side, as if she had been running her hands through it repeatedly, and her lipstick was worn off in the center. She gripped a designer purse in her lap hard enough that the leather creaked under the pressure of her fingers.

Nate entered with Pierce close behind to shut the heavy door with a solid thud that made Zoe jump.

"Ms. Kaplan," Nate said, keeping his voice low and soft, the voice he used for jumpers on bridges. "I'm Agent Holloway, this is Detective Pierce, and thank you for coming in."

He sat opposite her and placed his bandaged hands on the table, palms down, making sure she saw the injury.

"Am I in trouble?" Zoe asked, her voice thin and uncertain. "The officers said this was about safety checks."

"You're not in trouble," Nate said. "We're conducting welfare checks on women working in the historic district, given the recent events."

Zoe nodded with a movement so jerky it looked mechanical. "The murders, yes, terrible."

She said the word *terrible* without any weight behind it, like a line reading from a script she hadn't rehearsed.

"We're tracing the movements of the victims," Nate said. "Looking for connections, common acquaintances, places they frequented."

"I don't know any of them," Zoe said quickly. "I just moved here."

"The art world is small," Pierce said from the corner. "People talk, and people meet."

"I keep to myself," Zoe said, her eyes flicking to the two-way mirror, then back to Nate's hands. "What happened to you?"

"Work accident," Nate said. "Ms. Kaplan, we've had reports that a man might be targeting women with your profile—someone presenting himself as a patron of the arts, someone wealthy."

Zoe went very still, her hands tightening on the leather of her bag.

"Savannah is full of wealthy patrons," she said.

"This one focuses on history, on antiques and daguerreotypes, and he operates out of a townhouse on Jones Street," Nate said.

Zoe's chin lifted, the defensive posture immediate and unmistakable. "You mean Evan."

"Evan Carlisle," Nate said.

"Mr. Carlisle is a respected member of the Historical Society," Zoe said, her tone shifting to become haughty, almost rehearsed. "He's a gentleman who has nothing to do with whatever you're investigating."

"You've spent time with him," Nate said.

"He's helping me with a research project," Zoe said. "His private collection is unparalleled, and he's been incredibly generous with his time."

Nate watched her eyes, noting how, under the harsh fluorescent lights, her pupils were blown wide, swallowing the blue of her irises when they should have been pinned in a room this bright.

"Did he offer you a drink?" Pierce asked. "Food or anything else?"

Zoe stood up halfway, then sat back down with a thump. "Evan is cultured and refined, not some predator in an alley."

"We found three other women, Zoe," Nate said, leaning forward. "We found them, and they looked just like you—blonde, intelligent, isolated."

"Coincidence," Zoe said, but the word came out airy and dismissive while a small, vacant smile touched her lips. "Evan explained that small minds would try to diminish him because he operates on a different level. He is protective, walks me to my car, checks on me."

"Does he?" Nate asked. "Or does he track you?"

"He cares," Zoe said, her voice going soft again, almost dreamy. She looked past Nate, focusing on something that wasn't in the room. "He understands things like time and beauty, and he says I have an eye for what lasts."

Nate felt a chill crawl up his spine that had nothing to do with the A/C as he heard Carlisle's script coming out of her mouth. *What lasts.*

She was quoting him word-for-word. He gave a microscopic shake of his head at Pierce, knowing reason was useless here because Carlisle had bypassed her critical faculties. If they told her the truth, she would run straight to Jones Street to warn him.

Pierce stepped away from the wall and moved to a side cabinet, opening it to pull out a heavy canvas tote bag.

"We understand," Pierce said, her voice neutral and professional. "Mr. Carlisle sounds like a good friend, but we have a job to do." She placed the bag on the table.

"This is part of a pilot program for women in the district," Pierce said. "It's got a reinforced liner that's good for transit, and there's a pepper gel canister on the key ring, so take it."

Zoe looked at the bag and touched the canvas with tentative fingers.

"I don't need this," Zoe said. "Evan protects me."

"Think of it as peace of mind," Nate said. "For us—if we know you have this, we can focus our resources elsewhere, and it signals to our officers that you're part of the safety network."

It was a lie layered on a lie, but it worked because it appealed to her new sense of importance.

Zoe hesitated, then nodded slowly. "It's a nice bag."

"It is," Pierce said. "Why don't you transfer your things and see how it feels?"

Zoe opened her designer purse and began to move items with methodical precision—a wallet, a cosmetic case, a set of keys. Then she pulled out the notebook, black leather with *The Carlisle Collection* titled in silver pen on the cover, and slid it into the canvas tote.

Nate looked at the tote's bottom seam, knowing that buried inside the lining, stitched between the Kevlar and the canvas, was a military-grade GPS transponder with a battery life of forty-eight hours.

Zoe stood up, slung the bag over her shoulder, and smoothed her silk blouse before looking at her reflection in the darkened glass of the two-way mirror. She preened for just a second, checking her appearance for an audience that wasn't there.

"Am I free to go?" Zoe asked.

"You're free," Nate said.

"Thank you, Agent Holloway," Zoe said, her voice distant again and floating. "I'll tell Evan you said hello."

"You do that," Nate said.

Zoe walked to the door while Pierce opened it for her, and she stepped out into the hallway with her heels clicking on the linoleum before the door swung shut. The latch clicked.

Silence filled the room after Zoe left, pressing against Nate's ears like the weight of what they'd just done. Pierce turned back to the table and stared at the empty chair where Zoe had sat.

"She's going to tell him," Pierce said.

"I know," Nate said.

"We just sent a sheep back to the wolf, Nate."

"We sent a tracker," Nate said, unable to look at her while he stared at his own reflection in the mirror. "It was the only way," trying to convince himself as much as her. "She wouldn't have listened because she was already gone."

"She's breathing," Pierce said. "For now."

Nate pulled his phone from his pocket and opened the tracking application, watching a map of downtown Savannah fill the screen while a single green dot blinked and moved. East on Oglethorpe, toward the squares, heading for Jones Street.

"Get Rodecker," Nate said, his voice steady even as his stomach churned with cold acid. "Tell Alicia to prep the gear because we're on the clock."

CHAPTER

45

Nate Holloway stepped to the desk, shoving aside a stack of takeout containers and legal pads. "Bring the light over here."

Alicia Landry moved the brass desk lamp, and a yellow cone of illumination fell across the large architectural blueprints spread across the wood. They were copies of copies, tax assessor maps overlaid with Alicia's hand-drawn corrections from historical renovation permits.

"This is the '25 renovation update," Alicia said, her ink-stained finger tracing a line along the eastern wall of the property. "City records show he applied to reinforce the foundation, but look at the square footage."

Nate leaned in, the gauze on his hands brushing the paper. "It doesn't match the exterior dimensions."

"Exactly," Alicia said. "There's a four-foot discrepancy running the length of the pantry and the study—too narrow for a room, too wide for a structural wall."

"A passage," Nate said.

"Or a void," Alicia said, moving her finger down to the basement level. "A space to run pipes or hide a door. Here, the cellar extends past the footprint of the townhouse, under the carriage house garden. Common in the 1850s for coal storage, but Carlisle blocked off the street access in 1891."

Nate took a red marker from the desk and uncapped it with his teeth, then circled the area beneath the garden.

"The kill room," he said.

Pierce stood by the window, peering through the slats of the blinds at the street below, while Rodecker sat on the edge of the unmade bed, elbows on his knees, looking older tonight. The lines around his eyes were carved in shadow, pronounced and heavy.

"We have a window," Nate said. "Zoe's GPS shows she's in transit, and the clock starts when she crosses the threshold. We assume he isolates her immediately."

"He'll take her downstairs," Alicia said. "The tablets mention a preparation phase—he likes the underground environment because it's controlled and soundproof."

"Which gives us a problem," Rodecker said without looking up from the floor. "If he's downstairs, he won't hear a knock at the door."

"He'll hear this knock," Nate said, pointing to the front elevation on the blueprints.

"The distraction has to be aggressive," Nate said. "Karl, you're the face of the law tonight—you go to the front door, park the cruiser right in front with lights and no siren, and you bang on that door like you have a warrant in your hand."

Rodecker nodded slowly. "I can do loud—badge forward, official inquiry, and I'll tell him we have a witness report placing Zoe at the residence."

"He'll deny it," Pierce said from the window. "He's arrogant."

"That's what we're counting on," Nate said. "His arrogance is the only weakness we've found, and he thinks he's untouchable. When you knock, he'll come to deal with the nuisance because he won't want a scene on his doorstep. He cares about his reputation in the historic district."

"While he's dealing with me," Rodecker said, "you go in the back."

"The service entrance." Nate moved the marker to the rear of the property on the map, where a narrow, cobbled alleyway ran behind the row of townhouses, shadowed by high brick walls and overhanging oaks. "It's a direct line from the lane. Alicia."

Alicia reached into her cardigan pocket and produced a heavy iron key—long, the metal pitted with age, the bow intricate and scrolled. She placed it on the map, directly over the service door. It landed with a heavy *thud*.

"Standard lockset for the 1850s," she said. "I checked the hardware on the exterior during my recon, and he never updated the service door mechanisms. He relies on the privacy wall and the electronic security system for the main house."

"And the key fits?" Nate asked.

"It's a skeleton key from the same builder," Alicia said. "It opens the back door of the Sorrel-Weed House and the Mercer House service entry. It'll open this."

Pierce stepped away from the window, moving to the table to stand shoulder to shoulder with Nate. She smelled of nervous sweat and mint gum, and her manicured fingernail traced their path on the map.

"Entry point here," she said. "Service door—we clear the servants' corridor, which is forty feet of straight hallway with no cover."

"We move fast," Nate said. "Quiet and fast."

"Then the kitchen stairs." Her finger tapped the stairwell symbol. "Down to the cellar level, which is the choke point. If he has cameras, he'll see us on the stairs."

"He won't be looking at monitors," Nate said. "He'll be looking at Rodecker."

Pierce checked her bulky tactical watch, synchronized to the atomic clock, then looked at Rodecker.

"Timing," she said. "We need to be precise."

"Alright, at go," Rodecker said. "I engage him and keep him talking."

"We enter," Nate said. "Two minutes after he opens the door gives him time to move from the cellar to the foyer, which puts him on the main floor while we go underneath him."

"If he hears us," Alicia said, her voice dropping, "he'll come back down."

"Then we hold the stairs," Nate said, "but we have to get through the cellar door first."

Alicia pointed to a thick black line on the cellar diagram. "The inner door—the one leading to the wine storage and the secure room. In the 1980 renovation permits, he installed a steel fire door there with electronic mag-locks."

Nate frowned, looking at the electrical schematic Alicia had pulled from the city archives.

"A key won't work on a mag-lock," Nate said.

"No," Alicia said. "But this will."

She pointed to a small square symbol on the north wall of the cellar, near the base of the stairs.

"The main breaker panel," Alicia said. "He upgraded the service to 200 amps in '95 to run climate control for his collection, and the panel is right here, before the steel door."

Nate tapped the location. "We cut the power."

"Fire code," Pierce said, nodding. "Mag-locks are fail-safe—if the power cuts, the magnet releases so people don't get trapped in a fire, and the door pops open."

"It also kills the lights," Nate said. "We go dark."

"Better for us," Pierce said. "We have tac-lights, and he has night vision, probably, or he knows the layout, but darkness creates confusion."

"It also triggers the alarm," Alicia said. "The battery backup on the security system will sense the power loss and send a silent signal to the monitoring company."

"Response time?" Nate asked.

Pierce did the mental math. "Private security calls the house first, gets no answer, then they call dispatch. Priority two alarm—patrol cars will roll in eight minutes, maybe twelve if they're busy."

"Five minutes," Nate said. "We have a five-minute window inside that room before the cavalry arrives."

"And when they arrive," Rodecker said from the bed, "they aren't coming to help you—they're coming to arrest burglars."

The room went silent, and the weight of the statement settled over them. The air conditioner compressor kicked off, leaving a sudden, ringing quiet.

"That's the reality," Nate said, looking at each of them. "We're crossing the line—there's no warrant for this, no judge signing off on exigent circumstances based on a hunch and a history book. We're breaking and entering, and if we fire a shot, it's attempted murder."

"Or actual murder," Alicia said softly.

"Or actual murder," Nate agreed. "If we're wrong about what he is, we go to prison, and if we're right, we probably still go to prison, but the killing stops."

Rodecker rubbed his face with both hands, the sound of his rough palms against stubble like sandpaper. "I'm three years from a pension, and Linda wants to buy a boat."

"You don't have to do this, Karl," Nate said.

"Yes, I do." Rodecker dropped his hands, his eyes clear. "I saw Booker Hayes walk out of that jail, saw the look on his face, and I'm not letting another one die because I followed the handbook."

A buzzing sound cut through the tension.

Nate's phone vibrated against the wood grain of the nightstand, the screen lighting up and casting a blue glow on the ceiling.

Nadia Lopez.

The name pulsed on the screen. He could picture her in her Quantico office, or maybe at her apartment, bag packed, waiting for him to come to his senses. She was the lifeline, the career he had built, the sanity he had clung to for fifteen years. Answering meant hearing the recall order was signed, meant hearing her beg him to come home, meant listening to sense.

And if he listened, Zoe Kaplan would die.

Nate reached out, his bandaged fingers clumsy as he tapped the screen, not sliding the icon to answer, but pressing the button to send the call to voicemail.

The phone vibrated again, a moment later—a notification. *New Voicemail.*

He swiped it away. *Delete.*

He placed the phone face down on the nightstand, and the screen went dark.

"Everything okay?" Alicia asked.

"Everything's fine," Nate said, his voice flat. "We're clear."

Pierce rose from the bed and picked up her backup weapon, a compact Glock 43. She ejected the magazine, checked the load with a *click*, and slid it back in, then racked the slide—*clack*—and press-checked the chamber, where a brass casing glinted in the gloom.

"I'm good," she said, holstering the weapon at her ankle. "Primary is full, two spare mags."

Rodecker stood and walked to the small writing desk by the television, opened the drawer, and pulled out a piece of Marshall House letterhead. The pen in his hand scratched out three quick sentences, without hesitation, and he folded the paper once, wrote *Linda* on the outside, and slid it back into the drawer.

"Just in case," Rodecker said.

"You'll be able to tear that up tomorrow," Nate said.

"Maybe," Rodecker said. "But if I don't, make sure she gets it."

"I will."

Alicia sat in the corner armchair, an iron blade held across her lap—ugly and heavy, the metal dark and rippled from the folding process. It looked primitive against her cardigan and slacks, a relic from a time before gunpowder and due process.

She picked up the whetstone from the side table.

Shhhk.

She ran the stone down the edge of the iron.

Shhhk.

The sound was rhythmic, filling the silence—the sound of preparation, the sound of intent.

Shhhk.

Alicia stopped and closed her eyes, her lips moving. A whisper escaped her throat, low and guttural, the syllables strange and heavy with consonants that didn't belong in English. It sounded like stones grinding together.

"What was that?" Pierce asked.

Alicia opened her eyes—dark, focused. "An invocation, from the tablet. It consecrates the iron."

"Does it work?"

"I believe so," Alicia said. "That has to be enough."

She resumed the sharpening.

Shhhk.

Nate looked at them—a detective who had thrown away his badge, a cop who was ready to shoot a prominent citizen, a historian sharpening a sword, and a federal agent who had just deleted his career.

They were a disaster. They were the only hope Zoe Kaplan had.

"We go in," Nate said. "We get the girl, we document the room, and we end him."

"Heroes, criminals, or dead," Pierce said.

"Pick one," Rodecker said.

"I pick alive," Alicia said, not stopping.

Shhhk.

Nate turned back to the corkboard, his gaze landing on Sarah's photo—her smile frozen in 2010, unaware of the future, of the monster who would take her breath, of the brother who would burn down his life to avenge her.

The sound of the whetstone filled the room.

Shhhk, Shhhk, Shhhk.

CHAPTER

46

THE ELEVATOR DOORS SLID OPEN. Nate pushed through the lobby doors of the Marshall House and onto Broughton Street, where the night air fell on him thick and humid, smelling of river mud, exhaust, and the frying grease from late-night restaurants. Savannah did not cool down. It just sweated in the dark.

Turning right, Nate moved toward Bull Street, forcing himself into the current of the crowd. Tourists ambled in slow, aimless packs, holding plastic cups of beer and cocktails. Their laughter felt distant, distorted, as if coming from behind a thick pane of glass. They pointed at the architecture and stopped to read menus posted in restaurant windows, living in a city of historic charm, while he walked through a hunting ground.

He crossed the street and headed south.

Away from the commercial district, the darkness deepened between the squares. Amber streetlights cast long, warped shadows through the hanging Spanish moss, which looked like grey rags left to snag on the brick facades of the townhouses.

He reached Forsyth Park, where the fountain at the north end sprayed white water against the night, illuminated and endless.

A saxophone player busked on the corner, the notes low and mournful against the traffic noise. Nate walked past the music, past the open lawns where students threw frisbees during the day, his focus fixed on the Confederate Memorial.

The bronze soldier stood high on his pedestal, staring north. Nate looked beyond the monument to the patch of grass between two massive live oaks, where Bill Shaw had slipped on the blood, where Caroline Marsh had been arranged like a piece of art.

A young couple stood on the grass now, maybe twenty years old. The boy held a smartphone at arm's length while the girl leaned into him, her head on his shoulder, smiling brightly for the camera. They shuffled their feet, trying to frame the monument in the background.

"Smile," the boy said.

The camera's flash was a violent burst of white that momentarily bleached the color from the brick pavers and the grass.

Nate watched them huddle over the phone, laughing at something on the screen. They were standing on the exact spot where a woman's throat had been torn out, the soil beneath their sneakers having soaked up liters of her blood. They didn't know. Or worse, they did, and this was murder tourism—a selfie with a ghost.

A knot of acid tightened in his gut. He turned away.

He walked back north, his pace quickening as if he could outrun their ignorance. He crossed Liberty Street and entered Chippewa Square.

The Oglethorpe monument dominated the center, its bronze figure surveying the traffic. This was where Lucy Phelps had died, invisible in life until she became a headline, now just another story for the guides.

A modified hearse, painted black for the paying customers of a ghost tour, idled at the corner. The loudspeaker crackled.

"And right here," the guide's amplified voice dropped an octave for effect, "is where the Vampire of Savannah claimed his latest victim. Some say if you listen closely, you can still hear the screams..."

A collective intake of breath from the passengers gave way to nervous, excited giggles.

Nate gripped the iron railing of the square. The metal pressed hard against his bandages, and a fresh fire bloomed in his palms. He wanted to drag them off that bus, to unseal the crime scene photos and force them to look at what a human throat becomes when it is destroyed by teeth that had no right to exist.

They weren't screaming. They were buying tickets.

The trolley groaned as it drew away, the laughter receding down the street. At the base of the monument, two children chased each other around the stone plinth, their own laughter high and shrill. Their parents stood nearby, consulting a map on a phone, oblivious.

The kids were running over the exact spot where four white candles had burned.

The city digested tragedy, chewing it up until it was just another anecdote for a brochure. The blood was scrubbed from the stone. The police tape came down. The tours arrived on schedule.

He couldn't look anymore. He walked away, letting the city's rhythm carry him until he found himself in the relative quiet of Madison Square, where the trees were thicker, and their canopies blocked the amber light. He sank onto a wrought-iron bench set back from the path, shadowed by a magnolia. The metal was cool against his legs.

He took his phone from his pocket and stared at his own hollow-eyed reflection in the dark screen. He swiped it open, the sudden light stinging his eyes, and opened his contacts.

He scrolled past Nadia's name and stopped at *Mom*.

It was late. She might be asleep. But Margaret Holloway hadn't slept deeply since the night Sarah didn't come home fifteen years ago.

He pressed call. It rang twice.

"Nathan?" Her voice was clear, alert. She had been waiting.

"Hey, Mom."

"Are you okay?" The question she always asked. The one he could never answer honestly.

"I'm fine," he lied. "I just... wanted to hear your voice."

A silence hung between them, heavy with fifteen years of unspoken grief, with the knowledge that he was in Savannah, doing the one thing she had begged him not to do.

"You're still there," she stated.

"Yes." He leaned forward, resting his elbows on his knees, picking at a loose thread on his trousers with a bandaged thumb. The urge to tell her everything rose in his throat, thick and choking. He wanted to tell her about the lavender sprig on Nicole Gladman, that the man who killed Sarah was real, and that it would end soon. He wanted to tell her monsters were real, but they could be killed.

But he couldn't. She would think the grief had finally broken him. Or worse, she would believe him, and the fear would destroy her.

"Nathan," she said softly, "your father asked about you today."

Nate stopped picking at the thread. He dug the heel of his shoe into the gravel path, grinding a small divot. "He did?"

"He saw the news about the detective. The fire. He knows you're in the middle of it. He won't say it, but he's proud. He knows you're trying to make it right."

Make it right. Was that what this was? Or just vengeance in the clothes of justice?

"I don't know if I can, Mom." His voice fractured. "I don't know if anyone can."

"You do what you have to do," Margaret said. "That's who you are. That's who Sarah knew you were."

Sarah. Her name hung in the humid air. He looked up at the Spanish moss overhead, a tangle of cobwebs in the dark. He could see her walking through these squares, laughing, wearing her locket, holding a sketchbook. She had walked these same paths, breathed this same heavy air.

"I have to go," Nate said, the conversation a burden he could no longer hold.

"Okay."

"Mom?"

"Yes?"

"I love you." He said it with the finality of a courtroom testimony. He said it like a goodbye.

He could hear her breath catch on the other end of the line. "Be safe, Nathan," she said, her voice breaking. She didn't ask him to promise. She knew he couldn't.

Nate lowered the phone and ended the call. The screen went black. He sat there for a long time, the cold device in his damaged hand, listening to the distant sounds of the city carrying on without him.

He took the stairs back to the second floor of the Marshall House, unwilling to face the confinement of the elevator. The lobby had been empty save for the night clerk, who hadn't looked up.

The key card made a loud mechanical click in the silence. He pushed the door open.

The air conditioning unit hummed, blowing cold, dusty air across the dim room. A single desk lamp cast a pool of yellow light over a mess of blueprints and books.

Alicia was asleep, slumped over the desk, her cheek pressed against the open pages of a text on Mesopotamian history. Her glasses had slid down her nose, and dark strands of hair had escaped their bun to fall across her face. Her fingers, stained with blue ink, still loosely gripped a pen.

She looked small, an academic who belonged in archives, not a slaughterhouse. And tomorrow, she would walk into one because no one else believed her.

Nate slipped off his suit jacket and moved quietly across the room. He draped it over her shoulders. She stirred, murmuring something unintelligible before settling back into the deep sleep of exhaustion.

He turned to the nightstand. The iron blade lay next to the hotel phone.

It was a crude, ugly thing. Black, dull, rippled with the marks of the hammer. The edges were rough, the handle a bare tang of metal wrapped in a dirty rag. It didn't look magical. It didn't look like a weapon capable of killing a four-thousand-year-old entity. It looked like a piece of scrap.

He picked it up. The weight was surprising, heavier than it should be, the balance forward toward the tip. His bandaged fingers wrapped around the cloth handle.

Doubt washed over him, cold and paralyzing.

He was a Federal Agent who dealt in evidence, forensics, and behavioral science, who put men in prison based on facts. Now he was planning to murder a man with a primitive sword because of a story in a history book. Harran would have him committed. Nadia would weep. This was a delusion born of grief. Carlisle was just a man—a sick, brilliant, sadistic man—and Nate was about to throw his life away on a ghost story.

He looked from the blade, which seemed to absorb the light, to the corkboard.

He saw the photo of Nicole Gladman, her hair arranged just so, the lavender in her hand. He heard Stevie Ralston's voice: *He would have eaten us.* He saw the forensic reports detailing impossible blood volume, the lack of pooling, the bite marks that matched a cold case from 1950.

Rationality had failed. Science had no answers. The law was blind.

Carlisle had walked through history untouched because men like Nate refused to believe in things that didn't fit in a file folder.

Nate tightened his grip. The pain in his burns flared, sharp and real. This wasn't a delusion. It was the only truth left.

He placed the blade back on the nightstand. It made a heavy *clunk* against the wood. He looked at Sarah's photo one last time.

"Tomorrow," he said to the quiet room.

The jail cell smelled of industrial disinfectant and unwashed bodies, a cold, sharp odor that stuck in the back of the throat. The fluorescent lights hummed without pause, drilling into the skull.

Booker Hayes lay on the thin cot, staring at the pockmarked concrete ceiling. From down the block, a man was shouting, a rhythmic, incoherent plea. *Let me out. Let me out. I didn't do it.*

Booker didn't shout. Shouting didn't help.

He closed his eyes and pictured Monterey Square, the bench under the oak, Lucy holding her bag, and smiling when he brought her coffee. He pictured Nicole Gladman with her camera, her focused expression as she looked at the warehouse door.

Gone.

The police said he killed them. The TV called him a monster. His lawyer wanted him to plead guilty.

But the FBI agent had looked him in the eye. *I will fix this.*

Men made promises. Most broke them. But Nate Holloway had looked at him like he was a man, not a piece of trash to be swept off the street.

Booker rolled onto his side, facing the cinderblock wall, and drew his knees to his chest. He didn't have much. A record. Bad memories. A few dollars in an envelope. But he had a feeling.

A storm was coming. He could feel the pressure dropping.

He hoped the agent was ready.

Booker closed his eyes tighter, trying to block out the shouting from down the hall, and waited for the lock to turn.

CHAPTER

47

Ruby Tatum sat in the kitchen behind the forge, listening to her husband cough in the bedroom—the wet, labored rattle of a man whose lungs were filling with what they shouldn't. She stared at the yellow Formica counters peeling at the corners, linoleum worn through to the backing in front of the sink.

Six to eight weeks. Hospice can help manage pain.

The oncologist's words circled in her head. The young doctor with smooth hands and an expensive tie, who'd looked at the chart instead of at Zeke when he said it.

Four months ago.

The coughing in the other room stopped. Silence rushed back into the house, heavy and suffocating. Worse than the noise—in the silence, she found herself counting the seconds, waiting for the next intake of breath.

A floorboard creaked.

Zeke appeared in the doorway connecting the kitchen to the bedroom. He sagged against the frame, his left arm bracing the wood, veins standing out thick and blue against grey, damp skin. His shirt was soaked through, sweat plastering thin grey hair to his skull. He was hollowed out—skin and stubbornness and nothing else.

Ruby didn't move. She watched his chest rise and fall in jagged, shallow movements. He was fighting for every cubic inch of oxygen.

Zeke pushed off the doorframe and took a step, then another, his boots scuffing against the linoleum. He didn't lift his feet, shuffling toward the table with the focus of a man walking a tightrope.

"Couldn't sleep?" His voice was a wet rasp, full of gravel.

"Haven't slept in four months," Ruby said. "Not since they told us."

She didn't rise to help him. She saw the impulse in her own hands, the urge to reach, and forced them to stay on the table. An offered arm he hadn't asked for would break him more than the cancer—he needed to make it to the chair on his own.

Zeke reached the table and gripped the back of the vinyl chair opposite her, knuckles turning white. He lowered himself slowly, wincing as his hips settled and his spine took the weight. He let out a long breath through his nose.

He looked at her and reached across the table, covering her hand with his.

His palm was rough, callouses thick as leather pads, stained with coal dust and iron oxide. But the hand was cold—the heat that used to radiate from him, the furnace warmth that made her kick the covers off in winter, was gone.

They sat in the quiet while the refrigerator compressor started in the corner. A car drove past on the street outside, tires hissing on damp pavement.

Ruby stared at their joined hands, her skin wrinkled but pink, alive, while his was translucent, the skin loose over the bones, spotted with age and sickness.

She tightened her jaw. "You're planning to go help them."

It wasn't a question.

Zeke didn't flinch or pull his hand away. His thumb brushed the back of her wrist in the slow, rhythmic motion he had used to calm her for decades.

"I think they have the translation wrong," Zeke said, his voice rough. He stopped to swallow, his throat clicking. "The curse—it requires a hand of death."

He pulled his hand back and tapped his own chest, a dull sound.

"I'm dying, Ruby. Have been since February. This gives it meaning."

"You don't even know where they'll be," Ruby said. "You can't just go wandering around Savannah looking for a ghost story."

"I'm not wandering." Zeke's mouth twitched in the direction of a smile. "That thing's been tied to Jones Street since before either of us were born. The stories your daddy told, the ones Elaine Colfax drank herself stupid trying to forget—they all end up in those houses."

She shook her head. "Stories don't give you an address."

"Their fed does," Zeke said. "Address was right there on his work order—Marshall House on Broughton." He tapped the table with one knuckle. "I go there first. If they've already moved, I follow the trail uphill. That kind of man doesn't hunt in trailer parks, Ruby. He hunts where the money sleeps. It always runs to Jones."

Ruby pictured the map in her head—Bay Street, up through the squares, into the moneyed quiet of the historic district. "You won't make it that far."

"Then you drive me as close as you can," he said. "You drop me near the squares and park where you can see the Jones Street front. If it breaks loose, you'll know where I went."

Heat rose in her chest, a sharp pressure that made her want to scream at him, to tell him he was selfish, to sweep everything off the table and hear it clatter across the floor. She wanted to tell him that six weeks was still six weeks, and they were her six weeks too.

But she looked at his face.

The exhaustion was etched into the lines around his eyes, the pain a constant frequency in the set of his mouth. He was tired, so tired of being a patient, of being a tragedy, of waiting for the fluid to fill his lungs until he drowned in his own bed.

For the last four months, he had been shrinking while the world acted upon him. Doctors stuck needles in him, nurses charted his decline, and the disease dictated his schedule.

Last night, forging the blade for that FBI agent, he had been big again—he had been Ezekiel Tatum, and he had forced the metal to submit.

"You're the most stubborn man I've ever known." Her voice cracked. Tears pushed against the back of her eyes, hot and stinging.

"You knew that when you married me." The corner of his mouth lifted in an expression that didn't reach his eyes.

Ruby looked at his hand on the table, where the tremors were back, a fine shaking that vibrated through his fingers. He was hiding it, pressing his palm flat against the wood, but she could see the tendons jumping.

She reached out and covered his hand with both of hers, pressing down to still the shake. She felt the small bones under the skin, brittle.

"If you do this—" She paused to correct herself. "When you do this."

Zeke watched her and waited.

"I want you to know it wasn't just your choice," Ruby said. She sat up straighter, the wood of the chair pressing into her back. "It's mine too. We made this together."

She squeezed his hand hard enough to hurt.

Zeke stared at her, his eyes clear for once, not clouded with pain medication and fatigue.

He turned his hand over under hers and gripped her fingers. His movement was shaky, but he didn't drop her. He brought her knuckles to his lips, his mustache scratching her skin, his lips dry and cool. He kissed her hand and held it there for a long moment.

"Forty-seven years," he said, his breath warm on her knuckles.

He lowered their hands but didn't let go. He looked at her, not past her, not at the doorway or the window or anywhere else.

"Best thing I ever made," he said.

Ruby let out a breath she felt like she had been holding since the diagnosis, the anger draining away to leave a hollow sadness and a terrifying clarity. This was the end, the real end—not the slow fade in a hospital bed with morphine drips and pitying looks from the neighbors.

This was fire and iron.

She traced the vein on the back of his hand with her thumb, watching it roll dark blue under the loose skin.

"I'll make sure they know," she said. "After."

"It doesn't matter if they know—matters that it's done."

"It matters to me," Ruby said. Her voice was fierce. "I won't have you be another casualty, another old man who died in the confusion."

Zeke squeezed her hand again, his grip weaker than it had been a minute ago. The adrenaline was fading fast, and the crash was coming.

"Okay," he said softly. "Okay, Ruby."

They sat in silence as the shadows in the kitchen's corners began to stretch and thin. Grey light pressed against the window over the sink. The world outside was waking up—delivery trucks starting their rounds, the tide turning in the river.

She watched him: the angle of his jaw, the way his ears stuck out, the soot smudged on his forehead from yesterday's work. She looked from his face to their hands locked together on the table.

"I'm ready," she lied.

Zeke nodded and looked at the window.

"Almost morning," he said.

"Yes," Ruby said. "Almost."

She didn't let go. She held on as the light changed, held on as the kitchen grew brighter, watching the man she loved. She would hold on until the time had run out.

CHAPTER

48

THE SCREEN of the iPhone was the only light in the living room. It cast a sickly blue pallor over Zoe Kaplan's face as she stared at the message bubble, grey on the left, blue on the right.

Please come over.

Zoe blinked, her eyelids weighted and scratching against her corneas. She looked at her thumb hovering over the glass. She could not recall typing those words. She could not recall unlocking the phone. She could not recall making the decision to invite him into her sanctuary.

But the words were there. Delivered. Read.

The apartment was silent. It was a silence that felt pressurized, the air thick with the humidity that the struggling window unit couldn't quite cut. Cardboard boxes, taped and labeled in Sharpie, sat stacked against the far wall. *Kitchen stuff. Books. Winter clothes.* She had been here for two months, but she hadn't unpacked. A temporary life. A transient existence waiting for permission to begin.

Her thumb moved to the keypad.

Knock. Knock. Knock.

The sound was precise. Three raps, evenly spaced, neither aggressive nor timid.

Zoe's breath hitched. The knot in her stomach didn't vanish, but it was suddenly overlaid by a warmth that flooded her veins. He was here. He hadn't abandoned her. He hadn't let the police scare him away.

Her feet moved. *Monsters don't knock politely,* a part of her mind insisted. *You are in danger.*

But her hand reached for the deadbolt. Her fingers turned the latch. The metal clicked, a solid, mechanical sound in the quiet.

She opened the door.

Evan Carlisle stood in the hallway. The fluorescent corridor light washed out the color of his cream linen suit, making him look like a photograph from another era. He was perfectly still. No sweat beaded on his forehead despite the Savannah heat. His dark hair was swept back, impeccable.

He didn't smile. His eyes, ink-black and absorbing the hallway light, fixed on hers.

"You called for me," he said.

The voice was a physical sensation. It vibrated in her sternum, lower than the hum of the A/C, resonating in the hollow spaces of her body.

"I didn't..." Zoe's tongue felt swollen, too large for her mouth. The protest died before it reached her lips. "I mean, I don't remember..."

"May I come in, Zoe?"

The polite inquiry was a pressing weight. It demanded an answer. Zoe stepped back. It was a surrender masked as courtesy.

"Yes."

Evan crossed the threshold.

The air changed instantly. The temperature in the living room plummeted. The humidity froze, the moisture in the air turning crisp and sharp on her skin. It smelled of wet earth deep underground, and the cloying sweetness of night-blooming jasmine.

He turned and closed the door. The lock engaged with a soft, final snap.

The apartment felt smaller now. The walls seemed to lean inward. The white noise of the traffic on Broughton Street faded away, replaced by the sound of her own breathing.

"You're upset," Evan said. He moved toward her. He didn't walk so much as glide, his movements fluid and economical.

"The agent," Zoe managed to say. She wrapped her arms around herself, trying to hold her pieces together. "He brought me into the station. The Detective... they showed me pictures."

Evan stopped a foot away. A palpable cold radiated from him.

"Pictures," he said. The word tasted of dismissal. "Women who looked like me," Zoe said. Her voice trembled. "Women who were..."

"Women who were lost," he finished for her. He raised his hand.

Zoe flinched. *RUN. PREDATOR.*

But she didn't run. She leaned in.

His fingertips brushed her cheek. The shock of it gasped through her. His skin was ice. It wasn't the cool of a cold drink; it was the lifeless chill of marble in winter. It burned against her flush.

"They didn't have anyone to protect them," he said. His thumb traced the line of her jaw. "But you're not lost, Zoe. You're here. With me."

The panic in her mind went quiet. It was a heaviness that dampened the warnings. What remained was need. A hollow, aching hunger in her belly that demanded to be filled.

"I tried to break up with you," she said, the words slipping out without thought.

"I know." His lips quirked, a ghost of a smile that didn't reach his dead eyes. "And then you asked me to come over. Because you know the truth, don't you? You know what you need."

He leaned down. His mouth hovered next to her ear. His breath was cold, a winter draft against her neck.

"Tell me what you need, Zoe."

The command bypassed her logic. It went straight to the brain stem.

"You," she whispered.

"Show me."

Zoe took his hand. His fingers were long, pale, and hard as iron. She led him through the living room, weaving between the stacks of boxes that contained a life she hadn't bothered to unpack because she knew she wouldn't be staying. They passed the kitchenette. They passed the bathroom.

They entered the bedroom.

The only light came from the streetlamp outside, filtering through the cheap blinds in zebra stripes of orange and shadow. Against the far wall leaned the mirror.

It was an antique floor mirror in a tarnished brass frame. She had bought it at an estate sale her first weekend in the city. The old glass was slightly wavy at the edges, capturing the room in a silvered, dreamlike haze.

She stopped in front of it.

"Here," she said. Her voice sounded strange to her ears. Drugged. Sluggish. "I want to see everything."

Evan moved behind her. In the reflection, he loomed over her shoulder, a pale figure in the gloom. He placed his hands on her hips. The fabric of her sweatpants offered no protection against the chill of his grip. It soaked through to the bone.

"Then see it all," he said.

His hands moved up her torso. Zoe watched in the mirror as he lifted the hem of her grey tank top. She raised her arms, and he pulled the shirt over her head and tossed it aside.

Her skin was pale in the half-light. Her breasts were full, nipples already hard from the sudden cold of the room. Evan's hands settled over them. He didn't caress; he claimed. His fingers pressed into the soft tissue with bruising force. Her back arched without her permission, pressing into him.

Zoe gasped, her head falling back against his shoulder. The linen of his suit was rough against her skin. The cold of his hands on her breasts sent a spike of sensation straight to her groin—pain and pleasure fused into a single current.

"Keep looking," he said. The voice was ancient now. The cultured veneer was slipping, revealing something jagged underneath.

She forced her eyes open. She looked at the woman in the mirror. Her mouth was slack, eyes dilated until they were almost entirely black. She looked like a stranger. She looked like a victim. She looked like she was enjoying it.

Evan hooked his thumbs into the waistband of her sweatpants. He pushed them down. Zoe stepped out of them, kicking them away. She stood naked in the center of her room, shivering, while the man behind her remained fully clothed, armored in his suit.

He turned her. He positioned her hands on her thighs. He bent her forward.

Zoe stared at herself. The pose was vulnerable, animalistic. Her spine curved, her hips displayed. Behind her, Evan moved. The sound of a zipper. The rustle of fabric.

He positioned himself behind her with one hand gripping her hip while the other guided himself to her entrance.

"See what I do to you."

He entered her.

There was no gentleness, no preparation, only a dry, relentless friction that stretched her to the tearing point. Zoe cried out, the sound sharp and ragged in the quiet room as he began to move, setting a punishing rhythm. His hips struck against her buttocks with wet, slapping impacts, the friction burning while the coldness of him inside her was terrifying, a glaciated stone that numbed her nerve endings even as he set them on fire. She watched her own face in the mirror bounce with each thrust, hair falling across her eyes, her expression a mask of shock and awe.

She felt like she was floating near the ceiling, looking down. *That isn't me,* she thought. *That's just meat. That's just a body.*

Her hand moved. It wasn't a conscious decision. She reached up and pinched her own nipple, twisting the flesh hard.

Pain flared. Sharp. Bright.

"Harder," she gasped.

Evan growled, a sound that vibrated in her spine. He grabbed her hair, yanking her head back, forcing her to look into her own eyes in the glass.

She twisted both her nipples and saw herself in the reflection, doing things she'd never done before, being someone she didn't recognize. Free and owned at the same time. The breath tore out of her lungs in short, desperate gasps.

"You belong to me," he said. "Say it."

The words bubbled up from her throat, bypassing her mind entirely.

"I belong to you."

The release hit her like a physical blow. It wasn't warm. It didn't bloom. It broke. The orgasm was a jagged, convulsing spasm that shook her legs and left her gasping for air. She watched herself come undone in the mirror, her face twisting, her mouth open in a silent scream.

Evan stiffened. He drove into her one last time and held there.

She felt it then. Not warmth. An icy pulse. A transfer of cold that seemed to freeze her insides. It spread from her belly outward, numbing her organs, slowing her heart.

He withdrew.

The separation was abrupt.

With the physical disconnect, the fog was ripped away. One second Zoe was floating, and the next she stood naked in her bedroom, bent over, her thighs trembling, her insides aching with cold and friction, bruises forming on her hips.

The smell of sex and jasmine was suffocating.

She straightened up, stumbling. She grabbed the edge of the dresser to keep from falling.

What just happened?

The violation. The coercion. The fact that she had led him here, undressed for him, begged him. Shame, hot and acidic, flooded her throat.

She turned around.

Evan was already dressed. His suit was pristine. His hair was unruffled. He was fastening his watch.

Zoe grabbed her tank top from the floor and held it over her chest. Her hands were shaking.

"I need..." Her voice cracked. She cleared her throat. "I need to shower."

She backed toward the bathroom door. She needed to get behind a lock. She needed to wash the cold out of her body. She needed to call the police.

"No," Evan said. He picked up a bag from the floor near the closet. "We're leaving."

Zoe froze. She stared at the bag. It was a tan leather weekender.

"I didn't pack that," she said.

"I packed it for you," Evan said. "While you were occupied."

"Occupied?"

The word hung in the air. A gap in the timeline. He couldn't have packed a bag while he was...

He moved toward the door. "Everything you need is inside. We're going to my estate. The place I told you about. The garden is beautiful at night."

"I'm not going anywhere with you."

Zoe stepped back. Her heel hit the doorframe of the bathroom.

"You need to leave," she said. She tried for anger, but it came out as terror. "Get out of my apartment. Now. Or I'm calling the police."

She glanced past him, through the bedroom door, toward the living room. Her phone was on the kitchen counter. Thirty feet away.

Evan tilted his head. He looked at her with curiosity.

"You don't mean that."

"I do." She clutched the shirt tighter. "Get out."

Evan smiled. It wasn't charming. It was a baring of teeth.

"You won't call anyone, Zoe."

He moved.

One moment, he was standing by the closet, six feet away. Next, he was in her personal space, the air displaced by his passage hitting her face.

He gripped her wrist.

The cold was absolute. It burned like dry ice. Zoe screamed, trying to jerk away, but his fingers were steel bands. He didn't squeeze; he simply held.

"Let go!"

He raised his free hand. He placed his palm flat against her forehead.

Contact.

The world didn't go black. It went soft.

The sharp edges of the room blurred. The panic in her chest, the instinct to run, the horror—it all drained out of her. Her muscles relaxed. The shirt slipped from her fingers and pooled on the floor.

She looked up at him. The monster was gone. There was only Evan. Beautiful, timeless Evan. He was here to take care of her. He was here to take her away from the noise and the fear.

"We're going now," Evan said softly. "You want to come with me. Say it."

Zoe blinked. Her eyelids felt thick, luxurious.

"I want to come with you," she said.

"Good girl."

He released her wrist. He lowered his hand from her forehead.

The command held.

"Get dressed," he said. "Something comfortable."

Zoe moved like a sleepwalker. She pulled on her sweatpants. She put the tank top back on. She didn't notice the red finger marks darkening on her wrist. She didn't feel the soreness between her legs.

Evan held out his hand.

She took it.

He led her out of the bedroom. They walked through the living room, moving through the maze of cardboard boxes.

They passed the kitchen counter.

Zoe's eyes drifted to the canvas tote bag—the one from the station today.

She looked at it. A vague memory scratched at the back of her mind. A warning. She should... do something.

Evan's thumb stroked the back of her hand. The cold radiated up her arm, numbing the thought before it could form.

She looked away.

Near the front door, her canvas tote bag sat on the entry table.

"Take your bag," Evan said.

Zoe picked it up. She slung the strap over her shoulder. She didn't know why she needed it, but Evan said she did, and Evan knew best.

He opened the door. The hallway light spilled in.

"Ready?" he asked.

Zoe looked back at her apartment one last time. The unpacked boxes. The empty walls. The life she had been waiting to start. It looked like a set for a play that had been cancelled.

"Yes," she said.

They walked out together. The door clicked shut, locking the silence inside.

They took the stairs. The evening air outside was thick and humid, a blanket that smelled of exhaust and river mud. It should have been oppressive, but to Zoe, it felt distant. She was encased in a bubble of cold air that centered on Evan.

He opened the car door for her. A black sedan. Leather interior.

She slid into the passenger seat. The door closed with a solid, expensive thud, sealing her in.

Evan got in the driver's side. He started the engine. The air conditioning blasted, cold on cold.

He pulled away from the curb, merging into the traffic on Broughton Street. The city lights smeared across the windshield—neon signs, headlights, the amber glow of the streetlamps.

Zoe sat with her hands folded in her lap. The canvas tote bag rested at her feet.

Deep inside the bag, tucked into a side pocket, a small black device blinked once—a silent pulse of light.

Pulse.

Pulse.

Pulse.

Zoe closed her eyes.

CHAPTER

49

The alarm on Nate Holloway's phone vibrated against the wood of the hotel desk. In the dim room, the screen's glow illuminated the tactical map spread across the scarred surface. A single red dot pulsed at 465 Jones Street.

Nate picked up the phone, his hand strange in the blue light. White gauze bandages, wrapped tight to protect the burns from the warehouse fire, covered his palms and fingers. He flexed them, feeling the skin pull taut, sparking sharp, grounding pain through the nerves.

"She's there," Nate said.

Yolanda Pierce stood by the window, checking the load in her Smith & Wesson M&P for the third time without looking at him. Her stare fixed on the streetlights of Broughton Street, unblinking and focused.

"Stationary means two things," Pierce said. "She's talking, or she's unconscious."

"Or she's dead," Alicia Landry added from the chair in the corner.

The historian clutched the heavy satchel in her lap, inside of which, wrapped in layers of oiled cloth, lay the iron blade Ezekiel Tatum had forged. She looked small in the tactical environment, her hands gripping the leather strap until her knuckles turned white.

"We stick to the timeline," Nate said, holstering his Glock. The familiar weight of the weapon settled on his hip, a cold comfort. "Rodecker hits the front at eight-fifteen, which gives us fourteen minutes to get into position."

He looked at the three of them—a federal agent with suspended credentials, a detective risking her pension, a historian carrying a sword—and saw a bad joke waiting to become a tragedy. They were people about to die.

"Radio silence," Nate reminded them. "SCMPD dispatch cannot know we are there, and if this goes south, there is no backup coming."

Pierce nodded and holstered her weapon. "Let's go get her."

They filed out of the room, and the door clicked shut behind them, locking in the smell of gun oil and stale coffee. They moved down the back stairwell of the Marshall House, avoiding the lobby cameras with careful precision. The humid Savannah air, smelling of river mud and exhaust, hit them when they exited into the alley.

Nate led the way to the rental car, the red dot on his phone screen unmoving.

Detective Karl Rodecker sat in his unmarked Ford Explorer on Whitaker Street, engine off, windows down. The air felt heavy, saturated with moisture that refused to fall as rain. The digital clock on the dashboard read 8:13 PM.

Two minutes.

He wiped his palms on his trousers, feeling the dampness transfer to the fabric. Thirty years on the force, hundreds of warrants executed —he had kicked down doors and stared down meth addicts holding shotguns, but he had never felt this kind of cold in his gut. It wasn't the fear of dying but the fear of being wrong.

A manila folder sat on the passenger seat, and inside lay the letter to Linda, explaining the pension, the insurance, and why he did what he did. He hoped she never had to read it.

Rodecker's hand hovered over the door handle. In the side mirror, a tired man with grey temples stared back at him, looking older than he remembered. He got out of the car, adjusting his jacket to cover his weapon but leave the grip accessible. He clipped his badge to his belt, right next to the buckle, and the metal felt cold against his shirt.

He walked down the sidewalk, where gas lamps cast long, jumping shadows on the brickwork. Jones Street was quiet with the kind of silence money bought—high walls, heavy doors, manicured gardens smelling of boxwood and old wealth.

He stopped in front of 465.

A Greek Revival fortress, its white columns rose three stories into the darkness. The windows were dark, and the building held the stillness of a mausoleum maintained by a careful caretaker.

Rodecker walked up the stone steps, his boots making hard, scraping sounds on the granite. He stood on the mat and took a breath, holding it for a second to steady his heart rate.

He raised his hand.

Knock. Knock. Knock.

Three hard, police raps.

He waited—five seconds, then ten.

The lock tumbled, the sound heavy and intricate, machined steel moving against steel. The door swung inward.

Evan Carlisle stood in the threshold.

He wore an immaculate cream linen suit without a wrinkle in the fabric. He looked cool, dry, and perfectly composed, not like a man who had just abducted a woman, but like he was expecting a dinner guest who had arrived five minutes early.

"Detective Rodecker," Carlisle said, his voice low and smooth. "I believe my attorney made clear that further contact should go through official channels."

Rodecker planted his feet, keeping his hands visible. He did not cross the threshold.

"We have a witness placing you with Zoe Kaplan tonight," Rodecker said, his tone flat, professional. "I need to confirm her location and welfare."

Carlisle blinked, the movement slow and deliberate. "I'm afraid I don't know anyone by that name, Detective. Perhaps your witness is mistaken."

"Her cell phone GPS is pinging from this address," Rodecker said. "Right now."

Carlisle didn't flinch, didn't look nervous or check the street for backup. He just stood there, and then a slight shift occurred in his eyes—the pupils seemed to expand, swallowing the iris in black oil.

"Technology is notoriously unreliable, Detective," Carlisle said, leaning against the doorframe. "Cell tower triangulation can be off by several blocks, as you well know. You're fishing."

"I'm investigating a kidnapping," Rodecker said. "Step aside, Mr. Carlisle."

"You're welcome to call Miss Kaplan yourself," Carlisle offered. "Confirm she's safe elsewhere, if you'd like. But you aren't coming inside without a warrant, and we both know you don't have one—or you wouldn't be standing here alone."

Rodecker held his ground as sweat trickled down his back. The man in front of him wasn't human, and he knew it—Nate knew it—but the law required him to play this game until the screaming started.

"Call her," Rodecker challenged.

Carlisle smiled, but it did not reach his eyes. "I just told you—I don't know her."

The service alley behind Jones Street was a tunnel of shadows, the brick walls of the garden courtyards rising ten feet on either side. The air smelled of damp earth and rotting magnolia leaves.

Nate signaled with a raised hand.

Pierce and Alicia stopped, crouching by a heavy wooden gate set into the brick wall of 465.

Nate checked his watch—8:16 PM. Rodecker had engaged.

Alicia moved forward and reached into her satchel, pulling out the long, heavy, age-pitted iron skeleton key from 1847. She inserted it into the keyhole.

Nate held his breath. If the lock had been changed in the last century, this ended before it began.

Alicia turned her wrist.

Click.

The sound was loud in the silence as the internal mechanism shifted. The gate groaned as Alicia pushed it inward.

Nate moved first, weapon up, stock tight against his shoulder. He swept the small courtyard where a fountain bubbled in the center. White, night-blooming jasmine glowed in the gloom, its scent cloying, thick enough to taste. He moved to the servant's entrance at the rear of the main house—a simple wooden door.

Alicia stepped up and used the key again.

Another click.

The door opened.

They slipped inside, and the air conditioning hit them instantly—not comfortable cool, but a preservation cold of sixty degrees or lower. Nate's sweat turned icy on his skin.

They found themselves in a narrow servant's hall where the heart pine floor, polished to a shine, reflected the weak light from the exit sign. Nate pointed forward, signaling for quiet.

They moved in formation—Nate on point, Alicia in the center with the blade, Pierce guarding the rear. They passed a closed door to the kitchen, and Nate paused, listening.

Faint voices drifted from the front of the house—Rodecker's rough baritone and the other voice, smooth and arrogant.

Nate pointed to a panel in the wainscoting, one he recognized from Alicia's architectural drawings—the hidden access to the cellar stairs. He reached out with his bandaged hand, found the groove, and pulled.

The panel slid back, revealing a yawning darkness. A set of steep wooden stairs descended into the earth, and from the opening wafted a distinct smell—metallic, copper, old blood, and chemicals.

Nate looked at Pierce. She nodded.

He took the first step down.

CHAPTER

50

Zoe gasped as air rushed into her lungs, abrasive and scraping against her throat.

She opened her eyes to darkness, and candles flickered on a dresser across the room, casting dancing, erratic shadows on the ceiling. The smell hit her next—lavender, but not fresh—dried, dusty lavender mixed with something muskier.

She tried to sit up, but her body refused. Her arms were filled with lead, her legs heavy logs she couldn't move.

Drugged.

The thought floated to the surface of her mind through a thick, cottony fog.

She blinked, trying to clear her vision, and looked down. She was naked, her skin pale, almost blue in the candlelight, lying on top of a duvet cover that felt like silk against her back.

Where was she?

She remembered her apartment, the mirror, the cold hands.

Evan.

The name brought a surge of nausea, and the memory of the car ride flashed—city lights blurring, his hand holding hers. *Him* inside her again in the townhouse bed. The compliance. The violation.

She tried to move again, managing to roll onto her side and fall off the mattress. She hit the rug with a thud that jarred her teeth, and pain shot through her shoulder, sharp and immediate. The pain helped —the fog receded an inch.

She pushed herself up, her hands shaking, and looked around the room. High ceilings, heavy velvet drapes drawn tight over the windows, an antique wardrobe that stood in the corner—this was not her apartment.

A man's discarded white dress shirt lay on the floor. She crawled toward it, her limbs moving jerkily against the residual lethargy in her nerves. She grabbed the shirt and pulled it on, her fumbling fingers managing two buttons before they stopped cooperating. It hung to her mid-thighs.

She had to leave.

She crawled toward the door, the wood floor cold against her bare knees.

Voices.

She stopped, pressing her ear to the floorboards.

"...fishing," a low, smooth voice said. Evan.

"...investigating a kidnapping," another voice answered, rougher, louder.

Police.

The word was a spark, igniting the adrenaline in her blood. Someone was here, had found her—Evan was downstairs, talking to the police.

A cold certainty settled in her gut. *He will kill them. He will kill them and then he will come back up here.*

Zoe grabbed the doorknob and hauled herself up, her legs wobbling beneath her. She leaned against the doorframe and pulled the door open. The hallway was dark, and the voices were clearer now, coming from the foyer.

She took a breath, filling her lungs until they burned, and pushed the air out with everything she had left.

"HELP ME!"

The scream tore out of her throat, ragged and raw.

"SOMEONE HELP ME! I'M UPSTAIRS!"

Rodecker flinched. The scream hit him like a physical blow—terrified and undeniably Zoe Kaplan.

He didn't think. Training took over.

"That came from inside this house." His hand snapped to his belt, fingers wrapping around the grip of his Smith & Wesson.

"Step aside," Rodecker ordered. "Now."

He stepped forward, breaking the plane of the threshold.

Carlisle changed, and it wasn't a gradual shift but instantaneous. The bored, arrogant antique dealer vanished, and something else occupied the linen suit. He didn't step back—he stepped in.

He moved faster than Rodecker's eyes could track. One second, he was leaning against the frame, six feet away, and the next, he was inside Rodecker's guard. Rodecker drew the gun, clearing leather, and started to bring the muzzle up.

Carlisle's hand lashed out, a blur of motion, and pale fingers clamped onto Rodecker's right wrist. The grip stopped the gun's upward momentum instantly—the pressure was absolute, grinding bone against bone. The pain was blinding, but the cold was worse—not just skin temperature, but a deep chill that poured through his jacket sleeve.

Rodecker grunted. He couldn't aim, couldn't break the grip, so he twisted his hips and fired anyway.

BAM! BAM!

The shots were deafening in the enclosed foyer. The muzzle flash lit up Carlisle's face—his eyes wide, black, and empty. The rounds hit him in the chest, center mass, point-blank.

The impact threw Carlisle back two steps, releasing Rodecker's wrist. Rodecker stumbled back, gasping, and brought the weapon up to a proper Weaver stance.

"Get down! Get on the ground!"

Carlisle looked down at his chest, where two holes marred the pristine cream linen. The fabric was torn, the edges black with powder burns, and dark, red blood oozed from the wounds. Carlisle touched the blood, looked at his fingers, and appeared annoyed.

Rodecker watched the holes. The blood flow stopped—it didn't slow, it ceased. Under the torn fabric, the skin moved, rippled, and pink tissue knit together, muscle fibers weaving into place. The holes closed, and in three seconds, there was nothing left but smooth, pale skin visible through the ruined shirt.

Rodecker forgot to breathe. He had seen men shot, knew what a hollow-point round did to a human chest, and it didn't do that.

"You ruined the suit," Carlisle said. He looked up, his face devoid of humanity—the mask was gone. The thing looking at Rodecker was old and hungry.

Carlisle moved again, closing the distance, and grabbed Rodecker by the lapels of his jacket. He lifted him—Rodecker weighed two hundred and ten pounds, plus ten pounds of gear, but Carlisle lifted him off the floor with extended arms as if he were a child.

"No," Rodecker choked out.

Carlisle threw him, and there was no windup, just a violent extension of his arms.

Rodecker flew backward, crossing the ten feet of the foyer in the air. He crashed through a set of double doors leading to the parlor, wood splintering and glass panes shattering around him. Rodecker slammed into the plaster wall on the far side of the room, the impact driving the air from his lungs, and he heard a wet pop in his left shoulder.

He slid down the wall and hit the floor, his vision greying out at the edges. His gun skittered across the hardwood, spinning away under a sofa.

Gasping, trying to force air into his paralyzed diaphragm, Rodecker looked up.

Carlisle stepped through the ruined doorway and brushed a shard of wood from his shoulder. He looked at Rodecker with mild curiosity, then raised his foot and kicked him in the ribs—a precise, calculated blow. Rodecker felt three ribs snap, and he curled into a ball, wheezing.

Carlisle loomed over him, preparing to stomp.

Then he froze.

Carlisle's head snapped up, and he turned away from Rodecker, looking toward the back of the house, toward the kitchen. He tilted his head, his nostrils flared, and he sniffed the air.

A draft.

A draft coming from the cellar.

Carlisle went still, his predator focus shifting as he realized the mistake.

"A distraction," Carlisle said, his voice like grinding stones.

He looked down at Rodecker one last time, with no anger now, only dismissal.

"You were merely a distraction."

Carlisle turned, and he didn't walk—he blurred into a sprint toward the kitchen, moving with a speed that defied physics, abandoning the front door, abandoning Zoe.

Rodecker groaned, trying to reach for his backup ankle holster, but his arm wouldn't move. He watched the monster disappear into the depths of the house.

Zoe stood at the top of the stairs, and the house was silent now. The gunshots and crashing sounds had stopped, leaving only an oppressive quiet. She gripped the banister, her legs shaking so hard she almost fell.

"Detective?" she said, her voice a dry rasp.

No answer.

She took a step down, then another, moving faster until she reached the foyer.

She saw the destruction—the front door stood wide open, and the inner doors to the parlor were shattered, wood splinters littering the floor.

She saw the detective.

He was slumped against the wall in the parlor, his face grey, blood trickling from his nose. He clutched his side, his eyes open and staring at the ceiling.

"Oh god," Zoe sobbed. She ran to him, kneeling in the glass.

"Detective Rodecker?"

His eyes shifted, focusing on her through a haze of pain.

"Go," Rodecker wheezed, blood bubbling on his lips. "Run."

Zoe looked around. Where was Evan?

"He went... back," Rodecker gasped, pointing a trembling hand toward the kitchen, toward the back of the house. "Go."

Zoe looked at the open front door, at the street, at freedom, and then at Rodecker, hurt and needing help.

"I can't leave you," she said.

Rodecker grabbed her arm with his good hand and shoved her. "Run!" he coughed out. "Get out!"

Zoe scrambled back and stood up.

She ran.

She bolted through the open front door and hit the stone steps, nearly tripping, catching herself on the railing. She stumbled onto the sidewalk, the humid air hitting her face, feeling real, alive.

She ran into the middle of Jones Street, her bare feet slapping against the cobblestones, the men's shirt flapping around her thighs. Lights were coming on in the houses, and people were coming to their windows.

Zoe screamed.

"HELP! POLICE! SOMEONE HELP ME!"

She collapsed in the middle of the road and wrapped her arms around her head, waiting for the cold hands to grab her.

But they didn't come.

From deep inside the townhouse, from somewhere beneath the earth, rapid, controlled gunfire popped.

Then silence.

CHAPTER

51

NATE SWEPT the beam of his tactical light across the space, watching the wooden steps end at packed dirt that gave way to old brick.

"Clear left," Pierce said, keeping her weapon tight to her shoulder.

Nate moved forward as the beam cut the gloom, revealing the house's foundation where Victorian brick arches stretched into the shadows, supporting the townhouse above.

"The expansion," Alicia said from behind him. "North, toward the carriage house."

Nate swung the light. The brickwork shifted—newer mortar, though still decades old. The archway had been widened. They moved through it, and the temperature dropped, not the natural cool of a cellar but mechanical cold.

They entered a wine cellar that extended past the property lines Nate had memorized, where racks of dark wood rose to the ceiling, and dust coated the bottles in grey silt, thick and unbroken.

"Look at the vintages," Alicia said, leaning in close to a bottle. "Château Margaux. 1898, 1924, 1945."

"Souvenirs," Pierce said, moving with her back to the racks. "Just like everything else."

Nate ignored the wine and tracked the heavy black electrical conduit snaking along the ceiling—modern work with stainless steel clips bolted into antique brick, bypassing the cellar lighting to run deeper.

"Follow the power," Nate said.

They pushed on through the transition where wine racks gave way to industrial steel shelving, archival boxes stacked with obsessive precision, each bearing a white label with handwritten calligraphy in black ink.

Alicia stopped. "Estate Papers 1853-1870," she read, her hand shaking and the light trembling against the cardboard. "Daguerreotype Collection. Medical Instruments."

Pierce pulled a digital camera from her vest, the shutter clicking rapidly as the flash illuminated the dust motes. "He kept the receipts —every deed, every transaction."

"He's archiving it," Alicia said, gripping the handle of the iron blade. "He thinks he's the curator."

Nate moved past the shelves where the conduit led to the far corner and the brick walls met—no archway, just a modern steel security door set directly into the 19th-century masonry. Grey metal, featureless, with a small electronic keypad glowing green.

"Here," Nate said.

Alicia moved up, reaching for the skeleton keys before letting them drop against her satchel. "Magnetic lock, six-digit code."

"Don't need the code," Nate said.

He turned his light to the wall where the conduit ended in a grey breaker panel—a sub-panel for the climate control. He holstered his weapon and pulled his multi-tool, jamming the flathead driver into the latch and twisting until the metal popped open.

Rows of black switches. *Dehumidifier. Overhead Lighting. Ventilation.*

"Which one?" Pierce asked, checking her watch. "Rodecker engaged four minutes ago, and if he triggered a silent alarm, we have patrol units eight minutes out."

Nate scanned the breakers and found it bottom right—no text label, just a small round sticker with a red dot.

Fire code meant magnetic locks in confined spaces required a fail-safe, and when power cuts, the magnet releases.

"Do it," Alicia said, unwrapping the cloth from the iron blade.

Nate put his thumb on the red-dot breaker and looked at Pierce. "Ready?"

"Clear," Pierce said.

Nate flipped the switch.

The *snap* was sharp as the green light on the keypad died and the hum of the ventilation cut out, followed by a soft pneumatic hiss and the heavy *clunk* of the internal magnets disengaging.

The door popped open an inch.

Nate drew his Glock and hooked his boot around the edge of the steel door, pulling it wide as it swung outward on oiled hinges.

Nate's light cut into the blackness and hit white—sterile, blinding white.

"Moving," Nate said.

He stepped across the threshold with his weapon high, Pierce following close behind, and Alicia last.

Subway tiles covered the walls and floor, gleaming under the tactical lights, scrubbed and polished to a surgical shine. In the center of the floor sat a cast-iron drain with channels carved into the tile radiating out from it, designed to guide fluid.

Above them, steel tracks were bolted to the ceiling beams with meat hooks hanging from chains, empty but swaying slightly in the draft.

The smell hit him next—chemical, industrial bleach and formaldehyde, and underneath it all the sweet, rot-rich scent of a butcher shop.

"Clear," Pierce said, her voice flat.

Nate lowered his weapon and turned his light to the right wall.

"My god," Alicia said.

The wall was a gallery.

Framed photographs hung in rows with mathematical precision—dozens of them starting on the far left with small metallic squares, daguerreotypes showing ghostly faces in high collars.

Nate walked down the line, past sepia cabinet cards and grainy black-and-white silver gelatin prints, past Technicolor Polaroids and glossy 90s prints to high-resolution digital.

Every face different. Every face the same—blonde, petite, with eyes either terrified or vacant.

Nate stopped at the first frame.

Margaret Calhoun. 1890. Age 23.

He moved to the next.

Josephine Wilkes. 1905. Age 19.

The dates continued—1920, 1935, 1950, 1965—each one hammering against his ribs.

"He kept them all," Alicia said.

"Narcissism," Pierce said, crouching by the floor drain to photograph the dark staining in the grout. "He thinks they belong to him."

Nate reached the end, where the year shifted to 2025.

Caroline Marsh. 2025. Age 28.

Lucy Phelps. 2025. Age 34.

Nicole Gladman. 2025. Age 22.

And one more—a candid shot of a woman laughing outside an art gallery.

Zoe Kaplan. 2025. Age 29.

"He was done with her," Nate said. "Label was already printed."

He turned back to the center of the wall, where a gap in the timeline marked a larger frame, separated from the rows like a shrine.

Nate aimed his light, and the beam shook.

A student ID card with scratched plastic and a faded SCAD logo showed a girl with messy blonde hair and a smile that hadn't learned to be guarded.

Sarah.

Nate's lungs seized as the air in the room vanished, and he looked at the face he had tried to keep alive for fifteen years, looked at the date beneath it—2010.

"Nate," Alicia said, her hand gripping his arm. "Stay with us."

He couldn't speak because the killer hadn't just taken her life—he had curated it, framed it, hung it in a slaughterhouse like a specimen in a collection.

"Over here," Pierce said. "Trophy cases."

Nate forced his legs to move and walked to the opposite wall, where glass display cases sat on pedestals.

The first case held vials of hair—blonde curls tied with silk ribbons.

The second case contained jewelry: rings, cheap plastic bracelets, and diamond studs.

The third case displayed personal effects.

Nate looked down through the glass at lipstick, a keychain with a pink rabbit, a torn ticket stub, and, in the center, on a black velvet pad, a silver locket—heart-shaped, with a chip in the enamel near the hinge.

Nate's vision blurred at the edges as he gripped the edge of the case, his knuckles turning white, and he remembered buying it with landscaping money, remembered the smell of strawberry shampoo when she hugged him.

Beside the locket sat a cocktail napkin with an address in blue ink, and next to that, brittle and brown, a single sprig of dried lavender.

"He knew," Nate said, his voice a rasp. "When he came to my hotel room, he knew."

He wanted to smash the glass, wanted to burn the house down until nothing remained but ash.

"We have him," Pierce said, snapping a photo of the locket. "This clears Booker and proves everything—DNA inside the locket, fingerprints on the photos."

"We document," Alicia said, shaking now. "We document everything, then we end him."

Nate pulled his hand back and checked the chamber of his Glock, watching the brass casing glint in the light.

"Pierce," Nate said. "Get the floor, the drain, the hooks."

"On it."

"Alicia, get the dates and prove the cycle."

"Doing it."

Nate turned back to the shrine and raised his phone, taking a picture of Sarah's ID and then the locket—8:24 PM.

"Time's up," Nate said. "We move."

Above them, two gunshots cracked through the floorboards, followed by the sound of shattering wood and a heavy thud.

"Rodecker," Pierce hissed from behind him.

"Move," Nate ordered. "Go. Now."

Footsteps sounded on the stairs behind them—not the heavy boot-falls of a cop but light, fast, rhythmic.

Nate spun around, raising his Glock toward the open steel door, locking his elbows, and centering the sights on the black rectangle.

"He's coming," Nate said.

Two seconds to cover the stairs, boots on brick, moving through the wine cellar, and closing the distance between them.

"Back," Nate said. "Get back."

Pierce scrambled up with her weapon raised and moved left while Alicia retreated to the rear wall beneath the rows of dead women, holding the iron blade against her chest.

The footsteps stopped just outside the door.

No breathing, no movement—just a sudden stillness radiating from the dark as the temperature dropped further.

"Evan Carlisle!" Nate shouted. "Federal Agents! Show your hands!"

Silence.

Then a voice, smooth and cultured, layered with a fatigue older than the bricks themselves.

"You broke the lock," the voice said. "Parts for that mechanism are difficult to source."

A figure stepped into the light.

Evan Carlisle stood before them in a cream linen suit that was ruined—two ragged holes in the chest, the fabric stiff with blood—but the man himself looked uninjured.

He looked annoyed.

He stepped into the room as his eyes reflected the tactical lights with a flat, silver shine, looking at Nate, then Pierce, then Alicia holding the iron blade.

He didn't smile but looked instead at the broken lock and then at the mud on his white tiles.

"I haven't had visitors down here in some time," Carlisle said. "You're making a mess."

CHAPTER

52

Nate kept his weapon trained on the center of Carlisle's chest, the Glock 19M heavy in his hands and slick with the sweat of his own terror. He stared at the two ragged holes in the cream linen suit, dark stains radiating outward from the impact points and stiffening the expensive fabric. A man shot twice in the chest with hollow-point rounds did not stand with his weight evenly distributed, did not look annoyed, did not speak with a voice that carried no tremor of pain.

Carlisle brushed at the front of his jacket, his fingers coming away red. He looked at the blood on his skin with a detached curiosity before lifting his eyes to Nate.

His geometry shifted. The shoulders rolled back, the spine elongating with a wet pop of cartilage that reverberated off the subway tiles. The mask of the Savannah gentleman, worn for decades to charm board members and tourists, dissolved as the muscles in his face slackened and then pulled tight in new, wrong configurations.

Nate saw the eyes change first. The tactical lights mounted on their weapons cut through the gloom and hit Carlisle's face, but his pupils did not contract. They widened until the brown irises vanished, replaced by flat, reflective silver that caught the beams and threw them back like polished coins.

Then came the cold.

It rolled off the man in a physical wave, dropping the temperature in the kill room by twenty degrees in a second. Nate's breath misted in front of his face, the condensation clouding his sight picture as the smell of industrial bleach and copper vanished. A thick, cloying scent replaced it: night-blooming jasmine, wet earth, and beneath the flowers, the heavy, sweet stench of meat left too long in the sun.

Carlisle opened his mouth, but the jaw didn't just lower—it descended. A wet, clicking sound bounced off the tiles as the mandible unhinged, revealing canines that were not just sharp but long, serrated needles designed for gripping and tearing.

He wasn't pretending anymore.

Above them, faintly, the wail of sirens cut through the heavy floorboards. Zoe had made it to the street, and patrol cars were coming.

Carlisle didn't look at the ceiling. He looked at Pierce.

"SCMPD." Pierce's voice cracked, then hardened as she stepped diagonally, placing her body directly in the line of fire between Nate and the creature. "Get on the ground now."

She didn't wait for compliance or hesitate. She squeezed the trigger three times in rapid succession, the reports deafening them in the tiled room.

Crack. Crack. Crack.

Muzzle flashes lit the white walls in strobe-light bursts. Nate saw the linen suit jerk from the impacts, center mass, textbook grouping.

Then the space where Carlisle stood was empty.

Nate blinked, his brain trying to bridge the gap between one second and the next. There was no transition he could track, no movement the eye could process—just a blur of motion that disrupted the air pressure and popped his ears.

Carlisle was standing in front of Pierce.

He had crossed fifteen feet of space in the time it took a casing to hit the floor.

Pierce tried to adjust her aim, but her reflexes were human and too slow. Carlisle's left hand shot out and grabbed her by the throat, lifting her until her boots left the floor and kicked at the air six inches above the tile, her tactical vest bunching around her neck.

With his right hand, Carlisle backhanded her weapon with a gesture that looked effortless, like a man swatting away a fly. The heavy Glock flew from her grip, spinning through the air until it clattered into the far corner near the drain.

A raw, wordless sound tore from Nate's throat as he fired.

He advanced, closing the distance to eight feet while trusting his aim, pulling the trigger as fast as the slide could cycle.

Bam. Bam. Bam. Bam.

The rounds slammed into Carlisle's flank and lower ribs with wet, heavy impacts. Blood sprayed in a fine mist, coating the pristine white tiles behind the vampire as the linen suit tore open. Carlisle staggered, the force of the hydra-shok rounds pushing him sideways, his grip on Pierce slipping just enough for her to gasp.

Nate saw the wounds: gaping red craters in the man's side, tissue shredded, bone exposed. Lethal damage.

It had to be.

Carlisle looked down at his own torso, and the flesh moved.

It wasn't healing—healing took time, left scars. This was a reversal, the shredded muscle fibers reaching out and knitting together while the white of the exposed rib vanished under new meat. The skin surged over the open wounds, sealing them shut, and within three seconds, the skin was smooth and pale again. Only the blood-soaked, tattered linen proved Nate had fired at all.

Nate's brain refused to process the visual data. His finger froze on the trigger.

Carlisle turned his head and pulled Pierce closer to his face, her boots drumming against his shins while her hands clawed at his wrist, nails digging into skin that felt like cold marble. He inhaled deeply, pressing his face into the curve of her neck, eyes closing in what looked like ecstasy.

"You came into my home," Carlisle said.

The voice did not belong to the antique dealer—it was deep and layered, three voices speaking in unison, vibrating the bones in Nate's inner ear and carrying the weight of dust and stone.

Carlisle's lips moved against Pierce's skin. "You violated my sanctuary and photographed my collection. Did you think there would be no consequence?"

"Let her go." Nate shifted his aim, knowing center mass didn't work, and the heart didn't work, so he raised the sights to the bridge of Carlisle's nose—the kill switch.

He fired.

At the exact moment the hammer fell, Carlisle tilted his head, and the bullet missed the T-zone. It clipped the side of his temple, taking a chunk of flesh and hair with it, and Carlisle's head snapped to the side from the kinetic energy. Black blood smeared across his cheekbone.

For a second, Nate thought he had him.

Carlisle dropped Pierce.

She hit the floor hard, her knees cracking against the tile before she scrambled backward, boots scrabbling for traction on the slick floor. Her hand went to her ankle, reaching for the backup piece strapped there.

Alicia grabbed Nate's left arm and yanked him backward, her voice cutting through the chaos like a blade. "The door. Nate, the door."

He fought her and planted his feet. He wasn't leaving Pierce.

Pierce had her hand on the grip of the compact Smith & Wesson, and she was fast, one of the best officers he had ever worked with.

She wasn't fast enough.

The wound on Carlisle's temple was already closing as he looked down at her. He didn't lunge but stepped on her ankle instead, and the sound of the joint popping was sharp and dry.

Pierce cried out, a raw sound of shock.

Carlisle crouched, moving with a fluid, unnatural grace, and pinned her right wrist to the tile with one hand while the backup gun remained in its holster. With his other hand, he grabbed a fistful of her dark hair and yanked her head back, exposing the long, smooth line of her throat, the tendons straining against the skin.

Carlisle looked up and locked eyes with Nate. The silver shine in his pupils pulsed—a challenge, a lesson in impotence—and he wanted Nate to see this.

"This is what I am," Carlisle said, his lips pulling back over the gum line. "This is what you cannot stop with your guns and your laws and your rational explanations."

His jaw distended fully with the wet sound of cartilage popping, bone grinding against bone. The mouth opened wider than any human scream, and the elongated canines caught the harsh light of the flashlights.

"No," Nate said, barely a breath.

Carlisle descended.

He buried his face in her neck and tore.

The sound was wet and heavy: the distinct crunch of the trachea collapsing under a pressure it was never designed to withstand, followed by the high-pressure hiss of the carotid arteries giving way. Pierce didn't scream because she couldn't—the sound she made was a wet gurgle that bubbled up through the ruin of her throat.

Blood exploded outward.

It hit the white tiles in a hot, red sheet and sprayed across Carlisle's face, coating his eyes, his mouth, his ruined suit. He thrashed his head, ripping a massive section of tissue free before pulling back and spitting the piece of flesh onto the floor with contempt.

Nate stood frozen. His mind couldn't reconcile the image because it wasn't a crime scene—it was a process.

Blood poured from Pierce's neck but didn't pool, hitting the floor and running immediately into the grooves carved into the tiles, flowing in thick, red rivers toward the central cast-iron drain. The room was designed for this, the architecture serving the kill.

Carlisle stood up, looming over the body.

Pierce was still moving.

Her hands flew to her neck, fingers slipping on the wet gore as she tried to hold the edges of the wound together, tried to keep the life inside. Her legs kicked against the tile in rhythmic spasms, boots drumming a frantic, dying beat.

She turned her head.

Her eyes found Nate's.

They were wide and terrified, the whites bright against her dark skin, and she stared at him while blood bubbled from her lips as she tried to form a word. There was no accusation in her stare, only a silent, desperate plea for help he could not give.

A cold void opened in Nate's chest.

He raised the gun without aiming, pointed it at the monster, and pulled the trigger until the slide locked back with a final, metallic *clack*.

Bang. Bang. Bang. Bang.

Four shots at point-blank range.

The bullets hit Carlisle in the chest and stomach, and the vampire rocked back on his heels before looking down at the new holes in his shirt. He looked at Nate.

He smiled.

His teeth were stained crimson, blood dripping from his chin in dark ribbons. The smile was not human but a baring of fangs that promised nothing but the end.

"Now," Carlisle said, wiping his mouth with the back of his hand in the gesture of a dinner guest, "we can discuss terms of your surrender."

On the floor, Pierce's hands slid off her neck, and her arms fell to the tiles with a wet slap. The kicking stopped, and her chest hitched once before settling. The light in her eyes—the intelligence and the bravery and the life—went out, and she stared at the bottom shelf of the wine rack.

The flow of blood into the drain slowed to a trickle.

"Move." Alicia grabbed Nate by the vest and threw her entire weight backward. Nate stumbled, staring at Pierce's body because he couldn't leave her, couldn't leave her there with him.

"Nate!"

Alicia dragged him across the threshold, and they spilled into the corridor. She slammed her shoulder against the heavy steel door, which swung shut with a boom that shook dust from the ceiling.

There was no lock on the inside.

Alicia put her back against the metal, driving her heels into the dirt floor, and looked at Nate with wild eyes, her face streaked with dust. "Help me. He's coming."

Nate stared at the grey steel, still seeing Pierce's eyes, still hearing the sound of her throat tearing. The gun hung uselessly at his side, the slide locked open on an empty chamber.

From the other side of the door, they heard footsteps.

Tap. Tap. Tap.

They were slow and rhythmic, the confident, unhurried steps of a predator that knew the cage was closed, the prey was trapped, and there was nowhere left to run.

Nate dropped the empty magazine, and it hit the floor. He reached for a fresh one with hands that felt numb, shaking so hard he couldn't find the well.

"Brace it," Nate said, his voice sounding like a stranger's. "Brace the door."

He looked at the iron blade in Alicia's hand—dull, heavy, the only thing left—and he knew, with a cold certainty that settled in his marrow, that the guns wouldn't save them and the badge wouldn't save them.

He rammed the fresh magazine home and racked the slide.

The footsteps stopped, and the handle of the steel door began to turn.

METAL GROUND AGAINST METAL. The handle turned, the vibration traveling through the steel door and into Alicia's spine. She drove her heels into the floor and locked her knees, throwing every pound of her weight against the cold steel.

It did not matter.

The door pushed inward with a steady, hydraulic relentlessness that ignored leverage and the frantic resistance of a terrified historian. Alicia's boots slid through the dust, and she gasped as her shoes lost traction, stumbling backward until she caught herself on the edge of a heavy wooden worktable before scrambling toward the rear wall.

Nate stood in the center of the kill room, the air thick with the taste of copper and ancient dust. He held the iron blade low, his knuckles white around the leather-wrapped tang, while his ribs ground together like broken pottery with every shallow breath. He pushed the pain down, pushed everything down except the target.

Evan Carlisle stepped across the threshold.

He did not rush or storm into the room, but entered like a man returning to his study after a long evening. The heavy steel door swung loose on its hinges behind him, creaking once before settling into silence.

Blood had stiffened the cream linen suit into a black, crusty armor around his chest. Shredded fibers hung from the exit wounds where the hollow points had blown through the back of the jacket, but the skin visible through the tears was smooth, pale, and whole.

Carlisle stopped five feet inside the room. He glanced down at the mud from the alley that now stained his Italian leather shoes, then reached into his pocket and produced a handkerchief embroidered with the initials of a man dead for a century. He wiped a smear of Yolanda Pierce's blood from his chin and dropped the linen square, which fluttered to the white tiles, a splash of red on the scrubbed floor.

"Four thousand years," Carlisle said, his voice conversational, carrying no anger, only a terrible, crushing fatigue. He looked at Nate, then past him to the trophies lining the walls, and finally at Alicia, huddled against the tiles.

"I have outlived empires," he said, taking a step forward. "I have outlived languages and the gods they were used to praise. Do you think you are the first? Do you think you are special because you found a knife and a tablet?"

Nate adjusted his grip on the iron. The metal felt heavy, unbalanced, and crude—their only hope against a creature that should not exist.

"I have been hunted by Sumerian priests who knew the shape of my soul," Carlisle said, walking toward the center of the room and ignoring the weapon in Nate's hand as if it were a toy. "By Babylonian soldiers with bronze spears. By Persian witch-finders who brought fire to my door." He paused, letting the weight of centuries fill the space between them. "I survived Roman persecution and the medieval inquisitions. I survived the yellow fever that cleared this city for me."

He stopped and looked at Nate, the silver light in his eyes flat and hard.

"Now I have federal agents," Carlisle said. "With your guns, your forensic science, and your arrogance. You all believe you are the exception. You all believe you will be the one to finally close the case."

He shook his head.

"You are not."

Nate exploded from his stance without a scream or a telegraph, driving off his back leg and channeling every ounce of his remaining strength into a single, linear motion. He had trained for this at Quantico, practicing lethal strikes until the muscle memory was burned into his nervous system.

He covered the distance in a heartbeat and aimed for the heart.

The blade whistled through the air—fourteen inches of bloomery-smelted iron, sharpened to a razor edge, forged to kill a god. Nate put his body weight behind the thrust, locking his wrist and driving the point toward the center of the blood-stained linen.

Carlisle's hand moved in a blur too fast to track, his fingers clamping around Nate's right wrist with crushing force.

The stop was absolute. The kinetic energy of Nate's lunge rebounded through his arm, jarring his shoulder in its socket and snapping his teeth together, driving the air from his lungs. Nate strained, his boots slipping on the tile, his face contorted with effort as the muscles in his neck stood out in cords. He pushed until his vision greyed at the edges, until every fiber in his body screamed for oxygen.

Carlisle stood immobile. He didn't brace himself or strain, just held Nate's wrist in a grip that crushed skin and ground against the radius and ulna with the pressure of a hydraulic press.

"Bloomery iron," Carlisle murmured, looking at the blade hovering inches from his chest.

He pulled Nate closer, drawing Nate's hand forward until the point of the blade pressed against his own chest, directly over the heart that did not beat.

"Push," Carlisle whispered.

Nate screamed through clenched teeth and drove his legs into the floor, putting everything he had left into the metal.

The linen tore. The tip of the blade touched the skin beneath and stopped—it did not cut, did not puncture. The iron slid against the resistance of the body like a spoon pressing against a granite wall, skidding on the pale flesh without leaving a scratch. The skin was harder than the metal.

Carlisle leaned in, his face inches from Nate's, the smell of jasmine and rot overpowering.

He spoke. The words were not English, not any language Nate had ever heard—guttural, rhythmic, vibrating with a resonance that rattled Nate's teeth. Sumerian. A language dead for three millennia, spoken by a throat that remembered the taste of the Euphrates, and the sound made the air in the room thick, building a pressure behind Nate's eyes.

Carlisle twisted his hand.

The sound was wet and sharp, a dry snap followed by the grinding of bone on bone.

Nate's wrist shattered. Nausea rose in his throat as the pain—a spike of pure agony—shot up his arm and exploded in his shoulder. His knees buckled, and he dropped, gasping, the strength draining from his hand as the nerves severed.

The iron blade slipped from his useless fingers and clattered to the white tiles.

Carlisle did not release him. He looked at the broken wrist with mild interest, then at Nate's face, and said, "Disappointing."

He released Nate's wrist and, in the same motion, backhanded him with a blow delivered without effort but with the force of being hit by a car.

Nate flew backward and slammed into the glass display cases lining the far wall. The impact shattered the heavy panes, splintered wood, and buckled metal shelving as he hit the floor in a shower of glass and debris, sliding through the wreckage of the trophies.

Pain flared in his ribs, sharp and hot. He gasped, inhaling dust, and tried to push himself up, but his right hand hung useless at a sickening angle. His left hand scrabbled through the ruins, and his fingers closed around something cold and metallic.

He looked down. Lying in the dust, surrounded by shards of glass, was a small silver locket—Sarah's, the cheap jewelry he had given her for her sixteenth birthday. The chain was broken, and he couldn't look at it because the sight hurt worse than his wrist. He had failed her, come all this way, burned his life to the ground, and failed her again.

Movement in the center of the room drew his attention.

Alicia was scrambling on her hands and knees, lunging toward the iron blade on the tiles. Her lips were pulled back from her teeth, her glasses sliding down a nose slick with sweat, and she reached out, her fingers inches from the leather handle.

Carlisle took a single step and placed his Italian leather shoe on the blade, pinning it to the floor.

Alicia froze. She looked up at him, her hand hovering over the metal, her breath coming in ragged sobs.

Carlisle looked down at the weapon beneath his foot and tilted his head, studying the dark, folded metal.

"Old iron," he said. "Bloomery-smelted. Hand-forged. Quenched in running water." He looked at Alicia. "You did your research, Miss Landry. The Ashworth tablet, I assume?"

Alicia shrank back, pulling her hand away until her spine hit the leg of the heavy worktable.

"I watched that tablet being inscribed," Carlisle said. "In Ur. On clay still wet from the riverbank. The scribe was a man named Enki-nudu, and he had a lisp." He pressed down, grinding the blade against the tile. "The curse is real. This iron, forged in the old ways, could indeed end me."

He looked at Nate, who was struggling to sit up in the wreckage. Blood dripped from a cut on Nate's forehead, blinding him in one eye.

"But you are missing the fourth element," Carlisle said. He stepped off the blade and kicked it, sending the iron skittering across the tiles to rest against the far wall, a useless artifact.

"Your translation," Carlisle said to Alicia, "it said 'the hand of death,' didn't it? That was the phrase you pulled from the cuneiform?"

Alicia nodded, a jerky, terrified motion.

Carlisle shook his head, a small, pitying smile on his lips. "The Sumerian is more precise than that. Languages degrade, and meaning is lost."

He walked toward Nate, stopping just outside the debris field to look down at the broken agent.

"Not the hand of death," Carlisle said. "Not an executioner. Not a judge. Not a soldier." He tapped his own chest. "The cuneiform specifies *qāt mīt.*"

The words hung in the silent room. *Qāt mīt.*

"The hand," Carlisle translated, his voice low, "of one who is already dying."

Nate stared at him, the blood roaring in his ears as the truth settled over him like a burial shroud—the hand of the dying.

"The wielder must already be claimed by death," Carlisle said. "Not symbolically. Not bravely facing the end. Not willing to sacrifice themselves." He looked at Alicia. "Dying—biologically, irrevocably. Death must be in the bones, in the blood, in the failing flesh. The hand that holds the iron must belong to the grave."

He sighed. "Your professor translated the role but should have translated the condition."

The silence that followed was absolute. Nate looked at his empty gun ten feet away, at the shattered display case, at the door leading to the corridor where Pierce's body lay cooling on the dirt.

The dying. Not the brave. They had brought courage and skill and righteousness, but they had brought the wrong things.

Carlisle turned away from Nate, dismissing him as a threat, and turned toward Alicia. She was pressed against the white tiles of the rear wall, beneath the photographs of the dead women, her eyes wide, her hands held up, empty and shaking.

Carlisle moved toward her with a fluid, predatory grace, stepping over the iron blade without a glance.

"You understand now," he said. "Why I am still here. Why I will always be here."

Alicia slid down the wall, curling into herself, trying to disappear into the masonry.

"Please," she whispered.

"Begging is tiresome," Carlisle said. He reached out, his hand stained with Pierce's blood, the fingers long and pale, and reached for her throat.

Nate tried to stand, but his legs wouldn't work, and his ribs screamed. He watched, helpless, as the monster closed the distance, as the hand extended, as the end arrived.

Carlisle's fingers brushed Alicia's neck, and the cold burned her skin.

Nate closed his eyes, waiting for the sound of tearing flesh.

The silence stretched for a heartbeat, then two.

A sound came from the doorway behind Carlisle—a shuffle, a heavy, labored step, the rattle of plastic bottles in a pocket.

Carlisle froze. His hand hovered at Alicia's throat, and he turned his head, a muscle feathering in his jaw, annoyed by the interruption.

Nate opened his eyes.

Standing in the doorway, framed by the darkness of the corridor, was a figure who leaned heavily against the frame, his face grey and beaded with sweat. A bloody handkerchief was clutched in his hand.

CHAPTER

54

THE FIRST THING Nate registered was the sound from the doorway, a wet, rattling breath that cut through the cellar's quiet like a death rattle made audible.

Zeke Tatum leaned against the steel jamb, his chest heaving with the effort of each breath. He wore work pants stained with coal dust and a flannel shirt that hung loose on a frame stripped of its muscle by months of wasting illness. His face was grey, the color of old concrete. Sweat beaded on his forehead and dripped into eyes that were sunken and dark, hollowed out by pain and sleepless nights. He clutched a handkerchief to his mouth, pulling it away to reveal bright blood spotted against the white cotton, still wet from his lungs.

Nate watched from the floor, his vision swimming in and out of focus. The pain in his shattered wrist was a high-frequency whine that drowned out almost everything else, but he could still hear the pills rattling in Zeke's pocket with every labored breath. Morphine. Zofran. The chemical signature of the terminally ill, carried like coins for a ferryman who was already waiting at the dock.

Carlisle lowered his hand from Alicia's throat and turned slowly, the movement smooth and annoyed, like a cat interrupted from playing with a wounded mouse. He looked at the blacksmith, then at the blood on the handkerchief, and his expression shifted from irritation to curiosity.

"You," Carlisle said.

Zeke took a step into the room, his boots scraping against the concrete threshold. He did not look at the vampire. His eyes swept the kill room, taking in the shattered glass scattered across the floor, the broken federal agent bleeding against the tiles, the terrified historian pressed against the far wall. His attention landed on the iron blade lying where it had fallen against the far wall.

"Blacksmith," Carlisle said, his voice dropping an octave into something that resonated in the bones. He tilted his head, nostrils flaring as he drew in air. "I can smell it on you—the death, the rot working through your cells."

Zeke coughed, a deep, hacking sound that bent him double and shook his entire frame. He spat red onto the pristine white tiles, leaving a splash of color that looked obscene against all that sterile brightness.

"Rot," Carlisle said, stepping away from Alicia with the casual dismissiveness of a man abandoning a toy. "Your cells are failing, unraveling like cheap thread. You're spoiling from the inside out."

Zeke wiped his mouth with the back of a hand that trembled with a palsy not of fear, but of weakness, the kind that comes when the body begins its final shutdown. He straightened up as much as his ruined spine would allow. He looked small in the cavernous room, a man made of gristle and bone and dying tissue, something already half-claimed by the grave.

He finally looked at the man in the cream linen suit, meeting those silver eyes with the calm of someone who had nothing left to lose.

"Not spoiling," Zeke rasped, his voice thin and reedy, nothing similar to the boom of the man who had commanded the forge three nights ago. "Ready."

He moved. It was not a charge but a lurch, a stumble powered by momentum and desperation, the last gasp of a body that had already given everything it had to give. Zeke threw himself toward the far wall, his boots sliding on the slick tiles. He hit the floor on his knees, crying out as the impact jarred his wasting body, and scrambled toward the iron blade with clawed fingers.

Carlisle watched him with his head tilted, a scientist observing a rat in a maze. He did not intervene or move to stop him. He seemed to be observing a foregone conclusion, waiting for the punchline to a joke he'd already heard a thousand times.

Zeke's hand closed around the leather-wrapped tang of the blade, his fingers finding the grip worn smooth by his own hours at the finishing stone.

Nate tried to shout, to tell him it was useless without the condition, but his throat was full of dust and despair and the copper taste of his own blood. *Don't do it. Don't let him break you, too.*

Zeke used the wall to push himself upright, his legs shaking with the strain. He swayed on his feet, holding the heavy blade in both hands, arms trembling under the weight of iron that would seem light to a healthy man. The point wavered in small circles. He turned to face the vampire, shoulders squared despite the pain that must be eating him alive from the inside.

Carlisle smiled, an indulgent expression that made him look almost human for a moment. "Do you think you can swing that, old man? Do you think you still possess the breath to—"

"NARAM-EKUR!"

The sound tore out of Zeke's throat with a strength that should not exist in his ruined lungs, drawn from some reserve deeper than muscle or oxygen. It was not just a name but an indictment, an accusation hurled across four thousand years of darkness. The syllables hit the tiled walls and died, leaving a dead space in the air where sound should echo, but didn't.

Carlisle flinched. The vampire stumbled back a step, his hand flying to his chest as if he had been struck by something physical, something that left a wound. The arrogance vanished from his face, replaced by a shock so profound it looked closer to madness than surprise. The pupils of his silver eyes blew wide, swallowing the irises until only black remained.

"How?" Carlisle said, the word bleeding into a growl that contained harmonics no human throat could produce. "Who gave you that name? Who told you what I was?"

Zeke didn't answer, didn't waste his remaining breath on explanations. He shifted his grip on the blade, holding it in his left hand, and with his right, he seized the naked edge just below the hilt. He squeezed and drew his palm down the length of the iron in one deliberate motion.

The blade opened his hand to the bone. Blood welled instantly, dark and thick, flooding the fuller and running down the metal in rivulets that caught the overhead light. The pain didn't register on his face—or if it did, it was lost in the landscape of agony he already inhabited. He wrapped his bleeding fist back around the grip, his blood mixing with the leather, soaking into every crack and pore of the handle until the iron was slick and warm with it.

Qāt mīt.

The words from the tablet surfaced in Nate's mind with horrible clarity. *The Hand of the Dying.* The translation hadn't been metaphorical or poetic. It was a biological requirement, a magical contract written in blood and death. The curse demanded a wielder who was already part of the grave—someone who had one foot in the darkness and could bridge both worlds. Not just a dying man. A dying man's blood on the blade, his life force bonded to the iron, anointing the weapon with the only thing that could make it lethal to something that had cheated death for four thousand years.

Zeke looked at Alicia, his eyes clear for just a moment, the confusion and pain falling away. He gave her a small, grim nod—a farewell and a promise rolled into one gesture.

Then he charged.

It was a slow, lumbering thing from a man with minutes to live, a bull's rush powered by forty years of hammering iron and a lifetime of stubborn refusal to quit. His boots found traction on the blood-slicked tiles. The blade led, held low, angled upward, the point steady for the first time since he'd lifted it—steadied by purpose, by the knowledge that this was the only thing left that mattered.

Carlisle seemed paralyzed, pinned in place by the weight of his own true name, by the violation of rules older than civilization. He threw up his hands, summoning whatever power he still possessed, but the energy slid away from Zeke, unable to grip a man who had already accepted the end. The blood on the blade hummed, resonating at a frequency that made the air taste of copper, and the vampire's power broke against it like water against stone.

"No," Carlisle said, the English falling away, replaced by frantic Sumerian that hadn't been spoken in living memory. "No, you cannot do this. You are dirt. You are nothing. You are already dead."

Zeke hit him like a freight train running on fumes.

The iron blade punched through the cream linen suit with a sound like ripping silk. It slid between ribs that hadn't drawn breath in millennia, the bloomery iron parting ancient flesh as if it were paper. The impact drove them both backward, Zeke's legs churning, his weight behind the thrust, burying the blade to the hilt in the vampire's chest.

Carlisle screamed. It was a raw sound of animal terror, something primal that came from a place older than language. His hands clawed at Zeke's shoulders, fingernails tearing through flannel and flesh, leaving deep gouges that welled with blood. But Zeke didn't let go. He drove forward, didn't stop pushing until he felt the blade grate against Carlisle's spine, metal scraping bone with a vibration that traveled through both bodies.

Zeke's legs buckled. The charge had taken everything he had, the last reserves of a body already running on nothing. He collapsed against the vampire, his arms wrapping around Carlisle's torso, his weight pinning the blade in place. It became an embrace—violent and intimate—a dying man clinging to a monster, holding on with the stubborn, immovable determination of someone who knows this is the only thing he has left to do.

The scream that tore from the vampire's throat shattered every remaining piece of glass in the display cases, turning them into glittering shrapnel. It was a multi-tonal wail that pitched up and up, beyond human hearing, into a frequency that vibrated the fillings in Nate's teeth and made his bones ache. It was the sound of a four-thousand-year-old binding snapping, the chains of an ancient curse finally breaking.

The room shook with the violence of it. Dust rained from the ceiling beams, white powder falling through the air.

"Let go!" Carlisle said, his voice warping and doubling over itself, becoming multiple voices speaking in unison. "I am Naram-Ekur! I am the Favored of the Netherworld! I cannot end! I am eternal!"

"You end," Zeke whispered into his ear, breath hot against cold skin.

The disintegration began at the wound where the iron pierced his chest. No light, no fire, no dramatic transformation. Just entropy, the universe reclaiming what should never exist. Fissures of grey cracked across the vampire's chest, spreading like a shattered windshield. The skin didn't bleed or tear. It flaked, turning the color of dry slate and peeling away to reveal not muscle or bone but nothingness, an absence where substance should be.

The cracks raced up Carlisle's neck with increasing speed, covering distance in seconds. His jaw unhinged, stretching wide in a silent howl as his throat turned to dust, the scream dying before it could finish. The cream linen suit began to collapse inward, fabric folding on itself, no longer supported by the body beneath. Grey powder poured from the vampire's mouth in a thick stream. It erupted from the wound in his chest, a geyser of dust that smelled of ancient tombs and night-blooming jasmine and libraries that hadn't seen sun in centuries.

Zeke held on through all of it. He held on as the body he was embracing turned to powder between his arms. He held on as the arms clawing at his back dissolved into grit that pattered onto the floor. He held on until his hands slapped together behind a cloud of falling dust, his fingers meeting in empty air.

The vampire was gone. The suit dropped to the floor, empty of its occupant, just fabric and buttons. A pile of grey ash settled over the white tiles, rising in a small cloud that coated Zeke's face and stuck to the blood on his chin. The blade, no longer supported by the vampire's body, pulled free as Zeke staggered forward through the space where Carlisle had stood, the iron dragging from his grip and clattering against the tiles with a metallic ring.

Zeke swayed where he stood, alone in the center of the room. He was coated in the remains of a monster, covered in dust that had once been a man named Evan Carlisle. His right hand hung at his side, still bleeding freely from the gash that had opened it to the bone, his life painting the white tiles in a slow, steady drip. He blinked several times, looking confused, as if he had forgotten how to stand or what he was supposed to do next.

Then his knees gave way beneath him. He pitched forward, collapsing into the pile of linen and ash like a puppet with cut strings. He landed on his side, his ruined hand curled against his chest, his breath coming in shallow, wet hitches that rattled in his cancerous lungs. The effort had taken what little the disease had left him. The charge, the scream, the force of the kill—it had burned through the last of his reserves, and now the body was collecting what it was owed.

The distant sound of sirens grew louder with each passing second, their warning useless to a danger that had already passed, arriving too late to change anything.

Nate moved. His body was a map of broken things, each injury marked in pain, but he forced himself into motion anyway. He dragged himself across the tiles, using his good elbow to pull his weight, his shattered wrist cradled against his chest, his legs trailing behind him like dead weight. He ignored the agony in his ribs, the way each movement sent shards of glass through his side. He crawled through the broken glass and the dust and the blood, focused only on reaching the fallen blacksmith.

Alicia was already moving, scrambling out of the corner where she'd been pressed. She was weeping, her hands black with grime and ash, her face streaked with tears that cut clean lines through the dirt. She reached Zeke first, dropping to her knees beside him.

"Zeke," she said, her voice breaking on his name. "Zeke, please."

She tried to touch him, then pulled back, terrified of causing more pain or making things worse. The blood from his hand pooled dark and glossy on the tiles around him, mixing with the grey ash to form a sludge that looked too much like wet concrete. His breathing was worse now, each inhale a drowning sound, his destroyed lungs finally surrendering to the disease that had been eating them for months.

Rodecker appeared in the doorway, drawn by the silence that followed the screaming. He leaned against the frame, clutching his dislocated shoulder, his face the color of old parchment, drained of everything. He stared at the scene—the empty suit, the pile of ash, the dying blacksmith—and his mouth opened, but no words came out. He just shook his head, once, slowly, unable to process what his eyes were showing him.

Nate reached them, his arm giving out on the last pull. He pushed himself up to a sitting position with his good hand, his head swimming with pain and blood loss. He reached out and placed his hand on Zeke's shoulder, feeling the heat of the man's body through the flannel.

Zeke's eyes fluttered open, unfocused at first. They were cloudy, already losing their focus on this world, looking at something beyond what the living could see.

"Did it..." Zeke whispered, the words bubbling through the blood in his throat, wet and thick. "Did it work?"

Alicia leaned close, gripping his uninjured hand with both of hers, squeezing tight. "Yes," she said, her voice cracking with emotion she couldn't contain. "Yes, Zeke. It worked. He's gone. He's really gone. You did it."

A small smile touched the corner of Zeke's mouth, barely visible but there. The tension drained out of his face, smoothing the lines of pain that had been carved there by disease and suffering, making him look younger for just a moment.

"Good," he breathed, the word barely audible.

He looked at Nate, and his focus sharpened for one final second, cutting through the fog of approaching death. His eyes were clear and present.

"Make it..." Zeke rasped, fighting for each word. "Make it matter. Make sure they know."

His chest hitched, struggling for air that wouldn't come. "Tell Ruby..." he started, but the rest of the sentence dissolved into nothing.

The breath left him in a long, rattling sigh that seemed to go on forever. It didn't come back. His chest didn't rise again. The struggle ended. The light faded from his eyes, dimming until only blankness remained. The hand holding Alicia's went slack, fingers uncurling.

Ezekiel Tatum lay still on the floor of a kill room that had claimed victims for one hundred and thirty-five years, another body added to a count that should never reach this number. He lay in the ash of a monster, his blood still wet on the iron blade beside him—a testament to what one dying man could accomplish when he had nothing left to lose.

Nate bowed his head, closing his eyes against the sting of tears and dust that burned in the cuts on his face. He sat there, holding onto the dead man's shoulder, as blue and red lights began to pulse against the high windows of the house above, painting the walls in alternating colors.

"He's gone," Nate whispered to the empty air, though he wasn't sure if he meant Zeke or Carlisle or both.

Nate opened his eyes and looked at the scene with the cold assessment of someone who would need to write a report. He looked at the blade lying on the tiles, dark with Zeke's blood. He looked at the pile of ash that used to be a vampire. He looked at the dead man who had understood the assignment better than any of them, who had seen what needed to be done and did it without hesitation.

Qāt mīt. The hand of the dying.

Nate touched the handle of the blade with his good hand, feeling the leather grip now cold and slick with blood. It was just iron and blood now, the magic spent, the curse fulfilled and broken.

"We need a story," Nate said, his voice rough and damaged, barely more than a croak. He looked at Rodecker standing in the doorway. He looked at Alicia kneeling in the ash. "We need a story right now, before they get down here. Something that makes sense."

Alicia wiped her face with the back of her hand, smearing the grey ash across her cheek and leaving streaks. She looked at Zeke's body with an expression that was part grief, part determination, a stubbornness that dried her tears.

"He saved us," she said simply.

"He did more than that," Nate said, struggling to his knees with a grimace. "He finished it. He ended something that should never have existed."

He looked at the empty suit again, at the nothingness that remained of Evan Carlisle, at the dust that was already settling into the cracks between tiles. The monster was gone, reduced to ash that would blow away in the wind.

CHAPTER

55

HIS WRIST THROBBED in time with his heart, a dull, wet grind that pulsed with every beat. His ribs were worse, and every breath hitched against broken bone. The adrenaline that had sustained him through the fight receded, leaving behind a wreck of tissue and exhausted muscle. He forced air into his lungs and tasted copper.

"We have three minutes," Nate said, his voice sounding like gravel grinding in a mixer. "Maybe four."

He looked at Alicia, who was kneeling in the grey dust that used to be a man, her hands shaking so hard she could barely hold the plastic evidence bag. She wasn't crying anymore, had moved past grief into the cold, mechanical necessity of survival. She scooped the ash—grey grit and dust that shifted in the draft from the open door.

"Get all of it," Nate said. "Everything that looks like... him."

She nodded and scraped the tiles with a gloved hand, funneling the remains of Naram-Ekur into the plastic. The cream linen suit lay deflated and scorched on the floor, empty of the body that had worn it for decades. It looked like laundry dropped by a careless man.

Nate crawled toward Zeke, and the movement sent a spike of heat through his chest. He gritted his teeth and dragged his body across the slick tiles. Zeke lay on his side, anchored to the floor by the iron blade protruding from his back, his eyes open but vacant, staring at a point beyond the ceiling.

"I'm sorry, Zeke," Nate whispered.

Wrapping his shirt tail around his hand, he gripped the leather handle and wiped it down, scrubbing away the sweat and oil of the blacksmith's dying grip. He wiped the crossguard, then the pommel, making sure it couldn't look premeditated. It had to look like chaos, a desperate scramble for a weapon in a burning room.

Nate dipped the edge of his shirt into a pool of Carlisle's blood—the blood spilled before the transformation, when the bullets had hit flesh that was still pretending to be human. He smeared it on the blade's edge, then on the handle.

"Done," Alicia said, holding up the bag. It was half full of grey dust, and she sealed it before taking a permanent marker from her pocket and writing *Suspect Remains - Biohazard* on the plastic strip. Her handwriting was jagged.

"Pocket it," Nate said. "Deep. No one sees that until we're clear."

She shoved the bag into her jacket and looked at the empty suit. "What about the clothes?"

"Fire," Nate said.

He forced himself up, though the room spun and black spots danced in his vision. He stumbled toward the breaker box on the wall, the one with the exposed wiring they had tampered with to kill the lights. He flicked his lighter and watched the flame jump, small and yellow, against the stark white tiles. He held it to the frayed insulation of the old wiring until it caught, and a spark hissed, jumping to the dry, antique wall hanging next to the panel.

Nate grabbed the empty linen suit and threw it onto the growing flame. The fabric, dry and old, caught instantly, and fire curled the edges of the lapels before consuming the silk shirt. Within seconds, a localized blaze was climbing the wall, producing thick, acrid smoke that would mask the smell of the dust.

Rodecker stood at the top of the cellar stairs, leaning heavily against the frame, his left arm dangling uselessly at his side. His face was the color of wet concrete as he watched them work, his eyes glassy with pain, but he nodded. He understood the script.

He keyed his radio.

"Dispatch," Rodecker said, his voice flat, devoid of the horror below. "Officer down at 465 Jones. Suspect deceased. We have a civilian casualty. Send everything."

"Copy, Detective," the dispatcher replied, her voice tinny and distant. "Units are en route. EMS is two minutes out."

"Tell them to hurry," Rodecker said, letting the radio drop to his side. He looked down at Pierce's body in the corridor and didn't look away.

Nate limped to the wall of photographs as the smoke started to pool against the ceiling, hazing the harsh tactical lights. He pulled his phone from his pocket, his hands steady now, locked into the procedural rhythm.

Click.

A tintype of a girl with hollow eyes.

Click.

A silver gelatin print of a woman in a high collar.

Click.

The dates marched across the wall in fifteen-year intervals, cold math stretching back through time.

Click.

Zoe Kaplan, photographed from a distance, smiling at something out of frame.

Nate moved to the shelf of journals, leather bindings cracked with age. He opened one at random and found ink that had turned brown, the script precise and flowing. *Subject shows resilience. Blood volume adequate. Disposal planned for Tuesday.* He photographed the page, then the stack.

"They're going to take all this," Alicia said, standing beside him and photographing the property deeds on the desk.

"Let them," Nate said. "We just need the record. We need the proof for Booker."

The heavy thud of boots shook the floorboards overhead, and flashlight beams cut down the stairwell, blinding in the smoky air. Voices shouted, overlapping and chaotic.

"Showtime," Nate said.

"Police! Don't move!"

"Let me see hands!"

"Clear left! Clear right!"

SWAT officers in heavy tactical gear poured down the stairs, pushing past Rodecker. They swept into the corridor with weapons raised, sweeping the corners before they saw Pierce's body, the blood, and Nate and Alicia standing in the wreckage of the kill room.

"Federal Agent!" Nate shouted, holding up his badge wallet. It felt heavy in his hand, and technically, it was a piece of tin with no authority behind it anymore. In this room, covered in dust and blood, it was the only shield he had. "Scene is cold! Suspect is down!"

A SWAT sergeant lowered his rifle slightly, aiming it at Nate's chest rather than his head. "Identify!"

"Special Agent Nathan Holloway, FBI," Nate said. "This is Dr. Landry, civilian consultant. Detective Rodecker is at the stairs. We have an officer down."

The sergeant looked at Pierce, and his face tightened. "Secure the room," he ordered. "Get EMS down here now!"

Radios chirped. "Dispatch to Command. Victim Zoe Kaplan is secure in Unit 4. She's giving a statement. Alleges kidnapping and sexual assault. Says she heard shots."

Nate let out a breath he didn't know he was holding.

Zoe. She had held it together, and her statement gave them probable cause. It legitimized the breach, turning a breaking and entering into a rescue.

Medics rushed past the tactical team, carrying jump bags and a backboard. They knelt beside Zeke, and one of them checked for a carotid pulse, waited three seconds, and shook his head. He placed a black tag on Zeke's chest.

They moved to Pierce.

Nate watched, knowing what they would find, knowing the carotid was gone, the trachea severed. But watching them check, watching the medic's hands pause and falter, made it real in a way the fight hadn't. The medic looked up at the sergeant and drew a finger across his throat.

Another black tag.

Rodecker stumbled down the stairs, and a medic tried to guide him to a stretcher, but Rodecker shoved him away with his good arm.

"Don't touch me," Rodecker said. "Just pop it back in. Pop the damn shoulder and wrap the ribs."

"Sir, you need transport," the medic said. "You're in shock."

"I am not leaving this scene," Rodecker said, leaning against the wall and sliding down until he was sitting on the floor of the corridor, staring at his partner's body. "Fix me here, or get out of my face."

The medic looked at Nate, who nodded.

"Do what he says," Nate said.

The room filled with technicians, and the Evidence Response Team from the local field office arrived, wearing white Tyvek suits that made them look like ghosts in the smoky light. They began to grid the floor, placing yellow markers next to the shell casings, the iron blade, the pile of ash, and the scorched suit.

Chief Harold Dean descended the stairs like a man walking to his own execution. He looked small in the harsh lights, holding a handkerchief over his nose to filter the smell of death and ozone. His eyes swept the room, taking in the carnage, the victim photos, the dead blacksmith.

He spotted Nate, and his face flushed a dark red. He stepped over the yellow tape, ignoring the protests of a crime scene tech.

"You're done, Holloway," Dean said. "You're indicted."

"It's a crime scene, Chief," Nate said, not stepping back. "It's the end of your investigation."

Dean gestured at the room. "You broke into a private residence. You have a dead officer. You have a dead civilian. You have a fire." He pointed at the pile of ash. "Where is he? Where is Carlisle?"

"Fire consumed him," Nate said, his voice flat. "Struggle, a lamp went over. Electrical short. Old wiring. It went up fast. Synthetic fabrics. He burned."

"Burned?" Dean stared at the ash. "A man doesn't just burn into dust in five minutes, Agent. That's impossible."

"Forensics will sort it out," Nate said. "Maybe he fell into the chemicals he used on the victims. Maybe the accelerant he kept for disposal caught."

Dean stepped closer, smelling of peppermint and sweat. "I'll have you indicted for breaking and entering, felony murder for the officer, and obstruction. You went rogue. You got a cop killed."

Nate stepped into Dean's personal space, forcing the Chief back a step, and lowered his voice.

"Look at the wall, Harold."

Dean blinked. "What?"

"Look at the wall," Nate said, pointing to the photographs. "1890. 1905. 1920. Count the bodies, Harold. Then tell me you want to explain why Booker Hayes is sitting in a cell for this."

Nate grabbed Dean's arm and turned him toward the shelf of journals.

"Those are his diaries," Nate said. "Detailed confessions. Names. Dates. Locations. And right now, you have Booker Hayes sitting in a cell for three of these murders—murders that journals prove Carlisle committed."

Dean went still.

"If Booker Hayes spends one more hour in that cell," Nate said, "the lawsuit won't just bankrupt the city. It will end your career. It will end your pension. It will put you in prison for civil rights violations and obstruction of justice."

Dean looked at the photos, then at the ash, then at the dead man on the floor. He was doing the math, calculating the blast radius.

"What do we do?" Dean whispered.

"We tell the truth," Nate said. "Mostly. Carlisle was a serial killer who used elaborate identity fraud to span generations. He kidnapped Zoe Kaplan, and we breached on exigent circumstances. Pierce died a hero. Zeke Tatum intervened to save us."

"And the fire?" Dean asked.

"The fire stopped a monster," Nate said. "That's all the report needs to say."

A hush fell over the corridor outside as the officers parted. A woman walked through the gap in the uniforms, wearing a simple housedress and a cardigan, her hair pulled back in a severe bun. Her back was straight.

Ruby Tatum.

She didn't look at the police or the cameras flashing, but walked straight to the kill room door and stopped.

She looked at Zeke.

She didn't make a sound or collapse, just stood there with her hands clasped in front of her, looking at the body of her husband lying on the tile. She looked at the iron blade sticking out of his chest and at the blood on his hands.

She looked at Nate, her eyes dry and hard.

"Mrs. Tatum," Dean began, his voice taking on a practiced softness. "I am so sorry—"

Ruby raised a hand, and Dean fell silent.

She walked to Zeke's body and knelt in the blood and the ash. She reached out and touched his cheek, which was already cooling, and brushed a smudge of grey dust from his forehead.

"You stubborn old fool," she whispered.

She stayed there for a long moment before standing up. She looked at Dean, then at the detectives gathered in the doorway.

"Cancer," Ruby said, her voice carrying to the back of the room. "Stage four. He had weeks, maybe."

The room was silent.

"He found out the FBI agent was hunting a killer," Ruby continued. "He knew someone was in danger and couldn't sit in that house and wait to die. He wanted his last days to matter." She looked at the blade. "He made that. He made it to stop a bad man. And he used it."

She looked Dean in the eye.

"That's who Ezekiel was," she said. "That's what you put in your report."

Dean nodded, looking relieved. The narrative was perfect—tragic, heroic, clean.

"Yes, ma'am," Dean said. "That is exactly what we'll write."

The Medical Examiner stepped forward and knelt beside Zeke. He took several photographs of the blade's position before gripping the handle. With a wet, sucking sound, he pulled the iron from Zeke's chest.

He placed the blade in a long plastic evidence tube and sealed it.

"Bag him," Washington said to the techs.

Nate watched them zip Zeke into a black body bag, watched them lift him onto the stretcher. He felt a hollowness in his chest that had nothing to do with his broken ribs.

"Clear the way!" a sergeant shouted from the corridor.

Officers lined the walls of the narrow hallway, standing shoulder to shoulder and pressing themselves against the plaster to make room. They removed their caps.

Two paramedics carried a stretcher from the back of the hallway, another body bag.

Pierce.

As the stretcher passed the doorway of the kill room, Rodecker struggled to his feet. He winced as his reduced shoulder shifted, but he stood straight. His face was wet with tears he wasn't bothering to wipe away.

Nate stood beside him and tried to straighten his spine, ignoring the screaming of his ribs as he raised his bandaged hand to his brow.

Alicia stood next to them, her head bowed, her hands covered in grey dust.

The procession moved slowly, and the only sound was the heavy tread of boots. They carried her up the stairs, out of the darkness, and into the humid Savannah night.

The room began to empty, the urgency gone. Now it was just paperwork and processing, the GBI team dusting for prints on the display cases while a photographer documented the journals.

"Let's go," Nate said.

He grabbed his jacket without looking back at the ash or the blood.

They walked up the stairs, where the air in the house was cooler and cleaner. They walked out the front door, past the police tape, past the news crews shouting questions from behind the barricades.

They crossed Jones Street.

Nate sat down on the granite curb, the stone cool against his legs. Rodecker sat beside him, cradling his arm, while Alicia sat on Nate's other side, staring at her hands.

Blue and red strobes washed the night, stretching and jumping shadows against the brick facades of the townhouses. The radio chatter was a constant, low-level static.

"It's over," Alicia said, sounding surprised.

"Yeah," Nate said, reaching into his pocket and touching the plastic bag. The dust shifted under his fingers. "It's over."

Rodecker pulled a pack of cigarettes from his shirt pocket with his good hand and managed to shake one loose. He put it in his mouth but didn't light it, just sat there with the unlit cigarette bobbing as he breathed.

"What about Booker?" Alicia asked.

"Dean will cut him loose by morning," Nate said. "He has to. The journals clear him, and the DNA on the trophies clears him. He walks."

"Good," Alicia said. "That's good."

They sat in silence while the humidity pressed down on them. The smell of the marsh drifted in from the river, mixing with the exhaust of the idling cruisers.

Nate looked at the house one last time and thought about the dates on the wall. The pattern was broken, the interval ended.

CHAPTER

56

Russell Bennett smoothed the front of his charcoal suit jacket for the third time in a minute. The District Attorney stood behind the podium in the SCMPD briefing room, sweating under the glare of the television lights. The air in the room was thick with the smell of the nervous perspiration of men trying to save their careers.

Nate Holloway leaned against the back wall, arms crossed to relieve the pressure on his bandaged hands. Bennett adjusted the microphones, his knuckles white on the goosenecks, gripping the podium like a man trying to keep a confession from spilling out.

Bennett cleared his throat, and the sound snapped the room to attention. Reporters stopped checking their phones and raised their recording devices.

"Ladies and gentlemen," Bennett began, his voice smooth and practiced, the baritone of a man who spent his life convincing juries to believe the improbable. "Thank you for coming. We hold a significant development in the serial homicide cases that plagued our historic district."

Bennett's eyes flicked to the teleprompter.

"Forensic evidence processed over the last forty-eight hours led us to a conclusion regarding the identities of the perpetrators," Bennett said. He gestured to a large foam-core board on an easel to his right, which displayed a timeline of photos—the tintype from 1890, the black-and-white from 1950, the digital still from the 1985 interview. "We uncovered an elaborate, multi-generational criminal enterprise involving identity fraud and serial violence centered on the Carlisle estate."

A murmur went through the press corps.

"The DNA evidence, while complex, points to a closed familial loop," Bennett continued, leaning into the microphone. "We believe the crimes were carried out by individuals operating under assumed variations of the Carlisle name to mask their activities over decades. Edmund Carlisle. Edward Carlton. Evan Carpenter. A lineage of predation."

A lineage of predation. Nate heard the legalese for what it was—a way to package a four-thousand-year-old curse into a Rico case, glossing over the biological impossibilities, the identical bite marks, the unaging face.

Bennett wiped his upper lip. "The suspect known as Evan Carlisle was killed two days ago during an apprehension attempt at his residence on Jones Street. He initiated a violent confrontation with law enforcement officers and was killed in the subsequent fire that consumed the structure."

Nate's jaw tightened. Killed during apprehension. It sounded clean. It sounded like justice. It didn't sound like a dying blacksmith driving ancient iron through a monster's chest while a detective bled out in the hallway.

"Therefore," Bennett said, pausing for effect, "the District Attorney's office is dropping all charges against Mr. Booker Hayes with prejudice. Mr. Hayes was an innocent bystander who attempted to assist the investigation. He is being processed for release as we speak."

Camera shutters snapped in a sharp, mechanical volley. The narrative was set. The system corrected itself, or at least pretended to.

Nate pushed off the wall and slipped out the side door before the reporters could turn. The quiet of the hallway was a relief. He walked past the row of desks in the detective bureau, past the empty chair where Yolanda Pierce used to sit. Her nameplate was still there. A half-finished report sat in her outbox.

He kept walking.

The drive to the Chatham County Detention Center took twenty minutes. Nate drove the rental Ford Explorer with mechanical precision, his eyes moving, checking mirrors, checking blind spots—a habit he couldn't break. A trolley packed with tourists rattled down the cobblestones, their cameras pointed at the ironwork and oak trees. The city went on, oblivious.

The detention center sat on the outskirts of town, a sprawling complex of grey concrete and razor wire baking in the Georgia heat. Nate parked the Explorer in the visitor lot and sat for a moment, letting the air conditioning blast the last of the city's cheer from his face before getting out. Quarter to eleven.

Nate walked to the intake window and showed his credentials to the deputy behind the glass. The man looked at the badge, then at Nate's bandaged hands.

"I'm here to see Booker Hayes," Nate said. "He's being processed out, but I need a moment with him first."

"Sign here," the deputy said, sliding a clipboard under the glass.

Nate signed the logbook, then unclipped his Glock and placed it in the lockbox, followed by his keys and phone. The metal detector remained silent as he passed through.

"Through the second door," the deputy said. A harsh, grinding buzz rattled against the cinderblock walls as the heavy steel door clicked and swung open.

Nate walked down the corridor. The fluorescent lights buzzed overhead, casting a sterile glare on the mopped floors. The air smelled of industrial cleaner, failing to mask the sour tang of unwashed bodies. Inmates in orange jumpsuits moved with a slow, deliberate emptiness, their eyes fixed on the tiles.

A guard led him to a small interview room. "Five minutes," the guard said. "He's almost done with paperwork."

Nate sat on the metal stool bolted to the floor. The table was stainless steel, scratched and scarred by years of handcuffs and angry fingernails. He waited.

The door on the far side opened.

Booker Hayes walked in, wearing the standard-issue orange jumpsuit. It hung loose on his frame, too big in the shoulders, and his wrists were shackled to a belly chain that clinked as he moved. He looked tired. The lines around his eyes were deeper than Nate remembered from the other day, but his back was straight. He didn't shuffle.

"Agent Holloway," Booker said, his voice rough, like gravel tumbling in a dryer.

"Booker," Nate said. "Sit down."

The guard ushered Booker to the chair opposite Nate and locked the chain to the table ring, then stepped back outside, watching through the small square window.

Booker sat. He looked at Nate's hands, the white gauze stark against the grey steel table. He didn't ask. He just looked, then raised his eyes to Nate's face.

"They tell you?" Nate asked.

"Lawyer came by," Booker said. "Said the DA was dropping it. Said I could go." He said it without joy, just a fact, another thing happening to him that he couldn't control.

"It's official," Nate said, the words coming out flat and certain. "Bennett just announced it. Charges dropped with prejudice. That means they can't bring them back. It's done."

Booker nodded. He looked down at his own hands, resting on the table. His fingernails were clean for the first time since Nate met him, scrubbed pink by prison soap.

"And him?" Booker asked, the question barely a whisper.

Nate leaned forward, resting his forearms on the cold metal. "He's gone."

"Gone like arrested?" Booker asked. "Or gone like gone?"

"Ashes," Nate said.

Booker didn't blink. He held Nate's stare, looking for the lie, the police trick, searching the agent's face and reading the exhaustion, the grief, the flat certainty in those blue eyes.

"You sure?" Booker asked.

"I was there," Nate said. "It's over. You will never see Mr. Evan again. No one will."

Booker leaned back, and the tension went out of his shoulders all at once, as if a wire had been cut. He closed his eyes and took a long breath, inhaling the stale prison air, then let it out slowly. He rubbed his face with his calloused hands, the chains rattling against the table.

"He was... he wasn't right," Booker said. "The way he looked at people. Like they was food."

"I know," Nate said.

"And Detective Pierce?" Booker asked, opening his eyes. "She get my message?"

Nate looked at the scratches on the table, tracing a groove with his thumb. "She got it. She came for you, Booker. She came for Nicole and Lucy. She was the first one through the door."

Booker went still. He understood. He'd lived on the streets long before this, and he knew what past tense meant when a cop talked about another cop.

"She gone too?"

Nate nodded. "Yeah."

Booker looked away, staring at the concrete wall, his jaw working. "She tried," he said. "She was two hours late, but she tried. She listened when nobody else did."

"She believed you," Nate said. "She fought for you in the briefing room. Almost lost her badge trying to stop them from putting you in cuffs."

"Good police," Booker said. "Rare thing."

"Yeah," Nate said.

The buzz of the fluorescent tube overhead filled the quiet between them.

"What about the girls?" Booker asked, looking back at Nate. His eyes were wet, the rims red, but he held himself steady. "Lucy. Nicole. People gonna know what happened? Or they gonna bury it like everything else?"

"Their names are on the news right now," Nate said. "The DA is pinning it all on Carlisle. They aren't just bodies in the square anymore. They're victims. They mattered."

Booker nodded, swallowing hard. "Lucy liked the bread pudding," he said. "On Tuesdays. From the bakery on Bull Street. She always talked about it."

"I'll remember that," Nate said.

"When you write your reports, you put that in there," Booker said. "You tell them. She wasn't just a stray."

"I promise," Nate said.

Booker looked at his shackles. "When do I get out?"

"Processing takes a few hours," Nate said, then stood up, his knees cracking. "Tomorrow morning. First release. Someone will be there to meet you."

"Don't need a babysitter," Booker said.

"It's not a babysitter," Nate said. "It's a ride. And an apology. Whether the department wants to give it or not."

Booker looked up at him, and a small, sad smile touched the corner of his mouth. "You look like hell, Agent Holloway."

"I feel like it," Nate said.

"Get some sleep," Booker said. "You look worn to the bone."

"I will," Nate said, then turned to the door. "See you in the morning, Booker."

CHAPTER

57

THE SUN WAS BLINDING the next morning, beating down on the asphalt of the release lot and creating waves of heat that distorted the line of trees in the distance. The humidity was already climbing, sticking shirts to backs, making the air feel thick as wool.

Nate leaned against the hood of the Explorer, sunglasses cutting the glare. He'd changed his bandages, but his hands still felt stiff, the skin tight and angry.

Karl Rodecker stood next to him. The detective's left arm was strapped tight to his chest in a complex black medical sling, and his ribs were wrapped under his wrinkled button-down shirt. His face was grey, covered in three days of white stubble. He hadn't shaved. He hadn't slept.

"How long?" Rodecker asked, his voice raspy.

"Processing opens at eight," Nate said. "Should be any minute."

Rodecker leaned against the car, his breath catching as the movement pulled at his broken ribs. "I shouldn't be here," he said.

"You need to be here," Nate said, keeping his eyes on the heavy perimeter gate.

"I put the cuffs on him," Rodecker said. "I read him his rights, knowing it was bullshit. I let Dean parade him for the cameras."

"You were following orders," Nate said. "And then you helped break him out. You stood in that cellar, Karl. You paid the price."

"Yolanda paid the price," Rodecker said, his voice raw. "She paid for all of it."

The sound of a heavy mechanical latch clanked across the lot, followed by the sharp buzz of a prison alarm.

The pedestrian gate in the chain-link fence slid open.

Booker Hayes stepped out.

He squinted against the light, raising a hand to shield his eyes. He wore his own clothes—a flannel shirt too warm for the weather, faded jeans, worn work boots. He carried a clear plastic property bag containing a cheap burner phone, a wallet, and a folded photograph. Everything he owned.

He stood there for a moment, taking a breath of free air. He looked at the trees, the road, then at the two men waiting by the car.

He started walking toward them, his gait steady and unhurried.

Nate pushed off the car while Rodecker straightened up, fighting the pain in his side.

Booker stopped three feet away and dropped the plastic bag on the ground. He looked at Nate, then turned to Rodecker, taking in the sling, the grief carved into the detective's face like scars.

"Mr. Hayes," Rodecker said, clearing his throat. "Booker."

Booker nodded. "Detective."

Rodecker reached into his pocket with his good hand and pulled out a thick, white envelope, bulging with cash.

"This isn't..." Rodecker started, then stopped, looking helpless. "The department isn't going to do anything. You know that. They'll give you a bus token and kick you loose. This is from us. From the squad. The ones who knew Pierce."

He held out the envelope.

Booker looked at the money but didn't reach for it right away. He studied Rodecker's face, reading the guilt, the pity.

"It ain't gonna fix it," Booker said.

"I know," Rodecker said. "It's not a fix. It's just... it's what we got."

Booker reached out and took the envelope without counting it, then slid it into the back pocket of his jeans.

"Detective Pierce called me back," Booker said. "I left that message about the warehouse. She was late."

Rodecker flinched as if he'd been struck, his voice cracking when he spoke. "She was in a meeting," he said. "Politics. We were worrying about optics."

"She came through," Booker said. "She came to the house and went down into the cellar."

Rodecker nodded, unable to speak, his jaw working on words that wouldn't come out.

"She was good police," Booker said, like a benediction.

Rodecker looked down, swiping at his eyes with the back of his hand. "I'm sorry, Booker. For the arrest. For all of it."

"You take care of that arm," Booker said, picking up his plastic bag.

Nate opened the passenger door of the Explorer. "Get in. I'll take you wherever you want to go. Boarding house. Hotel. You got cash now."

Booker looked at the open car door, at the leather seat, then turned toward the road, toward the tree line where the Spanish moss hung heavy and grey.

He shook his head.

"I'm good," Booker said.

"It's five miles to town," Nate said. "It's ninety degrees."

"I been walking my whole life," Booker said. "I need the air. I need to not be in a box."

He turned toward the road, adjusting his grip on the plastic bag.

"You be careful, Agent Holloway," Booker said.

"I will," Nate said.

"And you," Booker said to Rodecker. "You stop carrying it. She wouldn't want you carrying it."

Rodecker looked up, startled. "Booker..."

Booker didn't wait for a response. He turned and started walking, his boots crunching on the gravel shoulder, moving with a loose, easy stride—the walk of a man who knew how to cover ground without spending energy he didn't possess.

Nate and Rodecker stood by the car and watched him go.

The heat made the air ripple and blur like water. Booker walked along the tree line, passed under the shade of a massive live oak, and emerged on the other side.

A city bus roared past, kicking up dust and diesel fumes. When it was gone, so was Booker Hayes.

"He's right," Rodecker said, touching the sling on his arm. "She wouldn't want me carrying it."

"Doesn't mean you can put it down," Nate said.

"No," Rodecker said. "I suppose not."

Nate closed the car door, the sound final—a heavy thud that punctuated the end of the morning. "Come on," Nate said. "I'll buy you a drink. Or coffee. Whatever the doctors say, you can tolerate."

"Whiskey," Rodecker said. "Doctors can go to hell."

Nate walked to the driver's side and looked one last time down the empty road. The sun was high now, burning the mist off the marsh. The shadows were retreating, hiding in the cracks and the deep places, waiting for nightfall.

CHAPTER

58

NATE SAT ALONE at the long laminate table, his hands folded on the surface, the bandages wrapping his palms bone-white against the fake wood grain. He didn't fidget or check his watch, his gaze fixed on the sixty-inch monitor mounted on the far wall where Assistant Director Jeff Harran sat, his face a high-definition mask of authority.

Two men in grey suits flanked Harran, their expressions as blank as their notepads. They belonged to the Office of Professional Responsibility, and they hadn't spoken in twenty minutes, just took notes with mechanical precision.

"Let's review the timeline of entry again," Harran said. His voice suffered from the slight digital compression of the secure feed, flattening the edges of his irritation. "You stated that at 8:15 PM, you heard screaming from inside the residence at 465 Jones Street."

"That is correct," Nate said, his throat feeling like he had swallowed glass—smoke inhalation didn't heal fast. "Exigent circumstances. A civilian was in immediate distress, and probable cause to breach was established the moment we heard Zoe Kaplan."

"And yet," said the OPR agent on the left, looking down at a file, "Detective Rodecker initiated a knock-and-talk at exactly that time. It seems convenient that the exigent circumstances arose precisely when your local asset was at the door."

"It was fortunate, not convenient," Nate said. "Rodecker's presence meant we had a sworn officer on scene to respond immediately."

"You entered from the rear," Harran said. "Through a service entrance, with a civilian—Dr. Alicia Landry."

"Dr. Landry was a consultant with specialized knowledge of the property's historical layout. We needed to navigate the structure quickly to locate the victim before it was too late."

"And the fire?" the second OPR agent asked, not looking up from his notepad. "The fire that conveniently incinerated the suspect and compromised the crime scene before forensics could process the basement?"

Nate saw his own reflection in the dark bezel of the monitor—a gaunt face, dark circles bruising the skin under his eyes. He looked like a man who had survived a car crash only to be asked why he wasn't wearing a seatbelt.

"The structure had wiring dating back to the 1920s," Nate said, the lie coming out smooth and practiced without a blink. He didn't think about the ash piling on the white tiles or the smell of night-blooming jasmine burning. "During the struggle with the suspect, a firearm was discharged and likely struck a junction box or exposed wiring. The fire spread rapidly due to the age of the materials and the chemicals stored in the room."

Harran leaned forward, his face filling the screen. "You understand how this looks, Agent Holloway—a suspect dead, a massive fire, no body recovered, just ash, and a federal agent running an off-book operation with a local detective and a history professor."

"I understand we recovered the remains of four victims from that property," Nate said. "I understand we found evidence exonerating Booker Hayes, and I understand the threat is neutralized."

"And Detective Pierce?" Harran asked.

The room seemed to get colder. Nate pressed his bandaged palms together until the pain sparked, sharp and grounding.

"Detective Pierce engaged a violent suspect to protect the lives of others," Nate said. "She acted with valor."

"She acted without backup," Harran said, "because you didn't call it in."

"There wasn't time."

Harran stared at him through the camera lens, the silence stretching out and filling with only the hum of the ventilation and the distant sound of phones ringing in the precinct bullpen outside.

Finally, Harran sat back in his chair and shuffled the papers on his desk in Quantico, the movement carrying a sense of finality.

"We're done here," Harran said, his anger replaced by a deep exhaustion that aged his face. "You are recalled to Quantico effective immediately. Your field credentials are suspended pending a full internal review, and you will surrender your service weapon and badge to the Chief of Police before you leave the building."

Nate nodded once.

"You'll report to the medical unit on Monday for a mandatory psychological evaluation," Harran continued. "Until that is cleared, you are on desk duty with restricted access and no active cases. Do you understand?"

"I understand," Nate said.

"This is a career-ender, Nate," Harran said, dropping the official tone. "You know that, right? You solved the case, but you broke the Bureau to do it, and we can't put you back in the field."

"I know," Nate said.

"Log off," Harran said.

The screen went black.

Nate sat in the quiet room, looking at the blank monitor, waiting for the crushing weight of his career ending to hit, for the panic about his pension or reputation. It never came. Instead, a breath he hadn't realized he was holding escaped his lungs, the tether finally cut. He stood up, the plastic chair scraping against the linoleum, and walked to the door without looking back at the empty conference room.

CHAPTER

59

In Laurel Grove Cemetery, Nate Holloway stood in the shade of a massive live oak. Rows of blue stretched across the grounds—hundreds of officers from Savannah, Chatham County, and the state agencies in formation, brass buttons catching the sun, trousers creased sharp enough to cut.

Chief Harold Dean gripped the podium, knowing exactly where the red tally lights were on the news cameras. He paused, wiped a bead of sweat from his forehead with a linen handkerchief that was too white, too clean.

"Detective Pierce did not just serve this city," Dean said, dropping his voice an octave to the practiced timber of command. "She was its heart, moving toward danger when others fled, giving the last full measure of devotion to protect the vulnerable."

Nate clasped his hands behind his back, the bandages throbbing inside the white cotton ceremonial gloves. The fabric felt like sandpaper against the burns.

Dean kept talking—sacrifice, duty, multi-agency cooperation, the swift resolution of a violent apprehension on Jones Street. He didn't mention the warehouse on West Boundary, didn't mention the cellar, didn't mention that Yolanda Pierce bled out in a hallway because the department was managing optics instead of dispatching backup.

The Mayor and Councilwoman Moffett sat in the front row, wearing dark sunglasses, offering solemn nods at the right intervals. Moffett slid her cuff back, checked her watch, and covered it again.

The lie was air-tight and seamless, glossing over the jagged edges of the truth until the surface was glass.

Dean stepped back, and Karl Rodecker approached the microphone.

The detective looked like a child wearing his father's suit, his left arm strapped tight to his chest, the black sling vanishing under the jacket. He had lost weight, and the collar of his shirt gaped at the neck. Grey skin, three days of white stubble, and he gripped the lectern with his good hand until the knuckles went white.

He didn't look at the cameras—just stared at the flag.

He pulled a folded piece of paper from his pocket with a shaking hand and smoothed it on the wood.

"Linda picked this," Rodecker said, voice like gravel in a mixer. "Yolanda... she liked this one."

He squinted against the glare.

"For I am already being poured out like a drink offering," Rodecker read. "And the time for my departure is near. I have fought the good fight. I have finished the race. I have kept the faith."

His voice cracked on the word *faith*.

He stopped, and the silence stretched, filled only by the distant hum of cicadas and the call of a grackle from the marsh. Rodecker stared at the paper for a long second, then another, before shoving it into his pocket and walking away.

The Honor Guard moved in sharp, geometric precision, snapping the flag taut over the casket and folding it triangle by triangle until the stars disappeared into the stripes. The leader knelt and presented the blue wedge to Pierce's mother.

Nate looked at the ground where a line of ants marched up the oak's bark. He focused on them—left, right, left—anything to avoid watching a mother accept a folded flag as payment for a debt the city refused to acknowledge.

The bar off Montgomery Street had no windows and smelled of stale beer, lemon polish, and fifty years of cigarette smoke trapped in the wood paneling.

Nate sat in the back booth on a vinyl seat taped with silver duct tape, the table crowded with wet napkins.

Rodecker sat opposite, the sling forcing him to turn his body and present his good shoulder to the room. A bottle of Jameson sat between them, half gone.

At the bar, a group of uniforms stood and one raised a glass to a photo of Pierce near the register.

"To Pierce."

"To Pierce."

Rodecker didn't stand, just poured two fingers of whiskey without toasting the room. He lifted the glass an inch off the table, stared at the amber liquid, and knocked it back before setting the glass down hard.

Nate turned his own glass, and the condensation soaked the gauze on his fingers. He hadn't touched the alcohol—Percocet and whiskey was a bad mix, and he needed his head on a swivel.

"Dean asked me to sign the papers on Monday," Rodecker said without looking up.

"Monday." Nate's jaw tightened. "Body wasn't even cold."

"Trauma leave transitioning to early retirement," Rodecker said. "Full benefits, kept my pension."

"Generous." The word tasted like copper.

"Paid me to keep quiet," Rodecker said. "They know I kicked that door in, and we didn't have a warrant. If I stay, I'm a liability, and every defense attorney in the state would tear apart my old cases."

"You saved Zoe Kaplan and stopped a monster."

"I got my partner killed."

Rodecker reached into his jacket and pulled out the leather wallet with his gold shield, setting it on the wet table. He spun it, and the badge rotated, gold catching the neon light from the beer sign—round and round.

"Thirty years," Rodecker said. "Thirty years carrying this thing."

"You carried it well, Karl."

Rodecker stopped the badge with his thumb, looked at it, then shoved it into his pocket out of sight. He signaled for another bottle.

Nate watched him, knowing there was no fix for this. The machine had chewed Rodecker up and spat him out with a check to keep his mouth shut, and Nate sat in the dark keeping watch.

The church in Thunderbolt smelled of old pine and hymnals—white clapboard, simple steeple, sunlight cutting through the dust motes dancing in the air.

Quiet, with no cameras and no press liaisons.

Nate sat in the back next to Alicia in her black dress, hands clutching her leather satchel. The pews were only a quarter full.

Ruby Tatum sat front and center with her spine straight, not touching the back of the pew. Navy dress, high collar, and she didn't cry—just stared at the plain pine box.

The pastor moved around the altar, an older man with a voice worn smooth.

"Zeke was a man of iron," the pastor said, nodding to the neighbors. "You heard his hammer and saw the gates on Abercorn. He built things to last."

He rested a hand on the wood.

"He fought his illness the same way he worked his forge," the pastor continued. "With patience, with heat, with strength."

Nate shifted, understanding the lie here was different—gentle, a privacy afforded to the dead. The pastor didn't know about the blade or the ash on the tiles.

Alicia twisted a silver ring on her finger.

"We have a guest who wished to speak," the pastor said, looking toward the back of the church.

Nate stood, and the floorboards creaked as he walked to the front. He placed a bandaged hand on the casket, feeling the cool wood beneath his palm.

He looked at the people in the pews, then at Ruby, whose eyes locked on his—clear and hard.

"I didn't know Zeke for long," Nate said, his voice sounding loud in the small space. "But in the short time I knew him, I saw a man who understood duty—not the kind you talk about, but the kind you do."

He swallowed against the tightness in his throat.

"He saw what was coming," Nate said. "And he didn't turn away. He stood against and was one of the bravest men I have ever known."

He nodded to Ruby, and she dipped her chin once.

Nate walked back to his seat.

They carried Zeke to the graveyard behind the church, where the heat sat heavy, smelling of pluff mud and salt. Cicadas buzzed in the pecans, a rising drone that drowned the traffic.

They lowered him into the sand.

The mourners drifted toward the fellowship hall for iced tea and condolences while Nate and Alicia stood under a pecan tree.

Ruby Tatum walked toward them carrying a long object wrapped in an oil-stained shop cloth.

She stopped, looking at Nate's hands.

"Mrs. Tatum," Nate said. "I'm sorry."

"Don't be," Ruby said. "He did what he intended."

She hefted the bundle and peeled back the cloth to reveal dark metal—bloomery iron, clean, with no blood and no ash. It looked like a tool again: heavy, dull, dangerous.

"I can't keep this," Ruby said. "I won't have it in my house."

"It's evidence," Nate said, though it wasn't—not to the Bureau.

"It's a burden," Ruby corrected, pressing the bundle into his chest.

Nate took it, and the iron was cold through the cloth. He felt the weight of it in his wrists.

"He made this to end something that needed ending," Ruby said, her voice flat and devoid of trembling. "He'd want you to remember that courage comes in all forms—sometimes it looks like a badge, sometimes it looks like a dying man with a hammer."

She looked at Alicia, then back to Nate.

"You finish it," Ruby said. "Whatever comes next, you finish it."

She turned and walked back to the church with her back straight, not looking at the grave or back at them. She walked straight and tall, a woman who had paid her price and refused to be broken by it.

Nate looked down at the weapon in his hands—iron and carbon, folded and hammered. It felt like it was humming.

He passed the bundle to Alicia, and she slid it into her satchel, the leather strap pulling tight against her shoulder.

"We should go," Alicia said softly.

"Yeah," Nate said. "We should."

CHAPTER

60

THE SUITCASE LAY open on the bedspread of the Marshall House hotel room, a standard-issue ballistic nylon carry-on battered from a decade of travel. Shirts went into the suitcase first, followed by socks, paired and rolled, the movements methodical—a routine that kept his hands busy so his mind didn't have to be.

On the desk, a stack of *New York Times* crossword puzzles sat in a neat pile. He picked them up, the cheap newsprint soft under his thumb, and thought about how he usually filed them, recording his times in a small notebook, obsessing over the ones that took longer than six minutes. He walked to the trash can and dropped the entire stack in, where they hit the metal bottom with a soft slap.

He turned to the corkboard wall, naked now, the red strings gone and the maps of Savannah already in the trash. He had turned the photos of Caroline Marsh, Nicole Gladman, and Lucy Phelps over to the case file, leaving only hundreds of tiny pinholes in the cork—the faint scars of an obsession that had finally burned itself out.

Nate picked up the leather satchel from the chair. From the night-stand drawer, he pulled out a manila folder, its corners soft and its paper worn thin from years of handling.

Sarah's file.

He held it for a moment, the weight familiar after carrying it as a part of him for fifteen years. He ran a thumb over the edge but didn't open it, knowing there was nothing left to read. The autopsy report, the crime scene photos, the theories—they belonged to the past now. The thing that had done it was ash.

He slid the folder into the satchel and zipped it shut.

His phone buzzed on the nightstand, the sound loud in the empty room, the screen lighting up with a single word: *Mom.*

He sat on the edge of the bed, the mattress dipping under his weight, and took a breath, held it, and let it out slowly before picking up the phone.

"Hey, Mom."

"Nathan." Her voice was quiet, not the voice of the schoolteacher who corrected grammar but the voice of a woman who had buried a daughter. "I saw the news—about the detective, about the arrest."

"Yeah," Nate said. "It's everywhere now."

"They're saying it's over," she said. "They're saying they found the man responsible."

"It's over," Nate said.

The line went silent except for the faint static of the connection, the distance between Savannah and Macon measuring more than just miles.

"Did you find what you were looking for?" she asked.

Nate looked at the empty spot on the wall where Sarah's photo had hung for weeks. He thought about the necklace in the evidence bag, the lavender sprig, the look in Carlisle's eyes when the iron pierced his chest—the ancient, terrified realization that he was ending.

"Yeah," Nate said, his voice raspy. "I did."

"Was it worth it?"

He looked at his hands, rubbing the bandages together, the friction sending a spike of phantom heat through his nerves—a reminder of the warehouse fire, of the cellar, of Zeke Tatum driving a blade into his own chest to save strangers. He saw Pierce's face as the light went out of her eyes.

"I don't know, Mom," Nate said, closing his eyes against the memory. "Ask me in a year."

"Come home soon," she said.

"I will."

He ended the call and placed the phone face down on the duvet. After zipping the suitcase with a final, definitive sound, he took one last look around the room that was just a hotel room now. He picked up his bag, left the plastic key card on the desk next to the lamp, and walked out, letting the heavy door click shut behind him.

Night had turned River Street into a different world. Tourists flooded the cobblestones, carrying plastic cups of beer and laughing too loudly, desperate to squeeze joy out of the oppressive heat that wouldn't break even after dark.

Nate moved through the crowd, feeling invisible in the way only the truly exhausted can manage. He found the bar at the far end of the strip, a place with rusted wrought-iron tables bolted to the sidewalk, facing the dark water of the Savannah River.

Alicia Landry sat at a table near the railing without her satchel, her hair loose and falling around her shoulders in dark waves, stripping away the severe academic look she usually wore. She looked younger and infinitely more tired.

Nate pulled out the metal chair opposite her, the legs scraping against the stone.

"You look like hell," Alicia said, without a smile.

"You don't look much better," Nate replied.

A waitress appeared, dropped a coaster, and looked at Nate with the bored efficiency of someone who had served a thousand tourists that night.

"Bourbon," he said. "Neat."

She nodded and vanished back into the crowd.

Alicia traced the rim of her glass, the condensation leaving wet tracks on her fingers. "I had my meeting with the board today," she said. "Crawley did the talking while Brandmeyer just sat there looking at his shoes."

"What did they say?"

"Administrative leave pending a full ethics review, which is code for 'don't come back.'" She took a sip of her drink. "They're sealing the archives—my research, my access, all of it gone. They said my involvement in a law enforcement operation resulting in a death brought 'unwelcome attention' to the Society."

"I'm sorry, Alicia."

"Don't be," she said, her eyes hard and bright in the dim light. "I knew what I was trading—a tenure track for the truth. It was a fair swap."

The waitress returned with a rocks glass filled with amber liquid and set it down without a word.

Nate picked up the glass and looked out at the river where a massive container ship was sliding past, a mountain of steel moving silently toward the ocean. Its lights cut through the fog, illuminating the chop of the water.

He reached into his pocket, pulled out his phone, and placed it on the table before taking a cocktail napkin and sliding it over the device.

Alicia watched him for a beat, then took her own phone and slid it under her purse.

"They recalled me," Nate said quietly, his voice barely carrying over the noise of the bar. "Suspended credentials, desk duty—I'm a file clerk now."

"We're dangerous to them," Alicia said. "We know the things that don't fit in the reports, the things that can't be explained away."

"We know the world is bigger than they think it is," Nate said. "And darker."

"Is it over?" she asked.

"For Savannah," Nate said. "For now."

He looked at her, really looked at her, and saw the toll the last few weeks had taken—the fine lines around her eyes, the tension in her shoulders. But he also saw a steel that hadn't been there before, forged in the heat of what they had survived.

Nate took a drink, the bourbon burning down his throat with a clean, honest heat.

Alicia picked up her glass and held it out, waiting.

"Until the next one," Nate said.

Alicia clinked her glass against his, the sound ringing clear like a bell in the humid night.

"Until the next one," she said.

They drank.

Nate set his glass down and looked back at the river where the container ship was almost gone now, just a collection of stern lights fading into the dark. The water churned in its wake, black and deep, hiding a thousand years of secrets in the silt, and the current moved relentlessly toward the sea, carrying everything with it.

CHAPTER

61

THE AIR at six in the morning was a grey haze that clung to the live oaks in Monterey Square, a heavy wet silence muffling the distant hum of traffic on Whitaker Street. Nate Holloway stood on the corner, hands shoved in the pockets of his charcoal travel suit, the wool damp against his wrists.

Through the fog, the edges of the Mercer-Williams House blurred into grey nothingness while the Pulaski Monument rose like a pale spike from the damp.

Watching the square, he did not move.

For three months, these streets had been his hunting ground, a maze of ghosts and patterns that led to a man four thousand years old. Now, quiet—the city waking up, stretching its limbs to sell its sanitized history to another round of tourists.

Collar turned up against the damp, Nate left the square for the narrow service alley behind the carriage house, where brick walls rose high on either side, blocking the morning light. Underfoot, hexagonal pavers buckled where oak roots pushed up from the earth.

He stopped at a patch of brick near a green plastic dumpster where weeds grew in the cracks, and a discarded coffee cup lay on its side. Nothing marked the spot where they found Nicole Gladman, nothing marked the spot where they found Sarah.

Nate crouched, his knees popping against the stiffness, and looked at the ground where no blood remained, no chalk outlines. The pressure washing crews had done their work weeks ago, blasting away the fluids and grime, leaving the bricks clean and indifferent.

He reached into his inner jacket pocket, his fingers brushing against the small, brittle object he had carried from the hotel room.

He pulled it out.

A single sprig of lavender.

The stem was dry, the tiny purple buds faded to grey as he held it between his thumb and forefinger. The scarring on his palm shone white and slick in the dim alley light as he rolled the stiff stem between his fingers.

Carlisle had used this flower, placed it on bodies like a signature to mock the dead and taunt the living, turning it into a mark of ownership.

Nate bent closer to the wall and found a deep crack in the mortar between two bricks near the base where the cement had crumbled away years ago. He pushed the stem into the gap, working it in until it held fast against the massive moss-stained wall.

The lavender stood upright, small and fragile.

Nate stayed in the crouch for a long moment, breathing in the smell of wet stone and garbage and river silt, and looked at the flower.

"Sarah Catherine Holloway," he said.

His voice was flat, absorbed by the brick—he did not whisper it but spoke it clearly.

The tightness that had lived behind his ribs for fifteen years loosened, though it did not disappear entirely. He had not saved her, had not answered the phone when it mattered.

But he had finished it.

He stood up and brushed a speck of dirt from his knee, looked at the empty space one last time, then turned his back on the alley and walked out to the street without looking back.

The haze in the square had lifted slightly so that the tops of the trees were visible now, Spanish moss hanging down like ragged grey curtains.

Nate walked toward the center of the square where Booker Hayes sat on a bench near the monument, facing the street. He wore a clean-looking military surplus jacket and new leather boots, though the toes were already scuffed grey from the pavement.

Nate approached, and Booker did not look up as he watched a squirrel dart across the pavers. Nate sat on the other end of the bench, leaving two feet of wooden slats between them, and they sat in silence while a street sweeper rumbled past on Bull Street, its brushes hissing against the asphalt.

Booker reached into his jacket and pulled out a crumpled soft pack of cigarettes, shook one loose, and offered it to Nate without turning his head.

Nate looked at it—he hadn't smoked since college.

He took the cigarette.

He needed something for his hands to do, his fingers restless and missing the weight of the files, the pull of the hunt.

Booker put a cigarette in his own mouth and produced a yellow disposable lighter, and with a flick of the wheel, a flame flared orange in the grey morning, catching the lines on his face. He moved the lighter toward Nate, who drew the harsh chemical smoke into his lungs, held it for a second, and exhaled a thin stream into the air.

"So it's over?" Booker asked, his voice rough like gravel rolling in a drum as he stared straight ahead.

Nate looked where he was looking—across the street, a tour guide in a top hat and velvet coat rehearsed on the sidewalk. He gestured at the Mercer-Williams House with a flourish, practicing his patter, pointing to a spot near the corner.

He smiled.

"For now," Nate said.

Booker nodded and took a long drag, the cherry of his cigarette glowing bright red.

"That guy," Booker said, gesturing with the cigarette toward the guide. "Making up stories, talking about ghosts."

"People pay for stories," Nate said. "They don't pay for the truth."

"Truth is ugly," Booker said.

"Usually."

Nate smoked, watching the city wake up as a jogger in neon spandex ran past with headphones in and a man in a suit walked a golden retriever that sniffed at the base of the monument. Normal people, living their lives on top of the pavement, ignorant of what lived underneath and how close they had come to the pattern.

On the bench, only he and Booker knew.

"What you gonna do now?" Booker asked, flicking ash onto the brick.

Nate watched it disintegrate.

"Go back to Virginia for desk duty and a mandatory psych eval—I'll probably get pushed out eventually."

"They don't like it when you go off script," Booker said.

"No, they don't."

Nate looked at Booker, whose face was lined and weathered but whose eyes were clear—he looked tired but not hunted anymore.

"You?" Nate asked.

Booker shrugged, adjusting the collar of his jacket.

"Same thing I been doing," Booker said. "Surviving."

He smiled, a crooked expression that didn't quite reach his eyes.

"But now I ain't got to worry about Mr. Evan," Booker said. "That's something."

"It's something," Nate agreed, though it wasn't enough, not justice. Booker had spent weeks in jail for crimes he didn't commit, a scapegoat to save tourism numbers, and now he was back on a bench. The monster was dead, but the machine was still running.

Nate reached into his inner pocket again and pulled out a plain white envelope thick with twenties.

He handed it to Booker.

Booker took it, felt the thickness without opening it or counting, and slid it into the deep pocket of his field jacket.

"My number is in there," Nate said. "Personal cell—it won't change. You need anything, you call, day or night."

Booker patted the pocket and looked at Nate, his stare steady.

"You find another one of them things," Booker said, "you let me know."

Nate looked at him.

"Why?"

"Because I watch," Booker said, leaning back against the bench. "That's what I do—I sit here, and I watch. I see things other people miss, the cars that circle too many times, the people who don't blink right."

He took a final drag of his cigarette, dropped the butt, and ground it out with the heel of his new boot.

"I'll watch for you, Agent Holloway."

Booker Hayes was invisible to Savannah, part of the scenery—the perfect sentry.

Nate extended his hand, and Booker looked at it, wiped his palm on his trousers, and took it. The grip was rough, strong, and warm.

"Thank you, Booker," Nate said.

"Be safe," Booker said.

Nate stood, dropped his own cigarette, and crushed it out, then straightened his jacket and looked at the square one last time: the live oaks, the moss, the deep grey under the branches.

He walked away with a steady ground-eating stride toward his rental car on Bull Street, not looking back at the bench or the alley.

CHAPTER

62

THREE MONTHS LATER

ALICIA LANDRY WALKED down the brick sidewalk of West Jones Street, holding a paper cup of black coffee from Gallery Espresso, the heat of the cardboard seeping into her palm.

She stopped across the street from number 465.

The townhouse was dark, a subtle "No Trespassing" sign and security system notice in the window replacing the yellow police tape that had been there months ago. The estate was in probate, a sealed mansion where the moss grew undisturbed and the shadows held their secrets.

A trolley turned the corner from Whitaker.

It was one of the hearse-style tour buses, painted black with fake gothic lettering on the side, its air brakes hissing as it idled at the curb and blocked the carriage stones. Alicia stepped back into the shadow of a massive oak, the bark rough against her shoulder, not wanting to be seen but needing to watch what came next.

"And here, ladies and gentlemen, we present the newest addition to Savannah's haunted legacy," the tour guide said, his voice crackling through an external speaker, distorted and tinny. He wore a top hat and a velvet coat that looked miserable in the persistent warmth. "The Carlisle House—home to the Vampire of Jones Street."

Camera flashes popped from the open windows of the bus, illuminating the dark brick for split seconds before darkness reclaimed it.

"Earlier this year, the FBI raided this very home," the guide continued, dropping his voice to a theatrical whisper that the microphone amplified into a boom. "They say bodies were found in a secret cellar, drained of every drop of blood, and the owner—a mysterious antique dealer—vanished in a fire that consumed the basement. But some say he didn't die."

A woman in the back row gasped; the sound delighted rather than horrified.

"They say he walks the halls at night," the guide said, pausing for effect. "Looking for his lost collection."

Alicia's fingers tightened around the strap on her bag, and she remembered the smell of the cellar—not the gothic romance the tourists imagined, but copper and bleach and rotting jasmine. She remembered the sound of Yolanda Pierce's throat being torn out, the wet slap of flesh hitting the tile, the ash that covered the floor after Zeke drove the iron home.

"If you look closely at the third-floor window," the guide said, "you can see a face looking back at you."

The tourists craned their necks and held up phones, buying a story the city had packaged from blood and horror and selling for thirty dollars a ticket. It was efficient and grotesque in equal measure.

Alicia pushed herself off the tree because she couldn't listen anymore, not when the guide started talking about a "shootout" and inventing details about heroic agents and supernatural resistance. He didn't mention the cancer-ridden blacksmith who sacrificed everything or the detective who bled out on the floor—those details didn't sell tickets.

She walked away, and the sound of the tour guide faded as she crossed Whitaker, replaced by the rhythmic chirping of cicadas in the canopy above.

Alicia turned into Monterey Square.

The light was failing fast now, streetlamps flickering to life and casting pools of yellow illumination on the hexagonal pavers. The Pulaski Monument rose in the center, a marble obelisk pointing at the darkening sky, and she scanned the benches until she found what she was looking for.

He was there.

Booker Hayes sat on the bench nearest the monument—the same bench where Lucy Phelps used to wait for handouts—but he looked different now. He wore new work boots with stiff, uncreased leather, and his coat was the same military surplus jacket he always wore, though it had been laundered and mended. He sat with his back straight, no longer huddled against the cold or the fear that used to define him.

Two men approached him from the Bull Street side—younger, disheveled, carrying heavy backpacks—transients new to the square.

Alicia stopped by a patch of azaleas to watch what would happen.

The younger men hesitated, looking at the bench and then at Booker, waiting for some signal. Booker didn't shrink away or withdraw his legs to make room but looked up at them and nodded once —a sharp, downward motion of acknowledgment without welcome.

The men nodded back and kept walking, moving toward the darker edges of the square near the Mercer-Williams House, accepting the unspoken claim.

Booker claimed the space, and the other homeless residents treated him with a deference that hadn't existed two months ago, before everything changed.

Alicia watched him reach into his pocket and draw out a pouch of tobacco and papers, his hands steady as he rolled a cigarette and lit it. The flame flared briefly against his weathered face before he took a drag and looked up at the spot near the monument where Lucy had been found. He touched the brim of his hat in a gesture that was part apology, part vigil—talking to her, maybe, or just keeping her company the way nobody had when she was alive.

Alicia felt the urge to go to him, to sit down and tell him that she knew what he carried and understood the weight of it. But she stayed in the shadows because he didn't need her pity—he had his dignity, and that was what Nate and Rodecker had bought him. It wasn't justice, not really, but it was respect, and sometimes that was all you could salvage from the wreckage.

She turned and headed north, toward Bull Street.

The cafe was quiet when she entered, smelling of roasted beans and old newsprint, a ceiling fan turning overhead and chopping the air into lazy currents. Frank Brandmeyer sat at a small table in the back corner, far from the plate-glass windows, wearing a tweed cardigan even though the temperature was in the seventies. He looked smaller than she remembered, as if the events of the last six weeks had aged him in ways that couldn't be measured in time. He was a creature of the archives, not the field, and the reality of what they had done sat heavy on his narrow shoulders like a weight he couldn't put down.

Alicia withdrew the chair opposite him and sat.

"You're late," Frank said, his voice a dry rustle of paper and dust.

"I got held up—traffic on Jones Street," Alicia said, watching him adjust his thick glasses. "Tour bus."

Frank winced as if she'd struck him. "They're calling him the Antique Dealer Killer now, and I heard a guide say he was a warlock."

"It keeps the tourists happy," Alicia said, taking a sip of her coffee and finding it cold. "Did you hear anything from the board ?"

"Crawley is cleaning house," Frank said, keeping his voice low as he looked at his hands folded on the table instead of at her. "They're auditing the access logs, going back ten years, wanting to know every document you touched and every file you reviewed."

"Let him look," Alicia said, her voice flat. "The relevant files are gone."

"He's asking about me," Frank said, still not meeting her eyes. "About why I authorized your access to the Ashworth collection, and I told him it was standard dissertation research."

"Will he believe you ?"

"It doesn't matter," Frank said, finally looking up, his eyes watery and magnified by the lenses but sharp underneath. "I'm retiring next month—effective now, really—and they're letting me save face by calling it a medical retirement."

"Frank, I'm sorry."

"I was tired anyway," he said, waving off her apology. "And you— did you hear from Charleston ?"

"Not yet," Alicia said, tasting the bitterness of rejection. "New Orleans rejected the application, said my research focus wasn't a fit for their current collection goals, though I think Crawley made calls."

"He would," Frank said, nodding. "He wants you exiled, turned into an academic persona non grata who can't find work anywhere."

A shadow fell across the table.

Alicia flinched as Frank jerked back and his elbow hit the table hard.

A man in a business suit walked past them to the counter, ordered a latte, and didn't look at them—just a customer, nothing more.

Frank let out a shaky breath and spoke in a voice barely above a whisper. "I see him everywhere, even though I know he's dead and you told me he's ash, but I see the suit and the way people stand."

"It gets better," Alicia said, though she didn't know if that was true or just something people said. "The hyper-vigilance fades with time."

"Does it?" Frank reached into the inside pocket of his cardigan, moving with deliberate care as he looked at the barista and then the door. "Or did we just finish a chapter?"

He slid a folded piece of paper across the table, keeping his hand over it and pressing it flat against the wood.

"What is this?" Alicia asked.

"I made a copy before they locked me out of the inter-library loan system," Frank said, his voice careful and measured. "It came from a contact in the Louisiana State Archives—a death registry from the French Quarter."

Alicia put her hand on the paper and slid it toward her, keeping it low in her lap as she unfolded it.

It was a spreadsheet with rows of data: names, dates, and causes of death.

1875 - Marie Laveau II (attributed) - Anemia

1890 - Unidentified Female - Found in Jackson Square - Exsanguination

1905 - Eloise Gagnon - Throat trauma - Animal attack

She ran her finger down the date column, and the intervals were precise—fifteen years between each death.

1920 - 1935 - 1950

"The pattern matches," Alicia said, her mouth suddenly dry. "It's the same cycle."

"Look at the victim descriptions," Frank said.

Blonde - Petite - 20-25 years old

"It's him," Alicia said, looking up at Frank. "Carlisle traveled, and we knew he traveled."

"Look at 1965," Frank said.

Alicia traced the line with her finger until she found it.

1965 - New Orleans - Three victims - Exsanguination

She paused, her mind working through the implications. "Carlisle was here in 1965 when he was Evan Carpenter, and he killed nine women in Savannah that year."

Frank nodded, his expression grim. "He couldn't be in two places at once, not with that volume of kills."

Alicia looked at Frank as the fluorescent light of the cafe buzzed overhead like an insect trapped in amber.

"There are others," Frank said, his voice barely audible. "The port cities—St. Augustine, Santa Fe, New Orleans—the oldest settlements."

Alicia stared at the paper, and the data didn't lie, couldn't lie. If Carlisle was active in Savannah in 1965, and an identical pattern was active in New Orleans in 1965, then Naram-Ekur was not the only one. The tablets had hinted at it—*Edimmu*, plural, not singular.

"How many?" Alicia asked.

"I don't know," Frank said, spreading his hands. "But the intervals could be synchronized or staggered."

"If they're staggered," Alicia said, working through the logic, "then one of them is active right now."

"Or waking up," Frank said.

Alicia refolded the paper and tucked it into the inner pocket of her satchel, next to the small notebook where she kept the translation of the destruction ritual.

"Thank you, Frank," she said.

"Be careful, Alicia," Frank said, standing up and buttoning his cardigan as if preparing for a journey. "You're not a historian anymore —you know that, don't you ?"

"I know," she said.

Frank walked out of the cafe and merged into the evening pedestrian traffic on Bull Street until he disappeared from view.

Alicia sat for a moment, finishing her cold coffee and tasting the bitterness of it. She thought about the tenure track she had lost and the quiet life of stacks and dust she had planned for herself—it seemed like a dream now, a story about someone else who no longer existed.

She left the cafe and walked north.

Her phone buzzed in her pocket, and she withdrew it to find a Google Alert waiting.

Atlanta Art Scene - Gallery Opening - "Trauma and Recovery" - Curator Zoe Kaplan

Alicia stopped on the sidewalk and swiped the notification open, though there was no photo of Zoe—just a blurb about a new exhibition featuring works by survivors of violence.

Zoe was alive and working.

Alicia thought about the email Zoe had sent two weeks ago, brief and professional: *Thank you for your assistance. I am processing what happened. I am taking time to heal.*

The words were clean and sterile, hiding the truth that Alicia knew too well. The nights were the hardest, when the phantom pressure returned to the throat, and the smell of jasmine appeared where there was none—that violation didn't wash off because it rewired the brain at a fundamental level.

But she was alive and fighting, and that was what mattered.

Alicia deleted the alert because it was better to let her go—Zoe was a civilian and deserved to forget.

She passed Trinity AME Church, where the doors were open for choir practice, and the sound of a hymn drifted out into the street: *Guide My Feet.*

There was a new sign on the lawn: *Rev. Simmons - Sermon: Justice for the Least of These.* Next to it, a flyer announced the quarterly meeting of the James Oden Foundation.

The community had scar tissue now, tough and knitting itself back together, and Oden's brother was making sure the marginalized weren't invisible anymore. The police were under scrutiny, the darkness had been exposed, and the light was disinfecting it.

Savannah was safer than it had been.

Alicia reached the edge of the historic district, where the river was ahead—black and churning—and the gas lamps flickered on Bay Street. The city looked beautiful in the way old Southern cities always did, with the ancient oaks draping their moss like lace veils and the cobblestones shining in the moonlight.

It was a perfect Southern postcard.

Alicia looked past it and saw the shadows between the trees, the storm drains that channeled to the river, the alleys where no tourists walked.

She touched the key again, then withdrew her phone and opened her email app to start a new message.

To: N.Holloway@gmail.com
Subject: New Orleans

She hesitated, her thumb hovering over the screen as she thought about what sending this would mean.

Nate was in Virginia, sitting at a desk and trying to be a federal agent again, trying to forget the smell of burning jasmine. Sending this email was cruel, dragging him back to a place he'd barely escaped.

She looked at the river.

If there were others, they were feeding right now, taking women who wouldn't be missed and charming archivists and paying off cops, existing forever on borrowed blood.

Alicia thought about the blade in her apartment and Zeke Tatum dying on the floor.

She typed:

Frank found records. 1875 start date. The pattern is identical. The timeline overlaps with Savannah. It wasn't just him.

She attached the photo of the spreadsheet.

I'm going.

She hit send, and the message swooshed away into the digital void. It was done.

Alicia Landry put the phone in her pocket and gripped the strap of her satchel, then walked toward the river and into the day, ready for the next interval.

AUTHOR'S NOTE

If you've read my other work, you know I tend to stay in the lanes of crime and thriller fiction. This book was a deliberate detour—one I've wanted to take for a long time.

I owe that impulse to Stephen King, whose ability to find horror in the ordinary has always fascinated me, and to the creative minds behind *The X-Files*, who proved that the strange and unexplainable could be grounded in characters you genuinely care about. Their work gave me the itch to try something outside my comfort zone, and I hope the result does their influence justice.

Writing this story was a real stretching exercise. There were moments when I wondered if I had any business wandering this far from familiar territory. But that discomfort is part of the point, isn't it? Growth doesn't happen inside the lines you've already drawn.

Thanks to the friends, family, and coworkers who read drafts along the way and didn't laugh me out of the room when I said I was writing *this* kind of story. Your encouragement and honesty made it better than it had any right to be.

To my family: thank you for your patience with the late nights, the distant stares, and the occasional muttering about things that go bump in the dark. Your understanding means everything.

And to you, the reader—thank you for following me somewhere new. I hope it was worth the trip.

Chris Binnix

ABOUT THE AUTHOR

CHRIS BINNIX is the author of several novels and novellas in the crime and thriller genre, including *Crimson Sand*, *The Interval*, *Digital Grave*, *The Farmhands*, and *Criminal Fortune*. His writing explores the darker corners of human nature with sharp detail, atmospheric settings, and characters that stay with readers long after the final page.

Long before he ever sat down to write a novel, he spent more than twenty years in marketing, training, and education, careers built on understanding people: what motivates them, what scares them, and what they're willing to do when the stakes are high enough. Those years of observation would eventually find their way into every character he created.

A lifelong admirer of noir detective stories, true crime, and tightly wound thrillers, Chris grew up on the kinds of books and films where shadows meant something, and no one was exactly who they appeared to be. When he finally turned to fiction writing, he brought that same sensibility to the page—stories where character complexity and tension converge, and where the line between right and wrong isn't always easy to find.

When he isn't writing, Chris can usually be found on a golf course or spending time with his family and friends.